Nigel turned away, letting his gaze fall on the crowd. There was honestly no way to determine who it was he was supposed to be meeting. Then the crowd near the salon door shifted to make room for new arrivals. A man ushered two women into the room, both of them beautiful, but it was the one on the right that captured Nigel's attention.

In a word, she was magnificent. Auburn hair tumbled in loose curls down her back, set off by the glittering gold of her dress. The material clung to her body with mouth-watering clarity, and Nigel felt his body respond to merely the sight of her. And then she stepped into the room, her face illuminated in the chandelier light.

His heart stutter-stepped, his mind refusing to accept the information his brain was intent on telegraphing. Melissa. Dear God, it was Melissa....

EXPOSURE

DEE DAVIS

EXPOSURE

HQN™

ISBN 0-7394-5834-5

EXPOSURE

Printed in U.S.A.

For JK and KP

EXPOSURE

The only thing necessary for the triumph of evil
is for good men to do nothing.
—Edmund Burke

PROLOGUE

Shchuch'ye, Russia

"TWO MORE MINUTES, and then we move." Khamis al-Rashid checked his watch on reflex. He was more than aware of the time, as every second counted, his dreams almost within his grasp.

"What about him?" Malik Barzani, Khamis's second in command, nodded toward the shadowy figure of Yuri Dynkin. Using the Russian was a calculated risk. He had helped with Khamis's enterprises before, but his motivation was purely financial, which meant that he couldn't be trusted completely. Still, he knew the compound and he knew where the R-VX was stored.

So for the moment, at least, Khamis was forced to rely on the man.

"We let him guide us to our objective, and then we'll reassess his value." Khamis's smile was hollow. He glanced down at his watch again, and signaled Dynkin. It was time.

The Russian moved ahead, guiding them through a maze of barbed wire and wooden fencing. Most of it was decrepit to the point of collapse, but occasionally they were forced to stop and use wire cutters to gain access. Beyond the fencing, the dark outline of the storage facility loomed. Five thousand metric tons of nerve agent housed in buildings that looked ready to collapse at the slightest hint of wind. The ex-Soviet Union had fallen hard, and nowhere was it more evident than Shchuch'ye.

Khamis smiled, this time with genuine amusement. What the infidels lost, the righteous gained. And in this case it would lead to personal triumph. He ducked under broken wire and stopped, surveying the compound, waiting to be certain that they were still undetected.

Malik slid to a stop beside him, his assault rifle aimed in the direction of the buildings. But there was no sound. The guards were underpaid and understaffed and, on a cold night like this, preferred the meager shelter of their barracks. It seemed Dynkin's intel had been correct.

Signaling Malik to split to the right, the two men moved forward, Khamis shifting to the left so that they flanked the building they were targeting. Dynkin followed on Khamis's heels, his machine gun held ready.

Silence reigned as they moved into place on either side of the building's double doors, and with a finger count of three, Khamis and Malik pulled open the doors, swinging around to face the yawning black opening.

Again nothing moved, and the three men donned gas masks before sliding inside and securing the door behind them. Pale tendrils of moonlight washed through the windows of the storage building, but it was not enough to guide them. Instead, Dynkin switched on a flashlight, carefully shielded so that it wouldn't be visible through the window.

Walking quickly between rows of wooden shelving, he steered them through the stockpile of chemical munitions, stopping at the back of the building in front of a tier of metal canisters.

"This is what you're looking for." He gestured toward the towering shelf and stepped out of the way.

Malik hoisted the leather satchel he'd been carrying onto a nearby table and, after inspecting the contents of the shelf, donned protective gloves and carefully removed three of the canisters, placing them in the case's specially constructed foam-lined interior. Once the R-VX was safely in place, he turned with a grin, giving a thumbs-up in the American manner.

The gesture sent a shiver of hatred running through Khamis, but he quashed it, knowing that out of control emotion could be a man's most dangerous enemy. With a nod at the other two men, Khamis gestured for them to begin making their way out of the building. Then with a last look around the warehouse, he followed, his A-91 trained on the door.

If Dynkin's information was correct, there wouldn't be anyone to question their exit, but he wasn't about to take the chance. Firing in a facility like the one here at Shchuch'ye would be risky. If any one of the munitions was hit, the resulting release of gas could easily knock out a sizable chunk of this godforsaken corner of Russia. But if it was their only defense, Khamis was willing to take the chance.

The chill air smacked his exposed cheeks as he pulled off the gas mask. The compound was still shrouded in silence. A swath of illumination from the barracks door cut across the dusty yard some two hundred meters to their right. But other than the flicker of light, there was no visible activity.

Apparently Dynkin had been right. Khamis waited until Malik had crossed the first barrier and was well on his way toward the second before motioning Dynkin to follow. The man shook his head and waved Khamis on, tipping his head toward the barracks, motioning with fingers to eyes that he'd keep watch.

Khamis nodded his agreement and slid through the barbed wire, following the same path as Malik, his friend visible in the distance, the dark shape of the duffel evident in the hazy wash of moonlight.

Behind him, the night suddenly exploded with noise, a siren splitting through the night, accompanied by the cutting illumination of a searchlight. Swiveling backward but still moving, he scanned the compound, counting at least eight guards emerging from the barracks. According to Dynkin there should have been only three.

Adrenaline surging, he searched for the Russian, only to find him still standing at the first barrier, his arms waving in either signal or surrender. There was no way to decipher which it was, and in truth it didn't matter. Dynkin knew too much and so, even if he was innocent, presented a risk too great to allow.

Raising the silenced assault rifle, Khamis centered on the Russian and took the shot. The man dropped without a sound. Khamis slipped the A-91 over his shoulder and turned to run, just as the first volley of machine-gun fire spattered across the dusty ground.

He cleared two more barriers and was under the third when the sound of helicopter blades filtered through the night air. The dark shape of the aircraft filled the sky, two beams of light sweeping the ground, intersecting and diverging as they passed over the turf below.

Far ahead, Khamis could see Malik as he ducked under the cover of a stand of trees. At least for the moment, his friend would be safe. Khamis crawled under the barbed wire and rolled to his feet, running all out toward the final barrier. Fifteen meters and he'd be there. The air filled with the noise of gunfire again, another volley from the machine guns.

Again he hit the dirt, crawling forward on his elbows, his weapon still grasped firmly in his hands, years of training making his actions instinctive. Five meters to go. The ground around him spit puffs of dirt, this time the gunfire coming from above. The searchlights were still moving, however, meaning the shots were preemptory. They hadn't found him yet.

He crawled under the fallen barbed wire and pushed forward, stopping as his coat snared on the wire. Reaching for his pocket, he cursed, remembering Dynkin had the wire cutters. The machine-gun fire was closer now, and he could hear his pursuers calling out to one another. With a surge of adrenaline, he jerked free leaving a large chunk of his coat behind.

Running now, bent double to the ground, he headed for the trees, grateful when the passing helicopter lights again missed him. It was dark in the woods, but he didn't stop. The rendezvous point was still a good distance away, and he had to move quickly—the plane wouldn't wait.

One of the canisters would be payment for the ride, and the fact that Malik had the satchel meant that Khamis was now expendable. There was relief in the knowledge that Malik would escape with the R-VX, but disappointment in knowing that he might not be able to see the mission through.

Still, there was a chance, and he ran on, oblivious to the tree branches that clawed at his arms and legs. He didn't bother to try to silence his footsteps. There was little point. Either he'd make the plane or he would die. It had always been an option, but one that he'd chosen not to dwell on. Unlike many of his compatriots, he was not keen on sacrificing himself for the cause. He'd already paid more than his share, and until he had achieved his revenge, he had no intention of dying.

Bursting from the woods, he raced forward, the dimmed lights of the plane directly ahead. Malik was standing by the wing, the precious satchel still clutched in his hand. Behind him, Khamis heard the swell of the helicopter and knew that he had only seconds.

Malik, too, saw the whirling rotors, and turned to board the plane, hands from inside the fuselage reaching out to pull him aboard. The little plane's engines roared to life, and it began to taxi, the helicopter's gunmen firing randomly, the distance still too great for contact.

Khamis ran forward, the moving plane quickly closing the distance between them. In seconds he'd be parallel to the fuselage door. Malik's face appeared, his arms outstretched, and with a flying leap, Khamis dove for the door just as the plane lifted from the ground.

His muscles contracted in protest as he whipped back and forth in the wash, but a second pair of hands joined Malik's and together they managed to pull him aboard, the plane soaring over the treetops, well out of range of the helicopter.

Antiaircraft guns flashed below, but only for a moment, and then silence reigned, the hum of the engine the only noise, the lights of the men below diminishing to pinpricks as the plane rose higher, finally disappearing altogether.

Khamis lay against the interior wall of the plane, his breathing still coming in gasps. Malik made the thumbs-up sign again and, despite his loathing for all things American, Khamis returned the gesture.

Praise Allah, they were safe, along with the nerve agent. There were still hurdles to overcome, the most important being access into the U.S., but his objective was righteous, and God was smiling upon him. Success was within reach, and the ensuing revenge would taste sweeter than sun-kissed *tamr.*

CHAPTER ONE

Gijón, Spain

NIGEL FERRIS LOWERED his binoculars and blew out a breath. Surveillance was not his strong point. He had neither the vision nor the patience for such endeavors, and yet here he was, waiting for Alberto Salvatore to make his move.

Nigel had been stuck here on the outskirts of town for the past week, watching the arms dealer and his henchmen come and go from their portside warehouse. His instructions were to observe, but considering the amount of activity in the past twenty-four hours it was fairly obvious that something was about to go down.

Salvatore supplied weapons of all sorts to the highest bidder with no concern as to the end use of his product. A menace in general, he'd come to the attention of MI6 when rumors surfaced of a potential arms deal with a particularly militant faction of the IRA.

Although things had been quiet of late in Northern Ireland, there was always the chance of someone stirring things up, and any movement along those lines had to be carefully monitored. Nigel, unfortunately, had drawn the short straw.

Or more accurately, he'd managed to piss off Jason Hardcastle, his immediate superior, by doing an end run around the man to work with Last Chance in America. The English government, though allied with the U.S., wasn't all that keen on its agents running willy-nilly over to the colonies at the whim of a man like Cullen Pulaski.

Not that Nigel had been responding to Cullen, anyway. It went far deeper than that. And the only reason he was sitting in Spain watching the world through the window of a dingy walk-up flat as opposed to finding himself on the dole was the fact that his superior's superior knew that, push come to shove, he'd always land on the side of Britain. He'd proved that fact in spades, and the resulting betrayal had almost cost him his friends.

But in the end, he'd managed to repair the damage, which was more than he could say for Hardcastle. The man would no doubt carry the grudge for eternity—or longer. The outcome being that Nigel could count on a series of lackluster assignments for the immediate future.

He lifted the glasses again to peer out the open window at the warehouse below. His contact with Spanish intelligence was working across the street in an equally inhospitable room. Of course, at the end of a long day, Enrique had a warm bed and a willing wife to go home to.

Not that location made any difference for Nigel. *Home* wasn't a word that had any particular meaning. He still had his family's estate in Gloucestershire but he hadn't visited it in years, leaving the upkeep to a series of caretakers. The only time he felt any sense of place at all was when he was with Gabe and Payton.

Tragic, but true. He grinned at his own morose turn of thought and forced himself to focus on the warehouse below. The black sedan out front was Salvatore's. He'd been inside for about twenty minutes, the timing atypical. In the three weeks Nigel had been observing the warehouse, Salvatore had only shown his face a couple of times, and then he'd never deigned to leave the confines of his car, the meetings lasting less than ten minutes.

Which meant that other than his proximity to the warehouse, and the fact that with a little digging its ownership could be traced to Salvatore, there wasn't a whole lot that could be pinned on the man. All of which signaled that this latest deviation in routine might in fact substantiate Nigel's feeling that something big was about to happen.

The headset at his elbow crackled with life, and he quickly put it on.

"Ferris, you there?" Despite the static, Nigel could hear the excitement in Enrique's voice.

"I'm here. What've you got?"

"A second car."

Nigel adjusted the glasses, focusing on the gray van pulling up to an open cargo bay at the end of the warehouse nearest the dock. Three men emerged from the sliding door, the driver remaining at the wheel. From this distance it was hard to make out the identities of the new arrivals. Their plates were Spanish, but that didn't signify much of anything.

"You recognize anyone?" Nigel whispered into the mouthpiece.

"It's hard to say for sure, but the man in the middle looks a lot like the photographs I've seen of Shamus O'Reilly."

O'Reilly was the head of a militant splinter group of the IRA. With only about forty members, the group was nevertheless a dangerous one, and if they were in fact here to buy arms, it proved beyond a doubt that they were far from ready to accept a peaceful solution to the troubles in Northern Ireland.

"What about the others?" Nigel strained for a closer view, but even with his powerful field glasses the faces were simply too far away.

"Nothing for certain. The shorter man could be Patrick Roan, but it's hard to say."

"Well, I can't see a bloody thing." Nigel lowered the glasses, his mind turning over the repercussions of directly disobeying an order—again. There really wasn't a choice. At the end of the day, he simply wasn't a sit-on-his-bum kind of man. "I'm going down for a closer look."

There was a pause, as Enrique considered the idea, then a chuckle. "I'll be right behind you."

Enrique, it seemed, wasn't too keen on sitting on the sidelines, either. Just as well, as Nigel had the feeling he might have need of the Spaniard's help before all was said and done. In a matter of minutes, the two of them were outside the warehouse, crouched behind a metal garbage bin.

"There are two main rooms and three ancillary closet spaces that pass for offices," Nigel said, drawing a map in the gravel at their feet. "My bet is that Salvatore uses the one on the west wall, closest to the water. It's the largest. If we come in through the northwest door, we ought to be able to use crates for cover to reach it."

Enrique studied the crude drawing and then nodded. "What about the driver?" He tilted his head toward the man now standing outside the van smoking.

Nigel smiled. "Looks like he could use a little nap."

Without waiting for agreement, Nigel slipped out from behind the trash bin and closed the distance between him and the Irishman. There was no mistaking the man's ethnicity, between his woolen sweater and his flaming red hair. His head was bent, his face averted as he tried to keep a match lit, the position giving Nigel the advantage of surprise.

Moving quickly on silent feet, he came up behind the man and, using pressure on the carotid artery, rendered the fellow unconscious in a matter of seconds.

"Well done," Enrique said, joining him at the van. "How long do you think he'll be out?"

"Fifteen, maybe twenty minutes. So we'll need to move fast." Nigel pulled his Sig Sauer from the holster at his back and slipped through the open door of the warehouse, squatting down behind a couple of discarded wooden crates.

Enrique followed, settling down next to him, the two men using cracks in between planks to survey the situation. This part of the warehouse appeared to be empty, although with the number of crates stacked everywhere it was hard to be certain.

The salty tang of the sea mixed with the crisp fall air, the resulting moisture clawing at Nigel's neck, making him shiver.

"Looks deserted," Enrique said, echoing Nigel's assessment. "The office is that way, *sí?*" He tilted his head toward the western wall, and Nigel nodded, already pushing away from the crate out into the open.

He paused for a moment, waiting for some noise signifying that the occupants of the warehouse were aware of their invasion, but everything was quiet except for the plaintive clanking from the rigging of ships in the harbor outside.

Working in tandem, the two men made their way through the warehouse, watching each other's backs in turn, finally ending up behind a metal container lodged just a couple yards from the open door of the west office.

As expected, the men were gathered inside, one of them speaking with a decidedly Irish brogue. As if to concur with Enrique's earlier speculation the man shifted slightly, the light hitting him full in the face.

O'Reilly.

Nigel hadn't been wrong. Something big was afoot. The appropriate question now being whether he and Enrique should try to do something about it. If they waited, the opportunity would be lost, and Nigel simply couldn't see letting the chance pass by.

He glanced over at Enrique, and again the Spaniard gave a nod of agreement. They were of like mind, at least. Not that it guaranteed them anything approaching success, but he simply couldn't conceive of an alternative.

There were five men altogether. Salvatore sat behind a desk, guarded by one of his henchmen. O'Reilly sat across from him, with one of his flunkies positioned near the door and the other leaning back against the windowsill.

Nigel edged closer, straining to hear the conversation.

"We are in agreement, then?" Salvatore asked O'Reilly.

The big Irishman shrugged. "As long as you can reassure me that I'll be getting what I'm paying for."

Salvatore nodded to his henchman, who crossed over to a table and lifted the lid off of a small wooden crate. Pushing aside some paper straw, he pulled out an XM8 assault rifle and tossed it to O'Reilly.

Nigel shot a look at Enrique, whose mouth had dropped open. They'd just moved from big to huge. The XM8 was an American prototype, the next generation of assault weapons for the U.S. military. The fact that Salvatore had the weapon at all meant that his connections were coming from inside the U.S.

"Impressive," O'Reilly was saying, his gaze focused almost lovingly on the rifle he held in his hand. "And you can provide fifty more?"

"Absolutely." Salvatore nodded. "Of course, as we discussed, I'll need half the money up front. A token of your good will."

"And the rest?" O'Reilly asked, still holding the rifle.

"It can be wired to my offshore account once you've received the shipment."

"And why should I trust you?" O'Reilly's eyes narrowed in speculation.

"Because I make my living by word of mouth. If I were to cheat you, *señor,* my word would be worthless, and that would mean the end of what is, believe me, a quite prosperous enterprise. It is to my advantage to deliver what I promise. Not the other way around."

O'Reilly studied the older man for a few minutes more, then nodded his head once in acquiescence, holding out the XM8.

Salvatore smiled. "Keep the rifle, *señor.* It is my gift."

Nigel wished he'd thought to bring a tape recorder, but of course there was no way for him to have known the magnitude of what he'd be uncovering. He looked again in Enrique's direction and smiled. The Spaniard, it appeared, had considered every possibility, the digital recorder in his hand silently immortalizing the exchange between Salvatore and O'Reilly.

Nigel turned his focus back to the office in time to see O'Reilly's flunky handing over an envelope full of American dollars—the first half of the payment.

As tempting as it was to do more than record the conversation, Nigel knew the best course of action was to retreat with the evidence and let other departments take over from there. Still, there was the small matter of the incapacitated driver. While no permanent harm had been done, there were sure to be questions. And the idea of letting O'Reilly simply walk away did not sit well.

An intake of breath pulled Nigel's attention from his internal debate and he spun around to find Enrique and one of Salvatore's men fighting for control over Enrique's gun. Nigel aimed the silenced Sig Sauer and shot once, the henchman instantly dropping to the floor of the warehouse, Enrique breaking his fall and stifling the noise.

So much for decision making. A groggy Irishman might be ignored, but not when one added in a dead man. Nigel met Enrique's questioning gaze with a nod, and the two of them inched toward the office doorway.

The meeting was on the verge of breaking up, the three Irishmen still standing in front of the desk, the two Spaniards behind it. Although there was no doubt that all five men were packing weapons, none of them had guns in hand. In fact, O'Reilly was still holding the unloaded XM8.

The odds certainly weren't in their favor, but then Nigel had survived worse, and they did have the element of surprise. After signaling Enrique, Nigel sucked in a breath, counted silently to five, and swung away from the container into the open doorway ordering the assembled men to freeze.

Of course the word had the opposite effect, sending everyone scrambling for their guns, and Nigel was forced to shoot two of O'Reilly's subversives before he could even get a bead on the two men he wanted most.

Salvatore's man got off a round, the bullet clipping Enrique in the right arm. Fortunately he was left-handed, and his responding shot took the man out before he even had time to realize what had happened. O'Reilly dropped the assault rifle, swinging around to face Nigel, his gun hand reaching for his holster.

"I wouldn't," Nigel said, the Sig trained at the man's head. "You'll be dead before you pull it clear."

O'Reilly nodded.

Enrique moved quickly to disarm the man, pocketing the Irishman's gun.

"Now Salvatore." Nigel tilted his head toward the Spaniard, shifting so that he had Salvatore in his gun sight, but the man had vanished behind the desk, the clatter of the opening drawer testament to the fact that he was now most likely armed. Instinct kicked in and Nigel dropped down, yelling for Enrique to follow suit.

A hail of bullets shot through the room, ricocheting off corrugated metal walls. Nigel rolled under the desk and came up firing, Salvatore only inches away.

The man's eyes widened as Nigel's bullet found home, and he convulsed once then dropped to the floor, his gun clattering as it spun out of his hand. Nigel rose slowly, his attention on O'Reilly and the possibility that he'd also had time to reach for a gun. But instead, the big Irishman drooped in his chair, eyes empty, a shilling-size hole in his chest blossoming crimson.

Nigel turned to congratulate Enrique, only to find the man clutching the envelope full of money to his chest, his gun trained on Nigel, his eyes narrowed in concentration. Blood had soaked through his sleeve, the quantity making it fairly certain the bullet had nicked an artery on its way through.

"You're hurt," Nigel said, ignoring the gun.

"It's nothing," the Spaniard scoffed, waving the revolver. "Just drop your gun and lie on the floor. I've no interest in hurting you."

"So what? Your plan is to take off with the Irishman's money?"

"It seems a reasonable goal." Again the man shrugged, but his gun hand was now visibly shaking, sweat breaking out on his forehead. "And I'll kill you if I have to."

"Come on, Enrique," Nigel cajoled. "You don't want to do this."

"Why not?" The man tilted his head, his expression glazed. "I've spent the better part of my life watching scum like this make off with all the money. Why shouldn't it be my turn?"

"Because I'm afraid that's simply not the way it's done, old boy." As he spoke, Nigel dropped to the floor again, rolling to escape the round Enrique fired, springing back to his knees and taking his shot.

The bullet entered Enrique's gun arm, the force of contact enough to drive Enrique to the ground, his weapon falling uselessly from nerveless fingers. Nigel slid across the floor and scooped up the gun, keeping the Sig Sauer trained on Enrique. "Sorry to do that, mate. But you really didn't leave me much choice."

A sound at the door had him spinning again, and Nigel wondered just how many bloody Spaniards were in the building.

"Seems like maybe you could use a little help." Payton Reynolds leaned against the door, the Beretta in his hand looking deceptively docile.

"Actually," Nigel said, standing up, his gun still pointed at Enrique, who was slumped dejectedly against the dead Irishman's legs. "I think I've got it all under control." He grinned at his friend. "What brings you to my neck of the woods?"

"Same old, same old." Payton shrugged. "Someone's commandeered several canisters of Russian VX. Intel has it targeted for the U.S. Cullen thought if you weren't too busy, you might be interested in helping us out. But of course if you haven't got the time..." He trailed off, his gaze taking in the bullet-ravaged office, his scarred face creasing with a smile.

Nigel nudged Enrique to his feet and the three of them walked out of the warehouse. The Spanish authorities had arrived and were already questioning O'Reilly's driver. Nigel turned Enrique over to them, along with the tape recording of the deal.

"Right, then," Nigel said, wiping his hands on his handkerchief, unadulterated pleasure washing through him at the thought of working with his friends again. "Seems I'm all yours."

CHAPTER TWO

"I NEED MORE EXPRESSION. Something that makes it look as though you're enjoying your work here." Melissa Pope adjusted her camera lens, the shot going wide over the woman's shoulder, focusing on the charts on the far wall.

The UN logistics officer beamed for the camera, her smile luminous. The photograph would have been wonderful, except that Melissa had gotten the shot she needed a half hour ago, and was now concentrating on the more inanimate parts of the office.

The last of the autumn sun beamed through the windows of the United Nations Secretariat, the glistening East River rolling placidly by. Each office here was very much like the next, cubicles and tiny offices fronted with metal dividers and standard-issue 1950s furniture. The only thing that seemed to have changed from Cary Grant's *North by Northwest* days was the addition of computer equipment. In this case, a state-of-the-art ThinkPad with seventeen-inch flat-screen monitor.

Clearly the IT department was intent on dragging the UN into the new millennium despite the dismal decor.

What Melissa needed was five minutes alone with the computer. But that wasn't going to be easy with this woman. Despite her glowing smile, she was in fact quite territorial. Every time Melissa moved too close to the desk or the information tacked on the walls behind it, Idina Meloski shot her "the look."

Of course the camera lens was impervious to that sort of thing, but it also wasn't able to turn on a computer and search through the files. What Melissa needed was a diversion. She scanned the office looking for coffee or water and found no beverages of any kind. Not even a cup. It wasn't exactly Sydney Bristow, but she had a hunch it would work.

Sucking in a breath, she began to cough, pulling all the way from her diaphragm for effect. Bending over for theatrical impact, she shot a look at the woman through her hair. Idina had risen to her feet, her eyebrows raised in alarm.

"Miss Pope, are you all right?"

Melissa nodded but continued to cough, straightening enough to hold out a hand gesturing that she needed water.

Idina swallowed the whole act, rushing from the office with the assurance that she'd be right back. Hopefully, it would take a little while to find a cup and water.

Melissa moved quickly around the desk to the computer, tapping instructions to bring up the woman's data directory. She'd already learned that most UN staff logged on to their computers first thing in the morning and stayed connected for the rest of the day, which meant that daytime was her best chance for access, averting the need to secure passwords, or try to end run past them.

Unfortunately, Idina's files looked pretty pedestrian. Not that she expected the woman to have labeled something *Subversive Efforts to Undermine the UN.* Still, there could be a clue, it was just a matter of finding it. With a couple of keystrokes she changed directories, again with nothing interesting to report. Standard requisition forms labeled sequentially, and a bunch of letters applying for various other UN positions. Apparently Idina wasn't all that satisfied with her job.

Popping a CD into the appropriate drive, Melissa ordered the computer to copy a series of files relating to Idina's most recent operations just in case there was a pattern there Melissa was missing. If nothing else she could compare it to similar files of other UN employees with the means to be a part of the smuggling operation.

While the files were copying, she entered a code her handler had given her, the miniprogram designed to find and open any encrypted files, but the resulting search came up empty. If Idina was working with terrorists, she certainly hadn't left a paper trail. Not that Melissa had really expected to find anything.

Although Idina's job as a junior logistics officer for UN Peacekeeping Operations gave her the necessary access to information that could be useful in the illegal transport of arms and munitions, she really didn't fit the profile of a woman on the take. And more importantly, she didn't have the necessary skill set to pull off a scam of this magnitude.

But Melissa had learned the hard way that acting on assumption alone was never enough in this business. It was the kind of mistake that could get a girl killed, actually, so she ran the program again, just to be certain. No hidden files. No secrets stashed handily on the office computer. Which meant either Idina was smarter than she looked, or she wasn't the one.

Melissa was betting on the latter.

Grabbing the CD, she slipped it into her pocket and was just rounding the desk summoning up a renewed chorus of coughing when Idina returned, water glass in hand, Alexi Kirov, her boss, following right on her heels.

If Idina was territorial, Alexi was expansive. He'd practically given her the key to the proverbial front door, partly, she suspected, because he didn't seem to care a whole lot about his job. Despite the fact that he was senior staff, his motivation had been left behind in his native Russia. Still, he was on the list, and sooner or later she intended to have a look at his files, as well.

Right now, however, she needed to do her best Camille. Coughing to beat the band, she took the water and gulped it, gasping for breath in a way she hoped signaled the choking was at an end. "Thank you," she panted. "I'm not sure what happened. Something went down the wrong way, I guess."

Idina fluttered around her, patting her back and mumbling what sounded a hell of a lot like Czech endearments. Melissa choked down some more water, and lifted her gaze to meet Alexi's. As always, it was difficult to read his expression. Amusement surely, but just for a moment she thought she saw something else in his eyes.

Melissa shook her head and smiled, patting the still-flustered Idina. "I'm fine now. Honestly. Sorry to have frightened you."

"Maybe you'd better call it a day." Alexi was still watching under hooded eyes.

"I can't." Melissa shook her head, patting her camera. "Deadlines. There are proof sheets to go over, film to develop, and I'd still like to get a few more shots before this light is gone." She waved absently at the window, wondering what in hell had made her think this assignment would be less stressful than her usual fare. Give her a war zone any day. At least there you were dodging bullets, not people.

"Surely you're allowed to take a break now and then?" Alexi sounded just a bit too interested for Melissa's taste, but she'd learned a long time ago never to say never when opportunity presented itself.

"Now and then," she grudgingly admitted. "In fact tonight I'm actually attending a party as a guest and not a photographer."

"What kind of party?" Idina asked, her mask of composure firmly back in place.

"It's in honor of the Swiss delegation. I'm going as the guest of my brother-in-law."

"Your brother-in-law?" Alexi asked, one eyebrow rising with curiosity.

"Yes, he's with the diplomatic corps. Assigned to Brazil at the moment, but he and my sister are here on leave."

"Not much of a holiday," Alexi snorted. "The Swiss minister is a noted bore."

"So tell me what you really think." The words were out before she realized what she'd said. Europeans, especially Eastern ones, were often slow to get American humor, and she usually tried to restrain from making flippant comments in case she was misunderstood.

She need not have worried with Alexi, though. His laughter erupted in full force. "I'm sorry, I spoke out of turn, but then that is, how do you say, *par for the course* for me."

"Well done." Obviously Alexi had a solid grasp on American slang. Part and parcel of a permanent assignment to New York, no doubt. "Anyway, regardless of the host's personality flaws, it'll be nice to leave the camera at home for once."

"And I'm sure you'll clean up beautifully." Again with the innuendo, and this time there was no mistaking the appreciative glint in Alexi's eyes.

Idina made a noise somewhere between a snort and a harrumph, making a play of moving the stacks of paper on her desk, her expression even more forbidding than usual. Melissa toyed with the idea that the woman was jealous, and then dismissed it. Idina wasn't the jealous type. And especially over Alexi Kirov. There was certainly still no love lost between the Czech Republic and the remnants of the Soviet Union, so despite the fact that he was good-looking in a blond and blue-eyed kind of way, Melissa doubted Idina was pining away for him.

Anyway, he had a weak chin and his handshake was a lot like a limp noodle. Not that a handshake was the be-all and end-all of a man, but it was a good indication of where he was coming from. Idina probably had the handshake of a National League linebacker.

Shaking her head at her own folly, Melissa drank the rest of her water and handed the glass back to Idina. "Let me just get a last shot of you at your desk, and then I really ought to be going." After all, there was a CD burning a hole in her pocket, and the longer she stood there chatting, the more likely it was she'd be discovered.

She'd been doing this kind of thing a long time, but sometimes she wondered how the hell anyone in the Company ever managed to take themselves seriously. Clandestine work was fodder for situation comedy, *Get Smart* being a lot closer to the truth than some of the more frightening flicks people thought of as tributes to the kind of work she did.

"Will you be back tomorrow?" Idina asked with about as much enthusiasm as if Melissa were a dentist holding a drill. Melissa clicked the shutter and then lowered her camera.

"No." She shook her head for emphasis, and the other woman immediately relaxed. "I think I've got everything I need from you. I might be back in a week or so for reshoots. But in the meantime, Alexi, I do still need to get some shots of you."

The Russian smiled, the gesture transforming his expression into something that bordered on charm, but then he frowned and looked down at his watch. "I'm swamped with detail work at the moment, everything due at once. So I'll have to check my calendar and then get back to you." She waited for him to click his heels and bow, but instead he tipped his head, his expression quizzical. "Why don't I phone you and we'll set a time?"

"Of course," she said. "I certainly don't want to do anything to interrupt your schedule. I can always shoot background rolls in the meantime."

"Wonderful." He seemed distracted now, as if his mind had preceded him from the room. "We'll talk tomorrow?"

"Absolutely." She nodded, shivering as his chilly gaze swept over her one last time. Maybe she'd been too flip earlier in dismissing the dangers of her job. Fingering the CD in her pocket, she nodded goodbye to Idina and turned to go, suddenly wanting nothing more than to get the hell out of Dodge.

"LOOK WHAT the cat dragged in." Madison Roarke contradicted her words with the warmth of her hug, as she embraced first Nigel and then Payton. Madison was a new mother, a profiler with the FBI and the wife of Nigel's friend Gabe. All three were difficult roles, but together they probably qualified Madison for sainthood.

"How's the baby?" The last time Nigel had seen Andrea Roarke she was about three months old, chubby, cheerful and very fond of tugging on his mustache.

"Not so much a baby anymore. She's pulling up and crawling everywhere in sight. And Gabriel swears she said *daddy.* Although I'm pretty sure it was only a burp." Madison's smile was beautifully maternal, and Nigel felt an absurd sense of longing. Fortunately, it never lasted long.

"How was the flight in?" she asked.

"Bumpy." Nigel hated flying and Cullen's private jet only made it slightly more palatable. "But as usual, Cullen's accommodations were top-notch."

At the mention of his name, Cullen Pulaski looked up from the document he was examining and smiled at the assembled company. "Nice to all be together again."

Cullen was a kingmaker of sorts, the kind of man who stayed behind the scenes but still managed to control almost everything he touched. Last Chance was no exception. His idea from conception, he left the dirty work to the team, but was always there for moral support and to provide an endless bankroll, which helped immeasurably when it came to cutting corners and actually getting things done.

"Almost all," Harrison Blake corrected, glancing up from his laptop. Harrison was a genius when it came to bits and bytes, his ability to manipulate a computer taking on more legendary proportions with each operation. He'd never met a puzzle he couldn't solve, and his tenacity had bailed them out on more then one occasion. "Gabe's flying in later today."

"And Sam won't be here for another day or so. She's trying to close out a case." There was a note of dejection in Payton's voice. For all practical purposes he was still a newlywed, but between his wife's job as an ATF explosives officer and his work for the CIA, the two of them were often separated for long stretches at a time, making Last Chance operations that much more attractive for the both of them.

"Well, since we've got a majority, why don't I go ahead and fill you in on what we know? Payton, you and Madison can brief your spouses when they arrive."

Payton nodded, his expression guarded as usual, his scar shining white in the fluorescent light.

"Works for me," Madison agreed.

Cullen laid down the sheaf of papers he was holding and crossed his arms. "Four days ago three canisters of R-VX were stolen from the storage facility in Shchuch'ye, Russia."

"R-VX?" Madison queried.

"Nerve agent." Payton's tone was grim. "One of the most deadly. VX can kill within minutes if inhaled or deposited on the skin."

"It was accidentally released in Utah in 1968, killing thousands of sheep, some of them as far as forty miles from where the gas escaped," Cullen said. "Imagine what that would mean in a crowded city."

"And worse still, it contaminates everything it touches, and remains dangerous for several days," Nigel added. "It was created by British scientists in the fifties. The only verified sources for its existence today are in the U.S. and Russia."

"Has it ever been used on humans?" Madison shuddered.

"Nothing verified," Nigel answered. "But there are stories."

"There was a village in Kampuchea," Payton said, his face hardening. "Everyone dead. Men, women and children. A couple hundred of them. They looked like macabre rag dolls littering the muddy streets, lying in their own excrement."

"Oh, God." Madison had obviously turned inward, her profiler's mind recreating the scene.

"It's bad stuff." Payton nodded. "Like smothering to death, only before it kills you, you sweat and salivate like a pig, your bowels releasing at whim, your muscles twisting and cramping until you're most likely praying for death. Basically, your central nervous system goes AWOL right before your respiratory system shuts down completely—paralysis, coma and then death. It's pretty frightening what humanity creates in the name of war."

"The *R* in R-VX is for the Russian variety, I take it," Harrison interjected, pulling them away from the horror as he typed the name into his computer.

"Exactly. The chemical makeup is apparently somewhat different." Cullen leaned forward, his palms pressed to the table. "But the effect is every bit as deadly."

"So why is it still in existence?" Madison asked. "I thought there were agreements to get rid of the stuff."

"There are," Cullen said. "But unfortunately chemical weapons aren't easy to destroy safely. And it can be quite costly. The deadline for destroying stockpiles is 2007, but there's little likelihood that either side will be able to meet that deadline."

"Which means that places like Shchuch'ye serve as one-stop shopping for terrorists." Payton's voice was filled with contempt. "The place is practically falling down, and the weapons are just lying on shelves waiting for someone to come along and pick them up."

"You've been there?" Cullen queried, his eyes sparkling with interest.

"Once." As usual Payton chose not to elaborate. Not that Nigel doubted him. He'd never been to Shchuch'ye but he'd seen similar facilities.

"But surely there's security?" Harrison frowned.

"Not much," Nigel answered. "The truth of the matter is that the new Russia simply doesn't have the money or personnel to deal with Soviet stockpiles, whether we're talking about conventional weaponry or chemical and biological ones."

"So someone just walked into the facility at Shchuch'ye

and helped themselves?" Harrison had stopped typing, his brows drawn together in frustration.

"More or less," Cullen agreed. "They had help. A man named Yuri Dynkin. He'd worked as a guard at the facility months earlier, and was fired for insubordination of some kind. Apparently, the man held a grudge."

"Or was looking to make a quick buck," Payton growled.

"I'm afraid we'll never know for certain. Dynkin was killed on-site. A bullet in the back."

"From which side?" Nigel quipped. "Not that it matters."

"No way to know." Cullen shrugged. "And unfortunately the rest of the party got away, along with three canisters of R-VX."

"Just the nerve agent?" Payton asked, his eyes narrowing in thought.

"No." Cullen shook his head. "The canisters are actually binary warheads."

"I'm not sure I'm following." Madison leaned forward, elbows propped on the table.

"Basically the warhead acts as a chemical reactor," Nigel explained. "Two substances are stored inside in separate containers. When the thing is detonated the wall between the two canisters collapses, the substances mix, and the nerve agent is formed."

"So all someone has to do is shoot the thing?" Harrison asked.

"Or blow it up. There are really any number of ways it can be used." Nigel sighed, the reality of the situation beginning to sink in. "Do we have any idea who took it?"

"No," Cullen said, tipping back his head and rolling his shoulders. "No particular group has claimed credit. But they had help from Hamas, so we're guessing Islamic extremists. And the chatter internationally seems to support the idea."

"So why were we called in?" Madison asked. "Surely

there are international groups more equipped to handle something like this."

"There are." Cullen nodded to emphasize the point. "But despite the fact that no one is claiming responsibility, we've got very credible intel that the stolen R-VX is headed for the U.S.—most probably here in New York. We believe the canisters are being routed through the Black Sea. I've got sources trying to confirm that fact now. But if we're right about the U.S. being the target, then we've got to move fast."

"It'll be like finding a bloody needle in a haystack." Nigel's frustration was echoed on the other team members' faces.

"Maybe not quite that bad." Cullen actually smiled. "The CIA has an ongoing covert investigation into the possibility that someone at the UN, specifically someone working for Peacekeeping Operations, has been using Peacekeeping transports to smuggle weapons and other illegal goods."

"Do they have proof?"

"Nothing verifiable, of course, or they'd have taken action. But I'm told they're getting close. They have someone working on the inside now. And I've arranged a meet. Her position is, as you can imagine, very vulnerable, so there's no way to just call her in. But her handler has arranged for one of you to connect at a diplomatic party."

"So who's going?" Harrison asked, looking like he'd rather eat nails than attend. Not that Nigel felt all that differently. Social dos weren't really his cup of tea, although they were often unavoidable in his line of work.

Cullen's gaze settled on Nigel.

"Not me," he groaned.

Madison laughed, although she at least had the good sense to hide it behind her hands.

"Unfortunately, you're the perfect choice," Cullen said. "It's unlikely that anyone will connect you with us, and you're certainly not American, which is a plus." He actually said it as if in normal circumstances being a non-American was a detriment. To date, Nigel had found the opposite far more likely to be true, unless one happened to reside in Nebraska. "Gabriel and Madison will accompany you. Madison's father will be there, so that gives them legitimacy."

"You knew about this?" Nigel asked.

"About the party?" she quipped with a debutante smile. "Yes."

"I didn't bring a tux." He sounded sulky and he knew it. But, bloody hell, he hated getting trussed up like an overstuffed pheasant.

"Not a problem," Payton said with a rare smile. "We're about the same size. You can wear mine."

"Wonderful." Nigel sighed, accepting the inevitable. "You said my contact is a woman?"

"Yes, but I don't know much more than that. As I said, they're trying to keep her exposure to a minimum. Anyway, she'll have a description of you. And there'll be a signal."

"The red salmon are running in Peru?" Payton's smile had turned to a grin. "Hell, why don't you just have her carry a neon sign or something?"

"Look, there wasn't much time to get this all arranged. And the thought was that the easiest way to deal with this was for her to find you, give you the signal—and then you can talk." Cullen waved his hand through the air in dismissal. "I'll leave the details up to you."

"So what is the signal?" Nigel asked.

Cullen had the decency to look embarrassed. "She'll ask how you like the weather in New York, and you'll respond that it's much colder than Spain."

"You'll be a regular Eliza Doolittle," Payton said with a laugh, and Nigel shot him a look, wondering what the bloody hell he'd been thinking agreeing to help out. This operation had disaster written all over it. He hated tuxedos, he hated society parties, and he hated playing James-fucking-Bond.

CHAPTER THREE

MELISSA WASN'T BIG on parties, especially the kind where she had to dress formally, but she had to admit that she looked pretty damn good in her sister's gold Ungaro. The dress, made from lace and gold embroidery, was barely more than a slip and much more revealing, but it clung to her curves as if it had been made for her.

She twirled in front of the mirror, watching the hem of the skirt flutter in the resulting breeze.

"You look beautiful."

Melissa jumped and then smiled at her sister standing in the doorway. Alicia looked elegantly regal in a shimmering white sheath that highlighted her flawless beauty. Nothing was ever out of place with her sister. She was the perfect diplomat's wife.

And Melissa's mirror opposite.

"Thanks. I feel sort of like a princess. Or the ugly duckling."

"Nonsense, you always look spectacular." Alicia walked over to adjust the shoulder line of the dress and fluff Melissa's hair. "This just highlights your beauty in a more sophisticated way."

French couture had a way of doing that.

Melissa smiled at her sister in the mirror. Despite their differences, the sisters were close, perhaps because they'd had only each other to rely on for so very long. Even Alicia's marriage to Aaron hadn't severed the bond—although the relationship had changed, no denying that. Alicia's first loyalty was to Aaron now.

Which was as it should be. But sometimes it still hurt. Anyhow, it was all for the best—Melissa's lifestyle didn't allow for long-term responsibility. Still, that didn't mean she couldn't make time for her sister. Unfortunately, between Aaron's postings abroad and Melissa's assignments, it wasn't all that easy, which was why she'd agreed to go to the party in the first place.

Now, however, it seemed she had a more pressing reason.

Ed Wyland, her handler, had called a few hours earlier with instructions that she was to meet a Brit at the party, Mata Hari style, and brief him on her investigation. It seemed harmless enough, but she hadn't told her sister about her dual existence and hated the idea that she could be forced to lie to Alicia in order to escape and meet with her contact.

The details were sketchy, but basically it boiled down to finding a tall, dark man with a mustache and an English accent. Not exactly a hardship assignment. She twirled for the mirror again, then stopped as her eyes met her sister's.

"Something's up." She turned to face Alicia, searching her face, the telltale quirk of a smile indicating her sister had a secret.

Alicia ducked her head, then looked up again, all hints of regality making way for an impishly crooked grin. "I'm pregnant."

"Oh, my God." Melissa let out a whoop and pulled her sister into a bear hug, mindless of the gowns they wore. "A baby?"

Alicia and Aaron had been trying for a long time with no success, making the news all that much sweeter.

"How far along?" She eyed her sister's still-trim figure.

"Almost three months. I wanted to wait to tell you until we got the doctor's okay."

"And everything's fine?"

Her sister nodded, and the two of them embraced again, Melissa surprised to feel a little twinge of jealousy. She'd never wanted to settle down. In truth, she couldn't. Not and keep up the hectic schedule she maintained between her photography and her work for the CIA. But, sometimes the idea held appeal.

Sometimes.

Alicia pulled back with a smile. "We're going to ruin our makeup. Not to mention our dresses." As always Alicia focused on the practical.

Melissa laughed. "I'll bet Aaron is over the moon."

"I am." Alicia's husband stood in the doorway, his genial face wreathed in a smile. "But I'm also worried that we're going to be late." Shooting a significant look at his watch, Aaron stepped aside and gestured toward the door. "Ladies..."

Together, they headed out for the party, Aaron wrapping an arm around his wife, pulling her close. Their joy was almost palpable, and for the first time in a long time, Melissa found herself wondering if the price of playing Mata Hari might not be a little too high.

THE PARTY WAS CROWDED, and thanks to an overzealous heating system, it was also hot. Nigel tugged at his bow tie, cursing again his agreement to come to the affair. The only bright spot in the evening was Gabe's return.

His friend had been working in California when the call from Cullen had come in, and he'd had to tie up a few loose ends before flying to New York. Looking at him, however, one would never know he'd just flown across the country. When Gabe was with Madison, his whole countenance softened, as if her mere presence soothed his soul.

A poetic thought, surely. Nigel shook his head and reached out for a drink as a livery-clad waiter passed by with a silver tray. Downing it in two swallows, he let the warmth seep through him as he searched the crowd for the woman he was supposed to meet.

There were any number of candidates, most of them well over the age of fifty and all of them clad in a myriad of jewelry that was too gaudy to be anything but real. A dowager with faintly blue hair approached, and he resisted the urge to turn away.

"I couldn't help noticing you," the woman gushed, her gaze following the lines of his tux from head to toes in a way that was decidedly hungry. "You're easily the most handsome man in the room."

As a come-on it was laughable, but considering the woman delivering it was old enough to be his grandmother it bordered on ridiculous. Yet somehow, the woman managed to make it seem like nothing more than an offhand compliment. There was definite admiration in her eyes, but there was also a hint of humor, as if she were in on the joke. And despite himself, Nigel smiled and held out his hand. "Nigel Ferris."

"Charlotte Northrup." She took his hand in both of hers, diamonds twinkling on her fingers. "I was just telling my friend Willie how bored I was, and then I spotted you." Her smile was warm, and just the slightest bit wicked.

"Nigel, sorry to interrupt," Gabe said as he sidled to the rescue, his lips twitching in a suppressed grin, "but Madison's father wants a word." Nigel had never even met Phillip Merrick, but just at the moment he'd have gladly kissed the man's feet.

"I'm afraid I have to go." Nigel squeezed Charlotte's plump hands and released them. "Perhaps another time."

She nodded, her smile sagging just the slightest bit.

Nigel leaned closer, his whisper conspiratorial. "I'd much rather spend time with a woman as lovely as you, but I'm afraid duty calls."

"I understand." Charlotte was beaming again, already sizing up a distinguished gentleman across the room decked out in full military regalia.

Nigel took his leave, following Gabe to where Madison was standing with her father. After a brief introduction, Phillip Merrick excused himself, crossing the room to converse with the Swiss ambassador.

"Thanks for bailing me out," Nigel said, turning to face the two of them. "I'm afraid Miss Northrup was rather intent on commandeering me for the evening."

"Charlotte's harmless, I assure you," Madison said with a laugh. "She's just a bit man crazy. She sits on one of my father's boards and, according to him, makes eyes at all the male board members. So at least you can take heart in the fact that you're only one of many."

"Apparently." Nigel nodded toward the woman, who was now busy chatting up the military man. His response was much more enthusiastic, however, and Nigel found himself hoping Charlotte had found someone worthy of her flirtation.

"Any luck locating your contact?" Madison asked.

"Not so far." Nigel shook his head. "It's such a crush in here I'm not really sure how I'm supposed to find her."

"Well, if I understand things correctly, it's not so much about you finding her as it is her finding you."

"Which could be the fatal flaw in the whole plan," Nigel offered. "It's not as if I'm one of a kind. Without a flashing arrow over their head, I've no idea how anyone finds anyone in this crowd."

"Cullen said she had a description." Madison shrugged. "Just give it a little time. She'll show."

"Right, she'll just walk right up and ask about the weather." He sounded petulant, but damn it all to hell, he hated this sort of thing. He was much better at hunting down arms dealers and drug lords.

"Considering your lineage, I'd have thought you'd be a natural at affairs like this one." Gabe's remark was meant to be teasing, but it hit home with an accuracy his friend couldn't possibly understand.

"Being born a peer doesn't guarantee much of anything these days except a great deal of debt and an antiquated notion of one's status in society. And unfortunately, despite my father's every effort, I never cared much about either."

Gabe's dark brows drew together in a frown, his expression regretful. "I'm sorry, Nigel, I didn't mean..."

"I know." Nigel forced a smile. "It's just old baggage. Nothing to worry about."

"Well, we like you just the way you are." Madison reached over to squeeze his hand.

"Warts and all?" Nigel laughed, trying to ignore the uncomfortable pressure in his gut. His father had been dead for years, but his disappointment with his son seemed to have a life of its own, rearing its ugly head at the most inopportune times.

"Exactly," Gabe said, sliding an arm around his wife. "Now what do you say we try and figure out which of the women here is your contact?"

Nigel nodded, relieved at the change of conversation. He trusted Madison and Gabe with his life, but that didn't mean he wanted to bare his soul for them.

He turned away, surveying the crowd. There was honestly no way to determine who it was he was supposed to be meeting. But standing with his friends in the corner wasn't going to help. So with a sigh, he moved toward another group of partygoers, working up the initiative to break into their conversation.

Before he reached them, however, the crowd near the salon door shifted to make room for new arrivals. A man ushered two women into the room, both of them beautiful, but it was the one on the right who captured his attention.

In a word, she was magnificent. Auburn hair tumbled in loose curls down her back, set off by the glittering gold of her dress. The material clung to her with mouthwatering clarity, and Nigel felt his body respond to the mere sight of her—and then she stepped into the room, her face illuminated in the chandelier's light.

His heart stutter-stepped, his mind refusing to accept the information his brain was intent on telegraphing. *Melissa.* Dear God, it was Melissa.

"ARE YOU COMING IN? Or are you going to put down roots right here in the doorway?" Alicia's voice was teasing, but at the moment that's exactly what Melissa wanted to do. Or more accurately, she wanted to dig a hole in the floor and let it swallow her up. "Melissa, are you all right?" Her sister's expression was worried now, and Melissa forced a smile she absolutely did not feel.

"I'm fine. Just a little case of the jitters. You know how I loathe these things."

Alicia searched her face, clearly unconvinced, but Aaron had already crossed the room to greet some colleagues, and was looking askance at his wife.

"Go on," Melissa urged her sister. "Really. I'll join you in a moment."

Alicia nodded and moved off in the direction of her husband, stopping to chat with several people on her way. Melissa watched as Aaron pulled her into his embrace, and then she stared down at the floor, willing her pulse back into something resembling normalcy. Surely her mind had simply been playing tricks on her.

She hadn't seen Nigel Ferris. Not here. Not after all this time. Surely even God wouldn't play that big of a joke. Her heart was pounding, seemingly oblivious to the fifteen-year gap between the past and the present.

She sucked in a breath, physically working to calm her racing pulse. It was a mistake. A man who resembled Nigel, nothing more. She'd been thinking about relationships earlier, envying her sister's happiness. It was only natural that her brain would conjure an image of Nigel.

"Melissa?" His voice hadn't changed. The same deep husky whisper, the same wonderfully clipped accent. It had excited her then, and it excited her now, despite the fact that she'd sworn off the man all those years ago. "It is you, isn't it?"

She lifted her eyes, her gaze colliding with the liquid brown of his. God, he hadn't changed at all. Well, maybe there were a few more lines around the corners of his eyes, and the mustache was certainly new. But his hair still flopped over his right eye in the exact same way that had always made her want to straighten it. And he still smelled of some exotic English aftershave.

"It's me." The words came out breathy, almost giddy, and she clamped her mouth shut on the off chance that more inane responses were in the offing.

Nigel's hand closed around her elbow and he steered her backward through the salon door and down the hallway, until they reached a small paneled study. He pushed her inside, then followed, pulling the door firmly shut behind him.

They paused for a moment, and then with a groan he pulled her into his arms and kissed her. Not a how-do-you-do-haven't-seen-you-in-a-while kiss, but a take-no-prisoners-I'd-like-to-fuck-your-brains-out kiss, and she reveled in the remembered feel of him. The taste of his lips, the strength of his arms, the texture of his skin brushing against hers. It was delightful and frightening all at once, her insides fusing together in a way she'd completely forgotten.

It was heaven.

It was *insane.*

With a sigh, she pushed back, her breathing still coming in gasps. Nigel, to his credit, looked equally shaken.

"I'm sorry." He held up a hand as if to ward her off. "I don't know what I was thinking. It's just that seeing you there like that, I…it was like…" He stopped, still searching for words.

"Like sliding backward in time," she finished for him, her stomach still doing the tango.

"And then some." His smile was endearingly crooked, the mustache adding a rakish touch.

"I like the mustache," she said, the words coming out on a more or less even note.

"Really?" He ran his fingers over it, then grinned. "I grew it just after leaving Special Forces. I thought it made me look older. Although now I don't suppose I really need the help."

They stood looking at each other for another moment, and Melissa had to fight the urge to throw herself back into his arms. "So what do you do now that you're no longer in the military?" As casual conversation it was better than "what's your sign," but considering the fact that they'd just exchanged a ridiculously passionate kiss it seemed a little stilted.

"I work for the government." A shadow flickered across his face, one that Melissa recognized. Whatever he did, he wasn't going to share it with her. Which was fine, all things considered, since she couldn't be honest with him, either. "I know you're still taking photographs. I see your byline from time to time."

She felt absurdly flattered that he'd been following her career. "It's a living." Again with the brilliant conversation. But then what did one say to a man that could have been *the one* all those years ago? That is if Melissa had been the type to want or need commitment.

"A good one, I'd imagine. Although I'd assume it means placing yourself in harm's way more often than not." There was real concern in his voice, and Melissa let the sentiment wash over her like a warm summer breeze.

"Well, at least at the moment, I'm safer than not. I'm shooting photographs for a book about the UN."

"Sounds interesting." His words were perfunctory, but there was an entirely different conversation going on at pheromonal levels, her body practically singing out its need.

"It is. Most of the time." She wondered what he'd say if she told him why she was really here, and then suddenly everything clicked into place. Almost involuntarily she took a step closer, her focus on his mouth, on the mustache.

"So—" she licked her lips, her breath sticking in her throat "—how are you liking the weather in New York?"

"Actually," he replied, his eyes narrowing slightly as he, too, took a step forward, the distance between them now only inches, "it's much colder than Spain."

CHAPTER FOUR

"YOU'RE CIA." NIGEL STEPPED back, feeling a lot like he'd just fallen into a fun-park house of mirrors. "How long?"

Melissa frowned and took a step back, too, the distance between them symbolizing a whole lot more than just physicality. "Since before I knew you."

"So you lied to me." The words came of their own volition, his mind trotting out a picture of Payton's first wife. Mariam, also a journalist, had lied about her involvement in espionage as well, the end result being five dead, including Payton's brother.

"No." Melissa shook her head, her expression cool. "I *am* a photojournalist—I've got the awards and scars to prove it." She indicated the remnant of a jagged cut on her arm. "And I wouldn't be very good at my other job if I spilled my guts every time I wound up between the sheets."

She was angry, and he supposed she had a right. She wasn't Mariam, but the revelation, if anything, had reminded him firmly of why he never allowed his emotions to become entangled. The past was just that—the past. And although in this case he remembered it with occasional longing, the fact changed nothing.

"I shouldn't have said that. I just reacted without thinking. Forgive me." The words were the right ones, but there was little emotion behind them, and her eyes narrowed as she studied him.

"If you're standing here discussing Spain with me, you must have a few secrets of your own."

"I'm with British intelligence." He owed her that much. Besides, she was right—the fact that they were standing here made them allies of sorts. "I've been with MI6 since I left the military."

Her frown deepened. "I thought this was an American operation?"

"It is, more or less." He smiled, attempting to lessen the tension stretching between them. "A task force called Last Chance. We're a ragtag bunch of recruits, actually. CIA, FBI, ATF…you name it, they're probably involved in some way."

"That still doesn't explain you." She crossed her arms defensively, but the tension seemed to have eased a little.

"There's no explaining me, really." He grinned ruefully. "But in truth, I'm here because two of the task force's chief operatives, Gabe and Payton, are my friends."

"I see." She nodded even though there was absolutely no way she could possibly understand. Their affair had ended long before he'd been assigned to Gabe's unit. Before they'd been betrayed. Before Kevin and the others had died.

He shook his head, dispelling the shadows that had haunted him for so many years. "The point is that, at least for the moment, we seem to be working on the same side of the fence. And according to Cullen, you've got information we need."

"That's what my handler said." She was frowning again. "Something to do with missing nerve agent?"

"Exactly. It was stolen from Russia several days ago, and we believe it's in transit to the U.S. Intel seems to indicate that your mark might be helping ours."

"I don't have a mark. Just a list of suspects as long as my arm." She sat down on a brocade chair, the rich material a perfect backdrop for her glittering gold gown. She wasn't beautiful in a peaches-and-cream kind of way. Instead, she had an almost Renaissance air with her pale skin and burnished hair. Her eyes were neither green nor blue but a curious mix of both, tilting slightly upward at the corners as if perpetually crinkled in laughter.

Her mouth, however, was the thing Nigel had always loved the most. Incongruent with the rest of her delicate features, her lips were full and lusty. Made for a man to kiss. In fact, just the thought of her mouth beneath his sent shards of pleasure slicing through him.

He ignored the sensation, however, pushing away his attraction. It was nothing more than a distraction and there were far more pressing matters at hand. "I understand. But it still might help if you tell me what you do know."

"Unfortunately, not much. I've only just started to dig. Which means the best I can do at the moment is tell you who *isn't* involved." She opened the small gold purse she carried and produced a folded piece of paper.

"I've divided it into people I've cleared, people I still have questions about, and people I haven't had a chance to investigate. Everyone listed here has access in some way to the various Peacekeeping shipments around the globe. Logistics and transportation seemed the obvious starting point. But of course there are also people at high levels within the Secretariat with the clearance to accomplish whatever they put their minds to."

"What tipped the CIA off to begin with?" Nigel leaned back against a desk, crossing one leg over the other, wishing he had a cigarette. Unfortunately, New York was currently on a smoke-free binge, which had left Nigel practically forced into cold-turkey withdrawal.

"A contact in Africa noticed some discrepancies with shipment documentations. Crates that were listed on the manifest but never arrived at the final destination. Further investigation showed similar situations in Southeast Asia and Bosnia."

"What was the explanation?"

"In Africa it was blamed on a military attack by opposing forces. In Cambodia it was simply noted as lost."

"And in Bosnia?" He tried to keep from staring at her mouth.

"It apparently suffered severe water damage and was abandoned at port of entry."

"Reasonable explanations."

"On the surface, yes. But at least one of the crates, Bosnia's, went missing about the same time that several large munitions were stolen from a facility in northern Russia. Add that to some of the intel that's been gathered, and talk of an insider at UN Peacekeeping began to take on credibility. Enough at least for me to start an investigation."

She held out the folded list, and Nigel reached to take it, careful not to let his fingers touch hers. "I'm sorry I wasn't able to get more, but I didn't know I was meeting with you until just before the party. This was all I could manage on such short notice."

"This will help tremendously. We're trying to keep this from going public as long as possible. For all we know, the stolen nerve agent is headed for somewhere else entirely. Until we have more definitive information we're trying to keep things close to the vest."

"I can understand that." She smiled, the gesture lightening her expression and making Nigel's heart twist. "I've spent almost my entire adult life hiding something from someone."

"Well, obviously you do it very well."

She flinched, and he regretted his words. They'd been meant as a flippant reply, but the remark had hit a nerve for them both, her lies to cover her work as much a part of their past as they were a part of the present. "It wasn't anything to do with us."

"There was no us." He sounded harsher than he'd intended, but it was the truth. "Not in the sense you mean, anyway. We always knew it was temporary, and pretending differently now is only going to make it harder when we have to walk away."

"And we have to do that?" She didn't sound convinced.

"You know that we do. Being seen with me would only

compromise your position. More so now than fifteen years ago."

She nodded, her eyes looking suspiciously bright, but Nigel didn't allow himself to dwell on the fact. It was difficult enough to see her again, and to think that their meeting was causing her pain was more than he could bear.

He twisted around to the desk behind him, grabbing a notepad and a pen. Scribbling hastily, he jotted down his phone numbers and the hotel where he was staying, then thrust it into her hand. "If you find out anything more—or if you need me—this is how to reach me." He wasn't entirely certain why he'd mentioned need. Maybe it was his overworked libido, or maybe he just wanted her to know that he still cared. Either way the words hung heavy in the air.

Melissa stood up and closed the distance between them, lifting her hand to stroke the side of his face, the contact setting off small explosions inside every nerve. "You look wonderful, Nigel. And for what it's worth, there was an *us*. Impossible maybe, but it was there. And I, for one, will cherish the memory forever."

He opened his mouth to answer her, to try and formulate something that resembled a coherent sentence, but she was gone.

ALL SHE NEEDED was to catch her breath, to ease the band of steel that seemed to have lodged itself permanently around her rib cage.

Forcing air in and out of her lungs, Melissa pressed her back against the cool paneling of the alcove under the stairs. She told herself it was only the surprise, the past reopened after all these years, but she knew it was more than that. It was Nigel. Pure and simple. He'd always affected her this way, robbing her of coherent speech and thought, pulling the very breath from her body.

It was a ridiculous notion, but one that was nevertheless absolutely true.

Damn the man.

She pushed off of the wall and straightened the narrow straps of her gown. She'd waited in the shadows until she'd seen him return to the party, looking devastatingly handsome in his tuxedo. She preferred him in jeans—or the altogether—but he certainly managed to fill out Armani nicely.

She shook her head, dispelling the image. She was a free agent. Her job required it and she preferred it that way. The decision had been made long ago.

Sighing, she walked down the hallway; her breathing, thank goodness, almost back to normal. The good news was that she'd most likely not see him after tonight. New York was a big city, and there was really no reason for their paths to cross again. Even if their investigations should intersect in future, she could always have someone else meet with him.

It was a cop-out and she knew it, but sometimes self-preservation was the name of the game. All that considered, they'd still have to share the same space for at least the next couple of hours. Fortunately, the room was a big one. But standing in the doorway, looking at the glittering throng, she felt as if it was just the two of them.

He was talking to a tall dark man and an equally stunning blonde, the three of them looking like something from the society pages—definitely not her world. In an odd way, the thought was comforting.

She stepped into the room, and as if he had some sort of radar, his eyes lifted to hers, his mouth curling slightly at the corners. It was a mocking salute, but there was an undercurrent she couldn't ignore, even with the distance between them.

"Melissa?" A soft hand touched her arm, and she jumped, the sound of her sister's voice breaking the spell. "Are you all right?"

"I'm fine. I just got a little hot, so I went outside for some air." As excuses went, it was pretty lame, but Melissa had learned through experience that the simpler the lie the better.

Alicia's frown deepened. "It's freezing outside."

"Bracing, actually." Melissa widened her smile, linking her arm through her sister's. "I was only out there for a minute. And now I'm feeling much better. What do you say we mingle a bit? You haven't introduced me to a soul." She actually had no desire to meet anyone. Hell, all she really wanted was to grab a taxi and put this night behind her. But that wasn't the drill. She needed to play the game, make certain that no one questioned her presence at the party.

Alicia, seemingly satisfied about her sister's well-being, steered Melissa over to a group of dignitaries. She sent a prayer heavenward that it wasn't Nigel's group. She'd work hard to play the game, but she'd be damned if she'd set herself up for more heartache. And at the moment, just being in the same room with the man was about the limit of what her overwrought nerves could endure.

"May I present out host, Jacques Ormond," Alicia was saying, and Melissa forced her thoughts back to the here and now.

Ormond nodded once, his smile perfunctory. Melissa returned the gesture, wishing she were better at small talk. Fortunately, she was spared the endeavor as Aaron joined the group, his arm encircling his wife, his attention centered on Ormond as they began a spirited discussion of foreign policy. Despite her secondary occupation, Melissa wasn't much interested in political philosophy. By her reckoning, it was politics that caused most of the problems in the world.

And she'd seen firsthand the atrocities that had been committed in the name of a political ideal. Seen the havoc wreaked on ordinary people and their lives. She shook her head, clearing her thoughts, and stepped away from the group, relieved to be on her own again.

Nigel had moved across the room and was now talking to an elegantly clad elderly woman. She'd most likely been a beauty in her day, and she wore the remnants of her youth well. Despite the age difference between the two of them, Melissa felt the familiar tug of jealousy and wondered how it was that a man she hadn't laid eyes on in over fifteen years could manage to upset her simply by talking to an octogenarian.

Strange world.

"You have been abandoned by your friends?"

The voice was deep and foreign. Melissa turned to find the dark brown eyes of a distinguished-looking man. "No. Actually I'm afraid you've got it backward." She forced a polite smile. "I'm the one who abandoned them."

"It is their loss then." His smile showed a row of evenly shaped white teeth. Not even Colgate Whitening would achieve that kind of gleam. Either he was wearing dentures, or he'd had his teeth capped.

She smiled at the ridiculous direction of her thoughts, and he mistook the gesture for an invitation. Reaching for her hand, he bowed slightly, his dry lips lingering a bit too long against her skin. "I am Hakan Celik." He straightened, his manners courtly, his dark hair and complexion making him seem exotic and slightly menacing, despite the smile.

Perhaps it was the fact that he was staring at her cleavage—what there was of it—or maybe it was just the night in general; either way, Melissa suddenly wanted nothing more than to escape.

"There is dancing." Celik smiled. "Perhaps you will allow me?" The question was obviously only a formality, his hand tightening on her arm as he led her over to the dance floor. Short of starting an international incident, she really didn't see any way out of it. At least she'd be concentrating on fending off his roaming hands rather than on the Englishman across the room. Her mother had been right—there *was* a silver lining to every situation, you just had to find it.

The orchestra was playing something Sinatra and she allowed herself to be twirled around the room. Actually Celik wasn't half-bad as a dancer, if she overlooked his palm warm against her butt.

"You work in New York?" As conversation went it wasn't exactly sparkling, but then Melissa had always found it difficult to be charming and dance at the same time.

"Yes." Celik smiled, the white teeth highlighted against his dark skin. "I am with the Turkish Consulate." He said it as if he expected her to be impressed, and so she nodded with what she hoped was an engaging smile. "And you?"

"I'm just a photographer." Definitely an understatement, but then she wasn't really a toot-your-own-horn kind of girl.

"Ah," Celik said dismissively, twirling her around, his hand massaging now.

Indignant, Melissa started to pull away, but then she saw Nigel dancing with the blonde, his smile warm and intimate. Gritting her teeth, Melissa tipped back her head, laughing as if Celik was the most charming man on the planet.

Two could play at that game.

The couples passed on a glide and Melissa shot Nigel a saccharine smile before batting her eyes at Celik in what she hoped looked like complete adoration.

The man, to his credit, looked a bit nonplussed but countered immediately with a slow and somewhat lecherous grin. "You are very beautiful, Ms. Pope."

"You know my name?" Flirtation vanished, as alarm flared.

"Of course. I make it my business to know the names of all beautiful women." His smile was slick. And although he was handsome in an Omar Sharif way, he was a little too polished for her tastes. Not to mention amorous.

She realized too late that he'd maneuvered them into a darkened corner of the room separated from the rest of the dancers by a row of potted palms. She shivered and tried to move from his embrace.

"I really should be getting back to my sister."

"Not quite yet, surely?" Celik's hands tightened on her

shoulders, and he pulled her close, his teeth flashing in the shadows as he smiled. "We've only just been acquainted, and I am certain there is much for us to learn yet."

The sentence had a decidedly sexual overtone. Melissa wasn't fond of making scenes, but she'd happily knee the man in the groin before allowing him to take advantage.

She cursed her own stupidity in letting herself be set up. Normally she'd have gone to all extremes to avoid someone like Celik, but she'd allowed her fractured feelings for Nigel to color her judgment, a stupid game of adolescent one-upmanship taking precedence over good sense.

Celik's breath was hot against her cheek, and with a sigh, she gave one last try for diplomacy. "I really do need to go."

"Not without a kiss." He bent closer, and she could smell brandy on his breath. Great, a lothario and a lush.

"Hopefully, this is going to hurt you more than it will me." Twisting to the right, she lifted her knee, and was just short of contact when Nigel's voice interrupted the action.

"Darling," he said, his cultured voice washing over her like a tonic, "I've been searching everywhere." His tone was proprietary as he slipped an arm around her, Celik's surprise giving way to anger.

The diplomat's eyes narrowed to slits, as he glared at the two of them.

"I'm sure you'll excuse us?" Nigel didn't wait for an answer, leading her away from the palms, back onto the dance floor, pulling her closer than absolutely necessary.

It seemed she'd fallen out of the frying pan and into the fire.

The music was slow, sort of undulating, and Melissa let her body lean into his, the contact too exquisite for words. They danced in silence for what seemed like hours, but was, of course, only minutes, and then he leaned close, his breath stirring the loose tendrils of her hair.

"You haven't thanked me yet."

His words broke through the languorous fog and she stiffened. "That's because I didn't need your help."

"Right." There was laughter in his voice, and the sound of it scratched along her nerve endings like a cat on tin. "You definitely had everything in control. One more minute and the man would have been howling bloody murder as he clutched the Turkish jewels. Not exactly discreet behavior."

Despite herself, she smiled. "Sometimes it takes a knee to get the point across."

"You should have known better anyway. Surely your radar is more finely tuned than that?"

"I was a bit distracted." She spoke slowly through clenched teeth; the man, as usual, caused equal measures of exasperation and exultation.

Nigel smiled, his eyes knowing, and pulled her closer.

"I thought we were supposed to be staying away from each other? Professional distance and all that."

"Well, I wouldn't be much of a gentleman if I'd allowed that man to get his hands on you."

"I'm not sure that *gentleman* is a word I'd have chosen to describe you."

"You wound me," Nigel said, the words belied by the laughter still crinkling the corners of his eyes. "Besides, you know as well as I do that sometimes being together is the best way to prove that there's nothing suspicious going on. And unless someone is onto you, I hardly think this is the place for prying eyes."

He was right, of course. But that didn't make contact between them any easier to bear. The music slowed, and they stopped moving, merely swaying in place, Melissa's breathing coming in short gasps. He bent his head, and she closed her eyes, knowing she was going to regret contact but completely unable to do anything about it.

Fortunately, fate had other things in mind, the shrill sound of her cell phone shattering the moment. She fumbled for her purse with shaking fingers, holding the flip phone to her ear.

"Melissa." Ed's voice was tinny sounding, cell-phone reception in the city an iffy thing at best. "I need to meet with you."

"Now?" she squeaked, Nigel's hand warm on her elbow.

"Yes." He was fading out. "It's imperative." He rattled off an address, and said he'd meet her in an hour. Melissa clicked off the phone.

"Something important, I take it?"

Too much had happened too fast, and Melissa, quite frankly, was having a hard time sorting through it. But whatever else was going on, there had been no mistaking the urgency in Ed's voice. "I've got to go," she said with a nod.

"This very moment?" Nigel frowned, as if he didn't quite believe her.

"Yes." She forced a smile she certainly didn't feel. "Duty calls. It was wonderful seeing you again. But if you'll excuse me, I really do have to go. I need to find my sister and tell her I'm leaving." Now that was a recitation worthy of Miss Manners.

Nigel tightened his hand on her elbow, his eyes searching hers. "You're sure everything is all right?"

The man of her proverbial dreams had just come crashing back into her life and once again, she was going to walk out the door without looking back. Nothing was okay—but she wasn't going to share the fact. "It's fine. Just part of being a photographer. They say jump—"

"And you say how high," he finished for her, still looking unconvinced.

"Exactly." They stood for a moment, their bodies revealing things their tongues weren't interested in verbalizing. Then with a resolute sigh, Melissa broke contact. "I really do have to go."

Turning away from him, she blindly pushed her way through the crowd, intent only on escaping the room before she lost it completely. The air outside was freezing, but it was nearly a half block from the consulate before she realized she'd not only forgotten her coat, she'd forgotten to tell her sister she was leaving.

She turned around, then stopped herself. She'd call Alicia from the taxi. Ed was waiting, and besides, if she'd learned nothing else tonight, it was the incontrovertible fact that as far as Nigel Ferris was concerned, she hadn't the slightest hope of controlling her emotions. And so, like Cinderella, she'd run from the ball. Only she wasn't interested in having the prince find her. No, far better to simply disappear into the night.

CHAPTER FIVE

"SO, WHO WAS the lady in gold?" Gabe's gaze was probing and appreciative all at once.

"Our contact." Nigel forced himself to focus on his friend. His gut instinct had been to follow Melissa out of the party, to finish what they had started. But his common sense overruled the thought. Despite the fact that he was still attracted to the woman, or maybe because of it, he needed to let her go. To keep the past firmly where it was supposed to be. "Although I'm not sure that she gave us anything all that useful."

"Anything is better than nothing." Madison joined them, linking her arm through her husband's.

"Well, according to Melissa, she's only just begun her investigation. Which means that she can't point to a guilty party at this point. She did provide a list of names. Suspects as well as those she's ruled out."

"It's a starting point," Gabe said, his brows drawn together in a frown. "You called her Melissa. Do you know her?"

"Of course he knows her." Madison smiled, her eyes gentle. "Didn't you see the way he was dancing with her?"

Nigel wished Madison wasn't quite as good at seeing things. But even if she hadn't been, Gabe would have ferreted it out eventually. So better to just tell them the truth—at least a version of it—and be done. "I do know her. Or more accurately, I knew her. It was a long time ago."

"But it was intense." As usual, Madison's perception was dead-on.

"Something like that," he admitted, staring down at his feet. "But I haven't seen her in years. In fact, I was as surprised as anyone to find her here, and more so when I realized she was our contact."

"You didn't know she was CIA, I take it?"

"You lot aren't all that keen on advertising your membership." Nigel shrugged with a nonchalance he most certainly didn't feel.

"But you had a relationship." Madison was as relentless as her husband.

"Yes." He nodded for emphasis. "Past tense."

"It didn't look past tense to me." Gabe shot a glance to the doorway. Melissa was gone, but it was almost as if some essence of her still lingered. Nigel could still see the coppery glint of her hair against the gold filigree of her dress.

"Well, it is." The very fact that he snapped at his friend was indication that it wasn't, although that in and of itself was a ridiculous notion considering she was gone. No doubt for good. Nigel sighed. "Look, it was a long time ago. I was practically another person. And apparently so was Melissa." His dry comment evoked a grin from Gabe, but Madison's expression was still quizzical.

"You cared about her a lot." It was a statement, not a question. Occupational hazard with Madison, but Nigel didn't like being dissected.

"Let it go." His voice was low and brooked no argument. Madison nodded her agreement, although there was something in her face that indicated the topic hadn't been retired permanently.

So he'd accept the battle and weather the war. He'd done it before.

"Hopefully she's given us something we can use. The honest-to-God truth is that we haven't got enough information to target anything specific. Even if we agree that the nerve agent is headed for the U.S., the number of potential entry points is almost limitless. Not to mention the fact that there's nothing concrete to tie any of this to a purported traitor at the UN."

"With luck, Harrison and Payton will be able to sort through the chatter and find some sort of lead. With Homeland Security on alert, it's much more difficult to get something into the U.S. than it was before 9/11, which should play to our advantage as it actually does limit access. For the moment, the possible manipulation of shipments through Peacekeeping is our best bet. And Melissa's list of suspects is a good start."

"The problem being that we're still shooting blind and the clock is ticking. Whatever has been planned, you know it's meant to happen soon." Nigel couldn't help the edge of dread that clawed at him. He hated racing against an unknown adversary, although he'd spent much of his adult life doing just that.

"All the more reason we move quickly." Gabe fidgeted with his bow tie, his mind already moving beyond the party.

"Sounds to me like it's time to make an exit," Madison said.

Gabe took the statement as permission and immediately headed for the door, Madison falling into step with Nigel as they followed. "She's beautiful, your Melissa."

"She's not my anything."

Madison smiled, her hand warm on his arm. "Sometimes fate throws the very things we're most afraid of right at our feet."

Nigel wasn't afraid of Melissa. He opened his mouth to tell Madison exactly that, but then shut it before he could issue the words. Truth was, she did scare him. Or at least the intensity of the emotions she aroused scared him.

But the fact wasn't relevant. Melissa was gone, and he had a job to do. And *fate* simply wasn't a factor he was willing to consider. At least not now—hell, not ever.

"I THOUGHT EVERYTHING WAS settled." Khamis exchanged a glance with Malik and then returned his attention to the man standing in front of him. Paulo Salvatore would sell his mother if the price was right. Khamis had been doing business with him for more than a decade, but despite the longevity of their association, Khamis didn't trust the man.

"Our network has been compromised." Paulo extended his hands in a shrug. The Spanish were lazy fools, but until now useful. "My father is dead, and Interpol is all over us. I myself only just escaped the bloodbath. Had I not been in Seville on business..." Again with the shrug.

"I don't give a damn what's happened to your network." Khamis leaned forward, his stance intended to be threatening. "We had an agreement and I expect you to honor it."

Malik shot him a questioning glance, his normally placid face marred with a frown. "Perhaps we should reconsider." His words were pitched low, for Khamis's ears only, but Khamis rejected the thought with a shake of his head. He'd worked too hard for this, and he wasn't giving it up without a fight.

"There must be an alternative," Khamis said, his attention centered again on Paulo.

"Perhaps." The younger man narrowed his eyes, his gaze assessing. "But it will cost you."

Khamis tightened his hand on the butt of the gun stuck in the waistband of his pants. It was tempting to shoot the arrogance off the Spaniard's face, but his cause would not be furthered by the action. Better to maintain control. At least until he had the information he needed. "We will meet your price."

"I don't want money." Paulo was clearly nervous now, his fingers fidgeting with a button as he worked up his courage. "Since my father's death, there are eyes everywhere. I need to disappear. To start over. I believe you can make that happen."

Again Khamis exchanged a look with Malik, his friend giving the barest of nods. "Consider it done."

Paulo searched his face, and then apparently satisfied, reached into his pocket for a slip of paper. "Call this number."

"And who exactly am I calling?"

"An insider with the UN. He'll be expecting you."

"And this man is to be trusted?" Khamis's eyes narrowed as he considered the change of plans.

"*Sí.* I've used him more than once to transport goods into particularly difficult regions. He'll make it happen. You have my word."

Paulo's word carried no weight with Khamis, but there was no point in sharing the fact. He reached for the paper, and once it was securely in hand, nodded toward his partner. "Go with Malik. As soon as I am certain that your contact is legitimate, we'll arrange for you to disappear."

Permanently.

But that, too, wasn't information he was prepared to divulge. He'd found through experience that people got rather rebellious when they thought they were about to die.

ED HAD PICKED one hell of a derelict place to meet. The shadow of the Brooklyn Bridge fell black against the diner, neon light refracting off the East River. Taking the time to change out of the gold gown had obviously been a good idea. This wasn't exactly a couture kind of joint.

She pushed through the door, the blast of warm air cloying. Shrugging out of her coat, she considered the coatrack and then rejected it, preferring not to share her coat's warmth with anything furry.

The place was sparsely occupied, not that she was surprised. A haggard waitress stood behind the counter making a new pot of coffee. Two teenagers dressed in chains, leather and a stunning array of body piercings sat at the far end of the counter, nursing slices of some kind of pie, and a wizened old man sat huddled in a booth against the far wall. His clothes were old and tattered, but she could see a spark of intelligence in his eyes.

Besides the four of them, the place was empty. No Ed. She

glanced at her watch to confirm the time. He should be here. With a sigh, she slid into a booth near the front of the restaurant, her back against the wall, her line of vision extending from the front door to the kitchen.

It was an occupational hazard, but she liked knowing the lay of the land. The waitress sidled over with a torn and stained menu, but Melissa waved it away, asking instead for a cup of coffee.

The woman nodded and returned to the counter, making a great display of pouring the coffee. Maybe she was ticked that Melissa hadn't ordered something more. Tips in a place like this were probably meager at best.

Not that any of it really mattered.

She leaned her head back against the wall and fought the urge to close her eyes. It was late, and by even the most conservative standards, it had been a trying evening, her emotions roller-coastering in and out of control with alarming intensity.

The waitress returned with the coffee and a tight-lipped smile, and Melissa ordered a slice of pie. She had no intention of eating the stuff, but somehow it soothed her sense of fair play to give the woman a little more business. Especially if she was going to be sitting here long.

She consulted her watch again, wondering where in the world Ed was. He was usually such a stickler for punctuality. She sighed, checked the watch again, and settled in to wait. The coffee, despite the fact that it was fresh brewed, had a nasty bitter taste. Still, it was hot and loaded with caffeine, so she drank it.

The pie arrived looking surprisingly tasty, and she allowed herself one bite. After all, a girl needed nourishment. Mata Hari-ing took a lot out of a person. She laughed at the thought, drawing a frown from the waitress and a smirk from one of the two teenagers.

Sobering, she shifted a little, enough so that she wasn't

forced to stare at the boys. She kept them in her peripheral vision, though. Not that she expected an attack from that quarter. It was just better to cover all bases. She took another sip of the acrid coffee and followed it with another bite of the pie. The apples were nicely coated with cinnamon and sugar, and the crust was amazingly flaky.

That, or she was just starving to death. Running into an old lover could do that to a girl. She considered the idea and then rejected it. The truth was, her appetite *had* been stimulated—but she wasn't hungry for food. She was hungry for Nigel, and the idea angered her as much as anything. Sure, there'd been the occasional night when she'd remembered their lovemaking with longing, but she'd always written it off to loneliness or the amazingly loud ticking of her biological clock.

Only tonight, the real live deal had presented himself, and there could be no denying the connection between them. She hadn't exaggerated the physical chemistry. It was still combustible even after all this time. But it remained gossamer thin, as well. Nothing that could ever be substantial.

They were two of a kind—he led a life of danger, and she walked a tightrope of duplicity. Neither good ingredients for happily ever after. Not that she wanted anything like that. It was just that seeing him had brought back so many memories.

Most of them wonderful.

She smiled at the thought and had another sip of coffee. Where the hell was Ed? The last thing she wanted to do was spend the middle of the night sitting in a derelict coffee shop mooning over a man she'd left fifteen years ago.

The waitress walked over to the old man and refilled his coffee cup. The pot was different from the one she'd been drinking from, and Melissa found herself wondering if perhaps the good stuff was only for regulars. More likely he was drinking decaf. Not a bad idea. Her nerves were jittery enough without caffeine.

As if to dispute the fact, she reached for the cup, tipped it in camaraderie toward the old man and had another swallow, the bitter beverage sending comforting warmth shooting through her body.

Laughing at her ridiculous musings, Melissa set the cup back on the table, dismissing both the old man and all thoughts of coffee. Ed had said their meeting was important. Something about new information. She wondered if finally they'd gotten a bead on the man behind the UN smuggling. If they had found the culprit it would mean an end to her investigation, which meant she was free to move on to other more interesting assignments.

She'd recently been offered an assignment in the Middle East, but had had to turn it down for the sake of her work at the UN. Boring from a photographic point of view, she was more than ready to see the last of the Secretariat and head off to points unknown. A bit of an adrenaline junkie, she needed the rush to keep her edge, and too much time in New York was not the ticket.

That and the fact that the desert was a great place to forget all about adolescent romantic yearnings. Nigel Ferris was just a man. And she was a woman who had better things to do than sit around drinking bad coffee waiting for some CIA pencil pusher to show up.

Ed usually chose out-of-the-way places for their meetings—they'd once met in a barn in Mogadishu—but this topped the charts. She checked her watch again, noting that he was fast approaching really late.

It had been a long night, and her head hurt. All she wanted was a warm bath, a warm bed—and…no she wasn't going to go there at all.

Shaking her head, she fumbled with her purse, her exhaustion making her clumsy. Finally she wrestled her cell phone out and flipped it open. Hitting autodial, she grimaced at the irony that number one was a man she hardly knew, a man whose sole job, it seemed, was to send her off to ferret out dubious information. In truth, Ed was Charlie to her Angel, although neither of them would have been cast in the movie.

The phone at the other end rang once, twice, three times and was then picked up by an automated voice that announced that the number wasn't available. She clicked the phone closed and dropped it back in her purse. It wasn't like Ed to miss a meeting, but nothing he'd said made her think there was any real reason to worry. They'd just missed each other somehow.

So until she could run him to ground, best to follow procedure. Retreat to a safe place, in this case, home. She stifled a yawn and reached for her wallet, extracting a ten to drop on the table. Probably a bit over the customary twenty percent, but she wasn't in the mood to wait for change. If it was important enough, he'd call her again, and they could meet somewhere closer to home. In a clean restaurant where they served better coffee. If not, then they could talk tomorrow.

She stood up, holding on to the table for a moment to clear her head. She couldn't remember the last time she'd been so tired.

She picked up her coat but didn't put it on. The heat in the diner was stifling and suddenly all she wanted was to feel the crisp fall air. The old man nodded absently as she walked by, and the waitress lifted an eyebrow. Other than that, she might as well have been invisible. A cold night in a cold city surrounded by strangers.

The wind outside was brisk, cooling her almost instantly, her head clearing in the damp air. She slipped on her coat and started to walk toward the corner. A streetlamp cast a bright yellow circle, the warm light beckoning, and she stopped in its glow, searching the street for a taxi.

Traffic, however, was nonexistent, and her stomach was beginning to reject the coffee, roiling in protest of the nasty stuff. With a sigh, she left the light from the streetlamp and headed downtown toward the subway. Late-night trains could be a bit dicey, but standing in the cold in a less-than-desirable neighborhood wasn't a picnic, either. The subway was simply the lesser of two evils.

She passed into the shadow of the bridge, the dark seeming to swallow up everything. The night air was strangely quiet for a city that never sleeps, and despite the fact that she wasn't a particularly skittish person, Melissa shivered, quickening her pace.

The buildings here were even more derelict than the ones surrounding the diner, many of them boarded up, all of them dark. There were boxes and blankets crowded onto stoops along the way. It was a hell of a cold night to sleep on the streets. Melissa wondered what they would do in a couple of months when the snow came.

Her head was pounding now, the rhythm threatening to rob her of rational thought. She checked a street sign, relieved to see that she only had a couple more blocks to go. Clutching her purse and trying to stay focused, she moved on, oblivious now to the street around her, the only important thing being to make the train.

Half a block farther, she stopped suddenly, her stomach clenching in agony, the pain enough to send shudders racing through her as she grabbed her gut. Frowning, she cursed the fact that she'd trusted the pie and tried to forge onward, but the pain was coming in sharp waves now, the contractions making her nauseous. An alleyway beckoned, and Melissa ran.

It might not be a nice neighborhood, but she'd be damned if she was going to throw up right there on the street. Bracing her hand against a brick wall, she bent double and let it rip, the evacuation immediately bringing relief.

When she found Ed, there was going to be hell to pay. Pulling a tissue from her purse she wiped her mouth, feeling weak but much better. Making a solemn vow never to eat apple pie again, she turned back toward the street, intent now on finding the subway stop and getting home.

But three steps later, she was hit again with the racking pains. This time she admitted she needed help, and with a concerted effort, dragged open her purse and pulled out her phone. She hit number one again, but the result was the same. No Ed. There was a risk to involving her sister, the invented explanations sure to bring all kinds of recrimination, but it beat the hell out of dying in the middle of the alley.

She started to call, but before she reached the first button, the nausea seized her again, and the phone went flying in her effort to avoid the regurgitated coffee and pie. This time there was no relief, just another wave of cramping and nausea, the alley starting to spin alarmingly.

She tried to brace her hands on the brick wall, but couldn't quite manage the task and ended up falling against it, then sliding down, her head pounding, dry heaves shaking her body with the force of a jackhammer.

She struggled for breath, the still-coherent bit of her mind struggling to decipher what was happening. She'd had food poisoning once in Istanbul, and although it had been horrible, she didn't remember it being this bad.

Maybe there were different kinds.

Frankly, she didn't care. All she wanted was for the pain to stop. She tried to push to her knees, but the effort was simply too much, instead she rolled over onto her side, with the hysterical thought that sitting amidst her own puke she'd easily be mistaken for a street person.

Hell, they probably smelled better.

Darkness edged forward from the corners of her vision, stealthily wrenching control from her conscious mind. She wanted to fight it, but the effort, it seemed, was beyond her control.

CHAPTER SIX

NIGEL STOOD at the window of his hotel room looking out onto Park Avenue. Its placid tranquility was a relief after the turmoil of the reception. Despite the fact that he'd spent the better part of his youth attending the bloody things, he'd never gotten the hang of them.

Maybe it was a character defect, or maybe it was because it had all been so damn important to his father, but either way he just wasn't up to anything requiring pomp and circumstance, whatever the hell that was.

If only he'd been a second son.

But that was Andrew's role, and he'd managed it quite nicely, keeping the family name in the newspapers on a regular basis. Not always in the best of lights, mind you, but front and center nevertheless.

Nigel blew out a breath, pushing thoughts of his wayward brother aside. They'd both made their beds ages ago, and there was no point in rehashing it now. Besides, the truth of the matter was that his wakefulness was no more the product of his family's peculiarities than it was the product of his dislike of social engagements. No, the fact was his nocturnal restlessness had everything to do with an auburn-headed siren by the name of Melissa.

She was the reason he was standing here in the wee hours of the morning staring out the window counting taxis, and the idea didn't sit well. Not because of anything she'd done. More because of what he hadn't done. He'd let her slip away.

Just like last time. And despite the fact that it had probably all been for the best, he couldn't help wondering if maybe he'd been wrong—if *they'd* been wrong.

He shook his head, smiling at his own flight of fancy. The fact that both Payton and Gabriel had found happiness in their respective marriages was apparently getting to him, the idea of a life of normalcy seductive. But Nigel had found that seductive things were rarely as advertised, in most cases turning out to be nothing more than disappointment.

No, it was better that she was gone. If any further contact was warranted, he'd send Payton. His mind made up, Nigel heaved a sigh and turned from the window. If he wasn't going to sleep, he might as well get some work done.

Pulling out the desk chair, he had a seat and picked up the folded paper Melissa had given him. He'd already gone over her list twice and nothing had jumped out at him, but sometimes it took repetition to recognize a pattern. So he read through it again.

She'd been thorough in her work so far, investigating each person with the meticulous care of a professional. Unfortunately, she'd spoken the truth when she said she'd only just begun and nothing she'd found so far pointed to a traitor. He threw the list down in frustration. Melissa hadn't known what exactly they were looking for, and she'd told him herself that she'd only had a short time to prepare. Maybe there was something more.

He smiled at the thought, not entirely certain if he was motivated by the thought of gaining further insight into UN trading practices or by the chance to see Melissa again. Considering his current physical state, it was probably the latter.

Angry at his ability to control neither body nor mind, he pushed back from the desk, half-inclined to pay a call on Payton. His suite was just down the hall, across from Harrison's. Cullen as usual had provided nothing but the best. But a quick glance at the clock stopped all forward motion.

It was too damn late for calling on anyone. Besides, Payton would suss out the reality of the situation in a heartbeat, and, at the moment, Nigel wasn't up to his friend's caustic comments. Which left the minibar. There was something disgusting about the little rows of bottles, as if they were play-pretend drinks, but it was way past time for room service, so baby bottles it was.

He pulled out two rounds of Maker's Mark and poured them in a glass. It still wasn't quite half-full, so he pulled out a third and added it to the mix. Probably ten quid a pop, but hell, Cullen was paying.

He sipped the fiery liquid. He loved a good bourbon. It was an American taste he'd picked up, much to his father's disdain, hanging out with Payton and Gabe. And he'd never given it up. It was exactly the medicine he needed. Enough little bottles and he'd be able to forget all about Melissa Pope—at least for tonight.

IT WAS COLD. Bone-shattering cold. And something was making a god-awful racket. Melissa worked to open her eyes, but neither of them seemed to be cooperating. She concentrated on her body, trying to assess what the problem was. She remembered waiting for Ed in the crappy diner and not a whole hell of a lot else.

Finally, through sheer force of will, her eyes opened, and she immediately shut them again to blot out the horrible spinning. Bile rose in her throat, and with it more memory. She'd felt ill and gone into an alley to throw up.

Carefully she opened her eyes again, this time steeling herself to wait out the spinning. Slowly the revolutions stopped and her vision cleared. The noise she was hearing finally took form and she realized it was her teeth chattering. Again marshaling her determination, she clamped her mouth shut and then relaxed slowly, the noise ceasing.

The alley was silent, the light dim. Because of the overhanging buildings it was hard to tell the time of day, but she'd guess early morning. Pushing carefully to her feet, she was relieved to find that, despite the cold and her shivering, her muscles were still responding to her brain.

She tried to conjure up a memory of something happening, but there was nothing. She clearly remembered the coffee shop. The pie and waiting for Ed. And more vaguely the walk toward the subway ending with her incapacitation in the alley. She must have passed out.

Looking down, she visually verified her story with the remnants of last night's bout with her stomach. Overall it was a pretty disgusting sight. She supposed she should consider herself lucky that the worst thing to have happened was a night spent passed out in an alley. Although, based on the pounding in her head, that wasn't exactly a good thing, at least the spinning and nausea seemed to have abated.

She searched the area for her handbag but turned up nothing. Add that to the cost of bad coffee. At least she hadn't had much money. And credit cards could be canceled. Still, it was not the best of situations.

She closed her eyes, her mind replaying the events of the previous night, and she laughed thinking about the difference between where she'd started the night—mixing with high society in French couture—and where she'd ended it—apparently sleeping it off in a garbage-strewn alley. Great.

The instant replay brought something else to mind. She'd dropped her cell phone. Maybe it hadn't been stolen. She knelt on the ground and felt around in the shadows, trying not to be squeamish, but when something rattled off to her left, she swallowed a curse, certain she'd seen two beady eyes watching her.

Blowing out a breath, she determinedly continued her search, her hand finally closing on hard, cold plastic. Her cell. Pulling back to a standing position, she flipped it open, grateful to see that there was still life in the battery.

She'd opened her caller directory and was thumbing down for her sister's number when a shudder of cold ripped through her. Automatically she pulled her coat tighter around her, and in the process touched something sticky.

Instinctively, she dropped the phone and jerked back, wrinkling her nose in disgust. She lifted a hand, not certain exactly what she was going to do, but the motion stopped midway as her eyes locked on her fingers, revulsion turning to alarm as she realized her hand was covered not with vomit but with blood.

She looked down at her coat, astonished to find that it was soaked in the stuff. Her heartbeat accelerated as she searched her body for signs of injury. There was nothing. No laceration or puncture, not even a scratch.

Rubbing her eyes, she tried to make sense of this newest development. Someone had practically bled out on her. Not a good thing. And not something one walked away from. She forced her breathing to slow, concentrating now on the scene. Pacing from one end of the alley to the other, she searched for a body. But there was no one there. Disappointment warred with relief—relief winning out in the end. Whatever had happened here, she was delighted not to be faced with an injured or dying stranger.

She searched the shadows of the alley again, this time looking for evidence of an altercation of some kind. Again there was nothing. No sign of struggle at all. Everything was coated with a thick layer of dust—if there'd been a fight, surely it would have dislodged something. She rubbed her temples, trying to think. Except for a bit where she'd passed out, there was no evidence of blood on the ground, either.

She stopped by the cell phone and reached down to pick it up, but hesitated once it was in her hand. Something was off here. Something beyond the fact that she was standing in the cold, covered with blood in an alley that had yielded neither a victim nor signs of a fight. The pieces just didn't fit. If she'd been attacked, then why wasn't she hurt? She certainly felt weak, but in an I've-just-thrown-up-my-guts kind of way as opposed to an I've-recently-been-in-a-knife-fight-with-a-street-person kind of way.

Then there was the whole call-from-Ed-who-didn't-show-up thing. She chewed the side of her lip, shivering again. *Ed.* She'd call Ed. Obviously her brain wasn't firing with all its synapses. Opening the phone again, she dialed with trembling fingers, and waited for the connection. The phone rang three times and was picked up by an automated voice requesting a message.

She waited impatiently for the beep, tersely explained the situation and clicked off the phone. Ahead of her, on the street, she heard the wail of a siren, and suddenly she felt the need to do something—anything—preferably as far away from here as possible.

She started for the street, and then looked down at her clothes again. She was a mess, and a noticeable one at that. Just walking down the street was bound to bring questions. Questions she didn't want to have to answer. She thought again about calling her sister but rejected the idea. She didn't want to involve Alicia until she knew what the hell was going on.

Turning away from the street, she noticed a courtyard behind a chain-link fence. Courtyard was an exaggeration, actually; it was more of a dingy space between buildings, but it was clear that someone considered it an amenity. There were a couple of stone benches, the browning remnants of summertime flowers, and a clothesline. It was the latter that interested Melissa, since it was strung with clothes.

She moved cautiously to the fence and peered through. There was no one around and, in the face of the frigid morning air, no windows open. That didn't mean there wasn't someone to see, but from this angle she could just make out the orange wash of dawn.

It was early. Hopefully everyone was snug in their beds.

She glanced down at her bloody clothes again and knew it was worth the risk. The fence was topped with the obligatory run of curling barbed wire, but she'd grown up in the Southwest and wasn't a bit afraid of the stuff.

Without giving herself time to consider the possible downside, she climbed the fence and gingerly straddled the wire. In less than two minutes she was up and over. So far so good.

The clothes on the line obviously belonged to a man—work pants and, thank God, a flannel shirt. After searching the tiny enclosure again for signs of life, she grabbed them both, along with an undershirt, and stepped back into the shadows. Thanks to the cold, she changed in record time, rolling her bloody shirt and pants into the coat.

It was tempting to abandon them, but she knew better than to leave anything traceable behind. With a granny shot, she tossed the soiled clothing back over the fence and climbed up, this time snagging her newly acquired pants on the barbed wire. Fortunately, they were made to be tough, and with a little maneuvering she managed to free herself without tearing them.

Back on the ground, she grabbed the ball of clothing and made her way out of the alley. She wasn't exactly a fashion plate, but the clothes fit more or less, and in this outfit she blended in with the crowd more than she would have in her bloodstained Burberry coat.

Not having money limited her mobility, but she was used to walking and, with a determination born of fear and cold, she made the hike to her Battery Park apartment in something less than half an hour, all the way trying to put the pieces of the puzzle together in some kind of logical order.

Not that she'd come up with much of anything. The facts were that she'd gone to meet Ed. He hadn't shown. The pie and/or the coffee had upset her stomach—actually that was an understatement—but the point was she'd lost her lunch in a rather big way.

From there, she'd apparently passed out, slept it off and been robbed. Conceivably, she'd fought off her attacker and been covered with his blood. The problem with the last bit was that she had absolutely no memory of anything like that at all, and logic told her that it wasn't the kind of thing she could have pulled off in her sleep.

Add to that the fact that her handler had gone AWOL, and that she was in the middle of an investigation concerning some potentially dangerous folks, and she was left with a less-than-appealing scenario.

She rounded the corner of State Street and skidded to a stop. There were two unmarked cars in front of her building. There was no way to be certain which agency the cars belonged to—but they were definitely law enforcement of some kind.

It wasn't that big a building—eight apartments, and she knew for a fact that two of them were empty. Of course that left five other possibilities besides herself, but considering the night's events, she didn't feel up to rolling the dice.

She stepped back into the shadowed opening of a building and tried to think what to do. Logic demanded she present herself at the door and let whoever was inside handle things. But years working undercover had taught her that assuming anything could leave you dead. So she held her ground.

She had no idea where Ed lived. It was better if they kept their relationship limited to the occasional meet, supplemented with phone calls. And since he wasn't answering the latter, that seemed to leave him out of the equation. Alarmingly so.

She'd worked with the man for a hell of a long time and nothing like this had ever happened. Sure there'd been some close calls along the way, but never involving him directly. And none that she couldn't sort out—eventually.

So that's just what she needed to do now. Sort things out.

But first off she needed a bath, new clothes and a warm place to think. She carefully unrolled the coat she still carried, and felt in the pockets of her jeans, hoping for cash.

Nothing.

Still, trying to keep an optimistic thought, she reached into the pockets of her coat, perseverance paying off in the form of a five-dollar bill and a wadded-up piece of paper. The money was like manna from heaven, and she resisted the urge to march straight into Starbucks for a grande mocha.

Not the wisest use of her very limited funds.

Biting her lip again, she clenched her fists and blew out a breath. Considering that last night had started out with an amazing kiss, it had certainly taken a decided turn for the worse.

If only Nigel were here. He'd know what to do.

The thought took a moment to crystallize, but when it did, she frowned and opened up the scrap of paper, staring down at the handwriting on it. Nigel's phone number.

She wasn't the sort to go running to a man for help, but at the moment she had to admit the idea was awfully seductive. And really, she had nowhere else to turn. Ed wasn't returning calls, and she couldn't risk getting her sister involved. But Nigel—well, in a way he was already part of this.

And no matter what lay between them, she'd trust him with her life. The decision then was simple. She pulled out her cell phone and dialed.

CHAPTER SEVEN

"IS EVERYTHING ALL RIGHT?" Payton asked. "You seem distracted."

"Just jet lag," Nigel said, stirring his eggs unenthusiastically. Truth was, it had been a spectacularly long night, and despite a shower and a couple of hours' sleep, he still felt as though he'd been run down by a lorry.

"And here I thought it was about a woman." Payton's mouth twitched as he ate his waffle.

"Gabe talks too bloody much."

"It wasn't Gabe," Payton was quick to reassure him. "It was Madison. And she only told me because she was worried about you."

"Well, there isn't anything to worry about. I ran into an old friend—who happens to be our contact in the UN investigation. It was a bit of a surprise, I'll grant you that. But anything remotely personal died a long time ago. So despite Madison's certainty that there is something more going on, I promise you there isn't."

Payton nodded, wisely refraining from further comment.

"Where's Harrison? Doesn't he like breakfast?"

"Up and gone," Payton said. "He's already at Cullen's offices. Something about his laptop not having the connections he needed. You know how Harrison is."

He did, actually, and despite his foul mood, he smiled. "Totally obsessed with anything involving seemingly inaccessible data."

"Exactly." Payton finished the last of his waffle, sitting back with a satisfied sigh. "Anyway, he couldn't wait to start digging."

"Well, I can't say that I blame him. The clock on this one is bound to be moving quickly. I spent the better part of last night going over Melissa's notes."

"Melissa? Is that her name?"

Nigel nodded, ignoring his friend's obvious curiosity. "She's been using her job as a photojournalist to investigate the possibility of a UN insider working to alter shipment documentation to allow for covert transportation."

"First timer?"

"No. Although it's the first I've heard about it."

Payton's face hardened, and Nigel knew he was remembering his first wife. Mariam had been a piece of work, romancing Payton only to use his connections to betray him. He still bore the scars—internally and externally—although Sam, his new wife, had gone a long way toward erasing at least some of the shadows.

"It's not the same, Payton. Honestly." Nigel held up a hand, not certain if he was trying to reassure his friend or defend Melissa. Both probably.

Payton shrugged. "Just watch your step."

"There's nothing to watch. What happened between us has been over for years." He stopped, realizing he was probably protesting too much. "Anyway, I won't be seeing her again."

"You can't know that for sure. What if she discovers something else that can help us?"

"Then you can talk to her." There was a finality to the statement that Nigel wished he truly believed, but six little bottles of Maker's Mark begged to differ.

Payton opened his mouth to argue, but Nigel's cell phone interrupted whatever caustic remark his friend had been going to make.

"Ferris," he said into the phone, expecting to hear Gabe or Cullen on the other end.

"Nigel?" The voice was almost a whisper, the trace of a tremor sending shards of alarm flashing through him.

"Melissa? Is that you?"

Payton leaned forward, concern replacing the beginnings of an I-told-you-so smile.

"Y-yes. Sorry, I'm having a little trouble with chattering teeth."

"What's wrong?" Nigel barked, cutting to the chase.

"I don't know." There was a note of frustration now. "Everything's gone crazy and I can't seem to make heads or tails of it. Look, Nigel—" she paused, and Nigel found himself holding his breath "—I think I need help."

"Tell me where you are."

"No." Her voice was stronger now, more decisive. "I'll come to you."

Visions of the firefight in Iraq and Mariam's betrayal flashed through his mind, but despite superficial similarities, Melissa wasn't Mariam. "Fine. I'm at the Regency, room seven-oh-one. Are you sure you don't need me to come and get you?"

Again there was a pause, as if she were considering his offer. "No. I need to keep moving. I'll be there as soon as I can. Funding is somewhat limited, so I'll be walking part of the way."

"Melissa? Are you sure you're all right?"

"No," she answered with a shaky laugh, "I'm not sure of anything right now. But I do know that I need your help."

"Right then, I'll be waiting." He held on, waiting for her answer, only to realize she'd disconnected. The thought sent a shudder of fear rocketing through him.

"What was that about?" Payton asked, leaning forward, his expression combined with his scar making him look formidable to say the least.

"No idea. She just said she was in trouble and needed my help. She's coming here."

"I'll wait with you."

"It's not necessary," Nigel said, surprising himself. "I'll handle it. You go on to headquarters and let everyone else know what's up. I'll report in as soon as I know what's happening."

"It could be a ploy," Payton said, his distrust showing.

"For what? She's one of yours, for God's sake. You're just projecting your past onto my situation."

"Well, the parallel is hard to ignore," Payton said, reaching over to sign the check.

When Payton's first wife had betrayed him—betrayed them all actually—she'd left half of the Delta team, including Payton's brother, dead. "I'm just saying you should still be careful. You said yourself you haven't seen this woman in years."

"Yes, but that doesn't mean I don't trust her." Nigel was more than aware that he had nothing current to base his feelings on, but he meant what he said.

"Fine." Payton shrugged. "You're a big boy, you'll take care of yourself. Just keep your eyes open and think with something besides your johnson."

Coming from anyone else the statement would have been insulting, but from Payton it was nothing more than common sense. He'd been there and done that and the cost had been beyond contemplation. Nigel not only understood, he sympathized.

"No worries. I'll be careful."

Payton nodded and stood up. "Just to cover all the bases, I'll run a check on her when I get to Cullen's. All right?"

The last bit was thrown in as pacification, but Nigel answered anyway. "Have at it. I'm more than certain you won't uncover anything the least bit questionable."

"We'll see." He said the words with a finality that set Nigel's alarm bells ringing.

He hadn't seen Melissa Pope in fifteen years, and now in less than twenty-four hours she'd managed to turn his entire world topsy-turvy—and that was before even knowing what had prompted her call.

MELISSA STOOD for a moment in the silence of the overhang, trying to decide if she'd done the right thing. Nigel had sounded concerned, but maybe she'd just wanted him to. No matter, the decision had been made, and whether she liked it or not, she needed help to sort through this thing.

Help from someone with no possibility of involvement.

Squaring her shoulders, she stepped out onto the street, turning her back on her apartment and the myriad of police vehicles. Whatever was happening there, she'd have to wait to find out.

Leave it to Nigel to be staying on the Upper East Side, well out of five-dollar taxi range. She'd told him she was going to walk, but visibility wasn't exactly something she relished, so maybe she'd risk the subway on the chance that if someone was looking for her, they hadn't had time to initiate a full-blown search.

The subway entrance was less than half a block away, and after checking for anyone suspicious, she darted down the stairs, using the kiosk to buy a MetroCard. One slide of the card and she was through the gate and bounding down another set of stairs, hitting the landing just as the train rumbled into the station.

The doors opened and she dashed inside, her instincts pushing her forward, even though she wasn't aware of being followed. She grabbed a seat and watched as a young mother ushered a toddler on while wheeling a baby carriage. No one else followed, although a man in a suit and overcoat passed her door and entered farther down the car.

The doors shut and the train rumbled off. The number five

was an express, which meant that there were only six stops until Fifty-ninth street. Then from Fifty-ninth and Lex she could either use the rest of her money on a taxi to the Regency or simply walk to Park Avenue. She'd make the decision once she was safely back on the street.

The train pulled to a stop at Wall Street, then almost before she had time to register the fact, pulled out again. No one had gotten off or on. Melissa pressed back against the cold metal of the subway car wall, keeping her gaze moving. The car wasn't crowded, but it wasn't empty either, and she couldn't shake the feeling that she was a sitting duck.

And unfortunately, she hadn't a clue who the enemy was.

The man in the overcoat had made his way closer to her seat, his gaze passing over her in a dismissing manner. Melissa contained a giggle, wondering how differently he'd have acted had she still been wearing her evening gown. Stifling her rising hysteria, she clutched her wadded-up coat closer, careful to be certain the bloody marks remained hidden.

The train next stopped at Fulton, the mother ushering her toddler off with one hand, pushing the carriage with the other. Really a phenomenal job, motherhood. Someday maybe she'd find time for it. Or then again, maybe not. She felt a moment's sadness but pushed away the thought. Her mother had always been opposed to crying over choices made, and Melissa prided herself on following suit.

Besides, there were more pressing matters at hand than lamenting the state of her biological clock. Two teenagers stomped onto the train, their black clothing making them look like rejects from a vampire movie. Only in New York.

The train lurched forward, and Melissa breathed a sigh of relief. Only four more stops. At the next stop no one got on, but the businessman changed his seat again, this time to the row facing Melissa's. He carried the *New York Times* and seemed engrossed in the business section.

Another mother, this time with a squealing preschooler, sat down next to her, the child reaching out sticky fingers to touch Melissa's balled-up coat. She jerked it away, and the little boy howled, his mother shooting Melissa a malevolent look. Again hysteria threatened as Melissa thought about what the woman would do if she'd let the child play with her bloody coat.

The train pulled out of the station and then almost immediately slowed to a stop, the garbled voice of the driver coming over the speaker, announcing a short delay. Her heart started to pound and she wondered if this was how a caged animal felt. But no one else seemed to be particularly bothered, so she forced her breathing to slow and tried to keep her mind on something else, her brain obligingly trotting out the image of Nigel and last night's kiss.

Not exactly calming thoughts…

Still, it beat the idea of an unknown assailant hands down.

And Nigel's kissing had, if anything, only gotten better over the years. Which meant of course that he'd been practicing, but she wasn't about to go there. In fact, she wasn't going anywhere—mentally or physically. Restless, she stood up and walked over to the map, double-checking the route.

They'd just passed City Hall, which meant that if they ever got moving again, there were only three more stops. The speaker crackled to life with news that they would be resuming travel in a few minutes, and as if spurred on by the announcement, the train lurched forward again. Melissa moved down toward the other end of the car, well out of the way of the sticky-fingered kid, stopping to hold on to a pole when the doors opened at Union Square.

It was tempting to get off, but it was a long walk from Union Square, and her remaining money still wouldn't cover cab fare. She was shaking now, the cold penetrating right to the bone. At least the subway car offered some warmth. Best to stay put, despite her desire to run.

Forcing herself to take a seat, she stared out the window at the beams and plaster passing by. Two more stops. The car was crowded now, and when they stopped at Grand Central, the subway car filled to standing room only. At least, she thought, there was safety in numbers.

Or was that an old wives' tale? The invading cold was obviously messing with her head, her responses seeming almost slo-mo. Next stop and she was out of here. The walk would be good for her, keep her blood moving and her brain clear.

She'd made it this far without incident, and she intended to make it the rest of the way. Then she'd let Nigel take over for a while. Get some sleep and a hot bath. The idea was seductive, just the thought if it making her head light. Or maybe that was Nigel. She couldn't really tell anymore, she was so damn cold.

The train jerked to a stop and the doors slid open, freedom beckoning. Summoning strength from God knows where, Melissa stumbled to her feet and out onto the platform, aware that an elderly couple were trying hard not to stare.

Attention was just what she didn't need, so with considerable effort, she forced herself to walk normally to the staircase, taking the steps one at a time in what she hoped was the unhurried rhythm of a person with nothing to hide.

At the top of the stairs, she pushed her way through the crowd. The station as always was bustling, and she consulted the signs overhead, trying to find the best exit. The Regency was at Sixty-first and Park—not all that far, but every inch mattered now, so she wanted to be certain she stayed underground until the last possible moment.

Finally she spotted the exit she wanted and, with more energy than she'd thought possible, she sprinted up the last set of stairs into the bluster of an October New York Saturday. Taking a moment to catch her bearings, she headed west on Fifty-ninth away from the crowds of Lexington.

Across the street she caught sight of the businessman still buried in his newspaper as he walked along. His London Fog raincoat made him look a lot like every other man on the street, and Melissa even doubted it was the same man.

Shaking her head, she dismissed him, concentrating instead on making her way to Park. Just a little bit more. The people had thinned out considerably, the tranquility of Fifty-ninth feeling almost lonely after the hustle of Lexington. She'd wanted out of the crowd, but here, suddenly, she felt exposed.

As if to emphasize the fact, the north wind whipped up the street, penetrating her meager clothing with icy fingers. She shivered and wrapped her arms around herself, still clutching her bloody coat and jeans. A Chanel-clad East-sider stepped out of her way, the look of disgust on her face something that Melissa would normally find funny, but today nothing seemed humorous.

The woman's repulsion had brought up an important fact, however—she was hardly likely to be allowed to just waltz through the front lobby of the Regency dressed as she was. Leave it to Nigel to choose a hotel with five-star attitude. Although truthfully, smelling like she did, she'd probably be turned out of a Super Eight.

She stopped in the shelter of a building's colonnade, praying a doorman wouldn't appear to shoo her away, and pulled out her cell phone. With trembling fingers she dialed Nigel's number and waited.

He picked up on the first ring. "Ferris."

"I'm almost there," she said, her voice nearly inaudible. "But they're not going to let me in. I'm a mess." That was an understatement, but she simply didn't have the time to explain further.

"I'll meet you out front." Nigel's voice was deep with concern and she blessed him for it.

"B…bring a c…coat, please."

"Right."

He clicked off, and Melissa closed her phone, pushing onward. The light at Fifty-ninth and Park cooperated nicely, turning green just as she reached it. She crossed to the northeast corner, preferring to keep to the opposite side of the street for now. She was afraid that if she stopped she'd never get started again, but she knew she needed to continue to use caution.

About halfway down the block, she could actually see the hotel, and hope blossomed warm in her chest. She stopped at the red light, moving to stand on the Sixtieth Street side away from the hoity-toity eyes of Park Avenue. Leaning back against a building, she struggled for breath, and was just pushing off again at the turn of the light when she saw the businessman standing just up the street.

There was no mistaking him. He'd lost the paper, and his dark expression was visible even from this distance. Melissa broke into a run, skidding out into the street heading for the curb on the opposite side. Something whizzed by her arm, leaving a trail of fire, and automatically she bent low, zigzagging like a drunk until she was safely back on Park.

Still running, she headed across the avenue, mindless of the honking cars whizzing past. She dodged around a taxi and stumbled up onto the median, turning as she did so to try to locate the shooter.

The street was empty.

The businessman had disappeared.

On a rush of adrenaline and relief, she sprinted across the southbound lane, the light in her favor this time. As she neared the corner, she saw Nigel, his face twisted with worry.

"Are you all right?"

"As well as can be expected considering someone just took a shot at me." She struggled for a look of nonchalance, but instead stumbled and would have fallen if his arms hadn't closed around her. She wanted to tell him more, to walk with him into the hotel, but given the proximity of safety, her legs finally gave out, the blackness she'd been fighting all morning surging up and encompassing her, her last cognizant thought that at least she'd managed to come this far on her own two feet.

CHAPTER EIGHT

NIGEL SWUNG her into his arms, not certain what to make of the scent that wafted up with her. She was disheveled to say the least, but what bothered him most was the bloodstain on her arm. She was clutching a coat, which seemed to be emanating the worst of the smell, but even unconscious, she clung to it fiercely, refusing to release it when he tried to dislodge it.

He'd searched the street the minute she'd mentioned a shooter, but nothing seemed out of the ordinary. He suspected her pursuer had at least temporarily abandoned his quest in view of the Regency's inaccessibility. It wouldn't stop him for long, Nigel suspected, but it would buy enough time to figure out what their next move should be.

Still holding Melissa close, he strode over to a doorman and explained the situation using as few details as possible. He'd have liked to have managed without help altogether, but he hated the idea of the spectacle they'd present if he just marched through the lobby and onto the elevator.

Fortunately the man was well trained and asked no questions as he led them through the service entrance and to the freight elevator. The back stairs of the Regency lacked the opulence of the guest's side of the hotel, but it was immaculately clean and relatively unoccupied. In just minutes, he was safely inside his room, Melissa stirring sleepily in his arms.

Her lips still had a bluish cast, however, and he knew he had to get her warmed up. The quickest way to do that was in the shower. Unfortunately, she clearly wasn't capable of doing it on her own, which meant a physical foray he wasn't completely certain she'd approve of. Still, given the choice between her anger and her sinking further into hypothermia, he'd pick the former.

He laid her gently on the sofa and sprinted into the bathroom to turn on the shower. That accomplished, he returned to the sofa and gingerly tore off the sleeve of her shirt, relieved to see that the bloodstain was the result of a bullet grazing her skin rather than something worse.

Next, he stripped her down to her panties and undershirt, trying not to think of the tantalizing skin that lay beneath the thin cotton. At the moment warmth was more important than modesty. If there was fallout he'd deal with it later. Right now he needed to get her body temperature back to normal.

To that end, he removed his shirt, as well, and then scooped her back into his arms. Her skin against his felt like ice, and he could feel the shudders rippling through her. It didn't take a genius to realize that she'd spent the night outside somewhere.

And been sick to boot.

Gingerly he stepped into the shower, letting the hot spray of water envelop them. Lowering her feet, he let her body slide against his until she was leaning back against him in a more or less standing position, then he locked his arms around her so that she could remain upright.

The water beat down on them both, the steam surrounding them like a shimmering curtain. Her eyes were still closed, but as the water began to work its magic, she moaned as the heat bit into her skin. The blue tinge receded, replaced by a healthy pink, and Nigel sighed in relief.

Carefully, bracing her against him with one hand, he reached for the soap and began to wash her, starting with her neck and shoulders, her skin silky beneath his callused fingers. Even that simple touch brought back memories, and he steeled his body, trying not to react to her tantalizing proximity. In the water, her underwear had become diaphanous, her breasts highlighted with mouthwatering clarity.

Gritting his teeth, he continued his washing, lathering her hair and neck, massaging away the remnants of whatever it was she'd endured. Next, he concentrated on the angry red contusion left by the bullet. It had already stopped bleeding, but the slug had left its mark on the tender skin of her upper arm. He fought against a surge of anger directed at her unknown assailant.

In New York City, anything was possible, but based on the fact that she'd apparently spent the night out in the cold, he'd have to guess that this was more than a random shooting. Most likely something related to her latest assignment. And if that were the case, then it meant her cover had been compromised.

Obviously someone either knew who she was, or simply wasn't taking chances. Either way there was no way to analyze the situation further until she could tell him what happened. Which meant he needed to concentrate on getting her warm and awake.

As if reading his thoughts, she sighed and turned around so that she was facing him, leaning into his warmth, her breasts pressed against his chest. Fighting the carnal heat racing through him, he concentrated on getting her clean, his hands skimming over her back and belly beneath the undershirt.

Unfortunately, the motion sent her shimmying against him, her pelvis rubbing against his penis in a provocative rhythm that threatened to be his undoing, but he persevered, tightening his muscles against the sensory onslaught, sheer determination his greatest ally.

Completely unaware of his plight, Melissa murmured his name on a sigh, and her eyes fluttered open. She smiled sleepily up at him, pressing closer, her lips parting for a kiss, then she froze, reality surfacing as anxiety flooded across her features.

"Why are we here?" she asked, her eyes narrowing in question as she tried to push away.

"To get you warm," he said, keeping his expression neutral as he pulled her back into the circle of his arms and the heated spray of water. "You were bordering on hypothermia."

She struggled for a moment more then relaxed against him, her mind finally wrapping around the logic of his words and accepting them. "The shooter."

Her words were almost too faint to hear, but he knew what she was saying, the red mark on her arm providing an all-too-real testament to her statement.

"As soon as I've got you warm, I'll go and see if there's anything left behind to identify him." Nigel knew that if he was right about this being something to do with her operation there wouldn't be anything to find, but he wanted to reassure her.

"You know better than that," she whispered against his chest. "There'll be no trace."

He should have known she'd be quick to assess the situation. She hadn't gotten where she was by being slow on the uptake. Hypothermia be damned. He stroked the back of her hair, the gesture stemming from a need to do far more than soothe her, and as if she too relished the contact, she leaned into him for a moment more, then drew a sharp breath and stepped back.

Nigel swallowed, trying to maintain focus. She was a beautiful woman, wearing her maturity with an ease one seldom saw, and it made his body tighten with a need that transcended the physical, creating a hunger that ran straight to his soul.

Suddenly uncomfortable in his own skin, he stared at the floor of the shower, working to pull his thoughts from his need to hers. Reaching over to the taps, he turned them off, the sudden cessation of the water leaving the room eerily quiet. Still avoiding her gaze, he stepped out onto the bath mat and grabbed a towel, handing it to her before retrieving another for himself.

"I didn't know what else to do." He felt foolish, as if he'd blundered into some sort of parallel universe where he'd regressed into adolescent insecurity. She'd always done that to him, stripping him bare of all pretense. It had been exhilarating and uncomfortable all at the same time, but just at the moment, the latter took the forefront.

"You did exactly the right thing." Her voice broke through his riotous thoughts, and he looked up to see that she'd stripped off her sodden undergarments and pulled on the hotel's toweling robe. "But then you always do."

He wasn't sure if that was a compliment or an insult, and so he let it pass, concentrating instead on removing the other robe from its hook on the back of the door. The corners of her mouth twitched as she turned her back, waiting for him to change out of his wet chinos. The maneuver was not as speedy or as graceful as he would have liked, but soon they were both clad in terry cloth and seated in the living room of the suite. A part of him wanted to be back in the shower, nothing between them but moisture and heat. But another part, a much wiser one, was grateful for the distance between them, and the thick camouflage of the toweling robes.

He was neither a saint nor a eunuch and even the desperation of her situation hadn't dulled the ache the sight of her naked body had elicited. He was, however, a consummate professional and, bearing that in mind, he turned his attention to the situation at hand.

"Do you want to tell me what happened?"

She chewed on her lip for a moment, gathering her thoughts. "It started with the call I got at the party." Two spots of color rose in her cheeks, and Nigel bit back a smile. At least he wasn't alone with his runaway emotions. Their gazes met, and a moment ticked by, the air full of electricity—and then it passed, the two of them safely back on level ground. "It was my handler. He said he'd found something important and that he wanted to meet at a diner near the Brooklyn Bridge."

"I take it something went wrong?"

"He never showed. And then when I left, I got horribly sick. The last thing I remember was losing everything in an alley."

Nigel frowned. "Food poisoning?"

"It's possible. The coffee was awful, and I did eat some pie," she said, her frown answering his. "But it happened really quick. I'd hardly taken ten steps before the nausea hit. I remember fighting to hang on to consciousness, but there was nothing I could do. One minute I was standing there puking my guts out and the next thing I know, it's morning and I'm freezing."

Nigel ran a finger across the line of his mustache, trying to sort out the pieces of the puzzle. "So you spent the night in the alley."

It wasn't a question, but Melissa nodded anyway.

"And then what happened?"

"I tried to call Ed, but he wasn't there."

"Your handler."

Melissa nodded. "I called the night before, too, when he didn't show up, but there was no answer then, either."

"Is he usually so elusive?" Nigel fought against an unreasonable surge of jealousy. He didn't know the man, didn't know Melissa's relationship to him, and he certainly hadn't the right to feel anything at all about the men in her life.

"No. He's actually sort of annoyingly prompt. The sort who never shows up to anything a minute late. That's what's got me worried." Melissa's eyes were dark with concern. "That and the fact that I woke up covered in blood."

The coat. Suddenly his brain grasped what his eyes had already seen. "Not yours." He knew it was true, but somehow he couldn't help saying it anyway. "Any idea whose it was?"

"None at all." She shook her head to emphasize the point. "There was no sign of a struggle, and no residual blood at the site. Just what was on my coat. I double-checked the area, but there was nothing."

"And the outfit?" Nigel prompted.

"I stole it." Melissa's smile was rueful. "There was a courtyard at the end of the alley. I scaled the fence and helped myself. It seemed the best solution."

"I'd have done the same." Nigel nodded his support, his mind still turning over the details. "Is that when you called me? After you'd changed?"

"No." Melissa threaded her fingers together, the knuckles turning white. "I headed home first. I thought stupidly that maybe there'd be a message there, or something to help me sort things out. But the place was surrounded by official-looking cars and I figured it'd be better to stay low until I knew what was what. That's when I called you."

"I see." He didn't really, but it was simpler to say that he did.

"You don't believe me."

"I didn't say that. It's just that the pieces don't seem to be coming together as a whole. We know that your handler—Ed—called. You're sure it was him?"

"Positive." She nodded, waiting.

"And you went to meet him, only he didn't show."

"Right. And while I waited I drank coffee and had a couple of bites of apple pie."

"Was there anything unusual about the food?"

"Nothing out of the ordinary. The coffee was bitter, which I thought was a little odd since it was a new pot, but this wasn't exactly Starbucks." She closed her eyes, trying to force the memory. "There were a couple of teenagers, you know the kind that make punks look like choirboys, and an old guy that looked like he came straight off the streets. Except for them the place was empty."

"What about staff?"

"All I saw was the waitress. She was the kind of woman that my mom used to say had been rode hard and put away wet."

"Any of the occupants show unusual interest in you?"

Melissa tipped back her head, thinking. "I don't think the kids even looked at me. They were too interested in their pie. Actually, that's what made me think of having it myself. The waitress was the usual monosyllabic type, and the old man was just drinking coffee. We made eye contact when I came in, but that's it." She frowned, holding up a hand. "One thing that struck me as off was the fact that the old man got his coffee from a different pot. At the time I wrote it off as decaf, but now..." She trailed off with a shrug.

"It's worth considering. Any vomit on the coat?"

"I'd imagine so, although it'll be hard to see with all the blood." She scowled at him. "What the hell difference does it make whether I threw up on my coat?"

"A lab might be able to analyze it. Figure out if you were poisoned."

"Sorry, I should have thought of that." Her expression was a cross between apology and dismay.

"It's all right, darling." The endearment slipped out before he could stop it, old times settling in like a well-worn rug. "It's not like you didn't have other things to deal with."

"I should have thought of it, though." She either hadn't heard his slip of the tongue or she was ignoring it. Either way Nigel was relieved. "At least I had the presence of mind to keep my clothes. They're wrapped up in the coat. Maybe they'll give us something more to go on."

"My thoughts exactly. We'll just get them analyzed for trace."

She glanced around the hotel room. "You carry a lab with you?"

"Right. I've just got it tucked away in the back room." Melissa's eyes widened, and Nigel laughed. "I told you at the consulate's party that I have some powerful friends. They'll be able to provide anything we need."

"I don't want anyone else involved in this." She started to stand, then seemed to think better of it and sat back in the chair. "I mean, after all, it was Ed who had me go to the diner in the first place." She paused, her gaze troubled. "That's why I didn't try to call anyone else at the CIA."

"How much did they tell you about Last Chance?"

"Not much more than you told me last night. It's a group of agents, mainly CIA, operating at the President's behest."

"Well, my friends may be CIA, but they're also a bit on the unorthodox side, so no worries about their alliances. We stand together—most of the time." Nigel pushed aside his regret; he'd made a mistake once, put country before Last Chance, and he'd not do it again. Gabe and Payton would never have done it at all. Their loyalty was absolute. "I trust them. And you can, too."

Melissa nodded, but he could tell that she still wasn't convinced.

"We've survived a lot, the three of us. The other members of the team, as well. If we ask them to keep this quiet, they will. It's as simple as that."

"So what? You just call them up, and we wait for the posse to arrive?" There was a little bit of sarcasm in her tone, and Nigel was pleased. Anger meant she was recovering nicely, and at the moment her health was his primary concern.

"No. We need to get out of here immediately. Whoever was shooting at you had to have seen where you went. Which means that sooner or later he'll find his way here. And I don't fancy running into him until we've got a better idea of what we're up against."

"So what do you suggest?"

"There's a safe house I know about. It's upstate a bit. I can arrange for a helicopter to take us there."

"Isn't that a little like blowing the bugle and letting everyone know where we're heading?" She still looked skeptical, and Nigel suppressed the desire to kiss her until it disappeared.

"Not in New York. Helicopter pickups are a dime a dozen. Besides, I'm good at this sort of thing, remember? You're not the only undercover operative in the room."

"And last night you were playing the part of the lush?" She tilted her head toward the empty minibottles on the table.

"Hardly likely with that lot. There wasn't even enough to give me a buzz."

She stood up, taking a step toward him, the static in the room stretching taut between them. "Were you having trouble sleeping?"

"Something like that." He moved toward her, the distance between them now measured in centimeters. "I ran into an old friend, and the memories were a little more than I'd bargained for."

"I see." She threw his words back at him with a crooked grin, her color now completely normal. It wouldn't take any effort at all to close the distance completely, but he'd been down this road before, and he knew with certainty that it couldn't have a pleasant ending. Truth was, he'd barely recovered from the last time the two of them had tangled, and damned if he was going to jump back into the fire without so much as a second thought.

It was important to protect oneself after all.

"I really should see to that arm," he said, purposefully stepping back, trying to ignore the flash of disappointment in her eyes. "I'll just get the first-aid kit."

CHAPTER NINE

MELISSA STARED AT THE BEDROOM door, trying to decide if she was angry or relieved. On the one hand, she couldn't help her reaction to Nigel—after all, it had been one hell of an affair all those years ago—but on the other, she'd learned the cost of such endeavors and had thought she was well past this kind of thing. She'd turned a corner, and quite honestly, she had no intention of ever looking back.

Only here he was not ten feet from her and all she could think about was running in there and begging him to make love. Considering the idea bordered on ludicrous, the better thing to do would be to hit the high road, but that meant she'd be on her own again. And despite the pull of the chemistry between them, she was still relieved to have Nigel on her side. Not that she couldn't have handled it on her own if necessary, it was just easier this way. Two heads and all that.

She shook her head and decided the whole dilemma had to be a by-product of stress. Spending a night in the cold hadn't exactly left her at her best. Add to that the blood and the shooter, and really a girl couldn't be expected to keep her emotions safely under lock and key.

She stood up, crossed restlessly to the window and stared down at Park Avenue. It was nearing noon, and the road was teeming with cars and taxis, the median in the center still bright with fall chrysanthemums. People were walking below, an uptown mix of society matrons, nannies pushing carriages, and businessmen with ears glued to cell phones.

Just an ordinary day.

"Sorry to be so long." Nigel's voice warmed her like a familiar sweater, and she turned from the window to face him. He'd dressed in khakis and a dark blue sport shirt, the clothes making him look both sophisticated and sexy. Whatever else he might be, Nigel Ferris was a gentleman and he looked every bit the part. "I wanted to go ahead with arrangements. The helicopter should be here in half an hour or so."

"They're coming here?" Melissa asked, more for something to say than for information.

"Right on the roof. I told you I had connections." His smile was crooked and her heart twisted with memory. "Now come over here in the light and let me look at that arm."

"It's just a scratch really." She waved it off, not entirely certain she wanted him touching her again.

"I know, but you still need to watch for infection. Come on." His smile grew a little more wicked. "I'm not going to bite." As if to underscore the fact, he lifted the roll of gauze and antibiotic cream, pointing at the chair she'd just vacated.

"Fine." She walked over to the chair and sat down, shoving up the robe sleeve. Unfortunately, it wasn't possible to push it up that far, and she was forced, against her better judgment, to drop the robe off her shoulder so that he could access the wound.

His touch was professional, gently probing the rut left by the bullet. "It's less red than it was in the shower. I think you'll be fine. Probably not even a scar."

She'd been shot before. More than once, actually, but never with the bullet specifically intended for her. She winced as he rubbed the antibiotic into the wound.

"Sorry. Almost done." He swiftly wrapped the gauze around her arm, securing it with surgical tape. "That should do for now."

He moved away, sitting in the chair opposite hers, the loss of contact sending shivers of regret racing through her. She pushed her riotous thoughts aside, concentrating instead on her surroundings.

The suite was a nice one, bordering on regal, and somehow it suited Nigel. The bedroom opened off a small sitting room, with the bathroom in between. Her nerves prickled at the sight of the bathroom door, sensory images of the two of them in the shower bringing her full circle stop to where she'd started.

Damn the man.

"I've called for some food and new clothes," Nigel said, bringing her attention back to the present. His expression was impassive except for the slight twitch at the corner of his mouth that signaled the fact that he'd accurately been following her train of thought. His mind reading was a trait she'd cursed fifteen years ago, and unfortunately it appeared the ability had not lessened with age. "I guessed at the sizes."

There was something very intimate in the idea of his buying her clothes, and her cheeks burned with the thought.

"It's going to be all right, you know." His face tightened with the words, all signs of flirtation gone, and she knew that if it were humanly possible he'd make it so. He reached out, and instinctively she responded in kind, their fingers touching, a pulse of pure energy arcing between them.

Then fortunately, or unfortunately—quite honestly she didn't know—there was a knock at the door and Nigel sprang to his feet, reaching for the Sig Sauer. Gun drawn, he motioned her back. "Who's there?"

"Room service," came the voice, and Melissa immediately relaxed, but Nigel stayed vigilant, moving so that he could see through the peephole.

Apparently satisfied, he opened the door, sliding the gun back into the holster at his back.

A young man with the hint of a beard and livery to fit a king rolled a food cart into the room, his gaze sweeping over Melissa to land nervously on Nigel. "Your breakfast, sir."

The sentence would have been perfunctory except for the fact that his voice broke on the second word, his focus on Nigel's now-empty right hand.

The kid had obviously clued in to the fact that Nigel had a gun, but he hadn't the slightest idea what to do about it. With a move worthy of James Bond, Nigel managed to smile reassuringly at the bellboy and flash some sort of credentials.

"Thank you, Walter," Nigel said, reading the boy's name tag. His smile had erased some of Walter's fear, but the kid still took a step back toward the relative safety of the door.

"The, ah, clothes you requested are in the sack underneath the table." Walter waved toward the cart, still edging toward the door.

Nigel reached into his front pocket, and the boy jumped again. Melissa swallowed a bubble of laughter.

"This is for your trouble," Nigel said, producing a twenty. In seconds, Walter's greed overcame his fear, and he stepped forward to snatch the bill away, his head bobbing with gratitude and a good measure of awe.

Now that the boy was fairly certain he wasn't going to get his head blown off, he was beginning to enjoy the situation. No doubt the incident would be greatly embellished and shared over beer with Walter's buddies.

"I'm sure we can count on your discretion." It was a statement, not a question, and if there'd been any doubt of the fact, Nigel's fierce expression sealed the deal. Walter nodded with a vigor that probably left loose teeth, and literally ran from the room. "That went rather well, I thought." Nigel lifted one of the silver lids and inhaled deeply.

The scent of bacon carried over to Melissa and her stomach grumbled in response. "Only if you count making the poor kid wet his pants as a victory."

"I really didn't mean to scare him." Nigel straightened and turned to Melissa. The intimate look was back, as if the two of them shared a private line, separate from the rest of the world.

"You were fine. After he's had a chance to recover, he'll dine out on the story for years."

They stood for a moment, communicating on a pheromonal level, then with a little shake of his head, Nigel broke the spell, reaching for the bag underneath the room-service cart. "Your clothes, milady."

Coming from him, it seemed truly chivalrous, and Melissa wondered why the hell she'd ever walked away. There were reasons, good ones to boot, but at the moment they all escaped her. She reached for the bag, carefully avoiding his fingers. No need in further inciting her already riotous nerve endings.

"Thanks. I'll change in the bedroom." She stood for at least three more minutes, trying to convince her feet to follow the command, then finally managed to move down the hallway. Ten minutes after that, she was sitting at the table wearing a pair of designer jeans and a Dolce & Gabbana T-shirt that accentuated every curve she had plus a few she hadn't even been aware of.

Nigel obviously had experience choosing women's clothing, despite his earlier protestations to the contrary. Not that she was about to acknowledge the fact.

The omelet he'd ordered was equally perfect, and despite her earlier stomach problems, she was enjoying every bite. Nigel, on the other hand, was still on alert, his gaze darting every few minutes to the windows and door. She supposed the movements ought to make her feel equally jumpy, but conversely she felt only a sense of contentment. As if she'd surrendered her problem.

It probably wouldn't last, but at least for the moment it was comforting.

"I talked with Payton Reynolds, one of the friends I was telling you about," Nigel said, his attention returning to her.

"The one with helicopter connections?" Again she found herself responding more because it seemed expected than because she really wanted an answer. Her brief burst of energy was fading fast.

"No." Nigel shook his head. "That's Cullen Pulaski—and he's more of an associate than a friend. Payton was with me in Iraq. Anyway, he's going to see what he can dig up. Try and trace your handler for one thing, and maybe find out who it was you saw at your apartment."

Melissa opened her mouth to protest, but Nigel held up his hand to silence her. "The more information we have, the better we can assess the situation. Payton will be discreet, believe me. You've no worries there. Until we know what it is you're facing, no one will have any idea that we know where you are."

"You think someone is trying to kill me?" They both already knew the answer. But she needed to say it out loud, to face the specter hovering between them.

"I'm afraid it seems likely. New York certainly has its fair share of people with guns, but generally you don't find them on Park Avenue taking potshots at pedestrians, and when you add the events of last night to the equation I'm not sure how you could think anything else. The big questions, of course, are who and why. Any ideas who might be after you?"

"Quite honestly, there are any number of possibilities." Melissa laid her fork on her plate, her appetite dissipating. "I haven't exactly been hanging out on the sidelines, you know?"

"But for the most part your work has all been undercover, right?"

"True." She nodded. "But that doesn't mean the information isn't available. Just a whole lot harder to obtain."

"And if your handler gave you up—"

"No," she interrupted, her anger surprising her. "I've worked with Ed Wyland a long time. There's no way he'd rat me out."

"There's always a way, Melissa." Nigel's expression was grim. "Even when people really care."

She blew out a long breath, knowing he was right. Still, she'd lay odds Ed would die before giving her up. At the thought she shuddered. "You think he's dead."

"I think it's a possibility." As usual he didn't sugarcoat his words, and for some reason she found that she was absurdly grateful for the fact.

"Which could mean I've been compromised."

"Again, I think it's possible. Look, we're not going to find answers sitting here speculating. Payton and the others will pull together whatever they can, and then we'll assimilate it and see where we are. Until then, the only thing we can do is lay low." He glanced at his watch. "The helicopter will be here soon. Have you had enough to eat?"

"More than enough." Her stomach was beginning to regret the whole thing actually, the reality of the situation back front and center.

"Right then." Nigel stood up, offering his hand. "Let's go."

She took it before she had the chance to think about what she was doing, the contact immediately sending waves of heat dancing along her skin. Whatever else was between them, she sure as hell couldn't deny the fact that there was chemistry present. Mind-numbing, explosion-causing chemistry, her brain cautioned.

Bragging or complaining? the little voice in her head countered, and Melissa grimaced.

It didn't really matter anyway. The fact was that she was here, and for the moment at least their lives were again intertwined. Time would tell what the repercussions might be, but in the meantime, despite the situation, Melissa was determined to enjoy the ride.

"So did you see this woman?" Payton asked, his attention on the tree line passing below them. He and Gabe were on their way to pick up forensic pathologist Tracy Braxton. She'd worked with them on several cases, and Nigel had requested her help.

Cullen had arranged a helicopter so that once they had Tracy, they could head straight to the retreat. Harrison and Madison had gone ahead in the SUV with various pieces of necessary equipment. For all practical purposes they were moving headquarters, at least temporarily, to a compound in the Upper Hudson Valley.

"Just when she came into the room. It was hard not to notice." Gabe raised an eyebrow with a shrug.

"A looker?"

"And then some. But not in the sultry way you're thinking. It was more about grace, as if she wasn't really aware of the package, you know what I mean?"

"The most dangerous type."

"Damn it, Payton, there's no need to be morose. You know as well as I do that we work in a small world. Nigel's running into someone from his past isn't exactly the end of the world."

"But she's a journalist."

"Photojournalist, actually. And she works for us." Gabe's expression turned darker. "Look, I don't blame you for seeing a parallel between your past and Nigel's, but that doesn't mean there actually is one."

"I know." Payton sighed, running a hand through his hair, wishing Sam were here. She had a way of calming his demons, allowing him to see the world as it really was, not as his nightmares would have him believe. "It's just that I can't help being cautious."

"So what did you find out?" Gabe sat back, crossing his arms, making the copter look small, despite the fact that it was built to carry at least twelve people in the lap of luxury.

"Not as much as I'd have liked. The dossier was sealed. But between my connections and Harrison's skills with a keyboard we got quite a bit. She was born in Dallas. One sister, Alicia, married to a midlevel diplomat named Aaron Rosenblatt."

"He's Jewish?"

Payton nodded. "Very low-key about it. I checked his dossier, too. But there's nothing out of the ordinary. Career officer with the foreign service. On the rise, but nothing extraordinary."

"What about the sister?"

"Even more bland. Not even a traffic ticket. According to the file, the girls were orphaned when they were still young. Raised by an aunt in Lubbock. The aunt apparently remarried and dumped the girls when they were close to college age. So the two of them moved to Austin, where Alicia met Rosenblatt and Melissa studied photojournalism. They appear to be close, but don't see each other much. Probably thanks to Rosenblatt's schedule and Melissa's assignments. Alicia and Aaron were at the party, though."

"I saw them when Melissa came in. Sister's good-looking, too. What about Melissa's dealings with the Company?"

"She's been on the payroll since she got out of college. Small stuff at first. Passing information, observational photographs, that sort of thing. Basically using her assignments to provide various levels of intel."

"I take it she's worked up to bigger things?"

"Yeah, according to the stuff Harrison finagled, she infiltrated a terrorist training camp in Afghanistan under the guise of journalistic freedom. She even managed to map the coordinates, and thanks to her work, the air force destroyed the place."

"Score one for the good guys."

"Something like that." Payton shrugged. "She worked Afghanistan for several more years and then got called home after 9/11. Her latest assignment has been working the UN to try and discover the identity of the suspected turncoat. From some of the reports I read, she's not too happy to be doing domestic duty."

"I hear that." Gabe's grin was commiserative.

"I thought you liked Homeland Security."

"In some ways I guess I do. But it's deadly dull compared to the old days." Gabe, like Payton, had spent the bulk of his career in the CIA working deep-cover operations overseas. Gabe's assignments had primarily been in Europe, while Payton's had been in Asia. And although Gabe's time in Delta Force as team leader had meant involvement in black ops, his path with the Company had been slightly more desirable.

Payton, on the other hand, had accepted assignments that no one else had been willing to carry out, one-man missions that often were expected to end in failure and/or termination. Of course they hadn't been counting on Payton.

"I can't say I'd like domestic duty beyond the occasional Last Chance case," Payton said. "But there's something to be said for staying this side of the firefight."

They were silent for a moment, each remembering. Payton was the first to shrug it off. If he'd learned anything it was that the past had to stay the past. "Anyway, there's nothing in Melissa's records to indicate she's anything but on the up-and-up."

"But you're still worried."

"Yeah, I am. I just don't want to see Nigel taken advantage of. Not to mention the fact that there's potential for our mission to be compromised."

"How do you figure that?" Gabe frowned, his brows drawing together in one black line.

"Melissa was Nigel's contact. So it follows if she's in trouble, it's pretty darn certain it will impact our operation one way or the other."

"I suppose there's validity in that," Gabe acknowledged. "But until we know all the details I don't want us jumping to conclusions. Especially based on something that has nothing whatsoever to do with Melissa."

"I hear you." Payton lifted a hand in supplication. "But I

can't shake the feeling that there's a hell of a lot more going on here than some old flame of Nigel's needing him to ride to the rescue. So if there is anything out there on Melissa Pope, I damn sure intend to find it."

CHAPTER TEN

THE HOUSE RESEMBLED a fortress more than anything. If Melissa had been in England or Scotland or maybe the Rhine Valley it wouldn't have seemed unusual. But here in the rolling hills of the Hudson Valley it seemed oddly out of place. Constructed of gray limestone, it rose out of the rock as if it had sprung from the ground fully formed.

Trees clustered around it like protective soldiers, and Melissa had no doubt that the compound would be all but invisible to the casual observer. The helipad consisted of an empty field, and as Melissa and Nigel ran from underneath the whirling blades, her primary thought was that getting out of the compound would probably be as difficult as getting into it.

Nigel's friend Cullen certainly liked his security.

She stopped underneath a large oak tree, grateful for the protection as the first spatters of rain hit the ground. The sky, which had been threatening all day, had finally decided to let loose.

In the distance, the helicopter rose into the air, and with a whir of blades disappeared into the clouds. "Will he be all right?" Melissa yelled above the rising storm.

Nigel nodded. "He's probably flown in a lot worse." His words were whipped away by the wind, and with a tip of his head toward the house, he slid an arm around her and they began to run, rain pelting down in earnest now.

There was no front drive. Nothing at all to allow vehicles of any kind, and Melissa wondered again if this were a fortress to keep people out or keep people in. She shivered, but

Nigel evidently thought it was the rain, because he tightened his hold, pulling her into the curve of his hard body.

The years had done nothing to soften Nigel Ferris, and some part of her was unaccountably pleased by the fact. They ran between stone pillars that parted the wall surrounding the compound, up a flagstone pathway onto the covered porch marking the entrance.

"So," he said, stopping in front of the door, "we're here."

It was the literal truth, and yet Melissa felt as if the statement had more meaning somehow, as if by stepping through the threshold she was moving into completely uncharted waters—both physically and emotionally. A part of her urged her to run as far and as fast as she could, but the part of her that had lived on the edge all these years knew that she'd already mentally crossed the threshold. There was no turning back.

"Let's do it."

Nigel nodded and then slid an elaborately carved rosette, situated just to the right of the door, to the side. Beneath it lay an electronic keypad. Nigel entered a series of numbers, waiting twice for answering beeps, then finishing with an additional three-number code. The door, apparently a facade, slid silently into the wall in response, the entry hall yawning cold and sterile.

"Don't worry, it gets a lot better from this point on." Nigel smiled down at her and ushered her into the anteroom. It reminded her of the Haunted Mansion at Disney World, and she half expected the floor to drop out from under them.

But instead, after Nigel punched another set of numbers into an identical keypad, the wall on the far side opened to reveal a much more inviting entryway. This one was paneled in walnut, with rich Turkish carpets lining the wood-planked floor. There was an ornate credenza bright with inlaid wood against one wall, and a gilded mirror opposite it on the other.

"I don't think we're in Kansas anymore," she murmured to no one in particular.

"I warned you." Nigel shrugged, his hand warm against her elbow as he escorted her to a room that opened off the wall with the mirror.

Again the decor changed, this time superimposing a high-tech operations room over a stately British study. A fire burned merrily in an open hearth, the logs supported by large brass andirons shaped like lions. Above it, the tranquil English countryside prevailed in what could only be a J.M.W. Turner original.

Across from the mantel, one would have expected tattered and extremely comfortable armchairs footed by hounds of some sort, but here was where the picture went askew. Instead, a forty-two-inch plasma screen adorned the wall, flanked by four smaller ones displaying various outside angles of the fortress.

Below them rested an elaborate bank of computers, servers and monitors that even Bill Gates would envy. There were machines there that Melissa couldn't even put a name to, their functions no doubt off in the realm of *Star Trek* or *Babylon Five.*

The fortress, it seemed, came with state-of-the-art security.

And like all good fantasies there was a man behind the curtain. Or, in this case, perched upon a swiveling stool that was oddly twisted but no doubt ergonomically correct.

The stool spun and a flop-haired boy-next-door face appeared, eyes narrowed slightly in speculation. "You must be Melissa."

He said it as if he already knew her, and for a moment Melissa wondered at Nigel's discretion. But another look at the bank of computer equipment stilled that thought. This was a man who knew how to extract information. There wouldn't be much he didn't know.

"And you must be Harrison Blake." Tit for tat. She might not know much about him, but Nigel had briefed her on the team's members during the helicopter ride, so at least she was fairly certain of who he was.

"Guilty as charged." He smiled, but the gesture didn't quite reach his eyes, as if he hadn't quite decided what he thought of her. Which under the circumstances was probably more than fair. "Nigel says you've had a bit of trouble."

"Something like that," she hedged, not willing to open up without knowing first that he was truly on her side.

"You find anything?" Nigel asked.

Harrison shook his head. "I've got feelers out though, so it's only a matter of time before we hear something. In the meantime, you'll be safe here." He gestured at the security monitors and Melissa fought against a wave of claustrophobia. The truth was she didn't really know anything about the people Nigel worked with. Other than the fact that he trusted them.

Still, that had to count for something. She forced a smile. "I appreciate your help."

"Not a problem." Harrison shrugged. "Besides, I haven't really done anything yet."

"You will." Nigel clapped his friend on the back, ignoring the thread of tension hanging in the air. "Anyone else here?"

"Madison and Cullen are on a conference call with the White House." He tilted his head toward a closed door in the far wall.

"Cullen's here?" Nigel's brows rose in surprise.

"Yes." Harrison nodded, underscoring the word. "He arrived shortly after we did. And I'll warn you he's none too happy about this little foray to the countryside."

"It couldn't be helped." Nigel's gaze settled on Melissa, making her skin tingle.

"I understand. And so does Cullen, fundamentally, or you wouldn't be here. But he's still concerned that Melissa's problems could pull us away from our primary focus."

"I'm not going to let that happen." Nigel's face tightened with emotion, his face flushing with anger.

"Hey, I'm with you." Harrison held up his hands in submission. "I just thought you should know that Cullen isn't thrilled with the intrusion." He shot an apologetic glance at Melissa.

"Message received. But until I have a better idea what's going on, Melissa stays right here."

She started to interrupt, to tell him that she could make her own decisions thank you very much, but then stopped herself. It wouldn't do any good anyway, and besides, for the moment, this was exactly where she wanted to be.

"Besides, if I'm right we're going to find a connection between Melissa's troubles and our missing nerve agent. That's one of the reasons I brought her here."

For the first time Melissa considered the possibility that Nigel had a secondary motivation for helping her. The idea didn't sit well, but she had to accept that it was likely true to some extent. After all, they were dealing with a crisis situation, and it was a bit coincidental that just when she was beginning to narrow down her list of possible culprits, someone had tried to take her out of the equation.

"And until we rule it out," Nigel continued, "we've got to consider the possibility that the attack on Melissa was linked somehow to the missing R-VX and the insider at the UN."

"If there is one," Harrison added. "You haven't found anything yet, right?"

There was no condemnation in his voice. No emotion at all, so Melissa wasn't exactly sure why she felt guilty, but she did. "I haven't been looking very long. And these things usually take time."

"Which is, of course, exactly what we don't have." A man walked into the room via the doorway Harrison had motioned to earlier. Cullen Pulaski. Her initial impression was that he was an enormous man, but in truth, he was only of medium height, almost short, with curling brown hair headed toward gray. His eyes compelled attention, though. Brown like his hair, they were hard like polished agate. Reflecting only what he chose to let others see.

It was the depth of his gaze, combined perhaps with his stance, that made him seem bigger than he was. Sheer presence of personality. She suspected most people were a bit in awe of him. But she'd been around kingmakers before—many of them carrying loaded Uzis. So while she knew enough to be wary, she wasn't afraid.

"I just got off the phone with Marshall." He dropped the name as if he'd been talking to his gardener rather than the President of the United States. "Paulo Salvatore has disappeared."

Nigel frowned. "I thought he was being followed."

"He was." Cullen shrugged. "But not by our guys. Turf war. The Spaniards won. Anyway, they lost him somewhere in Turkey. One minute he was there, the next off the radar completely."

"So he's flown the coop?" Harrison asked.

"Or he's dead." Nigel's tone was cold, as if the man's life wasn't worth anything at all.

"It's a definite possibility, although to be honest I don't give a damn. What's important here is confirming what the hell he was doing in Turkey in the first place. We have reason to believe Paulo was up to something before he dropped off the grid." Cullen trailed off as he eyed Melissa.

"Would you like me to leave?"

Cullen's expression indicated that's exactly what he'd like, but Nigel intervened. "There's no reason for that. We're all on the same side."

Melissa wasn't at all certain of that, but Cullen nodded his acceptance. "Nothing said here leaves this room, understood?"

Melissa nodded.

"Fine." Cullen moved to sit in a chair near the computer banks. "Harrison's encountered some chatter that seems to verify the stolen nerve agent was indeed transported across the Black Sea. If it's true, the logical exit point would be through the Bosporus Strait."

"Istanbul." Nigel frowned, obviously considering the options. "And Paulo Salvatore was last seen in Turkey."

"Yes." Cullen's smile was merely a shadow.

"But there are any number of points of egress in the Black Sea. Some of them a bloody sight better for spiriting away chemical weapons than the Bosporus."

"Sometimes the obvious choice is the least likely to be questioned." Cullen folded his arms over his chest, his expression inscrutable.

"You've got something else."

Cullen nodded. "Your killing Alberto was the final blow to the organization. There's nothing much left. But that hasn't stopped Paulo from trying to pick up the pieces."

"So he's freelancing? I wouldn't have thought him capable of it."

"Neither did the Spanish." Cullen's tone was dry. "Which is no doubt why they lost him. But before they did, they tracked him to a meeting."

"In Istanbul."

"Actually it was a few kilometers away in Izmit. According to the Spanish, he met with two Arabic men for about an hour yesterday."

"Any idea who they were?"

"No. The Spaniards botched the operation. The only thing they've got is some really bad audio and some grainy surveillance photographs." Harrison's disgust was apparent. "They claim there's a reference to chemical weapons, but nothing to definitively identify our particular package."

"And the next thing we know, Paulo goes missing." Cullen's eyebrows lifted in supposition.

"Handy coincidence. But even if the meeting was about the stolen warheads, there's no way Paulo has the network to move them. Not after what we did." Nigel's face tightened for a moment, and Melissa shivered at the look in his eyes.

"I agree," Cullen said, "but intel supports the idea that he might have been acting as a middleman, a broker for someone who does have the necessary connections to transport the package."

"The guy I've been hunting," Melissa said.

"Exactly." Cullen nodded his approval. "There's no way to know for certain until we've gathered additional information, but it seems likely. Nigel's right, there's no way Salvatore could move the nerve agent on his own."

"But this is all speculation," Nigel said. "As far as we know these guys could have just been looking for arms."

"Maybe," Harrison agreed. "But I've got a gut feeling it's about more than that."

"When do you expect the photos?" Nigel's attention turned to Harrison.

"Anytime. I'm just waiting for clearance from the Spanish officials." Harrison's smile hid the steel reflected in his eyes.

"Don't mean to interrupt, but the helicopter just landed." The striking blonde from the ball entered the room, her smile dazzling. "Tracy's with them." She crossed the room to Nigel, her attention fixed on Melissa. "I'm Madison Roarke," she said, holding out her hand.

Melissa took it, surprised at the depth of compassion in the other woman's eyes.

"I understand you've had a bit of a hard time."

"Yeah, I have." Melissa found herself smiling, surprised how quickly Madison had put her at ease.

But then, Madison was a profiler with the FBI. Obviously the woman was good at what she did. Which seemed to be the case with everyone involved with Last Chance.

"I saw you at the party last night." She struggled to remember the rest of what Nigel had told her. "You're married to Gabriel."

"Right." Madison's smile widened. "And I'm Andrea's

mother. I'm afraid between the two, I've sort of lost my own identity."

Melissa very much doubted that, but she smiled anyway. "Is she here with you?"

"No. She's with my father. He dotes on her, so I suspect she's having a marvelous time." A shadow passed across her face, and Melissa wondered at her ability to continue her work while raising her daughter, the two tasks seeming at complete odds with one another.

"I limit the cases I take," Madison said, reading Melissa's mind. "But sometimes it's hard to say no."

"We simply can't operate without her." Cullen put an arm around Madison comfortingly, and Melissa envied the ease with which they all seemed to support one another. She'd spent most of her professional life on her own, oftentimes among the enemy, so she'd never had the chance to form the kinds of bonds these people obviously had.

"Cullen, if you weren't my wife's godfather, I'd swear you were trying to cut in on my action." Another impossibly large man strode into the room. This time the electric presence was backed up by the physical. She recognized him from the ball, and Nigel's description. Gabriel Roarke.

He pulled his wife into a bear hug, and the naked love on their faces left Melissa breathless. Passion mixed with adoration was heady stuff.

A second man followed the first. He, too, had a presence but, unlike Cullen and Gabriel, his was entirely physical. Pantherlike in his grace, he moved with a stealth that hinted of assassin. She'd seen enough to know. There was an unmistakable stillness in a hunter. And this man had it in spades.

"Payton Reynolds," he said.

Nigel's friend.

She met his gaze. Unlike Madison, his eyes held no compassion. This was a man who gave nothing easily. If she wanted his trust, she'd have to earn it. And judging from the skepticism she saw reflected there, it wasn't going to be an easy task, but then she wasn't a woman given to shirking a challenge.

Nigel had moved so that he was standing just behind her, his body heat wrapping around her, subtly protecting her, making her a part of the group by simple proximity. She appreciated the gesture but had no intention of hiding behind him.

"I've heard a lot about you." She hadn't actually heard all that much, but it seemed an appropriate response.

"I bet you have." Payton's smile was tight, a crooked little thing that was meant to intimidate. But then Melissa wasn't easily cowed.

They stood for a minute more, each assessing the other, then Melissa broke contact, stepping back into the circle of Nigel's warmth.

"Any word from Sam?" Harrison asked Payton, obviously trying to cut through the tension.

"I talked to her this morning." He sounded frustrated, his examination of Melissa for the moment seemingly forgotten. "She's coming as soon as she can get things under control. There's a serial bomber in Oregon. She knows who it is, but hasn't got enough evidence to nail him. So I'm afraid it's a waiting game."

Gabriel smiled conspiratorially at his friend. "If anyone can make the case, it'll be Sam. She'll be here before you know it."

"Excuse me?" A statuesque black woman stood in the doorway to the operations room, her expression a cross between amused tolerance and exasperation. "I hate to interrupt this little soiree, but I didn't skip out on critical work just to listen to old home week. Unless I missed the boat completely, I believe there's some urgency involved?"

"This is Tracy Braxton," Nigel said, his smile full of admiration. "She's one of the foremost forensic pathologists in the world. I thought maybe she could help us get to the bottom of what happened to you."

Melissa frowned, then nodded, understanding dawning. "The blood."

"Exactly." Nigel held up a gym bag with the her coat and clothes to underscore his agreement. "With a little luck Tracy will be able to help us figure where the blood on your clothes came from. Or at least narrow things down a bit."

"Thanks for the vote of confidence." Tracy's grin was infectious. "First he thinks I'm godlike, and then he hedges his bets."

"I'm afraid that's the way he sees all women." The words were out before she had a chance to think about them, and she immediately regretted the inference, but his friends only laughed, and to her relief, Nigel seemed unfazed by her pronouncement.

"I'll also need a blood sample." Tracy was already pulling a syringe from the black bag she carried. "Would you like to do it in here or in private?"

"A blood sample?" Melissa protested.

Payton's glittering gaze landed on her, his expression still speculative.

"Yes." Tracy nodded, apparently unaware of the subtext. "Nigel said that you might have been poisoned. I want to take a look at your blood as well as what's on your coat to see if I can find any trace elements that might confirm the fact."

Melissa squared her shoulders. She hadn't anything to hide, and she'd be damned if she'd let Payton get to her. "Fine. I'll do it here." She stuck out her uninjured arm, already clenching her fist.

It only took a minute. Tracy's expertise obviously extended to drawing blood, because Melissa hardly felt a thing. Or maybe she was simply too preoccupied with the fact that Payton Reynolds didn't trust her.

The idea certainly didn't sit well, which in her books left only one alternative. She'd simply have to prove the man wrong. Not that she gave a damn what Payton Reynolds thought of her. But she did care about Nigel. He'd taken a risk bringing her here, potentially compromising their operation. And she wasn't about to let him down.

So if Payton Reynolds wanted blood then she'd give him three fucking quarts.

CHAPTER ELEVEN

"EVERYTHING IS ARRANGED?" Malik appeared relaxed, but his eyes were watchful, the bazaar humming with life, crowds ebbing and flowing around the small tables fronting the Turkish café.

"We have agreed upon terms, but nothing can be done until payment is made." Khamis, too, watched the passersby, but other than the interest of a young boy at the next table, no one seemed to notice the two of them. There was a certain anonymity in crowds, and Khamis had always preferred hiding in the open.

"So we wait." Waiting had never been Malik's strong point, and Khamis smiled.

"On the contrary. We must move now. The diversion is in place. If the Americans are tracking us, they'll think the R-VX is moving through Istanbul. While they are busy scouring the city, our package will travel down the Sakarya to friends in Greece. And from there, on to the United States."

"And what about us?"

"We must arrive in America before the R-VX. From there final arrangements will be made."

"You make it sound simple."

Khamis's smile widened as he toyed with an almond blossom that had fallen from the vase at the center of the table. "Simplicity is nothing more than a state of mind. It helps to keep one focused—complications becoming mere triviality. Something to overcome and nothing more."

Malik laughed as he sipped his coffee. "I have never pretended to understand you, my friend, but I do trust you. So if you say we must move, then so be it. I assume all the necessary arrangements have been made."

"They have." Khamis tilted his head toward a small valise lying on the corner of the table, still idly twirling the little flower. "The briefcase contains documentation that will permit our entry into the country. Once there, all that will remain is to pay off our contact and await the shipment's arrival."

"Our timetable is intact?" Malik narrowed his eyes as he contemplated the dregs in his cup.

"It is. Although the change in plans has caused a slight delay, we shouldn't have to deviate from our original intentions. In a very short time the Americans will feel the sting of our mighty sword."

"And your revenge?" Malik asked, his face tight with emotion.

"Will be all the sweeter." With a simplicity of motion, Khamis closed his hand, crushing the blossom, its delicate petals disintegrating against his palm.

"RIGHT THEN." Nigel strode into Cullen's study. "I've made some calls, and if the warheads are in Istanbul, they'll find them."

"MI6?" Gabe queried, from an armchair near the fireplace. Cullen certainly knew how to make a room comfortable.

"A mix actually. Sort of a ragtag group of operatives I've worked with over the years. I suspect you know most of them."

"As long as they get the job done." Cullen was standing by the fireplace nursing what looked like a brandy. "I'd prefer one of you do it."

"So would I, actually. But you know as well as I do that by the time we got there, it would be too late," Nigel said, helping himself to an eighteen-year-old bourbon from the drinks table.

"Something just doesn't feel right about this whole thing," Gabe said, staring down into the amber depths of his drink. "I mean why the hell would Paulo take the risk of meeting with clients just days after his father was killed and his trafficking network collapses?"

"Maybe there was already a deal in place." Nigel shrugged. "That'd be something he couldn't ignore, despite the situation. In fact, given his propensity to play the big man, maybe it's his way of thumbing his nose at authority."

"Well, it worked," Cullen said, his disgust evident. But then he had never suffered fools lightly, and Nigel had seen the Spanish operating firsthand.

"Depends on where you're sitting. If the meet really was about the R-VX, the Arabs in question wouldn't want to take a chance on anything leaking once arrangements were made."

"So you really do think Paulo's dead?" Cullen asked.

"Yes, actually, I do. It's completely out of character for him to disappear. So unless I miss my guess, the vanishing act wasn't consensual." Nigel took a sip, letting the fiery liquid slide down his throat. It seemed a week had passed since the morning, everything literally happening too fast.

Melissa was safe for the moment, but they still had no idea what had happened to her. Tracy had returned to her lab to try to find answers, but it would be hours still until she had anything to report. Payton and Harrison were checking sources, while Melissa and Madison went over everything that had happened, in the hopes that Madison would see something the rest of them had missed.

And in the meantime, he'd been attempting to stop a stolen cache of nerve agent capable of wiping out literally hundreds of thousands of people.

"Well, Paulo, dead or alive, is the least of our problems," Gabe said, his words pulling Nigel away from his thoughts. "Whoever is behind the heist won't be sitting around waiting for our team to find them. They've come this far because they know what they're doing."

"All of which means we have to be on our best game." Cullen shot a pointed look in Nigel's direction.

"I know you're not happy about Melissa, Cullen. But until I have a better idea of what's going on, this is the best possible place for her, and you know it." Nigel waved his glass to emphasize the point.

"If I didn't agree, believe me, she wouldn't be here. But that doesn't change the urgency of the situation we're facing, and I can't afford to have you distracted."

"I'm not." Nigel closed his eyes and counted to ten, trying to contain his anger. Yelling at Cullen wasn't going to do anyone any good.

"Nigel, we've been down this road with you before." Cullen's expression was harsh and, despite himself, Nigel flinched.

"That's hitting below the belt, Cullen," Gabe said. "You know as well as I do that Nigel regrets what happened with Kingston. There were conflicting interests."

"And there aren't now?" Cullen's eyebrows rose with the question.

"I thought this was all behind us." Nigel blew out a breath, dropping into an armchair, his anger dissipating with the action. Maybe some mistakes were just destined to be revisited. Gabe had hit it on the head when he'd said there were conflicting interests. Nigel considered himself a patriot, had dedicated his life to the fact, actually. And when England's interests had gone against Last Chance's he'd sided with Queen and country. And almost gotten Madison killed.

It was a mistake he'd regret for the rest of his life, one that fortunately hadn't ended in catastrophe. At the end of the day he simply hadn't been able to abandon his friends. Some things went beyond even national allegiance.

"It's behind us," Gabe said with a sigh, running a hand

through his hair. "We just don't want you to get caught off guard."

"I'm not Payton." The minute the words were out, Nigel regretted them. The past, it seemed, was tangled with more than just his mistakes. Payton's first wife's betrayal colored their perception of all women—especially journalists. But Melissa wasn't Mariam.

Silence held for a moment, all three men studying their drinks.

"I'm sorry." Nigel shook his head, wondering if they'd ever escape the shadows of Iraq. "I didn't mean that. At least not the way it sounded."

"You'd just better be grateful Payton wasn't here to hear it." Gabe's smile was weak.

"Look. All I meant was that the situations aren't the same. There are similarities certainly between Mariam and Melissa, but the differences are far more consequential. Melissa is on our side. Hell, she's CIA." Nigel turned to face his friends. "And more importantly, I'm not in love with her."

"I think the jury's still out on that one."

If it had been anyone else but Gabe, Nigel would have been tempted to knock him into next Sunday, but Gabe knew him all too well, and truth be told he wasn't completely off the mark.

"The point is," Nigel said as firmly as possible, unwilling to let his thoughts go any further, "Mariam used Payton to accomplish her own goals, and she hurt him—hell, she hurt all of us—in the process. But Melissa isn't going to do that. Whatever is happening here, my gut is telling me that it's all related. And in getting to the bottom of what happened to Melissa, we'll be that much closer to finding the nerve agent. Or at least its intended point of entry into the States."

"All I know," Cullen said, his expression hard, "is that we've got to keep our eye on the ball. Connected or not, Melissa's problems are not ours. So while I'm not forbidding you from investigating, I am ordering you to keep perspective."

"That's not a problem," Nigel said. "And you can rest easy on the other point, as well."

"The other point?" The older man frowned.

"I'm not going to betray any of you. What happened before was a lapse in judgment. I was faced with a conflict of interest that led to a wrong decision. But I've more than proved my mettle since then, and I'm not going to do anything that would jeopardize either our mission or our personnel. Am I making myself clear?" Nigel's anger was back, his pulse beating syncopated rhythm against his temples.

"Perfectly." Cullen's expression was hard to read, part anger, and part something else. Remorse, maybe—or maybe that was just what Nigel wanted to see.

"Come on, guys." Gabe's voice was deceptively soft. "We're arguing over ancient history. What's done is done, and what matters now is finding the nerve agent before it can be released."

Nigel opened his mouth, but Gabe waved him quiet.

"And," he continued, "we need to find out what, if anything, Melissa's troubles have to do with our operation. To that end, we all need to work together to find out what happened to her, and why. Agreed?"

There was really no arguing with Gabe when he had made up his mind, and Cullen for once recognized the wisdom of the fact.

"Fine." He nodded, underscoring his agreement.

"Nigel?" Gabe wasn't really asking, and so Nigel nodded, as well. "Wonderful. Now what do you say we get back to business?"

Again Nigel nodded, then swallowed the rest of his whiskey, the alcohol searing his throat. Unfortunately, the burning in his belly came from a completely different source. And unlike a good bourbon, she wouldn't wear off after a good night's sleep.

Once, a lifetime ago, he *had* loved Melissa Pope. And the

honest truth was that he wasn't at all sure that he'd ever really stopped loving her. Which meant that there was more truth in Gabe's words than he wanted to admit.

Or maybe he just had one hellacious case of indigestion.

Only time would tell.

"SO YOU AND NIGEL WERE an item?" Madison was perched on a stool at the center island in Cullen's kitchen. Melissa sat opposite her, idly pushing around the remains of a cranberry scone.

"I think that might be overstating it." She studied the other woman for a moment, trying to decide exactly how much she wanted to say. Madison's curiosity was understandable. It was clear that she cared about Nigel. Clear that they all cared about him a great deal, so it followed that they'd want to know more about what was going on between Nigel and her.

Of course there wasn't anything present tense, just the past. And a part of Melissa wanted that to stay dead and buried, but considering Nigel was sitting in the next room, that was probably wishful thinking. Better a preemptive strike.

She looked up to meet Madison's patient gaze, realizing that the woman would probably see right through anything she said that wasn't at least based in truth, and the thought was enough to propel Melissa past her usual reticence to share personal information. "It was just a summer fling, really. We were both young and the world was beckoning, that kind of thing."

Instead of responding, Madison simply nodded, sipping from her coffee cup, while she waited for Melissa to continue.

Melissa sighed, thinking that having Madison for a friend had the potential to be quite disconcerting. "We met when he was still with Special Forces. Before he was assigned to Gabe's unit. He was on leave in Naples. I was doing a piece on the Amalfi Coast."

Madison raised an eyebrow, her expression almost an exact mirror of one her husband used. "A piece?"

"I was working undercover. Something to do with the infiltration of Cyprus patriots. But as far as Nigel knew, I was simply working on a photo spread for a travel magazine. Anyway, I was at the end of my run, and ready for some R & R myself."

"How did you meet?"

"Usual story," Melissa said, trying to keep her tone neutral. "I was meeting some friends at a bar—fellow journalists. Nigel was there with some of the guys from his company. There was a mutual connection between the groups and we all started drinking together. One thing led to another, and the next thing I know Nigel and I wound up on the beach talking about life and hopes and dreams and whatnot until the sun came up."

"Very romantic."

"I don't know. I suppose it was a little like summer camp. You know, the friends you make there aren't real. The relationships are fostered by a ticking clock and the need for connection. So everything is more intense, but once the summer ends, there's no longer anything to tie you together, and it all sort of fades away until there's nothing but the memory."

"I don't know." Madison shrugged. "Certain psychologists would contend those kinds of connections are more real. No societal bullshit to get in the way."

"Maybe," Melissa admitted. "Anyway, at the time we were young and the connection was intense. We spent a month together. All of it set against the glorious backdrop of the Amalfi Coast. We basked in the sunshine, lazed on the beach…you know the drill."

Madison nodded, her expression speculative. "But everything has to end?"

"Yeah. But we knew that when we started. I mean it wasn't real. It was just a moment out of time really. A break from the stress we both encountered during assignments. I can't say I didn't enjoy it. But I never had any illusions about where it would end. Nigel had to report back to his unit, and I was booked on a plane to the Middle East."

"But you could have seen each other again, surely."

"I suppose so. But then reality would have set in and the magic would have been lost."

"That's true in all relationships to some extent. We're programmed to believe that after we ride off into the sunset it's all happily ever after, but that's not really the case, is it?"

"Not for most people. Although you seem to have found it." The words came out on an almost wistful note, and Melissa immediately regretted them.

"Yes." Madison's smile was beautiful. "I have. But that doesn't mean it's all wine and roses."

"I don't know." Melissa shrugged, pretending indifference. "Maybe I'm not cut out for that kind of relationship."

"The kind you have to work for?"

"I guess in a way, maybe that's what I mean. I'm not exactly a nine-to-fiver, and more times than not, I'm standing smack-dab in harm's way. That's not the kind of life one builds a relationship around. And if there were conflicts of interest when Nigel and I first met, they're even stronger now."

"But surely we're all working on the same side?"

"It isn't that. It's the work itself. You said earlier how hard it was to juggle your family and your work. Well, I work undercover most of the time. Not exactly conducive to the white picket fence. So you tell me how I'm supposed to find time for a relationship?"

Madison's eyes narrowed. "You just find a way. Unless of course there's something more to it. Something you're not admitting even to yourself."

The woman saw too damn much. "Look, it's really simple. I've been on my own for a long time. My dad ran out on us when I was in grade school, and then my mom died just after that."

"So who raised you?"

"Officially? My aunt Kiki. But trust me, she was way too busy looking for husband number three to be much of a mother figure. I guess the truth is that I raised myself."

"What about your sister? Nigel said that you're close."

"We are. But when she got married everything changed. I mean, I'm really happy for her. Especially now that she's expecting, but before it was just the two of us, you know? And now, well, her first priority has to be Aaron. And I totally understand that, but it just reinforces the fact that nothing is forever."

"And that's what you want—forever?"

"It's more about what I don't want. I don't want to set myself up for failure. And I don't want to relive the past. What happened between Nigel and me is over and done with. I care about him in the sense that he's an old friend. And I trust him, which is why I'm here with you all, but that's as far as it goes."

"I see," Madison said, her expression pensive.

Melissa wondered if she really did. If anyone could get it, she suspected Madison was the one, but then she'd found forever with Gabriel, so maybe she couldn't really understand. Perhaps it would have been better if Melissa had just kept her mouth shut, but in the face of all her cascading emotions, she had to admit it felt good to talk to someone about it.

"There you are." Payton stood in the doorway, his eyes narrowed as he took in the two of them and their cozy tea party. Despite herself, Melissa shivered. There was an underlying stillness about the man that was downright unnerving.

"We were just getting to know each other." Madison smiled up at him, apparently immune to his intense scrutiny.

"Well, you'll have to put it on hold." His tone was clipped, his cold gaze settling on Melissa. "Cullen wants us all in the operations room. Harrison finally hit pay dirt regarding Melissa's situation. It seems there are a few things you've neglected to tell us—like the fact that you're wanted for murder."

CHAPTER TWELVE

THE TEMPERATURE in the operations room seemed to have dropped about twenty degrees. Or maybe it was simply the doubt in everyone's eyes. Payton Reynolds hadn't made any bones about his suspicions, but now Gabe and Cullen seemed to have joined in his distrust. Harrison, to his credit, seemed exactly the same, although she suspected he hid a lot behind his youthful dishevelment. Even Madison seemed a bit more wary.

But it was Nigel who upset her the most. There was a shadow in his eyes that hadn't been there before. A glimmer of doubt. She wouldn't have thought his opinion would matter—not after all this time—but it did. A lot.

Still, there was no sense in letting them know she was upset. Better to keep her silence, and wait to see what exactly it was she was being accused of—or more precisely, who she was supposed to have murdered. She shivered, despite her resolve, wishing suddenly for the warmth of Nigel's arms.

Damn it all to hell. She wasn't the kind to buckle under when the going got tough, and she certainly hadn't killed anyone, no matter what Harrison thought he'd found. Despite their connection with Nigel, the people in the room were strangers. For all she knew they were enemies. She'd allowed her feelings for Nigel to color her judgment, end-running around common sense in an attempt to let someone else deal with her problems.

Never a smart move.

And not a mistake she was going to repeat. It was too late for retreat, but she'd be damned if she'd let them lead her placidly to slaughter. Narrowing her eyes, she swallowed all fear and squared her shoulders, her gaze locking on Harrison. "So let's have it. Who exactly am I supposed to have killed?"

Harrison at least had the grace to look slightly embarrassed, and unless she was totally off her game there was a flash of admiration in Madison's eyes. Two out of five. Maybe she could change the odds.

"A Turkish consulate member named Hakan Celik." Harrison looked down at his notes. "He was found stabbed to death in his apartment."

"Did you know him?" Gabe's question was terse, but at least he hadn't asked her why she'd killed the man.

"No. Not really. I met him though—last night." For about ten lecherous minutes. "He was at the party, and seemed to think I was going home with him for the evening." She looked over at Nigel, despite her resolve for singularity.

"It's true." He shrugged, his eyes sparking with something that might have been hope. "The guy was hitting on her. I maneuvered her away."

"And you'd never seen him before last night?" Payton asked, his tone indicating that he didn't believe her.

"No. Never. I hadn't even heard of him." She let her gaze sweep across the room. "And I didn't kill him."

"Unfortunately the evidence says otherwise." Payton reached over to take the report from Harrison. "According to the forensics report, the weapon recovered from the scene has your fingerprints on it. Coupled with the fact that the strands of hair found on the body match your DNA, I'd say they've got a rock-solid case."

"You know as well as I do that evidence can be manufactured." This from Nigel, who, despite his doubts, was obviously not willing to convict her without at least a hearing.

Ridiculously, she felt relief. As if her knight had climbed back up on his charger—or at least was making an effort to do so.

"Look, I don't even know where the man lives. And if I did, I couldn't have been there. I was at a diner under the Brooklyn Bridge waiting for my handler."

"You went there straight from the party?" Gabe resumed questioning. It was standard procedure, but she'd never been the subject of it. At least not like this.

"I stopped at home to change clothes."

"Did anyone see you?"

For the first time she regretted her walk-up. "No. My building doesn't have a doorman. But there are security cameras. They ought to show my arrival."

"It's a start," Gabe said, making notes. "What about your handler? Can he verify your meeting?"

She opened her mouth to respond, but before she could speak, Nigel answered for her. "He's disappeared. Never showed up for the meeting and isn't answering his phone."

"So obviously something here isn't right."

Melissa shot Madison a grateful smile. She was capable of holding her own in a tough situation, but it was always nice to have allies and evidently Madison was suspending her disbelief—at least for the moment.

"Or a sign that Melissa is lying." Payton's cold gaze met hers, his scarred face completely devoid of emotion.

"Look, if you're so certain I'm guilty, why the hell don't you just turn me over to the authorities?" The words were out before she could stop them and she immediately wished them back. These people, despite their doubts, were her best hope. That or working it on her own. And at least for the moment, that wasn't an option she wanted to consider.

"Surely that's not necessary." Madison shot a significant look at her husband, who shrugged in response. "The truth is, we don't have all the facts. If you compare Melissa's story to the one Harrison has dug up, you have admit there are conflicts. I think the least we can do is check some of it out. You know as well as I do that if someone is trying to frame Melissa, turning her in would be playing right into their hands."

"We're not turning her in." Nigel's response was immediate, and there was no arguing.

"Fine." Payton looked as if he wanted to argue but didn't, his friendship with Nigel overcoming even his own reservations. "But we're going to check it out." There was no missing the fact that he still didn't trust her.

Which was perfectly acceptable since the sentiment went both ways.

"Not so fast." Cullen Pulaski stepped into the room holding a sheaf of papers, his hard gaze sweeping across them all. "Everything's been hushed up, but I've managed to get my hands on something more." He passed the sheets of paper to Gabe, who skimmed them and passed them on to Payton. Nigel moved closer to his friend, his hand already out.

"What do they say?" Melissa cut across the heavy silence, her heart pounding as if she were actually guilty of something. She'd lost precious time in that alleyway, but she knew she hadn't killed anyone. Still, that didn't mean the deck wasn't stacked against her.

Nigel turned slowly, his strong face unusually pale. "These are copies of letters the authorities found at Celik's apartment." He held the letters out in mute testimony. "Correspondence from you to Celik. According to what I'm reading here, the two of you had quite a scam going. You pretend to dig around to find the traitor, when all the while you're in bed with the man—quite literally, if these are to be believed. But apparently it wasn't enough, and you wanted more."

"I didn't write any letters. I didn't even know the man."

"I'm afraid these tell a different story." Gabe snagged the letters from Nigel just as he would have dropped them.

"They're typewritten?" Madison came to stand beside her husband, looking down at the letters. "Is there a signature?"

Gabe thumbed through the lot, then shook his head.

Madison chewed on her lower lip, her brows pulled together in concentration. "Nothing at all here to indicate that the letter was actually written by Melissa. Anyone with a word processor could have done it."

Nigel's head jerked up, the flare of hope evident again. "Did they check the originals for prints?"

"Yes." Cullen consulted a report he still held. "Celik's are all over them. Melissa had a partial. It's a match, but not a perfect one. It was too smudged."

"Like maybe someone transferred it," Madison said. "All right. Before we hang anyone, let's sit down and look at the facts."

Nigel nodded. And Melissa was surprised to find herself breathing again. She hadn't realized she'd stopped.

Payton looked totally unconvinced, but he also nodded his consent. Harrison shrugged, and Cullen pulled out a chair. Apparently she was going to have her fifteen minutes.

"So here's how it stacks up." Harrison shot her another apologetic look. "There's a murder weapon with a clearly identified print and a strand of hair. Then there are letters and a partial."

"Weapon and motive," Payton said, his tone more probing than accusing. "Is there a time of death?"

"No autopsy yet, but they're thinking it was between midnight and three," Cullen said, again referring to the report.

"So there's opportunity," Gabe said almost under his breath.

"But she was at the diner waiting for her handler." Nigel crossed his arms, his tone defiant.

"Who has conveniently gone missing," Payton said.

"I'd say that's a point in Melissa's favor." Madison faced Payton. "If he really did place that call, then that makes him our primary suspect."

"Assuming she's telling us the truth." Gabe's words held no malice. "All we have right now is her word."

"Which, as a CIA agent, ought to count for something," Madison insisted.

"Besides, there is proof," Melissa said, glaring at the assembled company. "There were people in the diner. The waitress, a couple of kids and an old man. All we have to do is find them. They should remember me."

"It's a start," Gabe said. "But it's not enough."

"What about the fact that she was sick?" Nigel asked. "Have we heard anything back from Tracy? If we can prove she was poisoned, that'll go a long way to verifying her story."

"No news yet," Cullen said, checking his watch. "But I assume we'll be hearing something soon."

"Look," Melissa said, standing up. "I didn't know this man. I didn't send him letters. I didn't collude with him to transport illegal goods, I didn't blackmail him and I didn't kill him. What I did do was go to a party, run into an old friend—" she emphasized the word, shooting a pointed look in Nigel's direction "—and then get a call from my handler.

"He wanted to meet. So I left the party, went home to change and then headed for the diner. He never showed, and after drinking really bad coffee and eating some pie, I gave up and headed for the subway. Only I never made it, because I had to stop and puke my guts up in an alley. The next thing I remember was waking up in a blood-soaked coat, freezing my ass off, feeling a hell of a lot like a train had just run through my abdomen.

"I managed to pilfer some clean clothes, made my way to my apartment, saw the conflux of people and decided I needed help. So I called Nigel and met him at his hotel. But not before someone tried to kill me. And through all of that, I might add, I carried the blood-soaked clothing in the hopes that they'd provide some sort of clue as to what the hell was going on. If I was the killer, do you think I'd have hung on to evidence like that? Do you think I'd have run to the very people that were going to be looking for me?" This time her gaze landed squarely on Payton.

"I am not a stupid woman. And I do not make stupid mistakes. If I had been going to kill Hakan Celik, I certainly wouldn't have left a trail of evidence a mile wide in my wake. I may not be black ops, but I've been in this game for fifteen years, which means I've learned a thing or two about clandestine operations. If I murdered someone, believe me, no one would know about it." Melissa sank back into her chair, the anger that had been buoying her dissipating almost as quickly as it had come.

"Melissa's right. We need to figure out what's really going on." Harrison seemed to have swung over to the home team. "And the first order of business is to find Wyland."

"Actually, the first order of business would be to take over the case," Nigel said. "It's the only way to be certain that someone isn't constantly nosing about in our business."

"It's not our business," Cullen said. "We have our own situation and frankly it's more important."

"But the letters prove there was a transportation ring. Even if Melissa's involvement was faked, someone knew enough about her assignment to know what it was she was looking for. And what better way to stop her than to frame her as an accomplice in the very matter she's supposed to be investigating?" Madison crossed her arms, her gaze traveling around the table, settling finally on Cullen.

"So you think that this is all related?" Cullen asked.

"I don't think we can make the mistake of assuming it's not."

"But what if Melissa did kill Celik?" Payton asked, but there was a thread of something that hadn't been there before. He was giving her the benefit of the doubt.

"Then we'll be able to watch her." Gabe's pronouncement should have made her angry, but she knew that, like Payton, he was allowing for the possibility that she might be telling the truth.

"So she stays here, and Cullen arranges for Last Chance to take over the investigation." Madison's tone didn't permit any dissention.

"Is that what you want?" Nigel's gaze met Melissa's, and a shiver traced its way along her back. She needed him to believe her. It was more important than she could have ever imagined. And so she'd stay if for no other reason than to prove to him that she was trustworthy.

"Yes."

"I'm going to object on principle," Cullen said. "Not so much because I don't think there's merit to your argument, Madison, but because I think there are bigger fish to fry here. However," he sighed, "I know the way you all work, and if you've made up your minds, you're going to do this with or without my sanction. So you might as well have it. I'll call the President and make the arrangements. Of course, the other agencies will have to be kept in the loop. They'll be able to provide subsidiary help at the very least. And until we have something to corroborate her story, Melissa doesn't leave here. Is that clear?"

"We're agreed," Gabe said.

There was an implication in Cullen's last statement. They'd keep her whereabouts secret for now, but they'd also be watching her—waiting for the other shoe to drop. She should be insulted, but the truth was that if the situation were reversed, she'd be the skeptical one. They were professionals. And truth was, they were stepping out on a limb for her. No, for Nigel.

And that, in and of itself, was something precious. Not everyone had friends like that.

At least she'd never had any.

Well, maybe once, but she'd thrown it away. And now that she'd been given a second chance, she'd managed to arrive at his doorstep drenched in blood and accused of murder.

Wasn't life grand?

CHAPTER THIRTEEN

"SO HOW MUCH OF ALL THIS are you buying?" Payton asked Gabe, nodding at the super, who opened Ed Wyland's apartment with barely restrained curiosity.

"Let's just say I'm giving her the benefit of the doubt." Gabe shrugged, then pushed past the super into the handler's apartment. It wasn't much, a three-room walk-up with a tiny portico that passed as a balcony. "That'll be all." He shot the super a withering look. "We'll take it from here."

The man's frown was a clear indication of his displeasure. Payton waited until the super had shuffled through the door, then shut it behind him. It had taken more time than he'd have liked to cut through the bureaucracy that veiled the CIA's agent/handler relationships, but Cullen's perseverance had won the day and now they were standing in the man's apartment.

"You've got to admit that Melissa's record with the Company is exemplary. Not a *t* uncrossed or an *i* undotted."

"True, but the best subversives are very good at hiding their activities."

"Not that well." Gabe shook his head. "I think Madison's right. The evidence here is too damning. I mean, if she's that inept her record should reflect it. Add in the fact that her phone records show she did get the call from Wyland and I'm inclined to think she's telling the truth."

"It's not that I want to doubt her, Gabe," Payton protested, feeling like the heavy. "But she can't really explain any of it.

Top that off with the fact that no one at the diner remembers seeing her, and you've got to admit I'm not completely crazy."

"I'm not implying anything. I just think we need to gather all the information we can and then make an informed decision."

"If it isn't already too late." Payton knew he was being stubborn, but he wasn't about to take a chance on someone he didn't know. Even if Nigel swore her innocence. He knew firsthand how easy it was to let hormones override common sense.

"It's not too late. And as far as the diner goes, we've only got the waitress's word that Melissa wasn't there."

"And your problem with that is?"

"Simple," Gabe said, pulling open a drawer and riffling through the contents. "I figure that if it was a setup, the waitress had to be in on it. She's the only one who could have drugged Melissa."

"*If* she was drugged."

"Well that's the lab's purview and I guarantee you that if there was a toxin present, Tracy will find it."

"And in the meantime we chase shadows." Payton sighed, searching through the odds and ends thrown on the man's kitchen counter. Ed Wyland wasn't a believer in cleanliness.

"We'll follow up on the old man and the kids, but odds are against us finding them. They paid cash, and the waitress didn't exactly seem inclined to help us out."

"See no evil and all that?"

"Either that or I-am-evil-and-I'm-hoping-you-won't-notice. Seriously, I think we can't discount the possibility that the waitress was part of the whole scheme." Gabe as usual was talking sense. And the fact that he was siding with Melissa, or at least giving her a chance, lessened Payton's distrust. Gabe was a discerning man, and quite honestly, he wasn't carrying the same amount of baggage.

Still, it was worth being thorough. "So then maybe Wyland is the key?"

"His record is certainly nondescript. Nothing good, nothing bad. Which makes him a far better candidate for under-the-table dealings than Melissa."

"True," Payton said, considering the options. "He's been working with Melissa from the beginning?"

"Yes. He's been her only handler. But he's been with the Company longer than she has. He started in research and worked his way up from there."

"All of which would support the idea of a happy camper."

"Maybe. Or maybe he thought he should have been promoted faster and saw Melissa as cover for a nice little operation on the side."

"Then why let her be assigned to investigate it?"

"Not his call? Hell, I don't know."

"Well, don't look at me. I feel like we're running around in circles over something that shouldn't have been our play in the first place." Payton sighed and walked over to the table, thumbing through a stack of mail. "Nothing here but bills and advertisements."

"Phone bill?"

"Nope. Just Con Ed, and Hammacher Schlemmer." Payton stuffed them in his pocket anyway. "Let's check the other room."

Like the rest of the apartment, the bedroom was bland, bordering on boring. As if the man never looked at his surroundings. Or just didn't know any better. Payton pulled open the closet.

"Well, that explains a lot," Gabe said, eyeing the empty row of hangers. A large gap in the clutter on the shelf above the hanging rod stood testament to what had probably been home to a suitcase.

Payton jerked open the bureau drawers revealing scattered remnants of the contents. "Looks like he cleared out in a hurry."

"Which could fit any one of a hundred scenarios." Gabe

slammed his hand on the top of the chest. "We need answers and all we're getting is more questions."

"He couldn't have been operating on his own. I mean, he wouldn't have the contacts to run this kind of a black-market organization."

"Celik could have been his partner." Gabe leaned back against the bureau.

"And he turned on Celik and framed Melissa? There are a hell of a lot of holes in that theory."

"I'm just trying to fit the pieces together." Gabe blew out a long breath and pushed away from the chest of drawers.

"I know." Payton sat down on the end of the bed. "So what have we got? A CIA handler on the run. Another agent framed for murder."

"You're beginning to believe—"

Payton shook his head, cutting Gabe off. "I'm not buying into anything at the moment. But I do agree that this whole things smells."

"Let's look at this from another angle. If Melissa was working with Wyland or Celik, then what would be the advantage in her running back to the Company?"

"You mean the call to Nigel? Maybe she didn't know he'd bring us in?"

Gabe shook his head. "She had to have had an idea. She knew what he was working on. And she certainly couldn't have planned it ahead of time. There's no way she could have known that Nigel was going to be at the party. We didn't even know until just before time."

"All right, but there still could be an angle."

"You need Sam." Gabe slapped Payton on the back with a wry grin.

"What's my wife got to do with it?" he asked, glaring up at his friend.

"Lack of sex has made you one suspicious dude." Gabe's smile bordered on wicked.

"I fail to see the correlation." Payton scowled, standing up. "If anything I'm the only one seeing things clearly. One look at your wife and all you see is sunshine and rainbows."

"And you don't feel that way?" Gabe's eyebrow shot up in punctuation.

"Of course I do." Payton couldn't help his smile. Sam was his whole world, simple as that. "But it doesn't have to impair my thinking."

"Fine. We'll agree to disagree." Gabe laughed. "Right now, though, I think we need to finish our search and report back to the safe house. Maybe Madison and Nigel have had more luck."

"YOU DOING ALL RIGHT?" Madison stood in the security room of Melissa's building, her expression concerned.

"I don't think there's really a way to answer that question," Nigel said, grateful that the building super had left them on their own to review the tapes. It was amazing what the proper credentials could accomplish. That and underpaid staff. "At some gut level I never doubted her. But in the face of all that evidence…"

"A chink in the armor?" Madison's smile was full of gentle concern.

"Something like that." He shrugged, feeling suddenly uncomfortable in his own skin. "I don't want to repeat old mistakes."

"With Melissa or with us?"

"Both, actually. Well, more the group, I guess. I mean, I know it's all water under the bridge, but it can never completely go away, can it?"

"It has for me." There wasn't even a shred of hesitation in the statement.

"And you're the one who suffered the most."

"Actually, it's just the opposite. I'm the one who benefited the most. The way I look at it, Nigel, if you hadn't come back—if you hadn't told Gabe your suspicions—then I might be dead."

"But if I'd been honest from the beginning and not sent you all off on a wild-goose chase we might have nailed the bastard before you were threatened."

"Maybe," Madison allowed. "But you can't know that for certain. And there's no sense in trying to speculate on what can never be. The fact is, you came back, and in doing so you saved my life. It's as simple as that. So let it go."

"But what if I'm making the same mistake again? Placing my loyalty in the wrong place? It was a long time ago, Madison."

"Trust your instincts. They're good ones." She reached out to touch his hand. "I believe in them. And frankly, I believe Melissa. The whole thing just reeks of a setup."

"Payton doesn't believe it."

"Payton doesn't believe anything he can't substantiate in triplicate. It's just his nature. But that doesn't mean he's always right."

"I know that." Nigel ran his fingers over his mustache, a nervous gesture he'd never completely been able to rid himself of. "It's just that he could be, couldn't he? I mean, it would be far easier for me to let sentiment carry me away."

"Sometimes the heart has a way of seeing the truth even when it's buried in mud. Maybe you just need to trust it. That and the fact that we're going to get to the bottom of this one way or the other." With that she reached over to pop in a second tape. The first had shown Melissa leaving for her sister's, just as she'd said.

They fast-forwarded until they reached the time stamp indicating Melissa's arrival to change clothes. The footage was grainy, but in short order Melissa appeared as promised, the gold dress stunning even in black and white. Nigel swallowed, glancing sideways at Madison. Fortunately she hadn't seemed to notice his reaction.

Fifteen minutes further into the tape Melissa reappeared, this time dressed in jeans and her coat.

"She was telling the truth," Nigel said to no one in particular.

"At least about coming here." Madison punched a button to stop the tape, and then jotted some notes in a small notebook. "And the time frame might help once we get an actual time of death for Celik. Why don't I take this with us," she said, ejecting the tape from the machine. "Maybe there's something else here that will help. Someone who came into the building to access Melissa's apartment."

Nigel nodded. "It's certainly worth exploring."

"Great." She pocketed the tape. "Now, what do you say we get the notes from her investigation and get out of here?"

Melissa kept the disk hidden, so even with the authorities nosing about, there was a chance it hadn't been found. Not that Last Chance wouldn't have been able to access it, had it been discovered, but if it was still in the apartment it would speed things up considerably.

They took the stairs two at a time, stopping just outside the door to Melissa's apartment.

"On three." Nigel motioned to Madison, his gun drawn, and she nodded, her own piece at the ready. He counted slowly to three then swung through the partially opened door of Melissa's apartment. The lock was broken, ripped from the door frame with a savagery that spoke of impatience.

Not the work of the forensics team.

Although they'd been here, too. Leaving yellow tape and a pair of latex gloves as a calling card.

"It's clear." Nigel lowered his gun, checking out the room—or what was left of it. It had obviously been tossed, sometime between the authorities leaving and Nigel and Madison arriving.

"Not a pretty picture," Madison said, stepping into the room and holstering her gun. "Melissa isn't going to like this."

"I think we can safely assume it wasn't the good guys." Nigel reached over to right a vase that had somehow managed to escape unbroken. Even trashed, he could see the touches of Melissa in the decor. It was there in the bright colors and carefully chosen art.

"Sometimes the difference between the good guys and the bad guys is all point of view." Madison shrugged with a wry smile, stepping over a broken footstool. "She said it was behind the radiator, right?"

"Yeah, but it's the one in the bedroom." Nigel nodded, crossing to the bedroom. It hadn't fared any better—the linens tossed into disarray, cosmetics and books littering the floor.

The gold dress lay in a puddle at the end of the bed, and without thought he picked it up, lifting it to his face. It smelled of Melissa.

"Memories?" Madison's tone was banal, but there was a hit of mischief.

Nigel dropped the dress, moving over to the radiator, his face averted as he tried to avoid her perceptiveness. "She said it was between the windowsill and the pipes." He knelt down and slid his hand behind the edge of the radiator, fumbling to find the niche that held the CD. "Bloody hell," he muttered, withdrawing his hand, sucking at his skinned knuckles. "My hand is too large."

"Let me try." Madison dropped down beside him and slid her hand along the wall behind the radiator just below the windowsill. "There's an indentation." She shifted so that more of her arm slid in, then smiled, pulling out a CD. "Score one for the overly cautious. Whoever was in here, they missed her hiding place."

"And not much else." Nigel straightened, again taking in the mess.

"You think this was the work of the same person who took a shot at her?" Madison stood up, too, slipping the CD into the pocket with the security tape.

"It seems probable." He shrugged. "But the only way we're going to find out for certain is to keep digging."

"So why don't we go by Tracy's?" Madison said. "If she's got a time of death that conflicts with our tape, Melissa will be in the clear."

"And if not?" His heart sank at the idea, but he had to be prepared to face reality either way.

"Then we find something else to exonerate her."

"You really believe she's innocent?" He hated the note of desperation in his voice.

She reached over to cover his hand with hers. "Of course I do. She's your friend, after all."

It seemed as if Madison put extra emphasis on the word *friend.* Or maybe it was his mind working overtime. Seeing Melissa after all these years had thrown him for a loop. Not to mention the added bonus of the mystery surrounding her arrival this morning.

Walking on the edge was routine for him. And no matter the stakes, he prided himself on the fact that he never let emotion get in his way. So what the hell was going on now? It felt as if the wind had been knocked out of him with absolutely no warning.

He sucked in a breath, pushing his rioting thoughts deep down inside him. There was no room in his life for anything that compromised his ability to think quickly and accurately. And he'd do well to remember it.

"So," he said, "we head for Braxton Labs. Hopefully you're right and Tracy will put an end to this thing once and for all."

CHAPTER FOURTEEN

"YOU'RE GOING TO WEAR a hole in the floor if you don't stop pacing." Harrison leaned back against a computer console with a tolerant smile on his face.

Melissa stopped moving, running an agitated hand through her hair. "Where the hell is everyone?"

"Working. *For you.* Honestly, they haven't been gone all that long."

"Maybe I should call Nigel?" There was nothing she hated more in the world than waiting. It was like being trapped in a cage. In this case, a gilded one—but a prison nevertheless.

"They'll be back soon." Her jailer shrugged again and turned back to the computer screen. "In the meantime, why don't you help me sort through all this chatter? I've compiled everything that's been monitored in the last forty-eight hours, and now I'm trying to sort through it."

When she didn't answer he swiveled around to look at her again. "Come on. It'll take your mind off of things."

"All right." She sighed. Better to be doing something than to stare pointlessly out the window waiting for someone to return with news. "Tell me what you've got."

"It's all arranged by source and time." He waved at the screen. "What we're looking for is a pattern. Some obscure reference that gives us a clue where the nerve gas is or was headed. Or even better, something that hints at who was behind the heist."

"And you're going to get all that from these snippets?" Most of them didn't even make sense.

"That's the general idea. I didn't say it would be easy."

It meant a lot that he was trusting her to look at it at all, as if he'd already decided she was innocent. Or maybe he figured she was a captive audience and what she knew couldn't possibly go beyond the safe house. Either way, he was right. Helping him beat the hell out of brooding over her problems.

An hour later her head was spinning and they'd only made a tiny dent in the bits and pieces of intel recorded on the spreadsheet, and most of what they had spotted had been Harrison's doing. He was a marvel, seeing things that she'd never have noticed at all if he hadn't called her attention to it.

"Is this what you do when you're not working with Last Chance? Listen to the chatter, I mean?"

"God, no." Harrison laughed. "I'd never have the patience to do this full-time, believe me. I actually hack for a living."

"Computers?" Melissa asked, her brows raising with the question.

"Yup. I make my living breaking into other people's machines. Sometimes to prove that they need security. Sometimes to prove that they've done something they shouldn't have."

"Wow. I guess that really does make you the expert. I'm impressed. I'm pretty good with the latest photograph-enhancement software, but I'm afraid that's as far as my expertise goes."

"You use E.O.?"

"Yeah." Melissa frowned. Eyes Only was a program the CIA used for enhancing surveillance photography. "But I thought it was pretty top secret. How do you know about it?"

"Phoenix developed it. I didn't work on it, but I saw a demo. Pretty advanced stuff."

"Phoenix?"

"The company I work for when I'm not here playing superspy. Phoenix works with almost all the major government agencies, specializing in law-enforcement hardware and software."

"Sounds fascinating." And she was surprised to find that she meant it. There was something compelling about Nigel's friends. At first she'd thought it was merely their bonds as a group, but as she got to know them she was realizing that it was the players themselves that were interesting. Madison, Harrison, hell, maybe even Payton if they could get past their mutual distrust.

She hadn't met Sam yet, but she suspected there would be much to admire about the woman who had managed to capture Payton's heart. Like Nigel, he wouldn't be an easy man to tame. She smiled at her choice of words and Harrison shot her a quizzical look.

"Penny for your thoughts."

"Nothing worth sharing." She turned back to the computer screen studying the entries on the spreadsheet, frowning suddenly as words seemed to jump out at her. "Did you see this?" She pointed at an entry containing the word *dervish.*

"Yeah, I did," Harrison said. "It's mentioned two other times, as well." He pointed to the corresponding entries. "It mean something to you?"

"Maybe." Melissa squinted at the screen. "Dervish refers to a Muslim ritual of the Mevlevi sect called *sema,* performed by priests in a prayer trance to Allah. The Mevlevi believed that during the *sema* the soul was released from earthly ties so that it could freely and jubilantly commune with the divine."

"That's where whirling dervish comes from?"

"Exactly." Melissa smiled. "The priests turn independently, shoulder to shoulder, both around their own axis and around other dervishes, representing the earth revolving on its own axis while orbiting the sun or possibly God."

"How the hell do you know all this?"

Melissa shrugged. "I did a story on them once. Along with gathering a little intel on the Turkish resistance movement. Anyway, the ritual isn't the point. If this really is a code, then what matters is the interpretation of the word *dervish.*"

"So what does it mean?" Harrison's curiosity was apparent now.

"It means *doorway,* literally doorsill." Melissa paused to order her thoughts. "In spiritual context, it's a doorway from one world to the next. But in this context maybe it's referring to something more specific."

Harrison's eyes narrowed as he considered the idea. "All right. There are three references to dervish here. Maybe the pattern of three is significant." He switched the list to the big monitor overhead, highlighting the three references.

"Or maybe it's more simple than that," Melissa said, excitement rising. "Look at the first message. There are references to both the dervish and Istanbul. We'd already marked it as a possible link to our package. And here in the last message there's a reference to Galata Tekkesi."

"And that has significance?"

"Galata Tekkesi is a convent in Istanbul. A Mevlevi convent."

"So you think the nerve gas is being stored at the convent?" Harrison asked.

"I'm just postulating. But there is a connection between the whirling dervish and the monastery and if you include the reference to Istanbul and take it literally, then it's possible."

"But there isn't anything to tie in the nerve gas specifically."

"Oh, but there is." Melissa stood up, crossing over to the monitor. "Look at the second message. There's a reference to dervish and then to instruments. The Galata convent houses a collection of musical instruments used by the dervish. But if you translate this phrase literally—" Again she pointed at the screen. "It reads *instruments of death.*"

"The warheads."

"I realize it's a long shot." Melissa nodded. "But based on what you've been telling me about the way chatter works, I'd say it's worth considering."

"It's better than that," Harrison said. "There were three warheads. And three messages. And if you look at the timing, this fits right in with the idea that the R-VX was transported through the Baltic. See." He highlighted the dates and then clicked on another document showing a projected time frame for transportation. "I think you've hit on something big here. I'll take it to Cullen and let him decide how to proceed from here."

"Doesn't Nigel have men in place?"

"Yeah, but Cullen will want our team to direct." He grabbed the printout of the spreadsheet and started for the door, then stopped and turned around, his expression sheepish. "If I leave, you'll stay put, right? Technically I'm not supposed to let you out of my sight."

Melissa felt the hot wash of frustration in her cheeks. "I'm not going anywhere."

"Good." Harrison nodded, then ducked through the ornate door leading to Cullen's study.

It was tempting to try and outwit Cullen's security, tempting to just walk away from them all—before she allowed herself to get in any deeper. But in point of fact it was too late for that. So she sat down in the chair and started flipping through Harrison's notes again.

If she was going to be a prisoner, she might as well make herself useful.

TRACY BRAXTON'S LABS WERE state-of-the-art. Hidden amidst the crumbling brick facades of the meatpacking district, the outside of the building belied the modern technology inside. People all over the world called on Braxton Labs for answers to forensic questions. Last Chance was lucky to have her on their side. On more than one occasion she'd managed to pull the needle out of the haystack—proverbial or otherwise. And Nigel couldn't think of anyone better to prove Melissa's innocence.

Just at the moment, however, he'd rather have been discussing the case in her office, or maybe even by cell phone. Anything but standing here in the autopsy room looking down at Hakan Celik. The once-swarthy man was now pale as a ghost with an incision that ran from just below his neck to just above his groin.

"Sorry we had to meet like this, but I'm almost finished, and I had a hunch you wouldn't want to wait." Tracy took a tissue sample and dropped it into a specimen jar, carefully marking the contents before truly turning her attention to Nigel and Madison.

"Things are moving more quickly than we'd originally anticipated," Madison said with a smile, clearly more accustomed to autopsy tables than he was.

"The stakes have certainly risen." Tracy's pronouncement was matter-of-fact, neither condemning nor acquitting. "But I've got good news."

Nigel tightened a fist in anticipation. In his heart he'd believed Melissa, but somewhere in his brain there had remained an element of doubt. If he was lucky, Tracy was about to expel the notion once and for all. "You found traces of poison."

"Strychnine." Tracy's dark eyes met his. "Not much imagination, actually. It was garden-variety rat poison. Enough to kill a woman twice her size. I found traces in her blood and a much higher concentration in the remnants of her vomit. My guess is that it was in the coffee, although I don't have enough evidence to make a definitive conclusion."

"But you're sure about the poison," Madison asked.

"Absolutely." Tracy reached over to a counter behind the operating table and picked up a single sheet of paper. "Here's the documentation."

"So why didn't it kill her? If it was so much, I mean?" Nigel's heart had constricted to the size of a wadded-up Kleenex, Melissa's brush with death suddenly taking on frightening proportions.

"That's exactly what saved her. Whoever administered the poison overdid it. That, combined with the acidity in the apple pie, made Melissa throw up. And quite literally, vomiting saved her life." Tracy shrugged. "Sometimes it's just a quirk of fate."

"What about residual effects?" Nigel forced his breathing to slow.

"Shouldn't be any. Most of what she ingested she threw up. It wouldn't hurt for her to see a doctor though. Just to be sure."

"Seems odd that someone would use something so clearly traceable to try and kill her." Madison's brows had drawn together in thought. "I mean, if someone is trying to pin a murder on her, why in the world would they take her out in so obvious a way?"

"Suicide is one possibility," Tracy answered. "Melissa murders Celik here, and then in a fit of depression kills herself. Rat poison is an easy way to go."

"You're not saying..." Nigel's objection was clearly more intense than it needed to be and Madison reached over to pat his arm.

"She's only saying that someone might have thought that's the way it would play out. Two dead bodies, one of them clearly implicated in the death of the other. Open and shut."

"Except Melissa didn't die. And she didn't try to kill herself." The last was said for no one in particular but he couldn't stop the urge to vocalize it.

"I think we're all in agreement, Nigel." Madison's voice was soft but firm, her attention turning back to Tracy. "Did you find anything that might give a clue as to who poisoned her?"

"Nothing on the coat. And according to what Gabe told me, there were at least four people with an opportunity to put something in her coffee. Strychnine can take up to thirty minutes to work, too, so depending on the timeline, it's even possible that she ingested it before she got to the diner. Although I still hold that the coffee is the most likely culprit."

"What about the blood?" Nigel knew it was probably going to be damning but he needed to know.

"Definitely Celik's, I'm afraid." Tracy held her hand out in apology. "Perfect DNA match."

"So she had to have come into contact with him," Nigel said, feeling deflated.

"Actually, maybe not. The pattern on her coat is more consistent with pouring than rubbing. If she'd killed Celik and gotten his blood on her coat, it would most likely be from moving him or bumping up against him somehow. Maybe even bending over the body to check for life." Tracy demonstrated on the corpse with the casual air of someone who dealt with death daily. "The pattern would have been smeared and lighter in some places than others."

"But it wasn't," Madison prompted.

"Right. The stain saturated the coat. And based on Celik's injuries, I don't see how she could have gotten that much blood on her without help."

"So you think that someone poured the blood on her coat after the fact." Nigel blew out a breath, trying to find the pieces that secured Melissa's innocence.

"I can't say with certainty, of course, but the evidence seems to support something along those lines."

"But if someone followed her into the alley with the blood, wouldn't they have realized she wasn't dead?" Madison asked, still frowning.

"Odds are she was practically in a coma, so it's possible they could have mistaken it for death. It was dark, which would decrease visibility, and cold, which could slow respiration."

"But they'd have had to pick up her hand to secure prints for the knife and the forged documents." Somewhere along the way his brain had fallen into agreement with his heart. Melissa hadn't killed anyone. Period.

"It's possible, but it's equally likely that they got her prints off the cup or silverware at the diner," Tracy said. "It's fairly simple to transfer that sort of thing if you know what you're doing."

"But they'd still have to be in the alley to stain her coat. And I can't imagine not checking to see if she was dead," Madison said thoughtfully.

"Well, as I said, under those circumstances, it's not unrealistic for someone to have mistaken her coma for death. And even if they didn't, the amount of poison she'd ingested should have been a sure thing. It was just a matter of time."

"So we're saying that someone followed her outside the diner, waited for her collapse, then covered her with blood. And from there they went to the Turk's and planted the evidence." Nigel summed it all up, still trying to find the motivation. "Was there anything in Celik's autopsy to indicate that Melissa was involved?"

"Nothing. No fibers other than the two hairs they found on the scene. And no DNA under his fingernails. Although he was caught by surprise so that probably means he didn't have the chance to fight."

"But hair is easy to place at a scene," Madison said. "Were there any other prints?"

"None," Tracy said. "The place was wiped clean. Which runs counterintuitive to the fact that the knife had such a clear print and there were hairs at the scene."

"Not the kind of mistake a CIA agent makes," Nigel prompted.

"Exactly," Tracy agreed. "And there's more." She reached for the cadaver, flipping him over onto his back. "The knife entered the body here." She pointed to a blue-tinged two-inch wound just below his shoulder blade. "Based on the angle of the wound, I'd say that the killer would have to have been at least as tall as Celik, maybe even a little taller." She paused, her lips quirking at the corners. "Celik was six foot two."

The words hung in the air for a moment, and then sank in. Nigel smiled. "Melissa is only about five-six."

"So you're saying she couldn't have done this?" Madison studied the body for a moment and then looked up at Tracy.

"Not unless she was standing on a step stool. The body doesn't lie, and there's simply no way she could have inflicted this particular wound at this particular angle unless she were taller."

"What about heels?" Nigel needed to be certain. To cover all the bases.

"They'd have to have been eight inches or more." Tracy shrugged. "Even fashionistas don't wear them that high."

"All right then, we've got solid evidence for Melissa's innocence." Nigel rubbed his hands together in delight.

"Hold on." Madison raised a hand, her eyes still dark with concern. "While I believe everything Tracy's saying, it's still just one piece of evidence in the face of the prints and the hair, and those letters."

"You think she did it?" He seemed destined to repeat himself.

"No. But I don't necessarily think we have enough to prove it." Madison looked to Tracy for agreement, and she nodded. "So Melissa's still got to keep a low profile. If she surfaces, someone will nab her. Either the authorities who are being hounded to find a culprit for Celik's murder and the resulting diplomatic brouhaha, or the people who actually killed Celik. Melissa alive is a serious threat to whatever it is they're trying to cover up. What about the weapon? Can it tell us anything?"

"It was a hunting knife." Tracy held up a plastic bag with the knife inside. "Nothing particularly special about it, except that it didn't belong to Celik. Which indicates premeditation.

I'm running a check on murders involving the same kind of weapon on the off chance that there are priors."

"You can trace knife patterns to a wound, right?" Madison queried.

"In some cases. But the entry point has to be clean, and someone in forensics has to document it, including photographs and measurements. The degree of detail in an autopsy frankly often depends on the priority a case is given."

"Or the importance of the vic," Nigel said.

"So what you're trying to say," Madison said, ignoring Nigel's sarcasm, "is that even if the killer has used this weapon before, there may not be a record."

"The odds are against it." Tracy shrugged. "There are just too many variables. But as I said, I'll check into it and let you know if I find anything."

"What about time of death?" Nigel asked, still groping for something that would clear Melissa of suspicion.

"I've got a range. Can't do much better, I'm afraid. He'd been there too long." She glanced down at Celik, reaching out to smooth the guy's hair. It should have been a gruesome gesture but wasn't. "Conservatively, I'd say he was killed somewhere between twelve and two."

"And if you had to call it?" Nigel asked.

"I'd say one–one-thirty."

Madison turned to look at Nigel. "That puts Melissa in the diner."

"Potentially, without anyone to corroborate the fact." Nigel turned to Tracy. "Thanks for all your help."

"No problem." Her face softened for an instant and she reached out for his hand. "For what it's worth, Nigel, I don't think she did it. I just wish I could have given you conclusive evidence."

"Well, the poisoning and the fact that the killer was taller than Melissa is a start. Maybe we'll get lucky with the weapon hunt. And in the meantime, you can bet we'll be working overtime to try to figure out who's really behind this."

Tracy nodded, then hesitated, her dark gaze worried. "Hopefully you'll find something soon, because in the meantime, Madison's right. With Melissa alive, the killer's suddenly got a hell of a lot more to lose, which means she could be in real danger."

CHAPTER FIFTEEN

MELISSA STOOD in front of the fire, trying to sort through her tumultuous thoughts. She'd come into Cullen's study to call her sister, Cullen having arranged for a secure line. But now that the task was completed she couldn't bring herself to return to the others.

At least not yet.

Although the team's forays into New York had convinced them all of her innocence, the bottom line was that there simply wasn't enough evidence to counter what had already been falsely implied. Add Ed Wyland's apparent flight, and the shit was getting pretty deep.

Not that Melissa believed for a minute that her handler had gone anywhere willingly. Someone had forced him. And if that was the case, she had no doubts as to the ultimate outcome. Ed Wyland was dead. She could feel it in her bones.

She blew out a long shuddering breath, her stomach twisting. Twenty-four hours ago her life had been a hell of a lot more simple. And now…

Well, there weren't even words.

"Did you talk to Alicia?"

Melissa jumped at the sound of Nigel's voice, spinning around to face him.

"I'm sorry. I didn't mean to startle you, but you've been in here a long time. I thought maybe I ought to check on you."

She wasn't sure if she was delighted or insulted. He was

standing so close it was hard to breathe let alone think. "I'm fine. Just taking a moment."

"What did you tell your sister?"

"As much of the truth as I dared. I hate lying to her, but I'm afraid it's become somewhat second nature. She'd heard a little. Apparently, Celik's murder made the papers this morning, but it hasn't been tied to me. At least publicly."

"Cullen's work."

"I guess I should thank him." She'd have moved back, except to do so would mean stepping into the fire.

"Or me." Nigel moved even closer, his breath warm against her face.

She tipped her head, opening her mouth to dispute the fact, but it was too late. His mouth brushed against hers, the sensation beyond anything she'd ever experienced except with him.

She knew she should stop. Knew that there was only trouble ahead if the two of them continued, but she wanted his touch more than she could possibly have imagined. She pressed closer, deepening the kiss, opening her lips so that their tongues could meet, the taste of him more intoxicating than the best of wines.

She was kissing the boy she'd loved, but she was also kissing the man he'd become. A meeting of old and new in the time-tested way of men and women. It would have been laughable except that she was living it, loving it.

With a groan, he threaded his fingers through her hair, kneading her scalp, each stroke matching the movements of his tongue. She relished the contact, leaning into him, giving as much as she was taking. It was ironic, really; she hadn't felt like this in over a decade and with just one touch he brought it all back—every sensory detail.

She reared back, her heated gaze meeting his. "I can't do this."

"You're probably right," he admitted, his eyes tortured, "but I can't seem to stop."

They kissed again, then disengaged, both of them breathless.

"I know what you mean." Her laughter was forced, desire making her giddy. "This is crazy. I mean, anything we felt for one another was years ago, and now, well..."

He smiled, mustache twitching, and then kissed her again so thoroughly her insides ached with the contact. She sighed, not caring anymore what the proper protocol was. She wanted him, it was as simple as that.

One hand slid to her breast, and she sucked in a breath as his thumb found her nipple, circling in a proprietary way that made her weak at the knees. She wasn't a slut and she wasn't a prude, but no man had ever affected her in this way. And apparently time had merely heightened her desire.

The fire crackled, the sound seeming to intensify the heat between them. His other hand found the small of her back and then the soft curve of her ass, the cupping sensation almost more than she could bear.

Naked was suddenly an important word, all thought of modesty taking flight for the hills. Nigel was the one. The concept seemed suddenly like a blinding glimpse of the obvious, and despite the blaring warning resounding in her head, she wanted nothing more than to yield to the magic of his touch.

But fate was, as usual, not on her side.

Someone at the far side of the room cleared his throat, and Melissa sprang away.

"I'm sorry to interrupt." Harrison looked more than embarrassed, he looked as if he wished the ground would swallow him whole. "The video feed is ready. And your team is assembled as requested. All that's missing is you." He shot a pointed look at Nigel, who had the audacity to smile and shrug.

"Priorities, my dear boy."

In the moment, Melissa wasn't sure whether she wanted to strangle him or continue to kiss him, the former being the better decision by a long shot. Instead she opted for nonchalance, or her version thereof.

"You need to go."

The heat in Nigel's eyes quite honestly reduced her insides to a quivering mass of jelly, but her mother had taught her to hold her cards tight to the vest, and she'd be damned if she'd let him know the power he wielded.

"The team is in place." Harrison wasn't trying to support her position, but his words did exactly that.

"We're not finished here." Nigel's promise sent hot shivers racing through her.

"I'll be waiting." It sounded like a sex-kitten reply and Melissa hated herself for her weakness, but she wasn't about to close the door, her need as intrinsic as a heartbeat.

Harrison swallowed, his discomfort apparent, and suddenly the mood was broken.

"So everyone I requested is in place?" Nigel's attention was centered now on Harrison and the arrangements that had been made. There was a part of Melissa that applauded his concentration. She'd been working undercover too long not to recognize the importance of giving an operation first priority.

"Yes. And I've got a satellite connection that will allow you to command the team."

"Excellent," Nigel said, his accent making the pronouncement seem even more important. "Melissa?" he queried. "Are you coming?"

Damned if she'd miss the show. With a nod and a forced smile, she followed the two of them into the operations room, wondering if loving Nigel when he'd been Special Forces had been better or worse than loving him now.

She sighed, recognizing the implication of her thoughts. Maybe *loving* was an exaggeration. Wanting, certainly—but loving? Frankly the idea scared the hell out of her—and in her line of work, that kind of emotion was certain to be deadly.

NIGEL WALKED into the operations room, his heart still pounding in his throat. There was something intoxicating about Melissa Pope. All she had to do was walk into the room and he got a hard-on.

He could feel her presence now despite the fact that she was across the room. She'd taken a seat by Madison. He fought the urge to turn around and look at her, knowing that he was better off avoiding distraction. Gabe and Payton were already in place and Nigel blew out a breath as he crossed to the main console, taking the headphones that Harrison was offering.

The monitor above his head showed a hazy nighttime view of the outside of the monastery. A digital readout at the bottom left of the screen marked the time to the second. Three minutes to go.

"Haverton, you there?" Nigel slid into his chair, adjusting the headset so that the mike was centered in front of his mouth.

"Roger. Haverton here. Everything's ready, just waiting for the word." George Haverton had been in Special Forces with Nigel, following him to MI6 after his discharge from the military. They'd worked together off and on for over fifteen years. And although he didn't have the bond with George that he had with Payton or Gabe, he trusted the man completely.

"I assume by now you've been thoroughly briefed."

"And then some." Haverton laughed. "Your friend Payton isn't long on words, but he chooses them well."

Nigel shot a look at Payton, his friend's wry smile accompanied by a shrug. "He's definitely a to-the-point kind of guy. How many men do you have?"

"Eight. Two on each perimeter."

Harrison tapped a second monitor, this one with a blueprint of the building and property, blinking lights displaying each of the eight men. The monastery was actually an old hunting lodge. Octagonal in shape, it had been built in the 1400s, but a fire had destroyed it in the eighteenth century. A remodel in the late nineties had left the building functional but still somewhat run-down. It served as a museum and tourist haven, especially when the dervishes were dancing.

"Anyone spotted on guard?" Nigel studied the blueprint, then switched his focus to the live feed.

"Three that we've been able to identify. They're armed, but don't seem to be particularly on alert."

"Good. Much better that we catch them by surprise. My logistics expert—" Nigel smiled up at Harrison, who grinned back "—tells me the most likely spot for keeping the packages is the cells. The rooms are constructed of stone, and sit in a row on the first floor. They'll be easy to guard and more difficult to breach. You up to the task?"

The sound of Haverton's laughter filled his ears.

"All right then," Nigel said. "On my mark." He watched as the seconds ticked off the clock, and with a calm he didn't completely feel, ordered the team to go. "Move now."

The screen above him changed—the panel divided into four quadrants, cameras from each of the teams sending a signal. They crossed the grounds with no resistance, team one's camera revealing an old graveyard as they passed.

A guard appeared through a small garden gate in the south quadrant, but the team quickly disabled him, taking his weapon and rendering him unconscious. The same maneuver was attempted on the north side, but the man managed to break free and so had to be permanently silenced. Two down. Which, if their reconnaissance was correct, left only one armed guard inside.

Each of the four teams slipped inside the building, reconvening in the ritual prayer hall with no further incident. The room, like the building, was octagonal, with a balcony running its entire length. Shadows obscured the upper story from view, but the room was completely silent.

"The cells should be just beyond the door on your right." Nigel watched as the teams worked their way across the room, and through the door. The hallway here was narrow. Two team members stayed at the entrance on watch and the remaining six moved forward slowly, weapons at the ready.

The first cell was empty, as were the second and third. As they approached the fourth, a door ahead of them suddenly swung open, the third guard coming into view. He fired his semi, the volley of bullets whizzing down the hall, forcing the team members to scramble for cover. A second gunman appeared at the far end of the hall and opened fire.

"There are two men," Nigel barked into the mike. "One straight ahead at the end of the hall, and the second behind door number six."

Silence held for a moment, and then the men swung into action, Haverton making a dash for the fourth cell, drawing fire, his partner right behind him, gun blazing. The man at the end of the hall fell clutching his chest, and his partner burst out of the sixth cell, firing haphazardly at the approaching Brits.

A man from team three took aim and shot, the guard dropping to his knees, his machine gun clattering against the stone floor as he fell.

Several long minutes passed, then Nigel's headphone crackled to life. "Everything's secure here. Both guards are dead, and we've only got minor injuries."

"And the package?"

"So far nothing." Haverton's team was methodically searching the cells again, but as each room appeared in the camera lens, it was maddeningly apparent that they were empty.

"Damn it." Payton slammed a hand down on the desktop. "They're already gone."

"Or were never there." Haverton's voice echoed in Nigel's ear. "We're not finding any sign that there was ever anything here. And the dead men are definitely Turks."

"So what are you saying?" Nigel asked. "We've been taken for a ride?"

"Looks that way. The building is deserted. We'll search the rest of the place just to be certain. But I don't think there's anything here to find."

"Report in as soon as you've finished the search." Nigel pulled off his headphones and threw them onto the table. "Bloody wild-goose chase."

"Maybe I got it wrong." Melissa's voice was soft, regret coloring her words.

"No," Gabe hastened to reassure her. "You didn't. I had both the CIA and Homeland Security study the chatter you identified and they all agreed with your assessment. The fact of the matter is that we were played. Either the R-VX was gone long before they led us here, or it was never at the monastery at all."

"Most likely the latter," Payton said, his face dark with anger. "Fucking terrorists."

"Well it isn't going to do us any good at all to sit around lamenting our inability to recognize a decoy," Madison said, as usual the voice of reason. "What we need to do is figure out where the R-VX really went. And intercept it before it gets to the States."

The headset crackled with life again and Nigel picked it up. "What's up?"

"We've got an ID on one of the guards. He's a Turkish mercenary. Not working for the Mevlevi. I'm guessing we'll find similar stories when we ID the others."

"What about the live guard—he saying anything?"

"Unfortunately, I'm afraid he won't be talking at all. He managed to detonate a hand grenade. There's nothing left but pieces. I'm just grateful he didn't take one of our men with him."

"All right then, get the hell out of there before the officials arrive. We'll work through diplomatic channels to smooth things over, but it'll be best if you're not found on premises."

"We were never here," Haverton said, signing off. Nigel had no doubt that he'd manage to get his team out without leaving anything behind to identify who had been there. George was a bloody ghost when it came to these kinds of operations.

"So we're back to square one," Melissa said, her frustration mirroring his own.

"Maybe not. Haverton said they'd ID'd one of the guards. Maybe we can figure out who the hell hired him."

"Sounds like my kind of challenge." Harrison was already typing away at his keyboard. "I'll get the info from MI6 and take it from there."

"Good," Nigel said. "And in the meantime, I think we'd do best to concentrate on possible entry points for the R-VX here in the U.S. The odds of finding it at sea aren't very good. But as you said earlier, Gabe, it's a lot harder to get things into the States these days, so that ought to limit the options somewhat."

"Still going to be difficult." Gabe sighed. "But I agree. And I also think we need to follow up on Melissa's work. Assuming that Celik either wasn't the real culprit or that he had a partner out there somewhere, there's still another perp. And considering Celik's diplomatic connections, and the fact that they implicated Melissa, I'd say the possibility of a UN traitor is pretty damn high. So if we can find the turncoat, we just might get lucky and get a bead on the nerve agent at the same time."

"I REGRET THE NEED for such rash action. But believe me, it was unavoidable." The man across from Khamis sat back, his face cloaked in the shadows of the darkened bar, his air of superiority more about posturing than reality.

Khamis held tightly to his control. Anger served no one but itself, and he had enough problems without allowing his own weaknesses to contribute to the turmoil. Malik was showing similar restraint, although Khamis could see the mounting frustration in his eyes.

"You have taken action that could compromise my mission. That is not acceptable."

The Russian shrugged. They were such an arrogant race. Khamis wondered what the man would say if he understood exactly what it was he was transporting for Khamis. It was tempting to tell him, to wait for his reaction, but pride destroyed everything and Khamis was not a man to give in to self-indulgence.

"Let me be sure that I understand," Khamis said, leaning forward, his seltzer water untasted. "You have arranged for the death of a Turkish diplomat, and attempted to blame it on what you believe is an undercover agent of some kind."

"She is CIA, I'm certain of it. And I haven't *attempted* to blame her, Mr. al-Rashid, I have succeeded. Not only that, I have killed her."

Khamis's stomach tightened at the pronouncement. God would not be so unfair. It was his right to obtain justice. His right alone. "But there is no body."

Again Alexi Kirov shrugged. "She was administered enough poison to kill an ox. She is dead."

"Then why has there been no talk of it?"

"The Americans are afraid. There has been much talk of late as to the inefficiency of their so-called Homeland Security. A rogue CIA agent in bed with a Turkish traitor is not the best news copy." The Russian shot a surreptitious glance at Malik, for the first time looking faintly on edge. "But it will eventually come out. These things always do. And in the meantime, they believe they understand what has happened. They blame Celik and the woman for a supposed network transporting stolen goods."

"Which means the UN will be under greater scrutiny than ever." This from Malik.

"No. That's the beauty of my plan. I planted evidence that proves that Celik was operating the transportation network independently of the United Nations. The network was established using his diplomatic connections. The agent stumbled onto the operation but rather than expose him, she decided to ask for a piece of the action. Celik obliged her, and they worked together for a short time, but then she pressed for more, and when Celik refused, she killed him. The best lies are the closest to the truth. Don't you agree?"

"You said the woman was CIA. How can you know this for certain?"

"I had dealings with her handler. In a moment of weakness, he spoke too freely."

"And this man?"

"Is also dead."

"You killed them both?" Khamis raised a skeptical eyebrow, doubting the man had the fortitude for such a task.

Kirov shrugged with exaggerated nonchalance. "I have connections. And when I have a need, there are Russians here who are ready to come to my aid. Your people are not the only ones who command that kind of loyalty."

"You dare to compare your thugs to the faithful? We serve Allah. The Organizatsiya serves only its greed." Malik leaned forward, eyes flashing, and the Russian scooted back in obvious fear.

Khamis held up a hand, and Malik leaned back, his gaze still condemning.

"For your sake, sir, I'll choose to ignore your friend's outburst." Obsequiousness did not sit well with the Russian, and Khamis contained a smile.

Malik however was not amused. "I don't like any of this. The trail of blood is too wide."

"I assure you it has all been handled." The man bowed his head in Malik's direction. "The bases have been covered—to use the phrase of our American hosts."

"Surely there will be questions about the disappearance of two CIA operatives?" Khamis sat back, waiting.

"Perhaps. But none that can be answered. Maybe she killed herself in a moment of guilt. Maybe her handler did it? Or maybe she killed him. As long as the bodies are missing there is nothing to be done."

"And if the bodies are found?"

"The woman's will be damning. And the handler's will never be discovered. Trust me on that."

"Make no mistake. I do not trust you."

"But you need me." Kirov smiled, secure in himself again.

"I do not like it." Malik fingered the pocket of his coat, the outline of his handgun barely visible. "There is danger in risk always, but some odds are unacceptable."

Khamis considered the situation. Malik was right. But they'd come so far, the idea of backing out now seemed beyond comprehension. "You are certain that no one can trace the movement of the shipment?"

"I'm positive. I haven't survived in this game as long as I have without being careful. The shipment will arrive as promised. I can guarantee it."

"Do not make promises you cannot keep." Khamis's words held warning, but not surprisingly the man refused to take heed.

"There will be no problem."

Malik opened his mouth to protest, saw the look in Khamis's eyes and remained silent.

"Very well, we will expect delivery as promised. And you will inform us if things change in any way. If not, the consequences will be substantial. Am I making myself clear?"

The Russian's eyes narrowed as he met Khamis's gaze. Time passed as they engaged in a game of standoff. One minute. Two minutes. Three… Kirov dropped his gaze and Khamis smiled. "Then we have an understanding."

The man nodded, and stood up, his growing nervousness

now apparent in every gesture. He reached out to shake hands, and Khamis obliged him, tightening his fingers until he saw a flicker of pain. With a final smile he released the Russian's hand and watched as he hurried toward the entrance to the pub.

"That may very well have been a mistake." Malik's words were soft, but there was an edge that Khamis couldn't ignore. "The man is a danger to everything he touches. He leads with his emotions, not his head."

Malik's words hit home, and Khamis frowned at his friend. "There is no comparison between that man and me. You know better than most how carefully I calculate everything."

"I am not questioning your abilities, my friend. But when the heart is involved, there is always danger of making mistakes."

"My heart is dead."

"No." Malik shook his head. "It is withered. Blackened, perhaps, but not dead. If it were truly dead then revenge would not be so sweet."

"Perhaps you are right." Khamis buried his face in his hands. He needed closure, had needed it for a very long time. And now was his chance, months of careful planning coming together.

"Perhaps it is better if we call this off now, before we have passed the point of no return."

"No." Khamis jerked his head up, the word coming out louder than he had intended, people in the bar turning with curiosity. "I'm sorry. I should not have snapped at you. But we must continue. The risk is minimal. And as soon as we have the shipment, we will remove the Russian from the equation."

"But won't that cause more questions?"

Khamis shrugged. "Perhaps. But there will be no way to connect it to us, and even if they do work it out eventually, it will be too late. The damage will be done."

"And your revenge? With this last act, you will finally be at peace?"

"American bombs took everything from me. My wife, my children, my heart." He pounded his chest, the gesture underscoring his words. "I will never be at peace. But at least I will know that they have been avenged."

CHAPTER SIXTEEN

THE HOUSE WAS STILL, everyone in their respective beds. Only Melissa couldn't settle in and relax enough to sleep. A harvest moon shone through the window, the quiet of the countryside almost absolute.

It was beautiful here. Serene in an almost pastoral sense. If it weren't for the fact that someone was framing her for murder, she might actually enjoy this sojourn to the country. Of course, she wouldn't be here at all if it weren't for Celik's assassination and her subsequent poisoning, so the whole thought process was skewed from start to finish.

She sighed and turned away from the window. The room, like everything else at the safe house, was top quality. There was a massive marble fireplace, the coals banked and glowing, a comfortable leather armchair artfully angled to face both the bed and the fire. A mahogany four-poster the size of Manhattan made up with luxurious Italian linens completed the picture.

But despite the opulent surroundings, Melissa was still awake. A decanter of brandy beckoned, but she knew it would only enhance the feelings of melancholy that had been chasing after her all day.

Maybe she just needed a little air. Grabbing the leather jacket Nigel had rescued from her apartment, she headed out into the hall, moving with a stealth that was probably unnecessary but was as much a part of her as the color of her hair or eyes. The hallway was dark, and she stopped for a moment to regain her bearings.

Because the house needed to be impregnable, there were two security perimeters, one at the rock wall that surrounded the place and the other around the house itself. Since egress in and out was severely limited, Cullen had arranged for a courtyard. The cobblestone plaza reminded Melissa of small village centers in Europe.

She followed the left branch of the hallway, turning twice, trusting her instincts in the dark, finally finding herself at the archway that led out into the cool night air. Water from the fountain splashed contentedly in the center, the pool surrounding it dark green with reflected pinpricks of light from the stars above.

A breeze danced across the cobblestones, dry leaves brushing against them with an almost lazy air. The simplicity of sound and motion was far more pleasing than the luxurious appointments of her suite, and she settled down on a bench near the water, closing her eyes, allowing the rest of her senses to soak in the beauty of the night.

The wind caressed her face, its cold fingers soothing her tired soul. So much had happened in such a short time. She rubbed her sleeve absently where it touched the bandage on her arm, her thoughts turning not to the danger surrounding her, but to the man who had rescued her from it.

Nigel.

He'd been a shadow in her dreams for fifteen long years, but other than that she'd thought he was firmly relegated to her past. A lovely memory—nothing more. In reality though she'd obviously underestimated their connection. The chemistry between them was combustible to say the least. But sparks didn't necessarily mean lasting warmth. And she was at a point in her life where one-night stands had lost their appeal.

Even as she had the thought, she knew she was wrong. Nigel wasn't a one-night-stand kind of man and even if he were, given the opportunity she wasn't at all certain she had the strength to say no.

The idea of his mouth on hers, his hands moving along the smooth planes of her body, his penis hot inside her. It made her shimmy with need just thinking about it. Maybe all this overanalyzing was a bunch of crap, and what she ought to do was go find Nigel and scratch the proverbial itch. Put like that it was almost laughable, and despite the serious turn of her thoughts, she smiled, letting her hands trace the curves of her breasts, her mind giving in to temptation.

"Penny for your thoughts?"

The voice was straight out of her fantasy and she jerked to attention on the bench, searching the courtyard for its source. The telltale glow of a cigarette marked the spot, and with a heart-wrenching smile, Nigel stepped into the moonlight. "Thinking of me?"

"Hardly," she said, knowing full well that neither of them believed her.

"Well, I was thinking of you." He flicked the cigarette away, his gaze heated, a predator sizing up its prey.

Melissa swallowed and considered moving farther away, but rejected the notion. He'd just follow her, and truth was, this had been inevitable from the moment she'd laid eyes on him at the embassy party. Might as well sit back and enjoy the ride. "What exactly were you thinking?"

"Well…" He paused provocatively. "You were naked…"

"Interesting." She smiled, standing up to close the distance between them. "I was just following the same line of thought. Only it was you who was naked."

"Boring fantasy, that," he whispered, his hands coming to rest on her waist. "I much prefer my vision."

"You mean version." She tilted her head to look up at him, her breath catching in her throat as his eyes devoured her.

"No." His smile was slow. "I definitely meant vision."

There had been passion between them the first time they'd met, and nothing had changed, the resulting electricity an arc between them with an almost physical presence. She could feel it with every nerve in her body, anticipation building without even a touch.

One step and she'd complete the circuit. Body to body, lips grazing in the most wonderful of intimacies. One step…

And still she held her ground. Whether it was an attempt to resist him, or just an instinctual need to heighten her growing desire, she couldn't say. Either way her feet wouldn't move.

Thank God for Nigel.

With a groan that echoed her crescendoing emotions, he gathered her close, his lips finding hers in a kiss that was both provocative and punishing. It was as if the urgency that had been building between them for two days had reached implosion point and neither of them had the power to do anything but ride the cresting wave.

Melissa inhaled the familiar smell of aftershave, leather and tobacco—pure Nigel. "Maybe we should go inside."

He swung her up into his arms and strode from the courtyard back into the darkened hall, traversing the unfamiliar corridors as if he were at home. In just moments, they were inside her room, and Nigel released her, their bodies sliding against each other as she touched the ground, the friction almost unbearable.

She opened her mouth to stop things before they went too far, but swallowed the words instead, her uncertainty holding her captive.

"Melissa, I want to do the right thing here." Nigel's breath stirred the curls at her temples, the heat searing through her as if he had actually touched her. "But I'm only a man, and I can't take much more. So either throw me out now, or expect to see me here when you wake up in the morning."

She held his gaze for a moment, then reached behind her to shut the door, banishing all doubt. "I want you to stay."

A slow smile spread across his face as he reached for her,

his hands threading through her hair. They stood for a moment drinking each other in, and then he pulled her to him, this time the kiss gentle, almost serene.

She opened her mouth, tracing the line of his mustache, surprised at how soft it felt against her tongue. Then quickly as it had begun, exploration ended, their passion taking flight again as the kiss deepened, their tongues tangling together in a frantic attempt to find release.

Nigel pushed off her coat and reached for the hem of her T-shirt, lifting it over her head in one swift motion. Her nipples pebbled in anticipation and she thrust against him, closing her eyes as he bent his head, his tongue circling her breast, teasing, laving her until she was writhing against him, the building heat threatening to undo her.

He moved to her other breast and sucked lightly at first, then with building pressure, her body drawing tight, like the string of a bow just before the arrow is released. Pain mixed with pleasure, all of it colored with need. And she pulled his head up, kissing him with everything inside her, the past and the present coming together so that there was nothing but this man and his mouth upon hers.

His palms caressed the small of her back, then moved higher to rub her bare shoulders, finally sliding around them to cup her breasts, the motion of his thumb mimicking the circles of his tongue.

She pulled his lower lip between her teeth and bit lightly, the salty taste of his skin making her want to taste more. She kissed her way across the plane of his cheek to the curve of his ear, tracing the whorl with her tongue, his labored breathing assuring her that she was pleasing him.

His left hand dropped lower, sliding under the band of her sweatpants, his fingers stroking the silky hair between her thighs. She shifted on a sigh, moving her legs so that he had better access. And he slid a finger between the folds of her labia, his index finger unerringly finding her clitoris.

Softly he began to stroke, over and over, until her mind refused to function. The only thing that mattered was the sensation building between her legs as it ratcheted tighter and tighter, building and building until she thought she might explode. She hung there for a moment on the precipice, and then with a thrust of his fingers, he sent her over the edge.

She heard herself gasp, and bonelessly collapsed against him, her heart thundering so loudly she was certain that anyone within a five-mile radius could hear. His arms were warm, and he rained tiny kisses along her hair, and her cheek, settling again on her mouth with a sweet possessiveness that threatened to send her into convulsions all over again.

Still fighting for breath, she pulled away long enough to look up into his eyes, losing herself in the desire she saw reflected there. With shaking fingers, she unbuttoned his shirt, splaying her fingers against the hard muscles of his chest.

He shrugged out of his shirt, and then divested her of sweats and panties. The only thing remaining between them were his chinos, and with a tiny smile, she reached out and undid the button, then eased down the zipper.

He finished the job in short order, standing before her now totally naked. With an impish smile, she knelt, cupping his balls in her hands, circling his penis with her tongue, relishing the salty, masculine taste of him. She remembered everything, the way he smelled, the way he tasted, the velvety soft feel of the skin that covered pure steel.

Pulling him all the way into her mouth, she sucked, gently moving her hand up and down, squeezing in the way she remembered he'd loved. His groan was testament to the fact that she hadn't forgotten how to please him, and she sucked harder, establishing a rhythm, wanting to give to him as much as he'd given to her.

But instead, he reached beneath her arms and urged her upward, his mouth covering hers, his tongue thrusting now with a persistence that could only be a promise of things to come.

She pressed against him, his chest hair rasping against her already-aroused breasts, his penis caught between the hard muscles of his abdomen and the satin of her skin.

He massaged her buttocks, cupping them so that his fingers stroked the inside of her thighs. Her legs were shaking now, her passion beyond anything she'd ever experienced, fifteen years of waiting coming together into a need so powerful it was almost a tangible thing.

With a groan, he swung her into his arms again, carrying her to the bed. He laid her against the soft cotton sheets and covered her body with his own, his heart pounding against hers, his penis throbbing against the juncture of her thighs.

He kissed her neck, then the hollow of her throat, his tongue tracing the swell of first one breast and then the other. He paused at her nipples, sucking each with tender abandon, and then moved lower, stopping for a moment to taste the indentation of her belly. His hands caressed the tender skin between her legs, brushing lightly against her pubic hair, the teasing touch almost more erotic than if he'd been inside her.

His mouth dipped lower still, and she arched upward as his tongue found her soft center, stroking, lapping and sucking until the exquisite tension began to build again. As he began to suck her clitoris, his finger slipped inside her, moving up and down, hot spirals of desire washing through her.

"Please," she whispered.

He moved upward, his body sliding against hers, the contact a lifeline now that his mouth and hands were gone. Their eyes met and held, his asking, hers acquiescing. And in one swift movement he was inside her, his heat blending with hers until she was no longer certain where he ended and she began. Slowly he began to move, thrusting deep and then slowly sliding out until she lifted her hips in protest, wanting nothing more than to feel him back inside her again.

In answer, he slammed home with a force that sent her

senses reeling, then he put his hands beneath her rear, angling her for deeper penetration—in and out, in and out—each thrust reaching to her core, the spiral of heat full-fledged fire now, burning in intensity, pulling her onto the ledge again.

Higher and higher they climbed, until he pulled free and she thrashed with frustration.

"Wait," he whispered, as he pulled her up and settled her on his lap, her back to him, his hands cupping her breasts. "Lift up."

She followed his commands, lifting her body and then impaling herself on him again, relief and pleasure fusing together into heightened desire. "Now, Nigel," she gasped.

In answer, he took her earlobe in his mouth, sucking at the fullness there, his hands circling her hips as she began to move up and down, matching her movements to the rhythm of his thrusting. His fingers again found her clitoris, his thumb flicking against her tender engorged skin until she thought she'd surely fly apart.

But release danced just out of reach as they began their ascent, flitting higher and higher—taunting and teasing her. And still he moved inside her, up and down, in and out, everything but the feel of their bodies moving together vanishing into the night.

She could feel his mouth upon her earlobe, his thumb stroking her desire, the heat of his body pressed against hers, and the amazing friction of his penis as it moved inside her. And she relished it all, savoring every sensation, knowing that this was the only man she had ever wanted. The only one who could take her to this place.

And then as if in answer, the world shattered, the moon and the stars joining their dance until there was nothing but the joy of their union and the bright silvery light.

NIGEL LAY STILL, listening to the sound of Melissa breathing. She was asleep, her body curled into his as if it were a perfect fit. And indeed, maybe it was. But that didn't mean he had the right to pull her into his world.

The little voice in his head reminded him that she was already a part of it. By profession certainly, and now by necessity a part of Last Chance. But when this case was over, and one way or the other it would be, he'd be off to England, and she'd be back on assignment at some hot spot around the globe. Not that he was looking for anything permanent.

But if he were honest, he had to admit the idea was appealing.

Or maybe good sex had addled his brain. He rolled over, breaking contact, and Melissa sighed in her sleep, shifting so that she could snuggle close again. He stroked her hair, the strands satiny beneath his fingers. When he was with Melissa, nothing else seemed to matter. It had been like that fifteen years ago, and the intervening time hadn't changed things at all.

Besides, he knew that she was no more suited for a serious relationship than he was. After all, she'd been the one to walk away. He'd been angry then, but now he could understand. They were neither of them the type to treat love cavalierly, and yet neither could risk the vulnerability of letting someone in. There was simply too much danger.

Love changed the odds, and in his line of work, it was crucial to keep things tilted in your favor. Allow nothing that an enemy could use as a threat. Nothing. He'd learned that firsthand in Iraq with Mariam's betrayal and Kevin's death.

It was only Payton's determination to seek revenge that had kept him alive after his loss. But Nigel wasn't as strong as Payton, and this wasn't about a brother—although Lord knows he'd miss Andrew if anything happened to him. No, the truth was, this was about Melissa, and what would happen if he were to give her his heart.

Payton had found Sam. And the two of them had taken the risk, mainly because Sam simply wouldn't have it any other way. But Nigel still remembered how close Payton had come to losing Sam, as well. And that was pain Nigel wasn't certain he could have survived.

Gabe, too, had found his other half. But to do so he'd changed his professional objectives, stepping away from edgier assignments to safeguard his family. Madison had done the same, their decision made in tandem.

Compromise was the name of the game. And not one of Nigel's strong suits. It simply wasn't in his nature to turn down a challenge. And even if he could find the courage to walk away from his life with MI6, there was no indication that Melissa would follow suit. She'd made it more than apparent that she loved her job. After all, she'd left him for it once before in Italy. And he had no reason to believe that it would be any different this time.

The truth was staring him in the face. Impossible to ignore. Despite his inclinations otherwise, this could only be an interlude. Anything more would be disastrous. He sighed, turning to pull her close against him again, the smell of her hair sweet against his nostrils. Five more minutes, and then he'd leave.

The decision was the right one. He knew it as well as he knew his own name. But somehow he couldn't stop feeling that he was letting something precious slip through his fingers—something that only comes along once in a blue moon. Or in his case—maybe twice.

Unfortunately, a man made his choices in life, and sometimes, there simply was no going back.

CHAPTER SEVENTEEN

MELISSA WAS LATE getting to the operations room. First of all, she'd overslept. And then when she'd found that Nigel had already gone, she had stayed longer in bed, ruminating on exactly what his absence meant, and whether or not she should be concerned or relieved, both emotions demanding fair time despite the fact that they were diametrically opposed.

Now she stood in the doorway feeling very much the outsider. Everyone but Harrison was gathered around the conference table, but rather than discussing Melissa's notes projected on the screen above their heads, they were clustered around a small woman securely contained in the circle of Payton's arms.

Samantha Reynolds.

She was almost the complete opposite of her husband—angel to his demon. Tiny and blond, energy crackled around her. She carried an air of competence that one was born with. And even at this distance, Melissa could see the adoration in her husband's eyes. Payton Reynolds had been transformed. The lines of skepticism and speculation that were present when he looked at Melissa were completely gone in Sam's presence. Instead, he was actually grinning, a rare gesture from such an intense man.

Jealousy rippled through her, surprising in its intensity. She had just spent an incredible night of passion with Nigel, but this was something more. Something permanent. A covenant between two people.

Not exactly her cup of tea, despite her reaction. Every girl had a little Cinderella in her, that insane desire for a happy ending. But Melissa had learned a long time ago that happiness starts from the inside out. She'd worked hard to become self-reliant. And she wasn't about to trade that in because someone gave her one hell of an orgasm. Even if that someone was Nigel.

Relationships required constant attention. And even when well maintained, they could be ripped away without the slightest warning. She wasn't capable of withstanding that kind of loss. Just thinking about it made her weak at the knees.

Better to remain autonomous. Much better.

Squaring her shoulders, she summoned her courage and walked into the room. As if he sensed her presence, Nigel turned. His smile was genuine, but there was a touch of regret in his eyes. Maybe his thoughts were following the same lines as hers. Or maybe he was regretting last night. Either way, she was determined to move past it. To keep it light.

Unlike fifteen years ago, she couldn't simply run out the door. She needed Nigel. Needed his resources, his protection and, whether she wanted to admit it or not, probably his friendship. But that was all. She'd stay because she had no choice. But as soon as the coast was clear—she was gone.

Purposefully breaking eye contact, she smiled at the group. "Morning, everyone. Sorry to be late. I'm afraid I overslept."

"That's not surprising," Madison said. "You've been through a lot. Come over and meet Sam. She came in late last night."

"You must be Melissa." Sam's smile was warm as she offered her hand. "I hear you've had a rough go of it."

"Something like that." She returned the smile but still felt absurdly uncomfortable, as if they all knew what she and Nigel had been doing last night. It shouldn't matter either way, but it did. "I take it you caught your bomber?"

"Yeah. Took a little maneuvering, but eventually we managed to find the physical evidence we needed to tie him to the scene. Now it's just a matter of connecting the dots and I'll leave that to the suits."

"You haven't missed much here," Cullen said to Melissa, his tone mild. "We've mainly been playing catch-up—getting Sam up to speed."

"Sorry I didn't read the crib notes," Sam said with a shrug. "But there were better things to do last night."

Payton's eyes met his wife's, his gaze hot with the memory of what had obviously been a passionate reunion. Melissa automatically shot a glance at Nigel, then wished she hadn't, the sight of his crooked grin causing a deep flush of embarrassment.

Damn the man.

Gabe was grinning now, too, the three of them looking like cats who'd stumbled on an entire vat of cream. Madison and Sam were laughing, and once again Melissa was faced with the fact that she was an outsider. Everyone else shared a history. Some more than others admittedly, but all of them had commonality.

She, on the other hand, had never had anything like their kind of friendship. The only thing close was the relationship she had with her sister, and even that was stunted due to the fact that Melissa could never be totally honest with Alicia about anything involving her work with the CIA. The truth was, she had only herself to rely on. Until last night, that had seemed like enough.

As if sensing her discomfort, Nigel crossed the room and placed his hand against the small of her back as he steered her toward the table. "It's all right, you know. I always feel the same way when Gabe and Madison or Sam and Payton are together. And it's especially difficult when they're all here. It's enough to make one question one's priorities. But what's good for the goose isn't always good for the gander…."

His words were meant to make her feel better, but they didn't. With a sigh of exasperation, Melissa slid into the chair he offered and stared pointedly at the screen with her reports. "So where are we? I see you've been at my notes. Anything that points to a culprit?"

Taking Melissa's cue, everyone else found chairs again, and using a laptop, Cullen switched to a different image, this one enhanced with computer annotations. "Based on probability, we've narrowed your list of unknowns to seven, each of the names highlighted in red."

Melissa scanned the names, noting that most of them were people she also had suspected. "I take it you've already been through the list of those I'd rejected."

"Yes," Cullen said. "And I must say you did an outstanding job. Even Harrison and his magic computer couldn't find anything you'd missed."

Coming from him, it was high praise, but somehow it didn't matter. Everything just felt a little flat today. As if she'd spent all her joy last night, and now she was left with nothing more than middle-of-the-road emotions. "Thanks. But I'd feel better if I'd managed to get the goods on the real deal."

"Well you've significantly narrowed it down, and that helps," Gabe said, his gaze locked on the screen. "What we've got to do now is try and track things from both sides. The UN and the nerve agent's departure from Istanbul."

"But we have no solid evidence it was even *in* Istanbul, thanks to last night's failed attempt at finding the warheads."

"The presence of guards at least seems to indicate that we were on the right track," Payton said, his eyes narrowed in thought. "Add that to the probability that the nerve agent exited from somewhere in the vicinity, even if not Istanbul directly, and I'd say we've at least got a place to start."

"Unless these have something better to tell us." Harrison strode into the room waving a manila envelope. "The photos from the Spanish surveillance just arrived. You know, the ones they took just before they lost contact with Salvatore." He crossed to the computer and pulled a disk from the envelope. "Thank God for digital."

"I thought the footage wasn't any good?" Nigel sat back with a frown.

"That's what they said, but they don't know how to play with photographs the way Melissa does," Harrison said. "If there's something here to find, I'm betting she can find it." He slipped the disk into the laptop and the image on the screen changed again, this time to a grainy photo of what looked to be a Middle Eastern bazaar. "With a little help." He turned the laptop toward her, pointing to a CD case marked *E.O.*

"You got my software." For the first time she felt as if she had something concrete to contribute. This was home turf.

"Told you I knew the programmer." Harrison winked, and for a moment it was just the two of them until Nigel cleared his throat, the expression on his face enough to sober Melissa.

"Welcome to Izmit, Turkey," Harrison said, as usual oblivious to the undercurrents. He waved at the screen as Melissa moved the mouse over the picture, adjusting hue and saturation to coax the photograph into submission. In just a few minutes, the image grew noticeably clearer.

Payton studied the screen. "Unless I'm mistaken, the man by the fountain is the late, unlamented Paulo Salvatore."

"We don't know for certain that he's dead." Madison leaned forward to study the photograph."

"No," Nigel said, "but I'd make book."

Melissa studied the man in the picture. He had that slick European look. Tailored suit, dark glasses, gold glittering at his neck and wrists. Even in the heat of Turkey he managed to look perfectly pressed. "Is this coming or going?"

"Going," Harrison said. "There were two shots of him heading for the meet, but unfortunately they're so out of focus even you couldn't fix them."

Melissa switched to the earlier photos and, after trying a couple of quick fixes, nodded her agreement, switching back to the later picture of Salvatore. "This is why professional photographers should always be used on a stakeout. It's the only way to be certain you'll get what you need."

Melissa was preaching to the choir, but it had always been a pet peeve. She'd been called in many times to handle the photography side of an operation, but just as often, someone less qualified had been used, often with disastrous results.

And it wasn't as if you could just go in somewhere and retake the kind of shots necessary to get a conviction or identify a perp. Still, the CIA was a hell of a lot better than other countries—and she had the firsthand experience to back it up.

"Tell it to the Spanish," Nigel said with a shrug.

Melissa scanned the rest of the photos, making adjustments here and there. "Doesn't look like there's much here. A close-up of Paulo." She switched to the now-enhanced picture.

"There's nothing at all there to indicate who Salvatore was meeting," Harrison said with disgust, as Melissa cycled through the photographs again.

"Let's focus on the long shots," Melissa said, studying the one currently on the screen. "I think I can enlarge it without losing focus." She tapped out the instructions on the keyboard and the frame enlarged tenfold, the clarity if anything only improving.

Melissa searched the crowd, looking for anyone who seemed out of place. "It's possible they managed to catch someone in these crowd scenes. It's just a matter of searching through them for familiar faces."

"Good idea," Cullen said. "Can you slowly pan through each shot?"

"Sure." Again she tapped on the keyboard, the result being a slow sweep of the first photo. "Anyone see anyone they recognize?"

"Nothing." Nigel shook his head.

"Can you sweep through it again?" Payton asked.

Melissa obliged. "Gabe?"

"No. But that doesn't mean there isn't someone there. I see mug shots from our watch list on a regular basis. But I haven't been out in the field internationally for quite some time. Payton, you and Nigel are better bets at spotting someone."

"And Melissa," Nigel insisted. "She's got as much field experience as we do."

"Well, at least as far as visual identification." She shot a grateful smile at Nigel. Whatever did or didn't happen between them, he did care, of that she was certain. "Beyond that, I think your skill set is well beyond mine."

She turned back to the computer, framing a new photograph, first enlarging, then clarifying. "How about this one?"

They studied the photo inch by inch, but found nothing. The same was true for the next six pictures. Melissa was beginning to think her idea hadn't been all that brilliant, when something in the next photograph caught her attention.

This one was taken from a greater height, affording a different view of the crowded bazaar. From this vantage point, it was easier to see the café where Paulo had supposedly taken his meeting. Melissa scanned the crowd slowly, letting her eyes follow the natural ebb and flow within the photo. Something about a grouping on the far left of the picture tickled at her brain.

"Wait a minute." She signaled the others. "Let me zoom in on the area around the café tables."

"You think you see something?" Payton asked.

"Maybe." She moved the mouse and selected the adjustment she needed, waiting for the image to change. Obligingly, it clarified, this time showing a closer view of the front of the café. It was typically Turkish. Scattered tables decorated with colorful silk and a spray of almond blossoms. It was the man at the farthest table that captured her attention.

"There." She pointed at the monitor. "Can you see him?"

"I'm sorry, it's still too grainy." Madison shook her head in frustration.

"Hang on." Melissa chewed on her lip, enticing the computer program to work its magic and fill in missing pixels. "There. Got it."

Everyone stared at the Arabic man on the screen. Broad of face, with a slightly bulbous nose and a thick black mustache, he was much like others in the bazaar. Neither old nor young, the heat of the desert had creased his face well in advance of his years. His clothes were nondescript, a tunic and pants. Middle Eastern certainly, but not Turkish.

He sat with a friend, one fist clenched on the table, every muscle taut, waiting. He could have been anyone—except for his eyes. Here the photographer had inadvertently captured a glimpse of the man inside. Angry and haunted. As if he carried ghosts with him wherever he went. It was a quality she'd seen before in countless ravaged places throughout the world.

"I've seen him before," she whispered. "I know it."

"I wouldn't be surprised." This from Nigel. "I recognize him. His name is Khamis al-Rashid. An Islamic extremist of the first degree, he's rumored to be connected to al-Qaida, but no one has ever been able to tie him directly to one of their operations. Most likely his association is through a splinter organization. But there's no doubting the fact that he's deadly."

Melissa stared at al-Rashid, trying to remember why he seemed so familiar. Maybe it was just his expression. She'd worked the Middle East in some capacity for most of her time with the CIA. And she'd photographed a hell of a lot of people over the years. Maybe he was simply an amalgamation of all that she'd seen.

"I recognize him, too," Payton said. "Maybe seven years ago now, I infiltrated a smuggling operation in Uzbekistan. They were dealing in old Soviet weapons, including nuclear warheads. It was in everyone's best interest that they be stopped, but politically everyone's hands were tied."

"So you drew the short straw." Gabe tipped his chair back against the wall, his attention on Payton.

"Depends on how you look at it, I guess." He reached over to take his wife's hand. "At the time I thought it was a good way to keep my mind off other things. Anyway, the biggest buyers were from Middle Eastern countries."

"And al-Rashid was one of the arms dealers?" Cullen asked, staring up at the enlarged photograph.

"No. He was a customer. But as such, we researched him thoroughly. Like Nigel said, his connections were solid, and he was looking to buy a hell of a lot of merchandise. Particularly rifles and machine guns."

"And you sold them to him?" Madison asked.

"Absolutely. He wasn't the target. Sometimes the war on terror gets a little gray. Anyway, I do know that over the years, al-Rashid began appearing on more and more watch lists."

"Is he on ours?" Sam asked.

"I'll run the name. I don't recognize it offhand, but you have to understand these people are very good at using both disguises and aliases."

"Well, it wouldn't hurt to send a heads-up through proper channels, just the same." Cullen as usual was the voice of practicality.

"Already done," Harrison said, taking command of the laptop again.

"But we don't know for certain that this man is involved with the R-VX." Sam crossed her hands over her chest, her eyes narrowed in thought. "We don't really even know that Paulo Salvatore was involved. It's all just speculation."

"But it's a start," Cullen said. "I'll make sure that the right hand and left hand are coordinated on this. We want everyone and their brother on the alert for this guy. If for no other reason than to pinpoint his location and prove he isn't our man."

"He usually travels with a man named Malik Barzani. He's really the one we ought to locate. His expertise on munitions is on par with Sam's. If someone wanted to make sure the R-VX delivered bang for buck, he's your man."

"There's a man sitting with al-Rashid, but the shadows are too thick to see him clearly. Anything you can do to help, Melissa?" Madison asked.

Melissa pulled her attention from the screen. Something about al-Rashid seemed so damn familiar. "I can work magic, guys, but not miracles. I can't put a face on screen when there isn't one in the photograph. Sorry." She shrugged.

"Doesn't matter. You've given us enough to go on," Cullen said. "We'll take this as a two-pronged attack. Harrison and Madison can work on trying to find out more about Khamis al-Rashid and his friends, see if they can find a solid connection between them and the R-VX. In addition we'll work to pull out all the stops and try to find the man. And in the meantime, I want to continue to follow up on the possibility that someone working for the UN is involved. Which means we need to investigate the remaining names on Melissa's list. Gabe, I'll let you do some of the legwork there since you've got contacts through Homeland Security. Payton can help.

"Nigel, I want you to check out Hakan Celik. Search his office, apartment, whatever you need to do. I want to know if there's any truth to the allegations of his involvement in trafficking illegal goods, and if so, who his contacts were. If it's true, and we can find his associates, I'm betting we've got a shot at finding the R-VX before it's too late."

"What about me?" Melissa knew she wasn't a permanent member of the team, but surely she rated an assignment in light of the fact that her good name had been dragged through the mud thanks to these people.

"I want you to stay here out of sight. Let the others handle the legwork."

In other words, she was supposed to continue to play the role of princess in the tower. Like hell. But she wasn't about to take it up with Cullen. She was far better off waiting until later and then approaching Nigel. It wouldn't be an easy sell, but then she'd always liked a challenge.

CHAPTER EIGHTEEN

THE SOUND OF the beating helicopter blades was almost hypnotic, reminding Nigel of countless identical departures. Only this time, he wasn't entirely certain he wanted to leave. There had been no time for private conversation, and he was regretting his early-morning defection from Melissa's bedroom.

At the time it had seemed best to avoid the inevitable questions about what next. But he'd not thought they'd have gone without any discussion at all. He'd seen the question in her eyes and felt her withdrawing. And although he knew that should have brought relief, in actuality he felt nothing of the sort. Instead he had the distinct feeling that he'd sucker punched himself.

At least he had something to do. Maybe if he could figure out who'd really been helping Hakan Celik, he'd not only be able to get a bead on the location of the R-VX but he'd be able to clear Melissa's name once and for all.

In all probability it was too little too late, but he always felt better when he was working, and the present situation was no different. He ducked low and ran underneath the undulating blades, climbing aboard the helicopter with the ease of familiarity. He signaled the pilot when he was buckled in and felt the customary jerk as the machine lifted off the ground.

Maybe he wasn't really being honest with himself. A part of him did want to avoid the potential disaster of a relationship, the danger of a loved one being leveraged against him. But another part was also afraid of getting hurt again. Melissa had left him high and dry once before, and in all honesty, he'd not handled the loss well. And once he had recovered, he'd sworn never to repeat that particular mistake.

Yet here he was. Maybe distance was a good thing.

He leaned back against the upholstered seat, trying to order his plan of attack. There'd be a car waiting at the heliport, and from there he'd head for Celik's apartment. Cullen had secured the necessary approval for the search, but to be on the safe side, Nigel wasn't planning on announcing himself. Better to get in and out without raising curiosity from neighbors or anyone else who might have an interest in the building.

If they were right, and someone had framed Melissa, then Celik's was an obvious place for surveillance, if for no other reason than to be certain the ruse was working. Nigel leaned forward to look out the window, satisfied to see the cloud-studded skyline of Manhattan directly ahead. Almost there.

He sat back again, for the first time noticing that there was something oddly familiar about the pilot—the curve of the shoulders, the stray strand of long auburn hair.

Nigel moved forward with a speed that surprised even himself, landing in the seat adjacent to Melissa. "What the hell do you think you're doing?"

"Flying the helicopter."

"Well, that much was obvious. I meant what the hell are you doing *here?*"

"Coming with you." She shot him a saccharine smile and turned back to the instrument panel.

"I assume you're certified to fly this thing?"

"Yup. Learned the hard way—after my pilot was killed in a bush fight in Namibia. I either had to fly the thing out or walk. Considering people were shooting at me, I thought that flying seemed the better option. It was touch and go, but I made it. And after that it seemed prudent to learn for real."

"Bloody hell, is there anything you can't do?"

"Not much." This time her smile was more genuine.

"I assume you didn't hurt Cullen's pilot?"

"Quite the contrary, I left him quite happy." Nigel frowned, and Melissa laughed. "You've got a dirty mind. I told him Cullen was giving him the day off."

"I see," he said, counting to ten under his breath. The woman drove him absolutely, positively mad. "And Cullen—does he know about any of this?"

The skin on Melissa's nose wrinkled in protest. "Of course not. Do you think I'm crazy?"

"Yes, actually I do." And he wasn't the slightest bit certain if he loved the fact or abhorred it.

"Look," she said, keeping her attention on the instrument panel, "I couldn't stand another second in that fortified prison. It's my life on the line and I need to do something to make certain we find the answers we need to clear my name."

"Well, it won't do much good if you're dead," Nigel snapped, more than aware that had he been in the same position, he'd have done the same thing.

"No one is going to kill me, Nigel. I'm with you." Her faith would have been touching if her voice hadn't been laced with sarcasm.

"I'm more than capable of taking care of you, and you know it."

"Great, then there's nothing to worry about." Again with the nauseatingly sweet smile.

"The hell there isn't. This hasn't been approved by anyone. You've essentially stolen Cullen's helicopter, with me as an accomplice." He was talking nonsense, but she made him crazy.

"I've done no such thing. And you can tell Cullen it was all my fault when we get back. I just couldn't sit there staring at Harrison's computers while everyone else was out doing something useful."

"Harrison is more than useful, Melissa—his work is crucial."

"I didn't mean Harrison." Her eyes flashed with frustration. "I meant me. I'm the one who hasn't been doing anything useful."

"You finessed the photographs, and identified Khamis al-Rashid. That's something."

"It's not enough, and the man has nothing whatsoever to do with what's happening to me. Except maybe a subsidiary connection if he is in fact using Celik's network to transfer the stolen nerve agent. Anyway, unless you're going to force me to turn this baby around, or ditch me at the helipad, we're in this together."

"Fine." He agreed against his better judgment, but a part of him was happy to have her there. Happy to be bantering as if nothing had happened last night. Of course he knew that sooner or later they'd have to face reality, but in the meantime he was damn glad to have her sitting next to him. Not that he was going to admit it. "But we'll have to call Cullen."

"As long as you don't ditch me in the process."

"I said you could stay. *I* don't go back on my word, Melissa." He hadn't meant it to be a pointed comment, but for a moment the subliminal conversation was about a great deal more than whether or not she was going with him to Celik's.

"I didn't say you did." She returned her attention to flying the helicopter, but he could see by the set of her jaw that he'd hurt her.

"Look, I didn't mean to..."

She waved a hand, cutting him off. "It doesn't matter. Let's concentrate on finding out what we can about Celik, all right?"

"If that's what you want." He fell silent then, staring out the window at the George Washington Bridge. She'd always known how to press his buttons, and now evidently he'd mastered hers, as well. Hell of a thing, caring about someone.

"EVERYTHING IS AS IT SHOULD BE?" Khamis spoke softly into the microphone of his headset, his eyes trained on the building in front of him. Alexi Kirov's apartment was a third-floor walk-up in an old Brooklyn Heights brownstone. The building itself was a little run-down, but the neighborhood was pricey. Typical of Americans. They built up an area until all charm and history were lost, and then moved on like a swarm of locusts to devour whatever they found next.

Kirov wasn't American, but he'd made it more than clear that he wished he had been. The harsh allure of capitalism had worked its magic and now held the Russian firmly in its grasp, the false sense of security it afforded making him take risks that threatened not only his network but also Khamis's operation.

"I have the package." The headset crackled to life, Malik's voice sounding close by. He was, in fact, across the island in a loft in the financial district. The miracles of modern communication.

"Everything is accounted for?"

"All elements are present and secure," Malik assured him.

"Very well." Khamis nodded even though his friend could not see him. "Did you take care of everything at Celik's?"

"I planted what you requested, although I'm not certain I fully understand why."

"A ploy to flush out my quarry. You have everything you need for assembly?"

"Almost everything." Malik accepted the change of subject without question. One of the reasons they had remained friends for so many years. "One of the components was damaged in transit. I'll have to replace it."

"Can you do that without being traced?" Khamis asked, worry tugging at his gut.

"Of course, my friend. I wouldn't attempt it otherwise."

Despite the dire nature of the situation, Khamis smiled. "Very well. You get what you need, and I'll finish things here. We're so close, Malik."

His friend was silent for a moment. "Are you sure you want to proceed?"

"There is no choice. Everything has lined up in our favor. Allah has smiled upon us—we mustn't let fear pull us away from that fact."

"You mistake me," Malik said, his tone derisive. "I am not afraid. I would gladly die for our cause. But you must be sure it is truly Allah who is smiling and not a devil clouding your vision."

"My vision is clear. Proceed."

Again there was a brief hesitation, then a sigh. "As you wish."

Static surged as Malik disconnected, and Khamis reached up to switch the headset off. Perhaps Malik was right. Maybe he was letting his own desires cloud the truth. But he couldn't stop now. He had come too far. He would strike for both his cause and his family.

Only then could balance be restored.

He closed his eyes and opened them again, his mind now firmly centered on the task at hand. He'd been watching the building for most of the morning, counting its inhabitants as they'd left for work. According to his count the building should be empty. Or at least mostly so. Crossing the street, he kept his pace purposefully slow, as if he hadn't a care in the world.

He strode up the stairs to the brownstone and, using the device Malik had provided, was inside in no time. It was the second time he'd been in the building. The first had been on the heels of a young woman who lived on the first floor. He'd needed to make sure that there weren't security cameras, and as he'd expected, there was nothing.

The residents here spent their money on revitalizing the old building, not protecting themselves. Foolish arrogance. He took the stairs in easy strides, and again using Malik's electronic key, was inside Alexi's apartment in less than two minutes.

The Russian had few possessions, but those he did have were of the highest quality. A sound system with flat-screen television occupied most of the west wall. Blatant idolatry. Khamis stopped at a small desk between the bedroom and the living room. A date book lay open on top. The man was making it too easy.

Khamis grabbed a pen with one gloved hand, and then turned back a page or two. After studying Alexi's handwriting, he made a brief entry and returned the book to its original position. Turning toward the television, he scanned the room. The only other furniture was a sofa on the same wall as the door. The placement was wrong. The open door would provide a barrier. Better to wait in the bedroom.

Unlike the front room, there was more personality here. Bits of Mother Russia that Alexi no doubt believed bought him justification for his decadence. Soon he would not have any doubt which side of the battle he had chosen. If he believed in hell, then he'd soon be there.

Khamis pulled out his gun and sat on the bed. He was good at waiting. He'd waited so many years to put his plan in action. First ferreting out the needed information, information that Malik had believed he could never unearth. But Malik had underestimated Khamis's tenacity. In time his patience had won out and he'd found all that he needed to know.

The door clicked as the lock was sprung. Khamis tightened his hand on the gun, checking the silencer.

Footsteps moved slowly from the front door into the apartment. Khamis heard the television come on. American extremists lying about his people, claiming their superiority. Anger flooded through him, but he fought it down, knowing that it, too, was his enemy.

In the past few days he had pulled everything he could on Russian mob hits. It was important that he make things look exactly right. When Alexi was found, it must appear to be a contracted death. A double cross or perhaps simply another step in the mob's plan to undermine the UN.

By the time the authorities worked it out, Khamis and

Malik would be gone and there would be bigger problems for America to face.

He smiled, listening as Alexi's footsteps grew closer. Two more steps and…

The bullet ripped through Alexi Kirov before he even had time to open his mouth in surprise. He stood for a moment in confusion, trying to sort through what was happening, but before he could find his answer—he was dead.

Khamis stepped dispassionately over the body and picked up the appointment book. Ripping out the page he'd written on, he placed the book near Alexi's outstretched hand and then walked from the apartment. The hallway was empty and, after carefully relocking Kirov's door, he strode down the stairs and out into the street. One obstacle had been eliminated.

CHAPTER NINETEEN

HAKAN CELIK'S APARTMENT was in Tudor City. Close to the UN, the building was part rental, part owner with the accompanying hodgepodge of tenants. Celik lived on the sixth floor in a one-bedroom corner unit that actually belonged to the Turkish embassy. Melissa and Nigel had entered the building without incident, Cullen's magic having cleared the way.

They had identified themselves as real estate agents hired to list the apartment for the embassy. The fact that there were two rather than one didn't seem to faze the man at the desk, and they'd been given a key without further question. Melissa now stood in the living room of Celik's apartment, surveying the accoutrements of the man's life.

Except for the odd remnant of the NYC forensic team's examination, it looked as if Celik had just stepped out for a slice. There was an open soft drink can on the kitchen counter, the empty glass next to it still bearing traces of fingerprint powder.

The sofa was littered with magazines and junk mail. Evidently Celik hadn't been a believer in throwing out the trash. The floor in front of the sofa was covered with newspapers, most of them old.

"Either he wasn't here much, or the man was a slob." Nigel appeared in the doorway to the bedroom, the sound of his voice reminding Melissa of other things his mouth was capable of.

She pushed all emotion away. "It's hard to know where to start."

"If there's anything here, I'll wager it's either amazingly well hidden, or it's staring us in the face."

"Thanks for narrowing it down."

"No problem." Nigel grinned, his mustache making him look almost wicked. "You start with the newspapers and mail, and I'll check out the closets and radiators."

"Hey," she said, "hiding my files behind the radiator turned out to be a damn good idea. If I hadn't, they'd be in the hands of New York's Finest."

"That's why I'm checking them out," Nigel laughed, raising his hands in mock surrender.

Thirty minutes later, she knew a hell of a lot more about Celik's reading preferences than she'd ever wanted to know. The man definitely had a penchant for American pornography. Unfortunately, the preference did nothing whatsoever to help identify the man's true accomplice.

His bills had been equally unhelpful. There were a couple of unidentified cell-phone calls worth checking out further, but no calls to the UN or names that seemed familiar. She pocketed the bill for further examination.

"You finding anything?" she called into the kitchen, where Nigel was going through the cabinets. So far the closets had been silently unhelpful.

"The guy liked his cereal. There's like fourteen different kinds here. American overkill."

"He wasn't American."

"No. But Super Pops and Trix are. You'd think one corn-puff cereal would be more than enough for the world."

Melissa shrugged with a smile. "Capitalism at its best. You should see his choice in magazines, they run the gamut from *Playboy* to *Jugs*."

"Poor guy obviously wasn't getting any." Nigel's voice was muffled as he stepped into the pantry.

Melissa ignored the comment and turned her concentration to the piles of newspapers. Like the magazines, they didn't run to heavy journalism. The *Post* was a favorite, along with *Newsday* and the occasional copy of the *Star.* She sorted through them, stacking like copies together by date. It was unlikely that there'd be anything in his reading habits to suggest a connection to someone at the UN, but she liked to be thorough.

She'd worked her way to the far end of the sofa and the last group of newspapers when she picked up a copy of the *Wall Street Journal.* The lead article was about a proposed merger between two megaliths that threatened SEC rules. Nothing else on the front page seemed of value, but she put it to the side. If nothing else, the fact that it didn't fit with the rest of his reading material was noteworthy.

She sorted through the rest of the newspapers, then returned to the *Journal,* something inside her urging a closer look.

"Well, there's nothing in there. No loose ceiling tiles, floorboards or hidden compartments that I can find. Not even a stray key."

"There's not much here, either." Melissa looked up as Nigel walked into the room. "But this is kind of interesting."

"The *Wall Street Journal?* I find it a little dry."

Nigel had always been able to make her laugh.

"Well, that's actually the point. This is the only one here. And believe me its floormates are in a whole other class." She waved her hand toward the stack of *Newsdays.*

"Anything in the editorial copy?"

"Nothing to do with the UN. It's dated two weeks ago." She pulled out a couple of sections and tossed them to Nigel. "Have a look."

He took the newspaper and settled into an armchair, already thumbing through the pages.

Melissa picked up the front page and flipped through. "Nothing here."

"Nor here."

With a sigh, Melissa closed the newspaper, her gaze falling to the address label in the corner of the back page. "Hang on." Her heart started pounding and she reread it just to be certain.

Nigel had crossed to her side and was looking down at the label, too, a smile quirking the corner of his mustache. "I'll be damned. It *was* right under our noses."

According to the label, the newspaper belonged to Alexi Kirov.

"Kirov is on your list, right?"

"Yeah, I've met him, but I haven't had the chance to investigate him. In fact, I was trying to schedule a time the night of the party."

"Anything he said or did seem out of the ordinary?"

Melissa tried to think back. It seemed like decades ago rather than just a couple of days. "I didn't like him much. But that was as close as it came to him making me think he was the one."

"Sometimes instinct is your best ally."

"You sound like Madison." Melissa folded the paper and slipped it into her pocket with the phone bill. "So what do we do next?"

"We find Kirov."

ALEXI KIROV'S APARTMENT WAS a walk-up in a Brooklyn brownstone, and Nigel found himself wondering how anyone did it day in and day out. At least it was only the third floor.

There wasn't an on-site super, but they'd arrived at the same time as another tenant was leaving. This time Nigel's credentials had done the trick, and the woman had been only too happy to let them into the building and direct them to Kirov's floor. As they hit the landing, Nigel pulled out his gun.

"You think that's necessary?" Melissa whispered.

"I like to err on the side of caution. Besides, if Alexi is our man, there's no telling how he'll react."

"All right then." She reached behind her, pulling a .38 from her waistband.

"Where the hell did you get that?" he asked, frowning.

"Cullen's study." She grinned. "Desk drawer is a sure bet almost every time."

"Remind me to have a little talk with him about his security." Nigel knew he was reacting badly, but he didn't like the idea of Cullen leaving handguns lying about.

"It's not like I don't know how to use one. If I'd thought of it I'd have had you bring mine from my apartment."

"When in Rome," he mumbled, blowing out a long breath. "You ready?"

She nodded and together they moved down the hallway, Nigel flanking the left side of door, while Melissa took the right. Nigel reached over to knock on the door, not bothering to identify himself. Better to catch the bastard by surprise.

Nothing happened, and he repeated the action. Again nothing.

"Cover me." He waited for Melissa to move into position and then quickly picked the lock. He felt rather than saw her surprise but didn't stop to explain. There were a lot of skills a man in his position needed, picking locks being the least of them.

Leading with his gun, he cracked the door, then swung it open. At first all he saw was an empty apartment. And then he looked down. Alexi Kirov lay faceup on the floor near a small desk, a bullet hole marking what had been the center of his forehead.

Without thinking, he moved to block Melissa from entering the apartment, but she'd pushed past him, her face tight with anger.

"Stop treating me like some kind of hothouse flower. I know how to use a gun. In my business it's a necessity. People in war zones rarely stop to ask which side I'm on. They shoot first. I like to be able shoot back. And I've sure as hell seen a dead body before. Many of them a whole lot harder to stomach than this one."

"I'm sorry..." He trailed off, frustrated. He seemed to be apologizing a lot of late. "I guess I didn't think."

"The old testosterone just kicked in, right? Big man save little woman."

"It's not like that and you know it," he said, his anger matching hers. "It's perfectly natural to try and protect someone you care about. So don't ask me to stop, because I'm bloody hell not going to do it."

Her anger dissipated. "I didn't mean it like that. It's just that sometimes I get tired of being underestimated."

"Believe me, Melissa, I do not underestimate you."

She nodded, her gaze locking on Kirov. "What do you think happened here?"

"A professional hit, if I had to call it. Dead center, hardly any blood, and Kirov here doesn't even look surprised. I'd say he either knew his killer, or was dead before the fact registered." Nigel bent down to pick up a book lying near Kirov's outstretched hand, careful not to disturb any prints.

"What is it?"

"A day planner." Nigel flipped through the little book. "Looks like there's a page missing." He pointed to the jagged edge of paper next to the spiral binding.

"A whole day." Melissa stared down at the book, her brow wrinkling in thought. "Nigel, it's the same day that Celik was killed."

"So the question is, who tore it out?"

"I'm guessing the killer." Melissa walked over to the wastebasket and rifled through the contents. "Nothing here."

"So we've got a dead man and a missing diary page. Not a lot of help."

"Well, I'd say this is a pretty good indication that Alexi was involved in all this somehow. We've just got to figure out what his role was."

"Agreed." He pulled his cell phone from his pocket and started to dial, but before he could connect, something whizzed past his ear, his gut identifying it before his brain. "Get down," he yelled, diving for Melissa. They clattered to the floor, just missing Alexi's body, and together rolled to the corner, out of range of both the window and door.

"You hit?" he whispered into Melissa's hair. She shook her head, and he rolled off her to his knees, his gun at the ready.

"Where did it come from?" Melissa asked, holding the .38 with both hands.

"Window, I think." He nodded toward the open window in the opposite wall. Suddenly another slug slammed into the wall above their heads, the curtain undulating wildly.

"We should be able to make it to the door if we crawl," Melissa whispered. "There should be a blind spot there." She pointed to the floor about two feet ahead.

Nigel nodded his agreement, and then motioned for her to go first. She started crawling forward, using knees and elbows but stopped when another shot ricocheted off the baseboard.

"Move," Nigel hissed, following behind her in a low crouch, his gun trained on the window. Not that he had a prayer in hell of hitting anything. Whoever was shooting at them had the advantage of distance—and a high-powered scope on their rifle.

Melissa reached the door and was starting to rise up to open it.

"Wait," Nigel said. "Let me distract him."

She nodded, and he grabbed one of Alexi's shoes. "When I throw it, go." He counted silently to three and then threw the shoe at the window. Melissa yanked the door open and ran through it just as the leather of the shoe splintered from the force of their assailant's slug.

Nigel rolled past the window and through the open door in practically one motion, the two of them retreating to a windowless corner of the hallway. Melissa was breathing heavily but otherwise unharmed.

"That went well," she said, shooting him a crooked smile.

"Yes, but we've still got to get out of the building. If there's a back door, we're home free. Otherwise we'll be like sitting ducks when we emerge onto the street."

"It's a brownstone. There should be a garden of some kind."

"Great, then all we have to do is figure out how to access it. And we've got to do it fast, before whoever it is out there has time to work out our strategy and reposition himself."

Melissa nodded, already heading down the stairs, .38 still in her hand. Nigel followed, taking in both the landing above them and the landing below. The building was quiet, but he couldn't rule out the possibility that there was more than one shooter.

They reached the second-floor landing without incident. But as they turned the corner, the window in front of them shattered. Melissa hit the floor and Nigel moved back, out of range.

"He's still in the same location," Nigel said, picturing Kirov's apartment. "This window faces the same direction as the one upstairs."

Melissa nodded and crawled under the window to safety on the other side of the landing. "You're next." She angled herself so that she could shoot out the window if necessary.

He crawled past the window and leapt to his feet again, signaling Melissa to follow him down the stairs. It was darker here, the overhead light burned out, but he could discern the hallway below. The front door would be behind them. He tried to remember how much glass there was.

"Not much," Melissa whispered, reading his thoughts. "Just one window, about a foot square."

"All right, come off the stairs in a crouch and head toward the back of the hall. Hopefully you're right and there's a door to the garden."

Melissa hit the last stair, bending low as she ran down the hallway away from the front door. Nigel followed, moving backward, his eyes trained on the front-door window.

Suddenly the glass shattered, the window imploding.

"Get down," he yelled behind him as he automatically dropped to the floor.

The slug slammed into the left-hand wall.

Nigel fired twice at the door and then scrambled backward. A small French door marked the end of the hallway, and Melissa already had it open. "Go," he yelled. "I'm right behind you." Another shot rang out, this one whizzing past his ear. The shooter was on the move. Closer now. Maybe even as close as the front door.

He rose to a crouch and headed for the back door, another bullet slamming into the wall, this time about two inches from his head. It was tempting to stop and return fire, but he knew that would mean certain death. Instead he ran forward, stopping only long enough to slam the door closed behind him.

The garden was little more than a courtyard, and at least at first glance there was no other way in or out. Seconds ticked away as they looked for egress.

"There." Melissa pointed, already starting to run.

Nigel didn't see anything, but he followed her anyway, praying that she was seeing something he wasn't. She rounded two trash cans and disappeared from view. Nigel followed suit, relieved to see a slender alley leading out onto the street adjacent to the building. Behind him, he heard the door slam open, and the clatter of feet.

They were almost out of time.

The gate at the end of the alley was locked, but Melissa didn't hesitate as she boosted herself up and over. Nigel followed suit, as another bullet ricocheted off the wrought-iron grating to the left of his hand.

He hit the cement hard but rolled immediately to his feet, turning to fire once through the fence. Melissa was already sprinting down the block away from the building. From the opposite direction he could hear the wail of a siren. God willing, someone had called the cops.

Either way, they were out of here.

Unless their pursuer was deaf, he'd hear the siren, too. Between that and the fact that Nigel and Melissa were now sprinting up a very public street, he'd be forced to give up—at least for now.

Luck, it seemed, was still on their side. The question was for how long.

KHAMIS STOOD BACK in the shadow of the alley watching the woman and her friend run away. It would have been so easy to let the Russian pig take them. To end it now. But that would have defeated his plan.

Much better to stop the Russian.

He looked dispassionately down at the body at his feet. It was perhaps more of a chance than he should have taken. Malik certainly would not approve. But Malik wasn't here. And what he didn't know…

Khamis waited until the sirens faded into the distance, then pulled out his knife and reached down for an arm. It would be easier to dispose of the man in pieces. He smiled as he began to carve, thinking about the phrase they always used in American television. He dropped the arm into a trash bag he'd liberated from the garbage, and whispered to the corpse, "And now, my friend, you sleep with the fishes."

CHAPTER TWENTY

"WHAT IN HELL were you thinking?" Cullen's face had turned a mottled shade of red, and Melissa felt certain he was going to explode. His mood was matched by the rest of the team, all of whom were assembled in Cullen's study. "Exactly how the hell was I supposed to explain it if something had happened to you? You're not even supposed to be here."

"But nothing happened." Melissa shrugged with a nonchalance she didn't really feel. Actually, the whole thing had been a bit exhilarating. Watching Nigel at work. Working with him to keep themselves alive. It was the same adrenaline rush she had when she was shooting a war zone. Every move vital, every second precious.

"That's not the point." Cullen clenched a fist, lifted it, and then as if on second thought, let it drop.

"Maybe not," Nigel said, from his armchair by the fire, "but it is a fact that if Melissa hadn't been there, I'd probably be dead. We took turns drawing fire. That's the only way we got out of the building at all." A bandage shone white against his temple, the result of a bullet graze, and she rubbed the square of gauze on her own arm, thinking that they were a matched pair. For all the good that did them.

"Any idea who was doing the shooting?" This from Payton, who had been frowning at her from the fireplace ever since they'd convened the meeting. So much for swinging him over to her side.

"None at all," Nigel said. "We never got a look at him. It

all happened too fast. But from the looks of it, I'd say he was local talent."

"What makes you say that?" Gabe asked.

"Well, he obviously knew his business. Positioning and trajectories, that sort of thing. But if he were in our game, he wouldn't have missed. And he did. Several times."

"And here I thought we were just good at evasion," Melissa said.

"Well, there is that." Nigel's smile was tempered, but she'd take what she could get. The flight home had been a quiet one, and she knew that despite his attempts to side with her now, he wasn't at all happy with the fact that she'd been in danger.

She ought to feel contrite, but in truth, she didn't. After all her sister had always insisted that *obstinate* was Melissa's middle name.

"The truth is," Nigel continued, "that our skill set outweighed our assailant's. Not that I'm making light of the situation in any way. It was close, but I've seen worse."

"So we've got a tenuous connection between Hakan Celik and Alexi Kirov. But we can't substantiate it because Alexi is dead. Presumably by the same hand as Celik." Harrison stood up to pace in front of the window.

"And it looks like whoever offed Kirov also has it in for Nigel and Melissa," Sam added. She was standing close to Payton, the two of them looking very much as if they belonged together.

"My bet is that it was Melissa being targeted," Nigel said. "I would have just been collateral damage."

"But how the hell could they have known I'd show up at Alexi's?" Melissa asked, not liking the idea that she'd specifically been targeted.

"Two possibilities that I can see." Madison as usual cut right to the chase. "The first is that it was just coincidence. The killer was still there when you arrived, and seeing opportunity, took it."

"And the second?" Nigel asked.

"Someone is hunting her. If Alexi knew that she survived the poisoning—and I think that's a reasonable assumption since there was no body—then it's conceivable that he hired someone to finish the job."

"That would explain the gunman near the Regency." Nigel's forehead crinkled in thought. "But how could he have known Melissa would be at Alexi's?"

"Well, it would make sense that she'd try to get to the bottom of what happened. Clear her name. And since Alexi appears to have been at the center of the maelstrom, it isn't too big a leap to assume she'd eventually come to the source. Especially if you consider the newspaper at Celik's."

"A ploy to lead her to slaughter," Payton mused.

"It's possible." Madison shrugged. "I'm just trying to build a theory off of the facts."

"But why the delay? The sniper could easily have picked both Nigel and Melissa off when they entered the building." Cullen's question wasn't directed at anyone in particular, but Madison answered.

"Again there are two possibilities. You said there was a woman who let you in, right?" Madison turned to look at Melissa.

"Right. You think the shooter didn't want to involve a bystander?"

Madison shrugged. "It's certainly a possibility."

"But he didn't use a silencer, which is tantamount to sending an engraved invitation," Nigel said. "It seems like he wasn't all that worried about keeping his work a secret."

"Then, for some reason he needed you to find Alexi's body," Madison said, propping her chin on her hand.

"Maybe it was an attempt to frame Melissa again." Payton leaned against the mantel crossing his arms.

"Well, whatever it was, I don't see how it could have involved Khamis al-Rashid. Any progress on locating him?" Cullen asked.

"Nothing so far." Harrison sounded as frustrated as Melissa felt. "The man isn't exactly high profile. Russian intel put him in Kazakhstan as recently as last week. Which could conceivably have put him into position to steal the R-VX, but that's just conjecture on my part."

"Combined with the photographs in Izmit, I'd say it's pretty sound logic," Sam said. "Northwestern Kazakhstan is an easy access point to where the R-VX was stored, and it's also fairly easy to find passage from Kazakhstan through to the Black Sea. All of which fits the pattern."

"But even if that's true, we're still left with the fact that both al-Rashid and the R-VX have basically disappeared from the radar." Gabe tipped back his head, rubbing his temples.

"We'll keep looking," Harrison said. "We're fairly certain now that Alexi Kirov was the UN contact. Hopefully, we'll be able to find something in the shipments he controlled that links to one or the other."

"And I'm still waiting for background information on al-Rashid," Madison said. "History can go a long way toward explaining motivation, and once we have that, it'll be much easier to identify a target."

"So we're making progress," Cullen interjected hopefully.

"Not fast enough for my books," Payton said with his usual pessimism.

"Well, maybe I have something that can help." Tracy Braxton stood in the door of the study. With Cullen's help, she'd set up a partial lab here at the safe house, complete with state-of-the-art equipment and several of her staff. The rest of the work was still being done in the city, but Tracy's presence made dissemination of information move much more quickly. "A couple of things, actually." She held out a file, and Gabe took it. "I told you I'd run a check on the MO for Celik's murder."

"And you found something," Cullen prompted, his impatience obvious.

"I did. There were four murders in the last three years that involved the same kind of knife. Three of them were suspected mob hits. A guy named Johnny Jacko. He was never convicted, but there was enough to warrant an arrest in two of the cases. They never went to trial."

"Any idea what the guy's real name is?" Nigel asked.

"Yeah," she said, nodding at the file. "His name is Ivan Jacovitz. Russian mafia. Of course I can't prove he's behind Celik's murder. Only that an eight-inch serrated hunting knife seems to be his preferred methodology."

"It's a start." Payton reached over to take the file from Gabe. "If he's involved, believe me, we'll find out."

"Harrison, can you find the guy for us?" Gabe asked. "Or at least give us an address?"

"Sure." Harrison opened his laptop and started typing. "Should be fairly easy."

"You said you had two things," Cullen said to Tracy.

"Oh, right." She smiled, the gesture transforming. "I used indentations in the subsequent page to produce what had been written on the missing page from Alexi Kirov's planner." She dug into another file, producing a printout. "As you know, the missing day was the same as the one that Melissa was poisoned and Celik was murdered. There are a couple of routine notations. Meetings at the UN. I checked them out and they're legit. But here, in the margin toward the bottom—" she pointed to the reconstructed page "—there were scribbled letters—*I* and *V.* Based on the punctuation present, I'd have to say they're initials. Unfortunately that's all I've got."

Madison reached for the sheet of paper, studying it for a minute.

"What are you thinking?" Gabe asked.

"Well, maybe I'm being influenced by our previous discussion about the Russian mob, but one of the major families is run by a man named Igor Vetalav. We tried to nail him for a string of homicides about four years ago."

"Hey, I remember that," Harrison said, looking up from his computer. "It was about diamonds, right? A bunch of jewelers killed."

"Russian Jews, to be exact." Madison nodded. "But unfortunately we couldn't prove anything."

"How about Jacovitz? He have ties to Vetalav?" Nigel leaned forward, his eyes narrowed in thought.

"According to this—" Harrison tapped his screen "—he works for the guy. The FBI hasn't been able to substantiate it, but there is strong circumstantial evidence linking him to Vetalav."

"Nice work." Tracy sounded impressed.

"Hey, I can do better than that." Harrison's smile was lopsided and just a bit on the wicked side. "According to NYPD files the man likes to hang out in a Russian restaurant in Brighton Beach."

"So what do you say we pay this guy a visit?" Nigel was already halfway out the door.

"You don't need to go anywhere," Melissa said, following him out into the hallway away from the others, aware that she had no right whatsoever to tell him what to do but determinedly ignoring the fact. "In case you've forgotten, you were almost killed today. I'm sure Payton and Gabe can handle this one without you."

"You want me to just sit here and wait?" Nigel stopped, turning to face her.

"Welcome to my world." Melissa tried but couldn't keep the note of bitterness from her voice.

"Sorry, but there's no way I'm passing this one up. It's personal." His eyes met hers, and she shivered at the icy rage she saw there.

"Then please promise me you'll be careful." The words came out before she had time to think about how they sounded.

The ice vanished, replaced by smoldering heat, his breath warm against her cheek as he brushed it with his lips. "Nice to know you care."

"I WANT TO KNOW where you are." Alicia's voice sounded tinny on the satellite phone, even though she technically was only just down the Hudson.

"I'm staying with a friend." There was truth in that—a little at least.

"Who do you think you're talking to?" Alicia's displeasure had no trouble at all bouncing off the stratosphere. "I know you, Melissa. And despite the fact that you insist on keeping it in the dark, I am well aware that your job involves more than taking pictures in crisis situations. So don't even try to deny it."

"Fine, if it makes you happy I won't deny anything." There was a modicum of truth in there somewhere surely.

"All right, then tell me what the hell is going on?"

"I can't." Suddenly Melissa hated her life. Hated the deception, the danger. Hell, all of it. Well, maybe not everything. "I'm chasing a story. And if I tell you about it, I'll jinx things. All right? I just called to let you know I was okay."

"Are you with that man?"

She was tempted to pretend she had no idea who Alicia was talking about, but that was probably pushing things too far. "Yes, I am. And his name is Nigel."

"Is he a photographer, too?" Alicia still sounded suspicious.

"No. Related field. I told you before, he's a blast from the past."

"The man in Italy." Alicia sounded so certain, Melissa wondered if her life was that transparent.

"How did you know that?"

"Well, first off, there haven't been that many men. At least not that affected you so deeply. And second, I saw you with him the other night, remember."

"Save the good wishes, we're just working together. There's nothing else going on." Again with the lies, but she wasn't about to tell her sister she'd slept with Nigel. Not because she regretted it, but because it would only incite false hope in Alicia, who was perpetually praying for Melissa to find her own happily ever after, and certain that only a man could possibly provide it.

"Really?"

"Alicia—back off." As long as Melissa could remember, Alicia had been pressing her buttons. Her sister shouldn't be able to get away with it anymore, but somehow, despite that fact, it always managed to catch Melissa by surprise.

"For the time being. But I'm not giving up. In fact, why don't you bring him with you to the benefit at the Waldorf? You are still planning to come, aren't you?"

She could tell by Alicia's voice that she was going to be disappointed with her answer. "Oh, Alicia, I'm not sure I'll be able to make it."

"Melissa," Alicia cajoled, "we hardly ever get to see each other anymore."

"I hardly think a fund-raiser is the best of places to catch up."

There was truth in the fact, but her sister chose to ignore it. "You promised. Besides, I really want you there."

Ever since their mother had died, Alicia had been obsessed with breast cancer research. First spending all her time in the library, and then, as an adult, chairing events across the country to further research aimed at finding a cure. Melissa understood her reasons for involvement, but unlike her sister, Melissa wasn't comfortable openly discussing their mother's disease or her death. And despite the intervening years, she still wasn't comfortable attending Alicia's functions, the galas a constant reminder of all that she had lost.

"I know. But this is really important. I swear it."

"I see." Alicia could do icy better than anyone Melissa had ever met.

"Look, I'll come if I can, okay? And I'll even bring Nigel." She had no intention of doing anything of the sort, but at least it would appease her sister for the moment.

"Sounds like a plan." Already her sister sounded perkier.

"How's the baby?" Best to get her off the subject while Melissa was ahead.

"Fine. The doctor let us listen to the heartbeat yesterday. It was so amazing. You really ought to think about doing this, Mel. It's the most wonderful feeling, carrying a child."

Uh-oh, right back into shark-infested waters.

"Alicia, I've got to go. Give my love to Aaron. And stop worrying about me. You've got more important things to do, liking taking care of my new nephew."

"Or niece." Her sister's voice sounded dreamy now, and Melissa felt a tug of envy.

"I love you." That much was absolute truth. Alicia was the only real family she had in the world.

"Me, too, you," her sister said, and hung up.

Melissa sat in the wing chair staring into the fire, feeling more alone than she'd ever felt in her entire life.

CHAPTER TWENTY-ONE

THE RESTAURANT WAS LOCATED between a tailor and a grocery store that looked as if it had been pulled straight out of Soviet Russia. Nigel had seen the real thing on several occasions, and despite the fact that Russia was now a free country, there were places where it still felt decidedly old regime.

Apparently Brighton Beach was a satellite. Everything was written in Cyrillic here. Street signs, storefronts, even billboards. He half expected the KGB to round the corner and whip the riffraff into shape. The buildings had a third-world appearance, and it was hard to remember that the capitalist haven of Manhattan was merely a train ride away.

Blatnaya, roughly translated as *thieves,* looked every bit the part of a decrepit Soviet restaurant. Despite the city-wide ban on smoking, a haze filled the room, giving it a gray-blue hue and the pungent smell of tobacco and cabbage.

Men, most of them hardly more than boys, sat huddled together at tables scattered throughout the room. Waiters lazed idly near a long mahogany bar, testament to the fact that the word *restaurant* was meant as something less than literal, although there were bowls of borscht on several tables, and some unappetizing meat with potatoes that appeared to be the special. Despite evidence of food, vodka was clearly the main course here, bottles littering the tables as if they were upscale water, not ninety-proof diesel fuel.

The only real light came from the doorway, and at the moment Nigel was blocking it, Payton's substantial form filling in the gaps as he watched Nigel's back. Gabe had circled around behind the restaurant in an effort to make certain that all the exits were covered.

Nigel detested walking into a room of unknowns, all of them most likely carrying at least one weapon. It was a recipe for disaster—but then so was pretty much everything he did, and he'd lived to tell about it so far. There wasn't even a guarantee that Jacovitz was here, but the odds were in their favor. Gangsters, especially hit men, had a lot of downtime as a rule. And according to Harrison's intel, this was the place he most often frequented. Not exactly the Metropolitan Club, but then everyone had his own unique tastes.

Nigel's earpiece crackled to life—Gabe signaling that he was in place. With a nod at Payton, Nigel stepped into the shadowy room, his hand resting against the gun he'd stowed in his pocket.

Payton followed, their presence causing a ripple of unease in the crowd. Nigel scanned the faces, looking for one that matched the mug shot they had of Jacovitz. It was hard to tell in this lighting, but no one seemed to fit the bill.

He looked to Payton, who confirmed the fact. Nigel whispered the information into his microphone, and was debating retreat, when he noticed the bartender surreptitiously glancing at a closed door off to the left.

Maybe their quarry was holed up in a private room. Instinct screamed that they'd found their mark.

With a slight movement of his head, Nigel signaled Payton, who followed the line of his gesture to the closed door. His friend nodded in return, his expression grim, his scar making him look deadly in the faded light.

Sizing up the crowd, half of them with their hands conveniently out of sight, Nigel whispered instructions to Gabe and took a step forward, pulling a badge from his left pocket.

"Immigration." His carefully rounded consonants and drawn-out vowels successfully obscured his English accent, leaving him indefinably American. "We're looking for a man named Ivan Jacovitz?" He kept his tone pleasant, but there was an undercurrent that conveyed a completely different message.

Silence reigned, several men reaching for weapons. Payton, however, was ahead of the game as usual, shooting just past the ear of the most aggressive looking of the lot. Hands appeared. Thugs, in most cases, turned to jelly when cornered. It was a rule one could live by. However, there was still the matter of accessing the back room.

"Cat got your tongues?" Nigel smiled, knowing it conveyed little humor. "Too bad. I guess I'll just have to start checking green cards."

Gabe appeared briefly in the hallway leading to the back door, then stepped back again, disappearing into the shadows. Nothing like the element of surprise.

Several of the men were now sending furtive glances in the direction of the closed door.

"Anyone able to help us?" Nigel asked, surveying the room, waiting. Someone here would want out more than he wanted to protect Jacovitz. Nigel counted silently under his breath. One…two…three…four…

"He's in there," a tall, thin man whispered, his accent heavily Slavic. "Behind the door."

"Well done," Nigel said, producing his gun. "And now if you'll all just head for the nearest exit."

Most of the men rushed the exit, anxious to get out of the building before the situation deteriorated any further. Two men remained behind with the bartender, their hastily produced guns making their intentions clear.

"I wouldn't do that." Gabe stepped from the shadows, his gun trained on the biggest of the two. "It'd be a shame to damage the decor."

The man dropped his weapon, slowly raising his hands. Evidently he wasn't fond of the odds. Nigel bent to scoop up the handgun, and Payton motioned the other gunman to follow suit. But evidently he missed the fact that the odds were now three to one, because he fired in Gabe's direction, the shot going wide.

Payton dropped to the ground and fired, his bullet hitting its target, the man dropping before he had time to realize he'd missed. The bartender ran for the door, the unarmed gunman hot on his heels. Nigel made a move to follow but pivoted instead at the sound of the door behind him opening.

The gunfire, or maybe the bartender, had alerted the men inside the other room.

Shots rang out as two men emerged from the doorway, the first dropping to the floor, his cry of agony cut off as he drew his last breath. Nigel trained his gun on the second man, who had hit the floor also, but in defense not pain.

He rolled behind the bar, followed by a third man who slipped through the now-open door. None of them were Jacovitz.

Payton was closest to the door, crouched behind an overturned table, but he was also in the gunmen's direct line of fire. Gabe was about a meter off to Payton's right, behind an old jukebox.

Nigel was the closest to the bar, and with a nod at Gabe to cover him, he ran forward, keeping chairs and tables between himself and the gunmen. A bullet hummed past his ear, embedding itself in the far wall with a satisfying thunk. Better the plaster than his head.

Gabe returned fire, and the diversion worked, one of the gunmen moving around the far end of the bar to get off a shot. Nigel pushed upright and returned fire. The man fell, and for a moment there was silence, then all hell broke loose as the remaining gunman launched himself up and over the bar, the staccato sound of gunfire ringing through the restaurant.

It was over before it began, the second man landing half on, half off the bar in a spray of broken glass. Nigel and Gabe ran for the anteroom door, Payton behind them, only stopping long enough to make sure that the man on the bar was dead.

At first glance the room appeared to be empty, but then Nigel noticed the small window high in one wall. Hanging out of the window, squirming like a stuck pig, was the back half of a man, leather-booted feet moving to an invisible rumba in an attempt to wriggle through the tiny aperture.

Payton and Gabe each took a leg, and in moments, the second half of the man reemerged, the facial features identifying him as Jacovitz.

"Not exactly the most dignified of exits," Nigel said, trying to contain his laughter.

The man hardly looked like an assassin. But then looks were often deceiving. Gabe patted him down, removing not one but three guns, as well as the telltale hunting knife. It seemed the man preferred not to take any chances. Of course, he hadn't counted on Last Chance.

"Why don't you have a seat?" Nigel motioned to an overturned chair.

The Russian righted it and sat down, his expression making sullen appear sunny. "I have nothing to say."

"On the contrary," Nigel said, straddling the chair opposite the man, his easy demeanor intentionally deceptive. "I think you have a great deal to tell us."

The man's eyes narrowed. "I want a lawyer."

"You seem to be under the misapprehension that we're with the police," Payton said, his voice harsh against the quiet of the room.

The man blanched, but his expression remained impassive. "I don't care who you are. I have rights."

"Not with me you don't." Payton moved closer, and the man flinched.

"If I get hurt there will be hell to pay." The man's posturing was almost laughable, but Nigel gave him points for sheer bravado.

"I don't think you'll be caring one way or the other." Gabe obviously wasn't as impressed.

The Russian held Gabe's gaze for about three seconds then looked at the floor. "If I talk I'm a dead man."

Nigel tipped forward on his chair, sensing his advantage. "We're not interested in your organization."

That got Jacovitz's attention. "What do you want then?"

"We're interested in some work you did for a man named Alexi Kirov."

Surprise flashed in the Russian's eyes before he had the opportunity to successfully mask his expression. "I don't know who you're talking about."

"Sure you do," Payton said, cracking his knuckles for effect. "Slimy putz who works for the United Nations?"

"I might have met him," Jacovitz allowed. "It is a small world when you are Russian."

"It's a small world, period. Especially when you choose an identifiable weapon for assassination." Payton held up the hunting knife. "You used this to kill Hakan Celik."

"Why would I be interested in killing a Turk?" The realization of what Jacovitz had said hit about three seconds after the words were out of his mouth.

"We didn't say anything about a Turk."

"But his name…" Jacovitz shrugged in a valiant effort to achieve nonchalance. He failed—miserably.

"Is hardly a giveaway," Nigel finished for him.

The man eyed the three of them, particularly Payton, who was still holding his knife. Finally he blew out a long breath, all attempts at bravado draining away. "So I killed him."

"Why?" Gabe asked.

"For money." The man actually looked surprised, as if everyone traded human life for a bankroll.

"Of course for money," Gabe said, irritation coloring his voice, "but why work with Kirov?"

"We're friends." Again Jacovitz shrugged. "His family

knew mine in the old country. Over the years I help him now and then—for a price." The Russian smiled, a gold tooth glinting in the artificial light.

"Did he tell you why he wanted Celik dead?" Payton turned the knife slightly, the blade pointing at Jacovitz's throat.

"No." The younger man shook his head, his eyes glued to the knife. "Just something about a disagreement. I think this Turk he was working with Alexi on something. But I don't know what it was."

"And the woman?" Nigel asked, his voice cracking on the question, anger simmering just below the surface.

"I do not know what you're talking about."

Payton moved with a speed born of years of training, the knife leaving a bloody scratch along Jacovitz's throat. "Make no mistake, my friend, I have absolutely no reason to keep you alive if you lie to us."

"I never met her," Jacovitz said, rubbing at his throat, his eyes locked on Payton. "Alexi said only that she posed a threat. It was easy enough to frame her. I got what I needed from American CIA."

Gabe frowned. "What are you talking about?"

"Alexi had many friends. One of them was an agent. Ed something. I don't know. He was working with Alexi on something big. At least to hear Alexi tell it."

"And you talked to him."

"If you want to call it talking." The Russian's smile was cocky now. "In reality it was more of a persuasion."

"Where is he now?"

"Somewhere no one will ever find him." The man sat back with a swagger.

"And the poison?" Nigel managed to ask, his finger twitching at the trigger of his gun.

Jacovitz startled at the mention of the word, taking a moment to put it into context. "For the woman? It was enough to kill a cow. She never had a chance."

Nigel's anger fled in the face of his confusion. "You've seen the body?"

"Of course I have," the Russian bragged, but there was still wariness in his eyes.

Payton stabbed the knife on the table, neatly separating the man's index and middle fingers. A millimeter in either direction and a digit would have been severed. "I don't make idle threats, Jacovitz. The truth now, or I promise you'll be favoring your left hand—permanently."

"I have not seen the body. It disappeared. But I tell you there is no way she could have survived the amount of poison she ingested."

Nigel rose from the chair, his rage threatening to consume him. Gabe reached out to stop him, the contact clearing his head. He sank back onto the seat of the chair. "She isn't dead."

The man's reaction was of openmouthed astonishment, which meant that he hadn't known Melissa was alive. And more importantly, he couldn't have been the one shooting at them.

"If you didn't know she was alive, why the double cross?"

Jacovitz's eyebrows drew together in confusion. "I have double-crossed no one." It was a statement of pride. And again there could be no doubting the man's sincerity.

"You didn't kill Alexi?"

"No." The word hung in the room, seeming almost to have a life of its own. "I kill only for money. To do anything else is to risk heart over head."

"Someone could have wanted him out of the equation. Someone with bigger fish to fry?"

"No one. I swear it. The last time I saw Alexi, he was very much alive. He paid me for my work, and was quite jovial about our success."

"Well, he isn't smiling now," Gabe said. "He was shot point-blank with a modified Beretta. Sound familiar?"

"Could be the work of a colleague, but I cannot be sure. There are many such guns in this city."

"That colleague have a name?" Payton asked, still twirling the knife.

"I said before that I will not betray my countrymen."

"You gave up Alexi," Gabe cajoled.

The Russian spit at the floor. "He is, how do you say, bottom-feeder."

"Now there's the pot calling the kettle black," Nigel said to no one in particular.

Gabe leveled his gun. "I'm afraid you've just run out of time, Jacovitz."

The Russian paled and then held up his hands. "His name is Peter Stoeler. I can't say for certain that it was him. But he and Alexi, they have been known to quarrel."

"He works for Alexi, too?"

"Sometimes, yes." Jacovitz shrugged, breathing easier as Gabe released the trigger of the gun.

"Where can we find him?" Payton's eyes narrowed as he watched Jacovitz.

"He is usually here, but I haven't seen him at all today. He lives in a walk-up on Bridgewater. Over the *gastronom.*"

Nigel tightened his hand on his gun, his eyes meeting Gabe's, but his friend shook his head, and Nigel forced himself to relax. He'd like nothing better than to gut the man with his own knife. Payment for the hell he put Melissa through. But alive he could clear her name, and that had to mean something.

Gabe pulled out his cell phone to dial local authorities. Jacovitz took one look at the phone and dived to the floor. He reared back, a second blade flashing in his hand as he aimed for Payton. Fortunately, Nigel was faster, firing a second before the Russian could throw the knife.

Jacovitz grabbed his chest and, with a last slow exhale of breath, died.

Nigel reached down to pick up the fallen knife. "Lovely of you to give me the excuse." He stared at the dead man, wishing he'd caused the bastard a little more pain—for Melissa. Or maybe just for himself.

It was getting harder to separate the two. She was a part of him. There was no denying the fact, and while he might not be capable of giving her the life she deserved, he'd damn well make anyone who threatened her wish they'd never been born.

He walked out of the room, turning his back on the body—case in point.

CHAPTER TWENTY-TWO

"YOU WERE GONE a long time." Malik looked up from the warhead. Parts were spread everywhere, the components waiting to be reassembled into an even more lethal device.

"I ran into some trouble." Khamis threw his jacket and gun on the counter. "Alexi Kirov is dead."

"And that's a problem?"

"No. That was a delight. The man was dangerous to our mission. But with his death I set a trap. A circle that I hoped would lead those seeking answers from the true path."

Malik frowned. "Something went awry?"

"Not in the way you mean. My plan worked perfectly. Except that the hunters were not who I expected."

"You recognized them?" Malik's eyebrows raised in surprise.

"One of them—Melissa Pope."

"So she is not dead."

Khamis nodded, surprised at how calm he felt. "I have seen the man she was with before, as well. I believe he works for the British. But I cannot be sure. I have contacted Bashir to find out if I am right. But until we know for certain, we must tread carefully."

"Should we call off the operation?"

"No. We are too close to success, and I have faith in my ability to mislead. My clues will lead them in circles. Far away from us."

"Arrogance is a dangerous thing, my friend. You are certain you are not underestimating their abilities?"

"I am not discounting anything. That is why I maneuvered things so that the Russians will be blamed. And it has played out even better than I had supposed. Kirov must have arranged for someone to hunt for the missing Ms. Pope. He was there at the apartment shooting at her."

"I take it he had no success."

"Let us just say he is no longer a threat to anyone."

"But surely it would have been better—"

Khamis waved a hand, cutting his friend off. "By the time they work out what has truly happened, it will be too late."

He stood at the window of the apartment, looking down at the passersby. It was a quiet street, but still it was full of people. New York was like a living thing, vile and always hungry. It would be a pleasure to bring it to its knees. "Why are you taking so long?" He turned back to face Malik, who was carefully constructing the components of the warhead.

"Some things cannot be rushed." Malik didn't bother to look up from the wires he was separating. "If I allowed your frustration to affect my work, we would soon be worth nothing to our cause. Besides, I will be finished soon. You have made all the other arrangements?"

Khamis nodded. "Everything is in place. I have secured the necessary disguises." He motioned toward a uniform hanging on a closet door.

"And our escape?" Malik's interest was only passing, his attention centered on placing a laser grid over the device.

"I have secured tickets for you. First class." Khamis dropped the envelope on the table. "You will be traveling under an assumed name, of course."

Malik glanced at the ticket, puzzled. "You are not leaving with me?"

"No." He shook his head to underscore the point. "I want

you gone before the device is put into place. That way there will be no way to trace you to the source."

"But we agreed to see this through together."

"I cannot ask you to sacrifice your life, my friend. There is too much talent in those hands. Our people need you."

"But surely they need you, as well?" Malik laid down a pair of jeweler's pliers.

"Perhaps." Khamis shrugged.

"You must be gone before my device detonates." Malik's expression reflected concern and fear.

"I will be gone. Do not concern yourself. If all goes well, I have every intention of being far away from the seat of the explosion. But I will not be traveling by such luxurious means." He tilted his head toward the tickets. "I cannot risk being detected so close to detonation. So, I will avoid the usual methods of travel. As the warheads came in—so shall I go out."

Malik opened his mouth to say more, but evidently recognized the pointlessness of arguing.

"I promise you, my friend," Khamis said, "I will not place myself in harm's way unless it is absolutely necessary."

"I know that we are asked to sacrifice everything for the glory of Allah—" Malik's dark eyes were full of resolve "—but I do not want to lose you, too."

"Please understand, if I must die in order to secure our success, I will consider it an honor. We're so close to everything we've been working for, we must not fail now—no matter the cost."

"Sometimes the cost is too high." Malik sighed, then reached for the pliers.

"Not in this case, and if I must give my life to achieve our goal, then so be it."

"It is your goal, Khamis. Not mine."

"You do not mean that. This has been your dream, too."

"No." Malik shook his head. "I merely followed the orders of our superiors, hoping that Allah will bless me for my obedience."

"There is more to it than that, surely?" Khamis turned back to the window, his mind's eye replaying the fires and explosions, long-faded screams echoing in his ears.

"Perhaps if I look into the darkest corners of my heart, I, too, would find the desire for revenge. What hurts you, hurts me, and yet it is not the same. It was not my wife and children who were lost."

"No. It was not. But still they were your friends—your family."

He had known Malik since boyhood, their families close friends. It had been Malik who had urged him to make Kerea his wife. Malik who had celebrated the birth of each of his sons. They had joked that it was the beginning of a dynasty.

And then in one instant, everything was gone.

"Of course they were special to me. Why do you think that I have helped you hunt the people responsible for Kerea and the children's deaths? I care. But revenge is a double-edged sword."

"Revenge is righteous. And I will have mine or die trying." Khamis clenched his fists, fighting against his pain.

"Then may Allah be with you."

"And where was He on the day my family was slaughtered?" Khamis rounded on his friend, anger whipping through him like blowing sand upon a rock. But as quickly as it had come, it dissipated, leaving him empty inside. Malik was not the enemy. "I'm sorry. I didn't mean that. It's just that sometimes it seems too much to bear. When I close my eyes, I can see them, Malik. Hear their screams. Hassan was only three, Najid six. They were babies. Innocents. And they were slaughtered without a second thought."

"I share your pain, but you are not being honest with yourself. You brought them to the training camp, Khamis, even though you knew it to be dangerous."

"If it had not been for the American spying, the camp would have been safe. It was that information that caused the destruction of my family."

"You have no proof."

"Not before, no." Khamis narrowed his eyes, holding his anger close. "But Alexi Kirov confirmed it. I was right all along. Only when I have avenged my family can they rest in peace."

"Perhaps it is you who need peace."

"Believe me, there is no possibility of that." He shrugged. "So instead, why don't you give me the gift of making that thing work?"

Malik picked up the pliers again. "That will not be a problem. I can do this in my sleep."

"I pray that you do not, considering the repercussions should you make a mistake."

"Either way—" it was Malik's turn to shrug "—infidels will die. Isn't that the point?"

"Yes. But if we follow the plan, success will be all the sweeter."

Malik nodded, edging a metal container carefully into place, his attention returning to the work at hand. Khamis turned back to the window and the people walking below. One more day and the world would bow to him. He alone held the power to control a nation. Perhaps Allah had not forgotten him after all.

"SO THE BOTTOM LINE IS that you found the man who could prove that Melissa was framed and then you killed him?" Cullen asked, the muscle ticking in his jaw the only physical sign of his displeasure.

It was late, the fire in the study nearly gutted, but Cullen had just flown in from the city and demanded an update. The job had fallen to Nigel, Harrison and Melissa, the three of them having the misfortune of being the only ones left awake.

Sam and Payton had adjourned almost immediately after the men had returned from Brighton Beach, with Gabe and Madison excusing themselves a short while later. Melissa understood their need to be alone, to reaffirm that everything was still all right. Moments held against the day when quite possibly things wouldn't end as well.

She understood the need, and at a certain level, she envied the fact that they could so easily surrender to it. But she'd made her own bed, so to speak, and the reality was, she was happy with it. Or she had been—until Nigel had walked back into her life.

"If he hadn't killed the man," Harrison said, his eyes uncharacteristically cold, "Payton would be dead."

Melissa shivered at the thought, her mind's eye seeing not Payton but Nigel lying in a pool of blood. Determinedly she shook off the image, forcing herself to concentrate on the conversation around her.

"I acted in the moment." Nigel's grimace was indication of the strain of the day, and Melissa wanted nothing more than to ease his pain, but despite her desire, it was clearly not the time or place to do so. "Anyway, Cullen, the point is that we now know for certain that Melissa didn't kill anyone."

"But you haven't got any physical proof," Cullen said, driving home the obvious. "And unfortunately your word isn't likely to go very far in proving her innocence."

"Well, at least there's three of us."

"True enough." Cullen nodded. "But I'd feel better if we had something irrefutable."

"It's quite possible that we will," Harrison interjected. "We've got Jacovitz's knife, remember? If Tracy can tie it to Celik's wound, then that should be the ball game."

"And there's always a chance that Tracy's folks will turn up something at Jacovitz's apartment," Melissa added hopefully.

"Absolutely," Nigel concurred. "The man didn't strike me as the overly cautious type. With any luck the box of rat poison will be sitting under his sink."

"We'll keep a positive thought." Cullen shrugged with a frown. "But don't forget we've still got Kirov's murder."

"Well, I hardly could have been responsible for that one, Cullen." Anger flashed, heat staining the back of Melissa's neck.

"I didn't mean to imply that you were. But the fact that he's dead leaves us with a lot of unanswered questions. Specifically, how the hell this all ties together. Basically, we have a dead man we believe was using UN transports to aid black-market and terrorist operations, a second man, also conveniently dead, who is purported to have worked with Kirov, and now a dead member of the Russian mafia who claims to have killed Celik but not Kirov. And then as if matters aren't complicated enough, Melissa could very well still be in danger, and we haven't a clue where the danger is coming from."

"Well, if the threat originated with Alexi, then maybe she's safe," Harrison said.

"You're forgetting that someone tried to kill us today, and that Jacovitz swore it wasn't him." Nigel's tone was even more clipped than usual.

"So maybe Alexi was working with someone else? Someone who knew that Melissa had been sniffing around, and is equally interested in taking her out of the equation." Cullen frowned, obviously trying to assemble the pieces into some sort of recognizable pattern.

"But why would he have been working with two different people?" Melissa frowned.

"Maybe because his first flunky screwed up and left you alive." Nigel walked over to the drinks table and poured a bourbon. If it hadn't been for the muscle ticking at his jaw, Melissa would have thought he was talking about a stranger.

"Well, if Jacovitz is to be believed, it was your handler who gave you up." Harrison grabbed the poker and prodded the dying fire.

"For a price," Melissa said, shivering at the thought. "Jacovitz said he was dead, right?"

Nigel nodded, his expression if possible even more grim. "These guys were definitely playing for keeps."

"But none of this explains why Kirov was murdered." Cullen settled on the back of the sofa, opening and closing his fists reflexively. "I mean, if it was his operation, what motive is there for someone to take him out?"

"Maybe he double-crossed the mob." Harrison hung the poker on its hook and turned back to face them again. "Jacovitz seemed to think this Stoeler guy could have been involved."

"Did you find anything at his apartment?" Cullen asked.

"Nothing conclusive. But we did find ammo that matches the caliber used to kill Kirov. Without a weapon Tracy can't do much with it. But at least we can keep him in the running."

"Any sign of the man?" Cullen shifted, his eyes narrowing in thought.

"None at all. Tracy's people are canvassing the building. But there are only a couple of apartments above a grocery. All occupied by Russians. I doubt we're going to find the neighbors all that helpful."

"And thanks to your handiwork, Jacovitz won't be able to provide any further information. So we're potentially at a dead end." Cullen stood up. "What about Khamis? Anything there?"

"No link to the Russian mob, if that's what you're asking," Harrison said.

"And Kirov?" Cullen was like a bulldog, completely unable to let go of something until he'd talked it to death.

Melissa fought against her exhaustion, more than aware that she owed this man her life. If he hadn't opened the doors to his safe house, she'd have been handling this on her own.

"There's nothing to connect the two of them at this point," Nigel said, the muscle in his jaw still twitching.

"If there's a connection, I'll find it," Harrison said. "We've briefed the UN on a need-to-know basis, and in light of the threat, they're supposed to be sending me access codes to the Peacekeeping database. From there I'll be able to tap directly into Kirov's computer and the shipments he was handling. Hopefully there'll be something that will help us isolate an anomaly in one of the shipments. Something that could lead to recovery of the R-VX. Or if not, at least give us a heads-up as to where it might have entered the U.S."

"Timing is everything," Nigel said, the statement echoing all of their thoughts.

"It's never too late." Harrison's expression was a reflection of his usual optimism, but there was a shadow of doubt in his eyes. "Look, all we can do is give it our best. And to that end, if you'll excuse me, I'll head back in there and see if the UN has sent the codes."

"And if they haven't?" Cullen asked.

"There's always more than one way to peel an apple. I've also got the computer searching various databases using photos of our key players. It's possible that if they've used an alias, face-recognition technology can find them and provide us with new information."

"By all means, get to it." Cullen made a shooing motion toward the door. "The more connections we establish, the quicker we can fill in the pieces of the puzzle. I'll expect a full report in the morning."

Despite herself, Melissa smiled. Cullen definitely had a God complex, but he also had a paternal streak a mile wide. He might be angry that they weren't moving fast enough, but if anyone else dared to criticize the team, he'd be on them like a rottweiler on fresh meat.

"I think maybe I'll call it a night, too. I still need to check in with the White House." He nodded absently first in Nigel's direction and then in Melissa's, his mind already contemplating what he wanted to say to the President. "You two try and get some sleep."

Melissa turned to face the fire, trying to sort through her

jumbled feelings. Everything was so damn complicated. On the one hand she wanted nothing more than to be alone with Nigel. On the other, she was wishing herself at the opposite end of the planet.

Nice dichotomy.

"Hell of a day." Nigel's breath was warm against her skin. As usual he'd moved in silence.

She turned to face him, taking a step closer to the fire in an effort to keep distance between them. It was hard enough to think without him complicating matters by literally breathing down her neck. "I think we can safely say it wasn't boring."

"You all right?" His eyes echoed his concern.

"Actually, I was thinking earlier that in a perverted kind of way, today was fun." He opened his mouth to protest, and she smiled. "I don't mean that I enjoyed getting shot at. I just mean that it was nice to be back in action. Not just sitting on the sidelines waiting for someone else to save the day."

His answering smile was tempered with worry. "You could have been killed."

"So could you," she retorted, determined to keep things on an even footing. "Twice. But it's part of what we do, remember? And I for one prefer offense to defense any day, even if it means ducking a few bullets."

"I know." His sigh said more than words could possibly express, and Melissa felt her heart twist. "I can't deny that I feel any differently, but it's so bloody hard when the risks you take affect someone you care about."

There it was right out in the open. The question, of course, being what the hell they were going to do about it.

Silence hung heavy for a moment, neither of them willing to look the other in the eye. Then Nigel blew out a breath. "I shouldn't have let you come today."

"You didn't *let* me do anything." She kept her voice even, trying not to read things into his words that weren't there. But it was hard. "It was my choice to make."

"I know that, but if I hadn't brought you here, there wouldn't have been a choice."

She hated the sound of regret in his voice, hated the fact that she'd put him in this position. This, along with a million other reasons, was why she'd walked out all those years ago. "I called you, remember?" Her attempt at a smile fell flat. "You were my best bet. I needed help and you offered it. And all this was part of the package." She waved a hand at the cozy study.

"So what was I, just an added bonus?" There was a trace of bitterness in his voice she couldn't ignore.

"Of course not. But it isn't as simple as you're making it."

"We make of situations what we want, Melissa. You know that as well as I do."

"So now you're dispensing pseudopsychology? Relationships take work. Lots of it. And the primary requirement, as far as I can tell, is that the people involved be present a majority of the time. That isn't us, Nigel, and you know it."

"So where do we go from here?" He looked so sad, so uncertain.

She wanted to wrap her arms around him and tell him it would be all right. But it wouldn't. That was the crux of the problem. One or both of them was always going to be walking the line. And she simply wasn't up to taking the chance. She'd lost too much already, and she couldn't bear the idea of losing anything more—especially Nigel.

Better to keep her heart sequestered.

"Surely we can operate on a professional level. At least until we find the R-VX and figure out how all of it interrelates."

"And once everything is tied up with a neat little bow? What then?"

"We walk away." The words came out of their own accord, and the instant they were out she wished them back. Not because they weren't true, but because they sounded so final.

"Again." Nigel shook his head as if he couldn't quite make

himself accept the reality. But she could see in his eyes that he knew she was right.

She nodded. “I don’t see an alternative. Neither of us is going to retire, and neither of us can afford the risk of an entanglement. The cost would simply be too high.”

He opened his mouth to argue, but then changed his mind, his expression hardening. “I suppose you’re right. There’s no sense in starting something we can’t finish.”

She hated the fact that she’d killed the hope in his eyes, but she knew that eventually he’d have gotten there on his own. It was better that she did it now, before it could possibly hurt any worse than it already did.

She stared down at her hands, trying to think of something to say. Words that would make their parting easier. Make their working together less stressful. But nothing came to mind. She should have stopped things last night. Fought against feelings she knew couldn’t possibly last, but when she was with him it was so easy to forget all of that. To believe, if only for an instant, that there were happily ever afters.

“I’m sorry, I…” She looked up, still not certain what it was she wanted to say, but it was too late.

Nigel was gone.

CHAPTER TWENTY-THREE

PART OF HIM WANTED to smash the whiskey bottle against the wall, and another part of him insisted that it would be better to drain the thing first, while still another part of him—the part that carried his father's genes, no doubt—was reciting the disadvantages of ruining Cullen's priceless Oriental wallpaper.

So instead Nigel opted for pouring a measure of bourbon into a glass, removing himself from further temptation. Women were pains in the asses. At least one of them was. He settled into a wing chair by the fire.

The library was smaller than Cullen's study, but no less luxuriously appointed. First editions lined three walls, the fourth dominated by a massive fireplace that had to have been brought, stone by stone, from some Anglican stronghold. The room and all its opulence reminded Nigel of Laversham, and despite the fact that he usually avoided all thoughts of home, at the moment the surroundings brought a decided degree of comfort. At least things there were predictable. Unless of course Andrew was around.

He smiled, thinking of his brother. Although Andrew was considered the black sheep of the family with his tabloid exploits, Nigel sometimes wondered if his little brother wasn't by far the more normal of the two. At least he seemed content with his place in life.

Which was more than Nigel could say.

He lifted the glass, the desire to smash the Baccarat returning with a vengeance.

"Not usually the best way to solve problems." Madison stood near the doorway, a crooked smile lighting her face. "Besides, Cullen would have a fit."

Nigel lowered the glass with a sigh. "I wasn't really going to throw it."

"Right." Madison walked in to sit down in the leather chair opposite him. "So we'll just ignore my fortuitous timing. Thinking about the case, or has a certain redhead got you down?"

He started to lie and then thought better of it. Madison would see through him anyway. "Definitely the latter. I was lamenting the fact that I don't seem to know one bloody thing about women."

"I sincerely doubt that that's true. Can I have some of that?" She nodded toward the decanter of bourbon and Nigel obligingly filled a glass.

"So what are you doing up? I hardly think *you're* having relationship troubles."

"Well, not the sort you're thinking of anyway," Madison said, taking the glass. "I'm afraid I'm having serious munchkin withdrawal."

"Andrea."

"Yeah. I hadn't planned to be away this long. And despite the fact that Gabe did his best to relax me—" her grin was coy "—I'm still awake."

"And still missing your baby."

"Exactly." She took a sip. "Which is why I'm leaving in the morning. I hate to be a party pooper, but I think you all can handle this one on your own. Anything you need from me can be done by cell phone."

"You're leaving New York?"

Madison shrugged. "Seems prudent. We've got a cabin in Pennsylvania. We'll go there."

"Babies change everything." Nigel stared down into his drink, not certain to whom exactly he was addressing the statement.

"For the better."

"I know that." He looked up to meet Madison's somber gaze. "I knew it the instant I first held Andrea, and she isn't even mine. I admire you for what you're doing."

"Being a mother?" She paused, sipping from her glass, considering his words. "It's nothing out of the ordinary. More like the natural order of things."

"But you're able to put her needs above all else, and give up anything that gets in the way of that. Gabe would do the same."

"I suppose he would. But again, it wasn't much of a sacrifice. You'll understand someday when you have children."

"Somehow I don't think that's in the cards." He was back to staring into the amber depths of the bourbon. "Some people just aren't father material."

"Some people maybe," Madison agreed. "But not you. You'd be an amazing dad, Nigel. No question about it."

"But I haven't any of the skills, and I hardly lead a life suitable for child rearing."

"And I do?" Madison laughed. "Look, Andrea is Gabe's and my life now, granted. But that doesn't mean either of us has had to sacrifice ourselves. We still do what we love, we just make sure to keep family first."

"I've never had a family. At least not that kind. My father was more inclined to entertain the Queen than he was to have a meal with his children. We were to be seen and not heard, our only use our guarantee that the illustrious line of Laversham would continue on."

"My family wasn't all that normal, either." Madison set her glass down on the table. "You've met my father. He's not exactly *Father Knows Best* material. It isn't about where we've come from. It's about where we're going."

"I'm going nowhere fast, apparently. At least if Melissa has anything to do with it."

"And so we reach the crux of the problem." Her knowing eyes were assessing.

"She doesn't want me, Madison. It's as simple as that."

"Nothing is ever truly simple, Nigel. Especially where matters of the heart are concerned. Melissa has issues, but they aren't with you."

"Been doing a little profiling, have you?"

"Occupational hazard," she said with a laugh. "I can't help myself."

"So if her issues aren't with me, then who are they with?" Nigel sat forward, not sure exactly what to expect. "The boyfriends of Christmas past?"

"If you want my honest opinion, I don't think there have been any others, Christmas or otherwise. I think Melissa fell in love with you all those years ago in Italy."

"Right. And that would explain why she walked away without so much as a backward glance."

"It hurt you. I know that. But it hurt her, too."

"And I'm supposed to believe that because..." He let the words hang, reaching over to refill his glass.

"How much do you know about her past?"

"Melissa's?" He thought back on what she'd told him. "Her parents are gone. I think her mother died. She and Alicia are close." He shook his head. "I don't think she really said much more than that."

"Her father ran out on her when she was almost twelve. Alicia was eleven. Then three years later her mother died."

"I remember," Nigel said, "they went to live with an aunt. Right?"

"Yes. But the woman wasn't interested in children, especially girls. Melissa was the one who looked out for her sister when the aunt found a new husband and kicked the girls out of the house. The girls wound up in Austin, where Melissa worked two jobs to get them both through school."

"She's an amazing woman. But then I've always known that."

"You're missing the point." Madison's smile was tolerant, as if she were speaking to a slow learner. "Melissa has spent her whole life losing people she loved. First her father, then her mother and then her aunt. None of them leaving for the same reason, but all of them nevertheless bowing out just when she needed them most."

"What about Alicia? She's always had her sister."

"More or less, but in Melissa's mind I think she sees Alicia's marriage as another betrayal. Not that she begrudges her sister's happiness. More that she feels it's a withdrawal. A shift of loyalties if you will."

"But I don't see—" he began, but Madison waved him quiet.

"She ran out on you, Nigel, because she was afraid. Then and now. She believes that if she gives you her heart there will come a day when you'll give it back."

"But I'd never do that."

"You might not do it purposefully, but given the way you live your life, it's a distinct possibility that something could happen to you, and Melissa would lose you, even if through no fault of your own."

"But everyone runs those kinds of risks. Granted, some more than others. But still, isn't it worth the effort?"

Madison smiled. "So why are you sitting here?"

"Oh, bloody hell." He couldn't help his grin. "You haven't just been talking about Melissa's fears, have you?"

"Not all people are attracted to opposites, Nigel. Likes can also attract."

"But she told me in no uncertain terms that there couldn't be a future between us."

"And you're going to accept that? Let her make the decisions for both of you? Sometimes when someone runs away it's because they desperately want to be found."

"But she didn't run this time."

"Maybe not physically, but there are all kinds of running. Look, I don't mean to play Dr. Phil here, but get off your butt and go after her. What the hell are you waiting for? Fate's given you a second chance—take advantage of the fact. Don't let her go without a fight."

"But what if she's right? What if something does happen?"

"Then at least you'll have had whatever time there was. Life isn't about guarantees. It's about taking chances. So..." She inclined her head toward the door. "Go."

IF SHE WAS so all-fired certain about what it was she wanted in life, why the hell didn't she feel relieved? She'd nipped the problem in the bud, but instead of getting a good night's sleep, Melissa was standing at the window staring out at the night, wishing Nigel would materialize out of the mist.

Silly notion.

She was acting like a moonstruck adolescent.

She turned away from the window to the fire, the heat sending shards of memory slicing through her. Everything in the room reminded her of Nigel. The bed, the fire, the chair. God, she wanted him.

More than she'd have believed possible. But then she also wanted a gallon of Ben & Jerry's fudge brownie ice cream and she wasn't acting on that fantasy, either. Best to stick to safer harbors.

She sat down on the bed, staring at the flames, little pops and hisses breaking through the silence filling the room, giving an air, at least, of comfort. Last night she'd reached out for happiness, and barely twenty-four hours later she'd thrown it all out the window.

Her head was high-fiving with self-satisfaction, but her heart wasn't so certain. Maybe some risks were worth taking. She lived every day in the moment professionally. So why not live that way in her private life? So what if there could be nothing permanent between her and Nigel? She had now. Most people weren't even afforded that much.

She was cutting her nose off to spite her face, for fear of crossing a bridge she hadn't even reached yet. And apparently she was also the queen of the cliché. Smiling at her silly ruminations, she stood up, blowing out a breath and squaring her shoulders. Sometimes you just had to damn the logic and jump off the cliff.

Of course, that could hurt like hell.

She shook her head, cutting off the monologue. If she wanted any peace at all, she needed to find Nigel. To prove to him that she wasn't running away. Nothing had really changed. They still didn't have a future, but that didn't mean they couldn't at least enjoy the moment. Right?

With a sigh she reached for the doorknob, surprised when it turned in her hand. She jumped back as the door swung open, wishing she had the gun she'd taken from Cullen. This was supposed to be a safe house, but what the hell did she really know about any of them?

"I didn't mean to frighten you." Nigel stood in the doorway, his expression resolute. "It's just that you had your say, and now I want mine."

She opened her mouth to respond, but he shook his head, raising a hand to silence her.

"My turn."

She nodded and sank down on the end of the bed, her heart pounding for reasons she wasn't quite ready to acknowledge.

"I heard what you said earlier. Every word of it." His face tightened with the memory. "And for about an hour I bought into it. You're right, people in our line of work exist from minute to minute. Never really knowing what's going to happen next, or if we'll come out of it all in one piece. But just because we've chosen to live on the edge doesn't mean we're not allowed to be happy, to find peace wherever it might present itself. I don't believe that. If I did, I couldn't have fallen in love with you all those years ago." He sucked in a breath, his gaze colliding with hers. "I couldn't love you now. It's as simple as that. And I'll be damned if I'll just let you walk away without a fight."

Melissa stood up, joy and terror shooting through her in equal measures. "What did you say?"

"That I'm going to fight for us."

"No." Her voice came out on a tortured whisper. "Before that."

"I said that I love you." Nigel closed the distance between them, his hands on her shoulders, the heat in his eyes threatening to envelop her. "I can't promise you a future. Hell, I can't even promise you a present. But I know how I feel, and it's not something to be thrown out with the trash just because I'm afraid."

"You're afraid?" The idea seemed ludicrous. Nigel was the strongest person she knew.

"More than I've ever been in my life. But I can't let that be an excuse for losing you. Not if you feel the same way that I do." He waited, his eyes searching.

She licked her lips, her brain urging denial, but lying wasn't her style. "I don't know what I feel, Nigel." His jaw tightened, and she reached up to caress his face. "I'm not saying this right. I mean that I haven't ever felt this way about anyone before. I can't put a label on it. Not easily. But I can't imagine walking away from you now and never feeling like this again."

"So don't walk."

If only it were that simple. But then again maybe it was.

She stepped into his embrace, tipping her head back, offering him more than just her lips. "I'm here."

"I need more than that. I need to know where you'll be tomorrow."

"In bed with you?" She hadn't meant for it to be a question, but some part of her still wasn't sure, her fear threatening to consume everything that she wanted.

"That's a given." His smile didn't quite reach his eyes. "But it's your heart I'm worried about, not your body."

"I can't promise something I don't even understand myself. You of all people should understand that."

"I know that I'm tired of waking up alone. And if you'll give me the chance, I want to prove that I'm worth sticking around for." His vulnerability humbled her.

"Oh, Nigel," she said. "I've never questioned *you.* It's me I don't trust. I'm the one who's likely to run for the hills. And believe me, it has nothing at all to do with you."

"Then maybe I just need to hold you tighter." His arms closed around her, underscoring his words with searing intensity.

She released a breath, trembling beneath his touch. "I think that's a wonderful idea."

They stood for a moment more, linked by the heat of their bodies and the desperation of their need. In her whole life, she'd never needed anyone the way she did Nigel. And the intervening years between their meeting and reuniting seemed only to have cemented the bond.

She hadn't ever believed that a man and a woman could truly be fated—until now. And the thought made her shudder with possibility and fear. If she was wrong…

But she wasn't the kind of woman to live her life on regret. Nigel was here *now.* And she'd be a fool to turn her back on the one thing that made her feel whole. There would be consequences to pay. Of that she had no doubt. But she couldn't walk away. It was as simple as that.

"Kiss me." Her whispered words were more than an invitation. They signaled surrender. Wherever they went next, they'd go together. The decision was made and there would be no turning back.

He groaned and pulled her hard against him, his kiss possessive. His hands traced the contour of her back and butt, each stroke sending pleasure rocketing through her. She thrust her tongue against his, the taste of him exotic and familiar at the same time.

She pressed closer, reveling in the sensation of their bodies writhing together, pleasure in every undulating move.

Theirs was a dance older than time, the need to become one driving every move, every thought. Only with this man could she truly be whole.

He pulled back her shirt, mindless of the popping buttons, and she smiled, enjoying his frenzy—his need. Her breasts bared, she delighted in the friction of their movement against his chest, her nipples tightening into hot points of desire. As if sensing her need, he dipped his head, closing his teeth on one pulsing nipple, his playful nips sending streaks of heat racing through her abdomen to ignite an unquenchable ball of fire deep inside her.

He bit harder, and she arched against him, wanting more. Wanting him.

Fumbling with buttons and zippers, they moved backward toward the bed, each intent on stripping away all physical barriers. Finally naked, they stopped, content for the moment to rejoice in the fact that they were together, linked body to body—soul to soul.

Then need overcame emotion and Nigel pulled her up into his arms and laid her on the bed. For a moment she stared up at him, joy cascading through her with the strength of an orgasm. Then he was there, his body covering hers, propped on his elbows as he looked down into her eyes.

"You're sure?"

The question went much further than sex.

This was about commitment. They'd made no promises, but the covenant was there nevertheless. Spoken from the heart, she couldn't ignore it and she couldn't deny it, no matter what her rational mind was screaming.

He waited, his eyes shadowed with a vulnerability she recognized and cherished. She knew what it was like to always be on the outside looking in. Knew how it felt to be alone in a world full of people. And suddenly here in this room, she was certain that she'd never be alone again. If only she had the courage to seize the moment.

"I'm sure."

Nigel smiled then, shadows vanquished, and bent down to kiss her, his lips brushing hers with a touch of reverence. As if he was afraid of breaking her, of breaking the fragile bond they had just forged.

But if time couldn't take away the power of their connection, then neither could fear, and Melissa wanted more. Rolling so that she straddled him, it was her turn to tease and explore, her hands and her mouth tracing the lines of his hard body. There were scars, more than she could count. Reminders of the harsh life he led.

She kissed each in turn, soothing and exciting all at the same time. Wanting to know every inch of him. Needing to understand where he'd been, the man he'd become—the past and present blending together into one reality.

She tasted all his secret places, delighting in the feel of his skin against hers, the smell of his body as it mingled with her own scent to create something new and enticing. She circled his penis with her tongue, loving its velvety strength, and then sucked gently, delighting at his immediate response.

With a groan, he pulled her up, their bodies sliding together with exquisite friction, and then he flipped her over, his smile wicked now, his eyes burning with a passion she knew was reflected on her own face.

He kissed the soft skin at the base of her throat, and then traced a fiery line along her shoulder, then downward to the curve of her breast. Laving first one nipple and then the other, he sucked until she squirmed beneath him, her body arching upward, wanting him inside her—part of her.

Instead he let his mouth trail lower, his fingers still massaging her breasts. He kissed the soft skin of her inner thighs, his mouth teasing her, the white-hot spiral of desire ratcheting tighter with each stroke, each touch. She bucked against him, not certain whether she wanted to retreat or attack.

But he held her firm, allowing no rebellion, as his tongue

finally found home, flicking over her sensitive skin, driving her closer and closer to the edge. Sucking in a breath, she summoned her strength, and with a move worthy of a ninja, she managed to slide beneath him, hip to hip, his penis hot against her thigh.

"Now," she whispered. "Take me now."

His smile was answer enough, and in one amazing moment of heaven, he was inside her, each thrust deeper and stronger than the last. She moved against him, finding the rhythm, her body giving and taking as they moved together—strength against strength. Two halves of one whole.

And then there was no coherent thought. Just blinding sensation, far beyond pleasure or pain. The two of them joined as one, suspended amidst shattering brightness and consuming joy.

KHAMIS STOOD by the window looking out at the moon. The cold wash of light heightened the shadows, illuminating nothing. He had awoken from the nightmare bathed in sweat, his breathing labored, the pain almost beyond bearing. In his dream, Kerea had come to him, her dark eyes soft with passion, her lips full and moist. He had reached for her, his heart rejoicing in her presence, but as always, before he could touch her, she faded away. The shadows consumed her even as the heat of the bombs exploded around him.

Kerea was gone. He would never kiss her again. Never hold her trembling, warm body beneath his. He would never hold his sons. Never carry them high upon his shoulders. Never teach them to become men.

Everything was gone but the pain.

He leaned his forehead against the cold window glass, his mind lost in the past, lost in his pain. In one moment of betrayal, she had taken everything from him. His family, his life, his soul.

And by the cold heartless light of the moon, he swore again his revenge. An eye for an eye. What he had suffered she would suffer, too. By all that was holy, Melissa Pope would pay.

CHAPTER TWENTY-FOUR

BREAKFAST WAS a grand affair at Cullen's safe house, a buffet to fit a king served daily, complete with three kinds of eggs, steak, ham and biscuits so light Melissa would have sworn the cook was Southern. This morning she felt particularly hungry, due in no small part to the fact that Nigel had kept her up most of the night. Not that she was complaining.

"Sleep well?" Sam slipped in beside Melissa, helping herself to a generous portion of scrambled eggs.

"Fine." Melissa shot a sideways look at the other woman, trying to see if there was more to her comment than just a surface greeting. But Sam was reaching for bacon, her face devoid of any innuendo. "Or at least as well as can be expected under the circumstances."

"I can understand that. Standing knee-deep in alligators isn't exactly sleep inducing."

Melissa glanced over at Nigel, who was in deep discussion with Payton and Cullen, the latter waving his hands to emphasize whatever it was he was telling them. "I shouldn't have gotten you all involved in this."

Despite last night's reprieve, there was still the small matter of someone out there wanting her dead, and someone else walking around with enough R-VX to take out New York City. Even if she managed to escape the one, there was every reason to believe she'd be killed by the other.

But in all honesty, what scared her more was the possibility that Nigel would get caught in the cross fire. That by coming back into his life, she'd pulled him into the sights of a killer.

"There's nothing you could have done that would have made him walk away." Sam, it seemed, was channeling Madison.

"I could have resisted the urge to call him."

"No, you couldn't." Sam's eyes were kind. "I've stood in your shoes, believe me. And the good news is that Payton and I both lived to tell about it."

Sam grabbed a muffin and, without another word, headed off toward the dining room table, taking a seat next to Payton. Melissa watched as he absently drew Sam into the circle of his arm, effortlessly including her in his conversation. That's what Melissa wanted. What she'd yearned for most of her life. She wanted to fit.

To belong.

As if he'd heard her thoughts, Nigel looked up with a smile, his dark eyes devouring her in one slow sweep. He tipped his head toward the chair next to his, gesturing her over with a hand, his smile for her alone.

Secure in the intimacy of the moment, she walked to the table and sat down, realizing that she was no longer outside looking in. Despite all the evidence that had been stacked against her, this group of hardened operatives had persevered to prove her innocence. They'd done it for Nigel, there could be no question of that, but they'd accepted her in the process, and there was something humbling about the idea. Something powerful enough to break through the defenses she'd worked so hard to build.

Maybe there was hope. But before she could possibly consider the idea, she needed to find out who was hunting her—and why.

"So where are we?" Melissa asked, pushing all emotion aside to address the group at the table. "Anything on Alexi's shipments?"

"Harrison is working on it as we speak," Cullen said. "We've been talking about Khamis."

"Did you connect him to Alexi?" she asked, taking a sip of her juice.

"No. There's no intel to support any kind of relationship between the two men. In fact, at least on the surface, they had no commonality at all," Payton said.

"What Payton's dancing around, Melissa, is that Khamis apparently has a tie to you." Cullen's words cut through her with the surgical precision of a scalpel, her earlier thoughts of acceptance threatening to hemorrhage away.

"I've never met the man." She flinched at Nigel's touch, suddenly feeling as if she'd been ambushed.

"No one is saying that," he assured her, his tone placating.

"Then what are you saying?" She turned to him, trying to contain her anger.

"Khamis al-Rashid lived in Afghanistan, Melissa." Madison stood in the doorway of the dining room, her expression full of concern.

"I thought you were going home?" Gabe asked with a frown.

"I am." Madison's smile was gentle. "But I thought I'd hang around to be sure that Melissa was okay first."

"But I don't understand," Melissa said, trying to understand the importance of what they were telling her.

"His primary residence was an Islamic training camp in the mountains." She paused, her gaze holding Melissa's. "It was about three clicks north of Abu Khabab."

"But that was the camp I infiltrated."

Madison nodded. "Khamis's family was killed in the subsequent raid. His wife and two boys."

"Oh, my God." Melissa closed her eyes, her mind trotting out images of the children she'd seen running around the camp, some of them barely more than babies.

"They knew what they were doing," Nigel whispered, his hand on her thigh.

"No, they didn't," she said, pushing away from the table, all thoughts of breakfast evaporating. "Maybe their parents knew. But the children didn't."

"The price of war is always high, Melissa." Payton's tone was quiet but there was authority there.

"I know. I just haven't had it hit me in the face before." She walked over to the window, staring out at the golden fall sunshine. "How old were his sons?"

"Three and six." Cullen's voice held a surprising degree of compassion.

"They were just babies." She gripped the windowsill, trying to sort through her rushing emotions.

"Whose parents were training to be killers," Gabe said, his tone bordering on fierce.

"The sins of the parents." Melissa whispered the words but Nigel heard her, crossing the room, his hands warm on her shoulders.

"You aren't responsible for what happened there. You were just doing your job."

"Hell of a thing—killing children in the name of democracy." She stepped away from Nigel's embrace. "I'm sorry. It's not that I wasn't aware of what I was doing. And I'm more than aware that the world is a safer place without terrorists training to destroy it. But those boys were innocent, no matter who their father was."

"But the seeds of hatred had already been planted, Melissa." Cullen's eyes were kind. "Besides, nothing is accomplished without a price. You know that."

"And Khamis? What has it cost him?" Melissa turned to face her friends, searching for answers when there were none.

"While I don't condone the murder of children, Melissa, I don't feel any remorse for al-Rashid's suffering. Believe me, he'd gone to the dark side long before his family was killed." Gabe crossed his arms, his expression brooking no argument.

"So what about the connection? You think that somehow he's behind everything that's been happening to me?"

Payton shook his head. "Not directly, no. It doesn't track. If a man like Khamis wanted you dead, believe me, you would be."

"But I think it would be foolish to dismiss the correlation out of hand," Madison said. "If Khamis is behind the theft of the R-VX and if he's in bed with Alexi Kirov, I'd lay down odds that his actions are at least in part motivated by his need for revenge. According to Harrison, the general responsible for ordering the raid on the camp is dead."

"What happened?" Melissa asked, not certain that she really wanted to know.

"He was killed when terrorists bombed the Kuwait embassy." This from Gabriel.

"So what? I'm next?"

"We don't know anything for certain." Nigel's tone was soothing, but she wasn't interested in being pacified.

"But we know enough. Someone has been trying to kill me. We can't avoid that fact. And despite your confidence in his abilities, Payton, it's surely possible that Khamis just missed. Hell, everyone makes mistakes."

"Maybe, but I doubt it. According to the intel we dug up, he's been connected to several successful terrorist attacks, including a busload of American tourists in Dubai. Suffice it to say the man seems to be very good at what he does. And whoever's been after you has screwed up at least twice that we know of."

"That's wonderfully comforting." She wrapped her arms around herself, trying for a calm she most definitely did not feel. "That means I have two people out there hunting me."

"Which is why you have to stay here." Nigel reached to touch her, but she shook him off.

"I know you mean well, Nigel. But I'm damned sure not sitting here on my ass waiting for the bastard to come for me. We've covered this territory before. I'm fully capable of taking care of myself, and while I recognize that I need your help," she said, including them all, "I also need you to understand that I'm not going to play princess in the tower, waiting for someone to come along and rescue me."

"I didn't mean..." Nigel trailed off, holding his hands up in defense.

Her anger was out of place, and she knew it. But it was based on real feelings. Feelings of guilt for the children who had died in Afghanistan, and anger at the people who had put them in harm's way. And if she were honest, she was angry at Nigel, too. Hating the fact that his reaction to the situation was to try and sequester her away from the action.

"All right, Rapunzel," Harrison said with a smile, striding into the room, printout in hand, "I suggest you saddle up the destrier and hit the road."

"I take it you've found something," Payton said with the barest of smiles.

"Two possibilities." Harrison nodded. "A shipment bound for D.C. has mysteriously turned up in New Jersey. Port of origin was Istanbul. Seems like it's worth checking out."

"You said there were two things," Cullen prompted.

"Yeah." Harrison turned a page, scanning the document in his hand. "Another shipment arrived two days ago from Greece. The manifest doesn't match the shipping list Alexi has documented here. Seems there was an extra crate."

"The boat still in port?"

"No." Harrison shook his head. "And the shipment's gone, as well. But the Port Authority was able to provide an address for the miscreant crate." He held out a piece of paper, and Melissa grabbed it before anyone else had the chance.

"Looks like Melissa and Nigel are following up on the crate," Cullen said, apparently accepting her diatribe at face value. "Payton, you and Sam head for New Jersey."

Gabe opened his mouth to protest, but Cullen raised a hand. "I want you to take your wife home. Once she and the baby are settled, then you can meet up with us at headquarters in New York."

Gabe nodded, a modicum of relief washing across his face.

"Since Melissa is determined to leave the ivory tower, it seems New York is the most expedient place for us to confab." Cullen sighed. "So, everyone off to your tasks, and with a little luck, maybe we'll have answers before lunchtime."

Melissa glanced over at Nigel, not at all surprised to see displeasure. Despite his protestations to the contrary, she knew damn well that he'd prefer to keep her under lock and key until they'd found Khamis and the R-VX.

But since that wasn't going to happen, he'd be sticking to her side like a burr on a hound dog—and she had to admit she was damn glad to have him there. It was easy to talk a good game, but it was quite another to go out there knowing that she had one or more enemies who wanted her dead.

Especially since she'd only just discovered she had everything to live for.

THE NEW JERSEY DOCKS HAD a seedy appearance that wasn't helped by the quickly clouding day. The downside to life on the coast was that the weather could change in an instant—and usually did. What had started as a bright fall day was quickly descending into darkness, the smell of rain sharp in the cold air.

Payton skirted the car and nodded toward Sam, who was approaching the warehouse door from the right as he approached from the left. Both had their guns drawn, even though there had been no evidence that their arrival would be protested.

"Three cars around back," Sam said with a tilt of her head.

Payton nodded. He loved working with his wife. Partly because she was among the best he'd ever worked with, partly because they were so attuned to each other that their movements needed no choreography, and partly because it meant he could keep an eye on her.

An archaic notion at best, but there you had it. He smiled and watched her grimace in response, knowing damn well that she was, as usual, reading his mind.

"It's thoughts like those that make women run," she whispered, her smile countering any true negativism.

"I'm glad you didn't," he answered, inching closer to the doorway, his focus on the possibilities inside more than the conversation. He shifted slightly so that he could see through a small window. After double-checking the perimeter, Sam joined him.

There were two men in view, working with a conveyor belt. But three cars meant at least one more person in the building. "You see anybody else?" she whispered.

Payton shook his head, his eyes still searching the shadows along the far wall. "There's another room to the left. The door's open, but I can't see anyone."

"All right. I say we pop in for a visit. They don't look too concerned about security—that's a positive sign."

Payton gave the room one last look, and then motioned Sam back to the other side of the door. "On my count."

She lifted her weapon and moved into ready position. Payton counted to three and slammed open the door. The two men at the conveyor belt looked up in surprise, their eyes widening in fear.

"Federal authorities. Keep your hands in plain sight."

The two men obediently lifted their hands, a third man emerging from the office rubbing his eyes. Apparently he'd been napping.

"Here, here," he said, his voice rising with each word. "What the hell do you think you're doing?"

"We have reason to believe that you may have contraband goods stored here." An understatement, but no sense in alarming what appeared to be innocent bystanders. Payton stepped farther into the room, keeping his gun in plain sight. Sam followed him and then turned slightly so that her back was covered.

"No fucking way." The man was fully awake now, but still clearly befuddled.

"Is it just the three of you here?" Payton asked, hoping the question was out of context enough to get at the truth.

The guy opened his mouth to lie, then blew out a breath, evidently thinking better of it. "Yeah."

"Mind if we have a look at the shipment?" Sam said.

"How the hell do I know you're who you say you are?" For the first time the man's suspicion superseded his fear. "You come in here, guns drawn, yell that you're the Feds and we're just supposed to believe it?"

"I don't think you're exactly in the position to be asking questions, do you?" Payton knew he was overplaying his hand, but the guy was pissing him off.

"Maybe not." The guy deflated.

"Look," Sam said, ever the voice of reason. "All we need really is to understand why the shipment came here instead of going to D.C. as intended."

"Look, all I know is that I got a call in the middle of the night that a shipment was being diverted to our warehouse, and that I was to get my people out here ASAP."

"They didn't give you a reason?" Payton frowned.

"Something about a hurricane. I figured it must be Eloise. I mean, the news has been covering nothing else for days. If it hits Georgia as expected then that'd affect D.C., right?" He looked at them both askance, as if he needed their approval. Smart guy.

"You got anything to back that up?"

"Sure." The guy was starting to relax. "A fax from the harbormaster in D.C."

"All right. Why don't you show it to me?" Payton took a step toward the man and reflexively he backed up. Payton bit back a smile. "What's your name?"

"George."

"Fine, George, all you have to do is cooperate and we'll

be out of your hair in no time. Your guys speak English?" Payton nodded toward the two men, still standing frozen by the conveyor belt.

"Ermo does." George nodded toward the man on the right. "Horatio's not too good."

Payton nodded, thinking through the situation. He was beginning to believe the guy was on the level, but they'd need to check for verification, and since they were here, the shipment itself. Division of labor made the most sense, but he hated the idea of leaving Sam on her own.

She, on the other hand, apparently had no such qualms. She was already halfway over to Ermo, her weapon still drawn but now held at her side. "You want to show me the shipment?"

Ermo looked at his boss, and when George nodded, gave Sam a tentative smile. Despite the absurdity of the situation, Payton felt a tug of jealousy. He'd never gotten used to the fact that people responded to Sam in such a positive way.

"Tell Horatio to come with us," Payton ordered, his tone sharper than necessary. Sam gave him a know-it-all smile and then turned to go with Ermo.

Horatio seemed more reticent than Ermo to give in to trust, but he obeyed George's barked command and the three of them set off for the office. Once there, Payton settled Horatio in a rickety chair against the far wall, making sure that he had an angle on both men.

"All right, so where's this fax?"

George's hand was shaking now, and Payton had a moment's regret for scaring the shit out of the guy, but it was just part of business. Besides, it could be an act, and Payton was more the consider-them-guilty-until-proven-innocent type. "I've got it right here."

It took three tries through a towering pile of paper, but finally George produced the document. Payton scanned it quickly, satisfied to see that it did indeed corroborate the man's story. "Looks like everything is in order. We'll just finish checking the shipment and we're out of here."

As he reached out to hand the document to George, a movement in his peripheral vision sent him spinning toward Horatio. The man lunged forward, firing a gun he'd produced seemingly from thin air. The bullet went wide, but Payton's reaction was instant and deadly, the man's lifeless body falling to the floor. Payton swung back to face George, who was cowering in the corner with his hands over his head.

"Get up," Payton barked, just as Sam and Ermo appeared in the door.

"What happened?" Sam asked on an exhale of breath. "Are you all right?"

"I'm fine. Seems Horatio here thought he could use me for target practice." He smiled at his wife, the sentiment not reaching his eyes, then swung his attention back to George. "Want to tell me what that was all about?"

George shook his head, still huddled in the corner, Horatio's bullet lodged just a foot above his head.

"I think maybe I know," Ermo said, his somber gaze falling on his co-worker. "Horatio was illegal immigrant. Maybe he was afraid you were INS."

"Sorry, Ermo. Not buying. There's more going on than that." Payton lifted his gun, taking a calculated step toward the other man. "Why don't you save yourself a world of trouble and tell me what the hell is going on here?"

The younger man sighed, looked at George and shrugged. "We were using the shipment to smuggle heroin."

"The three of you," Sam prompted.

"No, *señora.* Just Horatio and I."

"Who do you work for?" Payton asked.

"Ourselves."

"Like hell." Payton took another step, backing the man into the corner.

"My cousin and I, we come here to make it big. To become

rich Americans. Only Horatio, he wanted to do it the easy way. So he gambled. A lot. Last month he told me he was in big trouble. Debt—how do you say—up to his ass? Some connected guys from Russia. Anyway, he needed money fast."

"So what, you made a deal with the mob that you'd sell heroin?"

"No. I told them we'd do whatever they needed us to do to work off my cousin's debt." Ermo shrugged. "They came to me two nights ago. Said there was going to be a diverted shipment. Something to do with weather. I was supposed to make sure the heroin was placed inside the shipment. That's all I know."

"You have a name?" Sam asked, her tone purposefully pleasant. Good cop, bad cop. Payton swallowed a smile.

"His name was Stoeler. Peter Stoeler."

Payton shot a look at Sam, instinct going into overdrive. "Any idea where the stuff was supposed to be going?"

"No." Ermo shook his head. "I was only to make sure it was placed in three marked crates."

"Show me the mark." Payton motioned Ermo toward the door, and Sam followed, George in front of her, still looking shell-shocked.

Ermo walked over to an open crate and gestured to a pockmark that at first appeared to be a flaw in the wood. Payton leaned closer and the burned wood took shape. A brand—an intricately linked *A* and *K*.

Alexi Kirov.

CHAPTER TWENTY-FIVE

"THERE'S NOTHING HERE." Melissa's voice echoed Nigel's frustration. They were standing in an empty lot fronting the East River. On either side there were abandoned buildings, but the land in front of them was empty, save for a collapsed dock and a junk heap in the western corner.

The north wind whipped across the open space, the salt-tinged air bitingly cold. Winter was coming. Nigel pulled his coat closer, and gingerly stepped out onto the dock, testing for soundness with each step. "Seems to be stable."

"Enough for a ship to anchor?" Melissa followed behind him, her arms crossed in an effort to fend off the cold.

"Maybe not a ship. But certainly a boat of some kind." He lifted a hand to protect his eyes as he looked downriver. Several warehouses were visible, one of them with a freighter docked off its pier. "Where did the original shipment off-load?"

"Brooklyn, according to Harrison's information." She came to stand beside him, her presence warming even without a touch.

"So that puts it directly downriver from here."

"Which means that it would be fairly simple for someone to take an undocumented crate and transport it here."

"Well, if that's the case there's certainly nothing here to prove it. Whatever came here—if it came at all—could be three states from here by now."

"Or right under our noses." Nigel turned back to the lot. "Maybe there's something over there."

Melissa followed his line of vision. “Besides trash?”

“Think about it,” he said, already striding toward the pile of junk. “If the R-VX was inside the crate, and if it was in fact delivered here, the recipient would most likely want to check it out and then transfer it to a more stable container. At least I know that’s what I’d do.”

“Which could mean the crate is still here.”

“Exactly. And if it’s here, then maybe we’ll get lucky and find prints. If not, at least we’ll have proof that we’re on the right track.”

“Now there’s the million-dollar question. The truth is that we could just as easily be on a wild-goose chase.”

“Precisely. Which is why it’s best for us to sort through everything here before making any conclusions one way or the other.”

“Lead on.” Her tone was resigned but determined, and Nigel reveled in the fact that he felt totally at ease with her, as if they’d been working together for years instead of a few days. Maybe Madison was right—maybe likes did attract.

The question now of course being could they turn that attraction into a permanent bond? Melissa hadn’t really committed to anything except not running away. Hell, he’d bared his heart and she hadn’t even said that she loved him. But then words weren’t everything. And she’d certainly shown him that she cared. And for now that would have to be enough.

That and the fact that she was still here with him. In a garbage dump—that alone had to mean something.

“So how do you want to do this?” Melissa was eyeing the refuse with disgust.

“Let’s break it into six quadrants. You start at the northeast corner and work south. I’ll start here at the southwest corner and work north. If the crate is here, it ought to be fairly recognizable. I can’t imagine there being time to break it down that much. And most likely it’s not buried under any of this.” He waved his hand toward the scattered trash. “There hasn’t been time.”

"Okay." She smiled, the gesture touching off a chain reaction of heat racing from gut to groin. Lord, he had it bad.

Forcing his attention onto the rubbish heap, he began systematically to scan the ground, occasionally stopping to kick aside a bag or box. Judging from the degree of rust and degradation, the site hadn't been regularly used for quite some time, which should make it easier to discern something recently added to the squalor.

He finished the first quadrant with nothing at all interesting to report, and had just started on the second when Melissa called out. "You finding anything?"

He looked up to see her standing knee-deep in refuse, sorting through a tottering pile with a stick.

"Nothing yet. So far everything looks like it's been here awhile." He stirred an abandoned oil can with his toe. "Maybe you're right and this is a huge waste of time, but it seems like it's better to be thorough."

She sneezed in answer and shot him a crooked smile. "At least it doesn't smell so bad here. The first quadrant I did really reeked."

Nigel frowned. "But you didn't find anything out of the ordinary?"

She shook her head and bent to pick something up, discarding it and then straightening. "Nothing that looks even remotely like it was part of a shipping crate."

"Right," he said, not certain what it was that was nagging at him. The third quadrant was as unproductive as the first two. He was just beginning to think the whole thing was indeed a massive waste of time, when he picked up the smell—and it was instantly familiar.

He was surprised that with all her war experience, Melissa hadn't sussed it out immediately. But then maybe it hadn't been as strong in her corner of the rubbish heap as it was here. Gritting his teeth and wishing he had a handkerchief or something, he rounded a tower of refuse to a semi-secluded corner of the area bordered on two sides by a rickety old hurricane fence.

The smell now was overpowering, and he fought not to gag.

There was an overgrowth of weeds, turned brown by the plunging temperatures. Nigel pushed them aside, grateful that he was wearing gloves. The crate was nestled in the shadow of an abandoned generator, almost indistinguishable from everything else piled there.

If not for the stench, Nigel doubted he'd have noticed it, but standing this close it was hard to ignore. Taking a deep breath for fortification, he stepped closer, pushing aside the weeds to look down into the open container.

The rats hadn't wasted time on their early Thanksgiving feast, and it wasn't easy at first to reconcile that what he was seeing was human, but one eye was still intact, and the lower half of the man's face, his muscles contorted into a permanent postmortem grin.

"Oh, my God." Melissa had followed, her gloved hand covering her nose. She stared down at the remains, her eyes widening as recognition dawned. "It's Ed." She turned to look at him, pain etched across her features. "Ed Wyland. My handler."

"SO WHAT HAVE WE GOT HERE besides a hell of a mess?" Gabe asked, pacing in front of the white board.

"Definitive proof that Wyland was playing both sides. And possibly a solid connection between Kirov and the alleged UN black-market network," Payton said, tipping his chair back against the wall. The team had reconvened in Cullen's New York offices, and spent the past hour or so trying to make sense of the various puzzle pieces, not the least being Ed Wyland's murder.

Melissa was still reeling from the find, trying to reconcile what she knew of the man with the picture the Russian had painted. It just didn't seem to fit, but then clearly she didn't know Ed as well as she'd thought, especially considering he'd potentially had a part in the plot to kill her.

"You don't know that he even knew about the attempt to poison you," Nigel said, his eyes dark with concern.

"You've got to stop reading my mind." She summoned a smile, determined not to let the latest episode in this drama deal her anything more than a glancing blow. "Besides, it doesn't matter if he was in on it or not. Payton's right. The very fact that Alexi knew he could use Ed to get to me indicates that he had to be in bed with Alexi to some degree."

"And paid the ultimate price," Sam said, looking at a forensic photo of the body.

"Don't forget that the Russian tied Wyland to Kirov, as well," Harrison said. "I don't think there's any way around the fact that the man was double-dealing. The question is whether he had anything to do with the theft of the R-VX."

"Doubtful." Payton shook his head. "My guess is that he was a bit player in Kirov's scheme. An insider who could provide information that allowed Kirov to stay one step ahead of attempts to uncover the network."

"Which was doubly useful once Melissa was assigned to the investigation," Sam said, her eyebrows drawn together in thought.

"Any chance Wyland was behind your being chosen to head the operation?" Gabe asked.

"I don't know. I don't think so. Ed has always seemed the consummate bureaucrat to me. I thought he was more a link between me and his bosses than the one making the decisions. But obviously I didn't know the man at all." Melissa tipped back her head, trying to hang on to some semblance of normalcy.

"I don't see that it matters anymore," Nigel said, jumping to her aid. "The man is dead. Whatever part he played in our little drama, I think we're all agreed that he wasn't involved with the R-VX. Which leaves us with Kirov and his network."

"And Khamis. He's got to fit into all of this somehow," Payton said.

"What about the crate Nigel and Melissa found?" Gabe stopped pacing to focus on Harrison. "Anything there?"

"Not a brand, if that's what you're asking." Harrison crossed his arms on a sigh. "But it is interesting that the crate was completely intact, except for a plank missing from the lid."

"Maybe it broke when the thing was pried open," Nigel suggested.

"Or maybe it was removed so that if it were ever discovered there'd be no link to Kirov," Payton said, reaching over to pick up two photographs. "The position of the missing plank is identical to the place on the other crate where we found the branded initials." He waved the pictures through the air for emphasis. "Might be a good idea to have Tracy's folks search the rest of the area for the missing plank."

"Already on it," Harrison said.

"I still don't see how any of this is getting us closer to finding the missing R-VX. Even if we assume that it was originally transported in the crate where you found Wyland, there's nothing to give us an idea of where the hell it went from there."

"True," Sam said. "But it does establish a time line of sorts. We know when the R-VX was stolen, and we're fairly certain the warheads were in the Istanbul area a couple of days ago. Or at least still on the move through that part of the world."

"How do you figure that?" Harrison asked.

"Because of the raid on Galata Tekkesi. That intel surfaced for a reason. If not because it was legitimate, then because someone wanted to create a diversion."

"And if it was necessary to create a diversion," Payton continued, "then we were close enough to have worried whoever was behind the theft."

"Khamis." Melissa leaned forward, resting her chin on her hand. "We have evidence that he was in Izmit, possibly meeting with Paulo Salvatore."

"And the timing of the meeting fits nicely into our time line." Sam stood up and crossed to the white board, noting each of the events in sequential order.

"We've still got nothing to prove a connection between Kirov and Khamis," Gabe said, studying the time line.

"I might be able to help there, actually," Harrison said. "I can't provide a definite tie, but I did some digging and found a connection between Paulo Salvatore and Kirov. It seems the two of them share an interest in polo. Kirov's first posting with the UN was in Geneva. While there, he was quite active on the European circuit. Salvatore still plays there."

"Or he did." Payton's expression was inscrutable, but there was no missing the implication.

Harrison shrugged. "I found several photographs of the two men together. And a couple of references in various society pages."

"Then at least we know they were acquainted." Gabe sat down at the table. "Which would allow for the connection between Alexi's network and Paulo's."

"And we can tie Paulo to Khamis through the meeting in Turkey. Which seems to indicate he was using Paulo's network," Melissa posited. "Conceivably for the R-VX."

"Okay, add to that the fact that the Salvatore operation was in shambles, thanks in no small part to Nigel," Payton said. "It is reasonable to assume Paulo would try and find an alternate route for the R-VX if he'd contracted to move it."

"And the undocumented crate in Brooklyn, along with the evidence of the network in New Jersey would verify that Alexi was indeed a player." Harrison's eyes gleamed with excitement.

"The arrival of the crate fits in the time line nicely," Sam added, writing it down on the white board.

"But not with Wyland's death," Gabe interjected. "He would have to have been killed before the shipment arrived."

"Unless Alexi kept him alive for some reason," Sam posed.

"And then killed him once everything was in motion with Khamis."

"That or maybe he and his Russian friends figured the dump site was a safe place to leave the body."

"Or were trying to leave a message." Harrison leaned back in his chair, still studying the white board.

"Either way, the man is dead." Payton as usual didn't mince words. "What's more important here is the fact that we have a link connecting Khamis to Kirov's network and the transportation of the R-VX."

"But if all that's true," Melissa interjected, "why would either of them risk bringing attention to the R-VX by targeting me?"

"Maybe we're looking at two unique situations." Sam stood up and walked over to the windows, leaning back against a sill. "Maybe Alexi realized you were onto him. Probably thanks to Ed Wyland." She looked at Melissa, her eyes full of sympathy.

"And so he decides to do something about it." Harrison nodded as his mind put together the facts. "Handling his problems with Celik at the same time."

"Meanwhile," Sam continued, "Paulo Salvatore is in desperate need of a secondary route for the R-VX in light of the heat on his organization."

"So he thinks of his friend, Alexi," Nigel said. "But Alexi has his own problems, with the chaos surrounding the attempt on Melissa and the murder of Celik. Still, he can't turn down a potentially lucrative deal, and agrees to go ahead with it. Paulo communicates with Khamis, not sharing any of Alexi's problems. And Khamis takes out Paulo, figuring one less witness. But then when Khamis arrives in New York, he finds out about the mess Kirov's created."

"But it's too late to cancel the shipment, so he waits until it arrives, then kills Alexi," Sam said, picking up the tale. "And tries to bring it full circle to the Russian mob, who conveniently have been in and out of the story enough times to provide at least confusion if not an out-and-out diversion."

"On the surface it's a good theory," Melissa said, "except that you're forgetting the fact that there's reason to believe that Khamis is the one who's out to get me."

"I'm sticking to what I said earlier." Payton's tone was grim. "If Khamis wanted you dead, you would be. The scenario we've painted here reeks of someone with a hell of a lot less field experience than Khamis al-Rashid."

"So we're completely discounting the connection between Khamis and Melissa?" Harrison asked, frowning.

"No." Payton shook his head. "We're just saying if revenge is on Khamis's agenda, he hasn't made his move yet."

Quiet reigned for a moment, and Melissa shivered.

"Look, there's no point in speculating about what hasn't happened," Nigel said, his dark eyes settling on Melissa. "What we need to do is find Khamis and the R-VX."

"Easier said than done." Gabe stood up again, hands on the table, his posture reflecting his frustration.

"Maybe not." Cullen walked into the room holding a photograph. "Harrison's face-recognition program just hit pay dirt. A man was photographed at an ATM in Manhattan a little over a year ago." He tossed the picture and another piece of paper onto the table. "The ATM was robbed and the tapes confiscated by police. The man was never a suspect, but he was questioned."

Melissa reached out to pick up the photo. The face was altered slightly, the bridge of the nose more pronounced, the hair lighter. But the eyes were the same.

"Could be a look-alike," Sam said, putting into words what they were all thinking.

"No way," Harrison said, studying the piece of paper. "There was a ten-point match. The program is designed to allow for nonstructural changes in the face. Eye color, hair color, prosthetics for the mouth or nose, anything easily altered." He handed the report to Payton. "This is definitely Khamis al-Rashid."

"What name was he using?"

"Francis Kennedy."

"Now there's a good Catholic name." Gabe's tone was dry. "Sounds like our man has a sense of humor."

"Let's hope he sees the humor in our finding him, then," Cullen said, his impatience showing. "Anyone interested in rounding up a terrorist? Thanks to New York's Finest, I've got Francis's address."

AT THE SOUND OF THE KNOCK, Khamis crossed the beautifully carpeted floor of his hotel room and, after checking the peephole, opened the door. The bellman smiled and offered to push the room-service cart inside. Khamis gestured for the man to enter, showed him where he wanted the cart and then slipped the man a ten-dollar bill.

It was just over twenty percent of the bill. Nothing overt that would make the man remember the delivery as anything other than routine. After closing the door, he walked back to the cart and systematically began to remove the items there, flushing the bulk of the food down the toilet, and stowing utensils and china under the bed.

He'd purposefully ordered things that were easy to get rid of, so that it would be days before anything odd was discovered. Housekeeping at the Waldorf was no different than any other hotel, the maids doing only what was absolutely necessary to clean the room. Checking under beds was not a daily occurrence, so it could be weeks before anything was found.

And even if it was, his alias was unlikely to be traced back to him. He looked in the mirror, smiling at his reflection. His hair and beard were shockingly red. So obvious he was all but invisible. Using mineral spirits he'd brought in a medicine bottle, he made quick work of the spirit gum attaching his false beard and mustache. Once he had them free, he removed his wig, putting all three into his duffel.

Using cold cream, this time provided by the hotel, he removed the pancake makeup, revealing the olive drab of his own complexion. The disguise completely discarded, he brushed a hand through his cropped and dyed hair, the blond streaks making him look both younger and of indeterminate origin. With a new eye color, he could easily pass as a citizen of almost any country. Most particularly America.

Returning to the room-service cart, he removed the soiled linen, stuffing it under the mattress, then retrieved a clean one from his duffel. Like the first, the Waldorf's emblem was embroidered on it, the replacement an exact copy except for a small change in dimension. The new one was longer on all sides, the result being that the bottom of the cart was totally concealed.

The difference in hem length was hardly noticeable, and Khamis smiled as he removed the copy, laying it carefully on the bed. First things first.

Crossing the room to the luggage stand, he carefully opened the suitcase housing Malik's bomb. Inside, it was nestled in a special fitting, although theoretically the thing was stable without the padding.

"No point in taking unnecessary chances," Malik had said, and just at the moment Khamis was inclined to believe him.

Khamis lifted the device, careful to keep it level. Everything was primed and ready. All he had to do was secure it to the room-service cart, maneuver it into place and set the timer. From there, it would be in Allah's hands, although Malik had done everything in his power to assure a successful conclusion. Even if discovered, the bomb would not be easy to disarm.

After setting the device on the bed, he flipped the cart and retrieved the roll of duct tape he'd brought with him. In short order, he had the bomb securely taped into place, the flashing red light indicating that it was armed.

The only remaining steps were to place the bomb at the target site and trigger the timer. Returning to the bathroom, Khamis popped in a pair of contact lenses, turning his eyes a faded green. Next he donned the neatly pressed uniform of a bellman, the outfit secured months earlier when a colleague had raided the hotel's laundry. Khamis added a pilfered name badge for authenticity and smiled at his reflection in the mirror.

He was ready. The end was near. And, as always, the final responsibility lay on his shoulders. He would have it no other way. It was his life's destiny to see that the plan met with success.

Whether he lived to tell the tale was another story. He hadn't lied to Malik—he had every intention of leaving the city, hopefully well before the nerve gas was released. But he had been at this too long not to accept the possibility that something could go wrong. A delay or an unforeseen complication would mean he must sacrifice himself for the cause—and his family.

He was more than prepared. He even had brought something to make certain that he would not survive in the case of an emergency. He reached into his bag, producing a bottle containing a single capsule. If he were to be caught in the explosion, he would no doubt die instantly, but he wasn't prepared to leave it all to chance.

Stuffing the bottle into his pocket, he walked back into the main room. With an official-sounding snap, he shook out the tablecloth, watching as it fluttered down into place, covering all evidence of the cataclysmic device it carried.

Turning back to the room, he made quick work of all evidence that could implicate him. The duffel was stowed beneath the cart for the time being, the empty suitcase thoroughly wiped for all prints. He'd been careful, everything dutifully sanitized, but one could never be too cautious.

Satisfied that the room was clean, he straightened the tablecloth and pushed the cart to the door. Opening it quietly, he checked the hall for occupants and, finding it empty, rolled the cart into the hall. He followed, squaring his shoulders, his best subservient smile firmly in place. After another quick glance to assure he was still alone, he produced the Do Not Disturb sign and hung it from the door.

That would keep prying eyes out of the room for at least thirty-six hours or so.

Pushing the cart down the hall, he shot a surreptitious glance at the tablecloth, his mind's eye seeing the bomb beneath. Malik's device was constructed to be easily transportable.

As with the original warhead, the two liquids were contained in separate compartments, rendering them harmless—until the force of explosion created inertia that would press the liquid contents of the front canister backward, bursting the wall separating the containers, the ultimate yield a deadly gas that would kill not only those present at the blast site, but anyone within a forty-mile radius.

It would be a victory for all true believers. And if it went as planned, his own personal vengeance.

The service elevator opened and Khamis rolled the cart inside. He pressed a button and waited as the elevator whizzed to the top of the building. With a ding, it slid open and Khamis rolled the cart out onto the vestibule of the eighteenth floor.

The recently restored Starlight Roof was the pride of the hotel. Touted as one of the most elegant venues in the city, it was perfect for his purposes. Overlooking Park Avenue, its glass roof offered the perfect place for an explosion to catapult deadly R-VX into the New York night. Pushing the cart into an empty adjoining room, he situated it behind a table, carefully lodged in the corner.

Invisible in plain sight.

Reaching carefully under the table, Khamis followed Malik's instructions to the letter, the feat accomplished in seconds, the formerly blinking light now shining steady. In a matter of hours, the world would be changed forever.

After a last adjustment to the tablecloth, he grabbed the bag beneath the cart and ducked into the bathroom. Changing into jeans and a sweater, he stuffed the uniform into the bag, and returned to the vestibule, this time to the main elevators.

He stepped inside and pressed the button for the ground floor, praising Allah for his good fortune. He had seen no one. Now all that remained was to exit the building and make his escape. On the fifth floor the elevator dinged open, an elderly man and his wife stepping into the car.

After a cursory glance, they dismissed him, concentrating instead on the numbers as they changed from floor to floor. Khamis resisted the urge to say something—to press his luck. He had learned long ago that control was everything. Control and normalcy. The elevator doors opened and with a wave of his hand he ushered the couple off, then followed, striding through the lobby with a renewed sense of purpose.

Outside a doorman hailed a taxi, and Khamis slid into the backseat, then leaned forward to give the driver instructions.

With that accomplished, he leaned back, closing his eyes, his wife's lovely face floating through his mind. "I do this for you, Kerea, my love. Only for you."

CHAPTER TWENTY-SIX

APPARENTLY FRANCIS KENNEDY wasn't hurting for money. His loft in the heart of the financial district had cost something close to four million. Terrorist dollars at work. The building itself was the usual warehouse facade, although this one looked as if it had been inspired by someone's idea of a warehouse rather than the real thing.

Either way, it wasn't the standard Manhattan walk-up. As well as a staircase, the building had an elevator that accessed all the apartments. The team had split into three components—Gabe and Payton on the stairs, Sam and Harrison watching the front and rear of the building, and Nigel and Melissa taking the direct approach via the elevator.

Surprise being the most important element, Nigel had disarmed the elevator's sound system, permanently putting the kibosh on the floor-announcing chime. According to the blueprint he'd studied, the elevator opened directly into the apartment on the tenth floor, which meant they had to be ready.

The stairs came out into a service area on the opposite side of the apartment, most likely behind a locked door, which meant that Gabe and Payton's arrival would be delayed at least for the amount of time it took them to deal with the lock.

For that reason Nigel had allowed extra time for them to get situated. The static in his earpiece solidified into the sound of Gabe's voice. They were in place.

"Ready?" Nigel glanced at Melissa, impressed as always with her relative calm.

"Let's do it," she said, shooting him a thumbs-up and stepping into the elevator. Seconds later the doors slid open on the ninth floor, a tactic designed to give them a moment for preparation.

"Next floor, lingerie and extremist bastards." Nigel hit the close-door button and leveled his gun on the door.

With a small lurch the elevator stopped at ten and the doors slid silently open again, this time revealing the interior of the loft. Moving with precision born of practice, Nigel entered the room, turning in surveillance while at the same time protecting both his and Melissa's backs.

She followed suit, taking up position on the opposite side of the open doors. Nothing moved, the only sound the steady drip of the kitchen faucet. The furnishings did not match the price tag on the apartment. Either Francis had spent all his cash on the loft, or he didn't give a damn about what was in it.

Since the man appeared to have overriding interests, Nigel assumed the latter. The loft hadn't been divided into rooms at all; the entire floor plan was visible from the elevator. Unless someone was hiding under the bed, the place was empty.

"It's clear," Nigel said into his mouthpiece, lowering his gun, disappointment washing through him. "No sign of any occupation."

"We're in," Gabe responded, stepping from behind a tattered screen, Payton on his heels.

"What do we do now?" Melissa's frustration echoed his own, but not finding Khamis didn't necessarily mean the end of the ball game.

"Let's see if he left anything behind." Nigel holstered his gun and began to search the apartment, the rest of the team joining in. Fifteen minutes later, it was more than clear that the place had been professionally sanitized. There was nothing. No food, no trash, no clothing, nothing at all to signal occupation.

"Maybe he was never here at all," Melissa lamented, dropping down on the sofa.

"He was here," Payton said, running a finger across a chest of drawers. "If someone hadn't been here recently there'd be dust. And this place is cleaner than the kitchen at Cipriani."

"Fat lot of good that does us." Melissa's tone was despondent.

"Tracy's folks are on the way," Gabe said, leaning back against the kitchen island. "I'll have them go over everything with a fine-tooth comb. This place is huge. Maybe they missed something when they were sanitizing it."

"Like this?" Payton held out a strand of filament wire, about two inches in length.

"Where'd you find that?" Nigel frowned, taking the wire.

"Between the wall and chair over there." He nodded toward a table and chairs sitting under the window. "It was caught under the baseboard. We'll need Sam to confirm it, but I'm fairly certain it can be used for circuiting a timer."

"Not the only use, though." Gabe blew out a breath. "And even if it were, it doesn't do a damn thing to tell us where the hell the bastard is now."

Melissa threw down the pillow, and Nigel took a step toward her, thinking she'd finally surrendered to her anger, but as he drew closer, he realized she was digging between the sofa cushions with both hands.

"Finding anything?" he asked, closing the distance between them.

She looked up with an embarrassed smile. "Men never think about cleaning under cushions, even the most fastidious ones. My sister and I used to find all kinds of things under my daddy's recliner cushions."

Nigel reached down to remove the seat cushion nearest him, the collection of dust and unidentifiable bits of refuse underscoring her thoughts. "I don't see how a rotting Cheeto is going to help us find Khamis."

"It won't," she said, "but this might." She held up her hand, a wadded-up scrap of paper between her thumb and forefinger. Nigel took it from her, carefully grasping it by the corner.

"Is there anything on it?" Payton asked, moving over so that he could see.

"Try to keep your prints off of it as much as possible," Gabe warned.

Nigel nodded, and shook the paper until it unfolded, keeping contact only at the original corner. The page appeared to have been torn from a notepad, half of it missing. But there were two words visible on the sheet. "It says 'stormy petrel.'"

"What the hell does that mean?" Payton spit.

"It's the title of one of my favorite books," Melissa offered, "but I hardly think that would have anything to do with Khamis."

"Isn't a petrel a bird?" Gabe asked, frowning over Nigel's shoulder at the crinkled paper.

"Yes, it is," Nigel said. "The storm petrel to be exact. They're seabirds. I've seen them in the Hebrides. There are around twenty species, I believe, occupying both the northern and southern hemispheres. They're sometimes called Mother Carey's chickens, although I've not got the slightest idea why."

"Ornithology," Payton said, "now that's a side of you I've never seen."

"I'm not sure about the Mother Carey part," Melissa said, her eyebrows drawn together in a frown, "but storm petrels are known as the sailors' friends. Supposedly they warn of approaching storms. It's considered unlucky to kill them, the legend being that each bird contains the soul of a dead seaman."

"Okay." Payton raised his hands in surrender. "You two clearly belong together."

"Well, they might just have something," Gabe said, taking the note from Nigel. "If a storm petrel is considered luck for seamen, then what better name for a ship?"

"Maybe, but why would Khamis have noted another ship?" Nigel asked, trying to work through the idea. "We know the unlisted crate came in on the *Argonaut.* Unless we've totally missed the boat, excuse the pun, I'm not sure where another ship fits into our scenario."

"What if it's an outgoing ship?" Payton queried, his expression thoughtful. "Maybe Khamis is moving the R-VX somewhere outside of New York?"

"Only one way to find out," Gabe said, turning on his headset. "Harrison, you there?" The headset crackled with life. "Yeah, everything's secure. Listen, we need to find out if there's a ship in the area by the name of *Stormy Petrel.* And if so, where it's docked, and more importantly—where it's going."

WITH THE PREPONDERANCE of clouds, there'd been no transition from night to day, the gray gloom giving way to the neon glare of the city in what seemed to be a matter of minutes. Across the East River the lights of Manhattan glistened in the moisture-laden air. Directly ahead the lights of the shipyards twinkled like a fairyland.

Except that fairyland had been invaded by the devil. Melissa stared out the window of the harbormaster's office at the wraithlike shapes of the tankers and freighters lined up along the quays. There was big money represented here, each ship's cargo providing an influx of capital to the American economy.

Warehouses lined the shoreline, each of them numbered according to pier. Pier thirty-five was dark, however, the water in front of the pier black and empty, the accompanying building a stark counterpoint to its thriving neighbors.

"According to the logs, the *Stormy Petrel* pulled up anchor about an hour ago. If it weren't for the weather she'd have reached open sea. As it is she's just left the mouth of the river." The harbormaster, a ruddy-faced man with the look of a sailor, pointed to the ship's position on the chart he had spread out before him. "You're sure you don't want me to call in the Coast Guard?" The man's gaze moved between the two women, his expression telegraphing his disapproval.

"Not yet. We need to see what we're dealing with here. Believe me, our combined experience is enough to deal with almost anything. It's better that we handle this our way."

The harbormaster raised his hands in defeat. "I was told to provide whatever you wanted and not ask questions." And the idea obviously didn't sit well at all.

"We'll be fine." Sam reached down to pick up a backpack containing her bomb gear. The harbormaster shot it a surreptitious glance and then looked away.

"Everything's ready." Payton appeared at the door, clad in a wetsuit, a tank of air dangling from one hand as if it weighed nothing at all.

Melissa pulled her jacket tightly around her and stepped out into the cold. It was raining, the fine mist almost a solid curtain, its icy fingers penetrating even the most water-resistant of coats. She and Sam followed Payton onto the dock and over to the wildly roiling boat. Gabe was at the helm, fighting to keep the boat beside the dock. Nigel was standing aft, his hand held out to help her into the vessel.

Once on board, she clambered over to a seat, hugging her coat around her. As Sam and Payton followed her, Nigel loosened the knot on the dock's cleat, throwing the rope to the floor of the boat with a signal for Gabe to go.

Gabe opened the throttle, and the boat, gaining buoyancy, ceased its violent rocking as it headed out into the river. It was amazingly quiet and, with no running lights, practically invisible in the misty night. Nigel settled next to her, his arm tightening around her, and for the moment she allowed herself to relax into his embrace.

It seemed as if aeons had passed since they'd reunited and yet it had only been days. She marveled at the fact that someone she'd known for such a short period of time could possibly mean so much to her. At least she couldn't fault him for being a boring date. She'd survived poisoning, found her handler dead and been shot at twice.

All that was left was to stop a terrorist from unleashing a weapon of mass destruction and find the courage to tell Nigel she loved him, the former definitely being the easier of the two.

The boat lurched as it slowed, and peering into the darkness, Melissa could make out the running lights of the freighter just ahead. She could see the glow of Sandy Hook off to her right, the swells of Raritan Bay bigger than the more protected harbor.

The Atlantic loomed ahead, the freighter steaming forward slowly, thanks to the rain and starless night. The spray was penetrating and Melissa shivered from the cold, her coat and sweater doing little to hold back the chill. Nigel stood up, bracing himself against the movement of the boat, and began to organize equipment, the most principal being a coil of rope attached to an apparatus resembling a crossbow.

Across from her, Payton donned a pair of flippers and a mask, and then carefully cross-checked his gear. The plan was for Payton to secure a line to the freighter, climb aboard and then lower a ladder for the rest of the team. Meanwhile, Gabe would keep the boat out of visual range, which thanks to the dark and the misty rain, shouldn't be all that difficult.

Payton nodded at Gabe to signal that he was ready, reached for the primed grappling hook, kissed Sam, and then flipped over the side of the boat into the churning water. Time seemed to tick by in magnified slow motion. No one spoke or even moved, the only physical sign of their concern being Sam gripping her arms as though she was literally holding herself together.

Finally, when Melissa was certain she couldn't stand a moment more, a tiny pinprick of light flashed three times off the bow of the freighter. Payton's signal.

Gabe started the boat, gliding silently toward the

freighter. Nigel moved a cushion and opened a storage bin, reaching inside to remove their weapons. Melissa reached for hers, checking the ammo and then sliding it into her holster.

Sam, too, took her gun and, after securing it, reached for her backpack, slinging it over her shoulders. Among other things, Sam was carrying a kit with injectable doses of atropine and an oxime called H-I6. While there was no true antidote for R-VX, the injection would slow absorption, allowing time for decontamination after exposure.

The boat slipped up next to the *Stormy Petrel,* Gabe adjusting the boat's engines to pace with the freighter. Payton was there, hanging off the end of the ladder, reaching out for the anchor rope Nigel tossed his way. Once the boat was secure, Payton climbed aboard, taking Gabe's place at the throttle.

Nigel was first off the boat, climbing the ladder to disappear about halfway up in the mist. Gabe followed next, then Sam and finally Melissa bringing up the rear. She stopped about a fourth of the way up the side of the boat and glanced down to see only empty ocean.

Payton had pulled away from the ship to await the signal to return.

Sucking in a breath, she continued to climb, the cold, slimy hull rough with barnacles. Two more minutes, and she was at the top, Nigel helping her over the railing. The four of them huddled behind a tarp-covered crate, Gabe and Nigel searching the decks using night-vision goggles.

"There's no one out here," Nigel whispered, his voice seeming loud even with the caterwauling of the wind. "Our best bet is to split up. If the nerve agent is here it could either be in the hold or with Khamis somewhere. As to the man, I'm betting on the crew's quarters, although we should probably check the bridge and captain's quarters, as well."

"What do we do about crew we encounter?" Sam asked, her shoulders hunched against the rain.

"Try to skirt them if possible," Gabe said, his goggles trained on the vast stretch of open deck. "If not, incapacitate them."

Sam nodded, and Melissa had no doubt that Payton's wife was totally capable of doing just that.

"All right." Gabe lowered his glasses, turning to face them. "I'll coordinate communication. Each of your transmitters is tuned to my frequency. Keep them on until you're in position, and then turn them off again until it's time to check in. That way we avoid intermittent noise and reduce the possibility that a transmission will be intercepted."

The plan made sense, but Melissa couldn't help wishing she could stay in contact with Nigel. One look told her that he felt the same, and the shared emotion was comfort of a sort.

"It's better that you come with me." Gabe had clearly seen the interchange. "That way there'll be no distractions."

She opened her mouth to argue but closed it before issuing a word. He was right. Protecting Nigel would always be more important to her than any other objective. She wondered for a moment how Sam and Madison managed. Maybe it just took time.

"Sam," Gabe said, the role of leader sitting well on his shoulders. "You head for the hold. Nigel, you take the bridge, and Melissa and I will scope out the crew quarters. If anyone gets into real trouble, don't worry about breaking silence. Just give a heads-up, and we'll come running."

Everyone nodded. Then Sam, on Gabe's go, moved away from the crate toward the portal leading down to the hold. She stopped for a moment behind the windlass, and then gathering her bearings, sprinted the final distance, disappearing into the darkness. Gabe waited for her assurance that all was a go, then motioned for Nigel to head out.

Melissa reached for his hand, trying to find the right words, but he shook his head to silence her, squeezing her hand instead, then moving out toward the bridge. She wished suddenly that she'd told him all she felt, that he knew just how much he meant to her, but there was no time for regrets. Better to get the job done, and then she'd tell him.

Gabe waited until Nigel reported his position and then gave Melissa a thumbs-up. It was a bit unnerving to leave the safety of the crate, the wind and rain reducing visibility. While the conditions worked to their advantage on one level, it was a detriment on another since it limited their ability to see what lay directly ahead.

Using the railing as camouflage, they worked their way midship, and then when they had closed most of the distance between the crate and the hatch leading below to the crew's quarters, Gabe signaled that he was going to move left directly across the deck.

Melissa held on to the rail, waiting for Gabe to successfully reach the open doorway. Two minutes passed, and her earphone crackled to life, Gabe instructing her to follow. Moving quickly and keeping low, she skirted the remaining distance between the rail and the hatch in record time, the dim bulb in the stairwell almost blinding after the driving rain on deck.

She opened her mouth to say something, but Gabe shook his head, motioning toward the stairs, and she picked up the sound of laughter from below. The crew, it seemed, was settled in for the evening. The big question was whether Khamis was among them.

Moving on rubber-soled feet, they started down the stairs, stopping every couple of rungs to make certain that they hadn't been detected. The hallway at the bottom had the musty smell of dried seawater and rust, the lighting here thankfully even dimmer than it had been on the landing.

A swath of light spilled into the passageway about ten feet in front of them, the laughter louder now. Gabe motioned for Melissa to stop, and he moved forward to the edge of the doorway. He waited about three beats, watching the occupants inside, and then moved swiftly to the opposite side of the door, motioning for Melissa to take his place to the right of the door.

She edged along the wall, heart hammering, and then after a fortifying breath, twisted her neck so that she could see into the room. Three men sat at a table playing cards, mugs of beer on the table.

Two of the men were in plain view, and clearly not Khamis, disguised or otherwise. The third man had his back to her, but he was too small to be a likely candidate. She tipped her chin in question, and Gabe nodded his agreement.

On the count of three, she dashed past the opening into the shadows of the corridor on the opposite side. Ahead of them, the passageway dead-ended, splitting to the right and left. Gabe motioned them to the left, but she shook her head, mouthing that it would be better if they spilt up and each dealt with one wing of the passage.

Gabe's frown looked suspiciously like a no, but then with a shrug he acquiesced and Melissa was pleased, as if she'd passed a crucial test. Gabe was acknowledging the fact that he trusted her to act on her own.

Five minutes later, when he'd disappeared around another bend, she wasn't as certain, but determination won the day and she continued to work her way forward. The first two rooms she passed were empty. Storage holds of some sort, one filled with old parts and equipment, the other with staples for the galley.

Ahead to her right another shaft of light lit the corridor, this one coming from the tiny window in a closed door. She could hear someone moving around inside, and drew her gun just to be on the safe side. Edging closer, she waited until the sound moved farther from the door, and then risked a quick peek.

The galley.

The man, a potbellied caricature of everyone's idea of a chef-cum-sailor, was chopping onions with a lethal-looking knife. Realizing that despite the dark and rain it was still early evening, Melissa increased her pace, not wanting to face the crew's dinner rush.

The next room was a dining hall, the tables set, the room thankfully empty. Directly across from the dining hall was a one-bunk closet that she assumed belonged to the cook, based on the culinary contents of his meager bookshelf.

Next to the cook's quarters was a narrow doorway that no doubt led to the lavatory. She paused at the door, but there was no sound. She was almost to the end of the corridor now, and so, moving past the bathroom, she edged along the wall until she could safely peer into the last room.

Inside, instead of the requisite tiered bunks, she saw a single bed strewn with a variety of clothing, as if the person who resided here had started to unpack, only to be interrupted. What was more interesting, however, was the fact that the clothing was not the typical fare of a seaman.

The skin on the back of her neck prickled and she spun around, her brain registering the sound of shoes on the metal rungs of a stairway. Confused, she studied the shadows and realized what she'd dismissed as a lavatory was in fact a stairwell. The door moved as someone on the other side began to pull it open.

Pushing away panic, she moved into the bedroom, frantically searching for somewhere to hide. A metal locker against the far wall seemed her best option. Without giving herself time to overanalyze, she stepped inside and pulled the door shut. Thankfully there were slits in the metal, so that she had a partial view of the room—the lower half.

She held her breath, praying that whoever was on the stairs had gone the other way. But luck, it seemed, was not on her side. The man, wearing polished brown loafers, strode into the room, humming an unrecognizable tune.

He moved over to the bed, and reached down to pick up a suit coat. *Oh, God,* Melissa prayed, *don't let him come over here to hang it up.* Someone was obviously listening to her prayer, because he simply looped the jacket over the back of a chair and then sat down on the bed.

The motion brought him into plain sight, and Melissa sucked in a breath of pure terror. The man's face was clearly illuminated—no more than three feet away. She started to turn on her mike, to call for help, but realized that any sound on her part could very well be overheard. And somehow, facing Khamis al-Rashid on her own wasn't her idea of a good time.

The best thing to do was to stay absolutely still and hope that dinner was sooner rather than later.

Minutes stretched, seeming like hours. Khamis simply sat on the bed, as if lost in thought, his head tipped downward so that his eyes were no longer visible. She tightened her hand around the .38, thinking that at least she'd have a fighting chance. Still, even with a weapon, she knew it was better to try to wait it out.

She closed her eyes, fighting for a calm she simply didn't feel, finally deciding that she needed to risk letting Gabe know where she was. The microphone switch was on her wrist. She shifted carefully to the right, the angle giving her the room to maneuver her arm. Slowly she moved it upward, and could almost reach it with her other hand when suddenly the locker door jerked open, a hand snaking forward to grab her gun hand.

With a yank, Khamis pulled her into the room, the pressure of his grip causing her to lose hold of the gun. It hit the floor with a metallic clang and spun out of sight under the bed. He ripped off her headset, neatly snapping it in two with his left hand. She pivoted against his weight, trying to unbalance him, but the bite of his gun against her side stopped her cold.

He swung her out to face him, his hand tight on her wrist, his expression so filled with loathing it made her flinch. "It seems, Ms. Pope, that we are destined to meet again."

CHAPTER TWENTY-SEVEN

THE BRIDGE WAS ACCESSED by a spiral staircase that reminded Nigel of the kind often found in old English towers. Clearly designed for shorter men, he had to bend almost double to make the curves which, due to the narrow design, were all too bloody frequent.

At least he hadn't met anyone coming or going. In these tight quarters a bullet would no doubt rebound until it managed to hit everything moving. Above him he could see a circle of light—the opening hatch.

There had been an easier route, an open stairway that led both down below deck as well as to the bridge, but the chance of meeting someone had been much more likely, and until he got the lay of the land, he preferred to remain incognito.

At the moment, however, he was regretting the decision, the muscles in his neck aching in accord. He ducked even lower to pass through the hole that served as a doorway, emerging onto a small landing directly outside the bridge.

The hallway extended to the left with at least three doors opening off the passageway. From this vantage point he couldn't see if it dead-ended or turned toward some other part of the ship. A series of dim bare bulbs were placed at varying intervals along the way, doing little to alleviate the gloom. Best that he explore the remaining rooms, but for the moment his attention centered on the closed door to the bridge.

A window afforded a view of the room. Nigel drew his weapon and, after rechecking the tiny corridor, returned his attention to what was happening inside. The com center was off to his immediate left, the steady circle of the radar showing an empty sea.

As intended, their boat was too small to be picked up. And even if it had been, evidently no one on the freighter would be paying attention. The navigational equipment was dated but immaculately clean. Unlike the rest of the ship there was no rust present on the bridge. Several small computers and an internal communication system were banked underneath a wide expanse of window, the rain lashing against the glass making visibility almost nil.

Against the far wall, a man sat with a mug of coffee and a nautical chart. To his right, closer to the window, stood a bearded man in a black turtleneck and yellow slicker. Ahab. Or at least his embodiment on this vessel. There was a certain stance all captains adopted—shoulders square, spine rigid. It didn't matter whether it was a tiny scow or an aircraft carrier, the captain was always recognizable.

This one was talking on a two-way, and Nigel wanted to know what exactly he was discussing. After a quick glance down the still-empty passageway, Nigel carefully cracked the door open, thankful that there was no accompanying squeak.

The room hummed with equipment, but the captain's voice carried nicely. Nigel leaned in slightly so that he could hear.

"The package is on board, and we're almost clear of the harbor." He paused for a moment, listening to the reply. Nigel could hear the static from the radio, but couldn't make out the words.

"No, everything is fine. The storm is slowing us, but the delay shouldn't cause problems. We'll be clear soon. No worries."

Again the radio's static filled the room, but as before Nigel could only catch the odd word.

The captain's accent was not recognizable, his travels no

doubt washing away any trace of origin. His hair was dark, his complexion somewhere between olive and black. Egyptian, maybe, but it was impossible to tell.

"I'll radio again in an hour when we've reached open water."

At least that confirmed the fact that they were leaving New York, the pertinent question of course being exactly where the hell they were headed. Their filed plans at the harbormaster's were for South America. But once on the open sea it was easy enough to divert to a secondary port as long as it was not the kind to question your arrival.

What he needed was a look at the charts. But how to accomplish the fact? He thought about trying to contact Gabe to see about Melissa, but resisted the urge. She'd only see it as him checking up on her, which he supposed to some degree was absolutely true. He glanced down at his watch, noting that they were all due to check-in in fifteen minutes anyway.

Better to maintain silence and figure out a way to get a peek at the charts.

Nigel could see a door just beyond the second man's head, the window indicating that it connected to an internal hallway. Since the command tower was small and roughly rectangular, it seemed entirely possible that this corridor led around to the second door. If that supposition held true, he should be able to see the charts. Waiting for a moment to be certain that the captain hadn't anything else relevant to say, Nigel carefully pulled the door closed, and began cautious navigation of the passageway.

The doors on his immediate right and left were closed and windowless. There was no light showing under either door, so with his Sig Sauer ready, he quickly checked both, one a secondary radio room, the other a storage closet. They were empty.

The final door was open, the darkened room revealing the

captain's quarters. As scrupulously neat as the bridge, there was nothing there to affirm the presence of either the R-VX or Khamis. However, the captain's mention of the "package" seemed to point to a positive answer.

As he'd hoped, after the captain's room, the passageway made a ninety-degree turn to the right, the hallway devoid of doors or windows. Making quick work of the distance, he made a second right turn, this time into a corridor identical to the one where he had begun. There were two doors in addition to the one leading to the bridge, as well as an opening that probably led to a staircase like the one he'd used to gain access to the bridge.

The first door led to another storage room, the second to smaller quarters probably reserved for the radioman. Thankfully, both were unoccupied. Moving quickly but still quietly, Nigel headed for the door to the bridge, then crouched beneath the window, ears straining for anything that would indicate one or both of the men were leaving.

There was nothing but the quiet hum of the ship and the soft babble of their conversation. Inching up slowly, Nigel peered over the bottom edge of the window. The captain had moved across to the computer bank, apparently plotting his course.

The table was less than three feet away, the man at the charts sitting in profile. If Nigel took the time he needed to focus on the maps, he'd risk being seen. Better to hold his position and wait for the man to move.

Five minutes went by, the men inside each absorbed in their separate tasks. Then the captain turned to the second man and said something involving the words "computer" and "bullshit." Nigel contained a smile, delighted as the chart man responded by pushing away from the table and going over to the computer bank, ostensibly to show the captain how exactly it was done.

With both men turned away from him, Nigel popped up

for a steady look. The chart was still far enough away that he couldn't see detail, but he recognized the line of the coast. The Arabian Sea. Not at all what he'd expected. Of course, for all Nigel knew, the man could merely be studying navigational charts, the one on the table nothing more than his latest assignment.

Still, considering whom they were tracking, it wasn't a fact he could ignore. Both Pakistan and Iran provided access to Afghanistan, which if intel was to be believed was the base of Khamis's operations.

Perhaps they were tracking their way home. But where the hell were they going to leave the package?

Nigel knew he'd seen enough. Best not to risk any more exposure. He checked his watch—nine more minutes until check-in. Maybe another quick search of the captain's quarters would yield something.

He crouched again and moved quietly away from the door, then turned to head back down the corridor. Before he had taken two steps, he felt the hard cylinder of a muzzle in his back.

"Move and you die." This time the accent was clearly Arabic.

"I'VE NEVER SEEN YOU before in my life." Strictly speaking, that wasn't exactly the truth. Melissa had seen his picture now on more than one occasion, but she had no clear memory of ever meeting the man live and in person, despite Madison's conjecture.

"How typical of an American to forget." He spat the title out as if it were a curse, his fingers digging into the skin at her wrist. "You gave my children candy."

An image of children crowding around her as she stepped out of her jeep flashed through her mind, the memory bittersweet. Their hopeful faces still sometimes haunted her dreams. "Where?" She knew the answer, but she needed to keep him talking, find the moment when she could break free and dive for her gun. With any luck Gabe had heard the struggle, or at least the snap of the headset. He'd alert the others. And then hopefully they'd be on their way.

Still, she wasn't about to sit idly and wait.

"In Afghanistan." The pain in his eyes was palpable, and Melissa's stomach clenched in response. "At the camp. You claimed to be there to interview our forces, but in fact, you were a spy. And because of you, my wife and my children are dead."

She wanted to retort, to say something to throw him off guard, but there was truth in his words, and she fought against a rising sense of guilt.

"Your people talk of the atrocities of terror, but think nothing of killing women and children with the drop of a bomb."

Reflexively Melissa lifted her chin. "Your camp was a training ground for killers. Men and women—even children—who gave no value to human life. Not even their own. In my opinion any death is one too many, especially a child's. But sometimes there are no alternatives."

"There are always alternatives." His grip had tightened to the point that she feared he would snap the bones, but she resisted the urge to cry out. She would not bend before this man.

"And did you consider those alternatives when you blew up a busload of innocent people?"

"What I did was for a higher cause." The fire in his eyes didn't flicker for a moment. The man was as deluded as they came, and despite the horror of his loss, he was her enemy. She'd do well to remember the fact.

"All's fair in war for your side, but not ours? Is that it?"

The blow came as a total surprise, the butt of his gun glancing off her cheekbone, the result a nauseating wave of dizziness. She stumbled, but he jerked her upright, the skin on the inside of her wrist tearing with the motion. Pain transmitted from nerve ending to nerve ending and she spit blood, fighting to regain control of her senses.

"You will remember that I have the upper hand. Your barbs have no effect other than to bring about your own pain."

"Is that why you didn't kill me with the poison?" The words were out before she had time to think about it. "To cause me more pain? And here I thought you meant me to die." She dared a look out the door, hoping against hope to see Nigel or Gabe riding to the rescue.

The doorway was empty.

"Had I attempted to kill you, Ms. Pope, you can be certain that you would be dead." His words echoed Payton's earlier pronouncement. Had it only been this morning? "Kirov was the one who poisoned you. It was he who fumbled the task. The man was a fool."

"So you killed him." Melissa's head had cleared, although her cheek still throbbed and her wrist burned where he held her.

Khamis shrugged. "He was no longer useful."

"And you say I have no respect for human life."

"He was not a child. And he knew the dangers of the game he played."

"So he deserved to die?"

"He was ruled by greed. My children were innocents."

"So were the people on that bus. I take it you're not big on an eye for an eye."

"Make no mistake, Ms. Pope." He twisted her arm, drawing her close. "It is what I live for."

Despite her attempt at bravado a shudder rippled through her, and Khamis smiled, enjoying her fear. Then in her peripheral vision she saw movement. Someone outside the door.

Gabe.

He motioned silence, then stepped back again into the shadows.

"Then why don't you just end it now?" She forced herself to meet Khamis's eyes, to keep his attention away from the doorway.

"There are greater rewards, are there not?" His smile was icy, his eyes even more frigid, and again Melissa shuddered.

Gabe appeared in the doorway again, this time motioning Melissa to move so that he had a clear shot at Khamis.

She shifted her weight, attempting to throw the man off balance, to force him to pivot toward the right, but he was much bigger and her efforts only resulted in his tightening his grip.

"Be still," he whispered, his eyes fixed over her shoulder. The locker. It was reflecting the door. Khamis knew that Gabe was there. She opened her mouth to warn him, but before she could utter a sound, bullets were flying.

Khamis dropped to the ground, pulling her with him, his weight pinning her to the floor. Transferring his weight to free his gun hand, he got off another shot just as Gabe appeared in the doorway, his shot ricocheting off the locker.

Gabe's eyes widened for an instant and then he stumbled to his knees, blood blossoming on his shirt. Melissa swallowed a scream, bile rising in her throat, watching helplessly as Gabe fell forward, unmoving.

"Is he the only one?" Khamis's voice was ragged in her ear as he jerked her back to an upright position, pulling her across the room as he retrieved Gabe's gun.

She fought for breath, fought for words. No way in hell would she give up Nigel and Sam, but this man was an expert and she was afraid that he would recognize her lie.

"I asked you a question." Again he backhanded her, but this time the blow missed her cheek, glancing off her ear. The violence settled her quandary—she'd lie like a pro or die in the effort.

"There's no one else. This was a reconnaissance mission. We didn't expect to find you here. We were just looking for the R-VX."

She couldn't tell whether he bought her half-truth or not, but at least for the moment there were no more questions. She swallowed against another wave of despair, trying not to think of Madison and the baby. Gabe had died because of her. And now Madison would pay the price.

"Come," Khamis ordered, pushing forward, forcing her to step over Gabe's body. "We will leave your friend to the rats, no?"

Tears flooded her eyes and she fought the emotion. If she was going to get out of this alive, she couldn't think about Gabe. Not now. She had to concentrate on other things. Like Nigel. Oh, dear God, she prayed, please let nothing happen to Nigel.

NIGEL EYED the three men in front of him, one holding a gun. They'd taken away his communication gear and his weapon, but for the moment at least they seemed more concerned with what to do with him than actually watching him.

So far he hadn't learned a whole hell of a lot, except that apparently the two others deferred to the captain in making decisions. And he in turn seemed intent on taking Nigel to someone else with even more authority. Most of their conversation was in an Arabic dialect he didn't recognize although there was also a smattering of English, mostly idiomatic, which meant they all probably spoke the language.

The man who'd caught him unawares had spoken his commands in English, and Nigel had heard the captain speaking fluent English on the radio. Nevertheless, for the moment at least, they seemed to be more interested in keeping their thoughts private. He was standing by the table, only a few feet from the door, but they were standing only a little ahead of him, and he didn't like his chances should he try to run.

Better to try and even the odds a bit. Best he could tell, there was only the one man with a gun, and interestingly enough, he'd pocketed Nigel's rather than giving it to one of his comrades. Nigel could feel the metal of the tiny derringer he kept strapped to his ankle. It had belonged to his father, one of the few things the old man had ever given him. Fortunately the sailors had been far too interested in discussing where he came from to perform a thorough search.

All he had to do now was figure out a way to retrieve it without anyone noticing. If he could take out the gunman, he could probably nail the other two before they had time to scramble for their guns. But all of it depended on safely retrieving the derringer.

There was no sign of any of the others. Nor had the jabbering sailors given any indication that they had discovered anyone else. Hopefully Melissa was having better luck. Actually, luck played no part in it. He should have been more careful. There was really no excuse for not having noticed the man before it was too late.

But then there was no point wasting time regretting what couldn't be changed. Better to concentrate on getting the hell out of here. Keeping his eyes on the arguing men, he backed up slowly until he felt the table against his legs. Moving slightly to the left he managed to get his fingers on the edge of one of the charts, and with a shove, he pushed it onto the floor, the rustle of paper drawing the eyes of his captors.

Waving his hands apologetically, he leaned down to retrieve it, his back to the men, and in seconds managed to palm the little gun. Turning with his best blank expression, he extended the map toward the gunman.

The man shook the gun, motioning Nigel to return the chart to the table, which he did with an exaggerated sense of concern. The captain eyed him curiously, looking for something out of place, but evidently he passed inspection because the man turned back to his friends.

The gunman, however, was not so quick to give up, his focus on Nigel's face. "Sit over there." He motioned with the gun to a chair near the other door, and Nigel shrugged his agreement. Three steps into crossing the room, he heard the gunman's voice as he rejoined the conversation.

It was now or never.

He fired the derringer, simultaneously diving behind the chair. He rolled back into position, the metal-framed chair offering at least a modicum of protection. Firing another round, he successfully brought down the gunman. The captain dove for cover, but there wasn't much available in the small bridge.

The third man hit the floor, crawling forward for the dead man's gun, but Nigel was faster coming up over the top of the chair, nailing the bastard with a single shot. Two down—one to go. The captain was all eyes now, evidently more brain than brawn, the seriousness of the situation dawning. Raising his hands, he stood slowly, surrendering.

Nigel was tempted to take him out, but knew it would be better in the long run to leave someone to answer questions. Besides, he might need a hostage. "Turn around." His terse order was obeyed immediately, and Nigel crossed to stand behind the man, retrieving both his gun and the dead man's on the way.

Using the butt of the Sig Sauer, he quickly dispatched the captain, successfully sending him to la-la land. Taking the man's belt, Nigel bound his hands and then gagged him with a handkerchief. That ought to hold him until Nigel could round up the troops.

His communication pack lay on the counter running beneath the bridge window. Scooping it up, he switched it to on, trying to raise Gabe. The static was deafening. And despite attempts to fine-tune the connection, there was nothing. He switched frequencies then, trying to raise Melissa, but again only got static, his heart rate ratcheting up as his imagination began to run amuck.

Switching frequencies again, he tried to get Sam. It took three tries, but finally he heard her tinny voice asking what was wrong.

"I've run into a bit of trouble. Two casualties and a man out of commission. I'm fine, but I can't raise Gabe or Melissa, and I'm not sure how many more of them there are. Have you had any trouble?"

"No. It's been quiet here. No sign of anyone at all. No R-VX, either, although I've only just started to look. Is it possible that Melissa and Gabe just have their mikes turned off?"

"Negative." Nigel shook his head. "Gabe at least should have had his on in case of emergency. Besides, if they were off, I'd get dead air. Instead I'm getting static." His heart was racing now, the thought of Melissa in trouble far more frightening than the situation he'd just escaped from. He needed to find her—and find her fast. "I'm going to try and find them."

"Do you want me to come?"

"Not yet." Better they didn't play all their cards until they knew what they were up against. "But keep this line open. I'll be in touch as soon as I know something."

"All right," Sam said, her matter-of-fact tone laced with the barest hint of worry. "I'll be waiting."

Nigel signed off without answering, already moving toward the main staircase leading directly below decks. The stairs were empty, thank God, and the staircase dumped him at the end of a hallway with an open door across from him and the passageway extending on to the right.

He cautiously stepped out of the alcove housing the stairs, taking a moment to size up the situation. The passage was empty, the bare bulbs giving it a gray-future-world kind of feel. He was just starting to move down the hall, when a groan from the room behind him sent him spinning around, the Sig ready.

Something moved on the floor just inside the door, repeating the groan. Nigel moved forward, his eyes fixed on the target. A dark head lifted, icy blue eyes meeting his.

"Jesus, Gabe." Nigel spoke the words on an exhale, rushing to his friend's side, memories of the bloody courtyard in Iraq parading through his mind. "What the hell happened?"

"Shot," Gabe managed, struggling to a sitting position. "Force of the thing knocked me out. But I think I'm okay. Just nicked my collarbone. Hurts like hell."

"Who shot you?" Nigel asked, helping his friend to his feet.

"Khamis. And he's got Melissa." Gabe struggled for balance. "Sorry."

"Fucking hell," Nigel said. "How many men have you seen?"

"Four, including a cook, not counting al-Rashid. They were up the hall a bit in a rec room. The cook was in the galley."

Nigel nodded, figuring one of them was probably the man who'd caught him at the bridge. Which meant three unaccounted for besides Khamis. The odds of there being more weren't all that great. It was unlikely anyone was out in the storm, and Sam had said the hold was unoccupied. "Will you be okay if I leave you here?"

"I can come."

"The hell you can. You'd only be a detriment and you know it." Nigel headed for the door, then turned back, reaching for the revolver he'd secured at the small of his back. "You have a gun?"

"No." Gabe shook his head. "He took it."

"Here, take this one." He handed the gun to Gabe. "The previous owner won't be needing it anymore."

"I take it you had your share of trouble, too?"

"Yes, but I came out on the winning side."

Gabe grimaced, and Nigel immediately regretted the remark, opening his mouth to say as much, but Gabe held up a hand, shaking his head. "I know. Just go."

Nigel ripped off his earpiece, tossing the entire unit to Gabe. "Call Sam. Have her meet you here. And if you can raise Payton, better call for backup."

Gabe nodded, sitting down on the bed, his color slightly better.

"All right then, I'll be back as soon as I can." *With Melissa,* he added silently to himself. *Please, with Melissa.*

CHAPTER TWENTY-EIGHT

NIGEL STEPPED out into the corridor, forcing himself to slow to a walk. He couldn't help Melissa if he allowed himself to be captured again. He was fairly certain Khamis hadn't taken her up the main staircase, because he'd have seen him, or at least heard him.

Moving as swiftly as he dared, he headed down the hallway. A small bedroom and what appeared to be the dining room were both empty, as was the galley, the cook obviously having moved on to something more interesting—hopefully not Melissa.

There were two storage areas right after the galley. The first was empty, and Nigel approached the second with something less than caution, assuming the small closet would prove no threat.

About a foot from the door, he came full stop, his fingers tightening on the gun. Someone inside the storage room was humming. His first thought was Melissa, but as he edged closer he realized that the voice was decidedly male.

Swinging into the room, his gun centered on the back of an apron-clad man. The cook. Flipping the weapon butt first, he struck the man on the side of the head, catching him as he fell to prevent noise. Once the fellow was laid out, Nigel grabbed a broom and snapped it over his knee. Taking the broken handle, he stepped back into the hallway, closing the watertight door behind him, then jamming the handle into the door's wheel latch, effectively locking the man inside.

Satisfied that for the moment at least all was secure, he surveyed his surroundings. The corridor continued straight ahead, but there was also a short passage to the right, ending at the hatch that led onto the deck. Light spilled out of a doorway near the end of the passage, most likely the rec room Gabe had spoken of. The room was empty, two beer mugs the only indication the room had recently been occupied.

Backtracking, he headed to the original corridor, this time taking the left side. This passage was darker than the others, several of the lightbulbs burned out, the resulting shadows both a liability and a blessing.

There were two rooms ahead on his right, one well lit, the other just a shadow against the wall. The first housed two bunks, the upper one occupied by a sleeping sailor, his even breathing assuring Nigel that at least for the moment he was no threat. Carefully pulling the door closed, he tied the door shut with a piece of twine, securing it so that Sleeping Beauty couldn't escape should he awake at an inopportune moment.

Content with his makeshift padlock, Nigel moved forward to the second doorway. Beyond that he could see the dim lightbulb illuminating a third set of stairs, leading no doubt to the bridge. If this room was clear, he'd have to face the fact that Khamis had discovered his handiwork, thereby upping Khamis's odds considerably.

Leaning back against the rusted wall, Nigel breathed deeply, trying for a calm he didn't feel, the thought of Melissa in the hands of someone like Khamis sending anger and fear coursing through him.

He waited a full minute, allowing the emotions to run their course. It was always better to face fear and then vanquish it, rather than pretend it didn't exist. Calmer, he inched toward the last door, his fingers tightening on the trigger of the Sig.

The soft murmur of voices reached him first, and then he recognized the faint light of a lamp. There were people in the room. The question was how many and whom.

Inching forward, he risked a quick look. The room was meant to be a parlor of sorts, a ragged sofa at one end and a couple of weatherworn armchairs at the other. A battered bookshelf stood in between, curiously devoid of tomes. It was a sad little room, but what interested Nigel most was the man standing near the sofa. He was motioning with his left hand, a lethal-looking Walther flashing in the light. Apparently he was talking to himself, or on a two-way because there was no one else visible.

Nigel held his breath, waiting for the man to stop talking—willing him not to turn around. As if by command, the man lowered his right hand, the two-way transmitter visible now. In one swift motion, Nigel crossed the room and rendered the man unconscious.

After rolling the man into a corner out of sight, Nigel grabbed the transmitter and dashed back into the hallway in time to see Sam rounding the corner on her way to Gabe. She stopped and started toward him, but he shook his head, motioning her back the other way. Better not to involve anyone else. Not to mention the fact that he would feel a hell of a lot better knowing there was someone to keep an eye on Gabe. He might not be mortally wounded, but it was a nasty injury nevertheless. Besides, all things considered, Nigel liked his odds.

Worst case, there was Khamis and the captain to deal with. Best case, the captain was still undiscovered and the only one he had to face would be al-Rashid. Of course, the fact that the bastard had the woman Nigel loved changed the parameters of the game a bit. But push come to shove, Nigel usually pulled the win out of the fire. And now certainly wasn't the time to go changing his average.

The staircase led as he'd expected to the U-shaped hallway flanking the bridge. Waiting for a moment in the shadows, he searched the hallway for signs of life, and then, finding none, stepped out into the corridor. The door leading to the bridge was almost across from him, and he ducked low in case his handiwork had been discovered. Crouching under the bottom edge of the door's window he had an unsettling sense of déjà vu.

Except this time he wasn't about to let anyone sneak up on him. He moved slowly until he could see into the bridge. The dead bodies were just where he'd left them. But the captain was gone.

Nigel swallowed a curse. If Khamis had found the captain, it was possible that he knew Nigel was here. Of course it was also possible that he had attributed the attack to Gabe. They were of a similar height and build. As long as the captain hadn't seen Gabe, it was possible Khamis would believe the problem had been handled.

Which still meant that Nigel would have a slight advantage. Unfortunately, there was no way to be certain. And to make matters worse, if Khamis believed the threat was over, there'd be no reason to keep Melissa alive. The thought was enough to send terror racing through him, his pace reflecting his inner turmoil. After first checking the radioman's room, and then the closet, he turned the corner, heading for the captain's quarters.

It was the only room of any size in the far corridor and, unless they were on the move, the most likely place for them to be holed up. The idea of Melissa in a bedroom with a murderous thug like Khamis was almost more than Nigel could stomach, but no matter how horrifying the thought of Khamis hurting her in any way, it wouldn't help Melissa for him to lose his cool and announce his presence.

To that end he slowed his pace, using his breathing to slow his racing heart.

The captain's room was just around the corner, and if both men were there, then the odds were definitely running against him. Still, he had the advantage of surprise, and that always counted for something.

Almost as if on cue the transmitter crackled to life. "Umbert, are you there?" The question was repeated twice, and Nigel was fairly certain he recognized the captain's voice. For a moment, Nigel considered trying an answer but discarded the notion. The odds were against his sounding anything like the now prostrate Umbert. No point in tipping his hand. Although Umbert's silence would certainly raise questions.

After turning off the transmitter, he made his way around the corner and, keeping his back to the wall, inched forward until he was just outside the door of the captain's quarters. Angry voices carried down the corridor, and Nigel fought to separate and identify the actual words.

"I assure you he's dead." The voice was low and clearly Arabic, although he was speaking perfect English. "I stepped over his body myself."

"Then how is it that we've lost contact with Umbert and the others?" The second voice was definitely the captain's. "I tell you, he has to be alive."

"Or there is someone else." Khamis's voice faded as he turned away from the door. "Tell me who else was with you."

"Just the man you killed."

Nigel recognized Melissa's voice, his gut clenching simultaneously with joy and fear. He had to get her out of there.

"There would have been more." There was a thread of anger in Khamis's voice.

"No. I already told you, we were certain that two could handle the job." Melissa's tone was taunting, and Nigel clenched a fist, wanting nothing more than to pound al-Rashid to a bloody pulp. But even if he had that luxury, there was still the captain to deal with. And of course the little matter of getting past both of their guns.

He considered the idea of going back for Sam, or to see if perhaps Gabe had enough strength to hold a gun after all. But even if his friend had managed to recover enough to help, there simply wasn't time to make it there and back. If they were questioning the silence of the crew, it wouldn't be long until they decided to confirm the fact. And in his absence, anything could happen—Khamis could move Melissa or, worse, kill her.

The thought spurred him into action, and for the barest of seconds he allowed himself to move forward enough to peer into the room. Melissa was standing almost dead center in front of the door, her face in profile. An ugly purple bruise glared from her left cheek, but other than that she seemed unharmed.

Khamis stood to the right of her, Melissa's body blocking any attempt Nigel might make to take the man out. He held a gun in his right hand, his hand like a vise around her wrist.

The captain stood opposite Melissa behind an oversize chair. He, too, held a gun, although his hand was relaxed. His focus, like Khamis's, was on Melissa and her insistence that there were no others on board the ship.

"What about my men?" he queried.

"I'm sure my colleague took them out. We separated in the passageway." She glanced first at the captain and then over at Khamis as if for support. "You saw him. He certainly fits the description. And believe me, he's more than capable of taking out a few sailors." Her face darkened, grief and anger mixing together as she glared at her captor. "Or at least he was—until you shot him." If words were venom, Khamis would be dead.

Despite the desperate nature of the situation, Nigel's heart lightened a bit. Melissa as usual was right on task, supporting the idea that Gabe had been the one in the bridge earlier. Nigel sobered on another thought. She was protecting him to the last, despite the fact that she had no way of knowing he was just outside the door.

God, he loved this woman.

He shifted back, leaning against the wall for support, running through scenarios in his mind, none of them seeming like a good solution. If he stormed the room, he risked Melissa getting shot. If he tried to pick the two men off one at a time, he risked them finding him first. It was a rock and a bloody hard place any way he looked at it.

"Hey." A whispered voice came from his immediate left. Nigel spun around, ready for defense and then relaxed as he recognized Payton's scarred face. "Sam said maybe you could use a little help."

"You're lucky I didn't blow your head off."

"I trust your reflexes." Payton shrugged.

"How's Gabe?"

"Sore as hell and a little groggy. Sam's with him. They're trying to get through to the mainland. What have you got here?" He tilted his head toward the open door.

"Khamis is in there with Melissa and the ship's captain. Both men have guns, and neither of them is a clear shot. To get Khamis we'd have to go through Melissa, and the captain is standing behind a wing chair."

"No time to wait for the cavalry. Sounds like we need to do something to change the odds." Payton's smile held a wicked glint, and Nigel couldn't remember the last time he'd been so happy to see someone.

"Exactly my thoughts," Nigel whispered, "but I haven't been able to come up with a damn thing."

"Emotion wreaks havoc with logic." There was no judgment in Payton's tone, only understanding. "What's with the transmitter?" Payton glanced at the walkie-talkie clipped to Nigel's belt.

"I took it off one of Khamis's henchmen," Nigel said. "Figured he didn't need it anymore."

"So maybe we can use it to our advantage." Payton risked an assessing look into the room and then pulled back. "I can create a distraction. Make them think their man is in trouble. With a little luck one or both of them will come running. If they both come out of the room, we'll divide and conquer. If only of them comes out, then I'll take him and leave Khamis to you. Piece of cake." His smile was crooked. "We've dealt with a hell of a lot worse and lived to tell about it."

With Payton standing there, it suddenly felt like old times, adrenaline pumping, the odds making it more interesting.

"There's a radio room up ahead. If you rig the transmitter there, and turn on some of the equipment, they'll recognize the sounds and know where the transmission is coming from. I'll duck around the corner." He tilted his head toward the hallway behind him. "With a little luck, we'll take them both at once."

"And if not, I have every faith in your abilities as a crack shot." Payton started to smile, then sobered. "Although the guy's obviously damn good if he managed to hit Gabe."

"I think it was luck more than skill." Rage flashed through Nigel, the image of Gabe covered in blood flashing through his mind, Melissa's brave voice playing simultaneously in his head. "And don't worry, I'm not likely to forget."

Or forgive.

Payton nodded, his expression hardening as he mentally focused on the task ahead. "Give me ninety seconds," he said, taking the transmitter, then checking his watch. "Starting now."

He was down the corridor in less than fifteen seconds, disappearing into the radio room without a backward glance. Nigel waited another twenty-five, then moved back around the corner to begin the countdown. Less than a minute to go. He watched as the second hand ticked down, his heart pounding in his ears. Ten seconds, five seconds, three seconds—

Nigel lifted his gun, his muscles tightening in anticipation. A door slammed down the passageway. A last-minute embellishment on Payton's part. Nigel strained into the resulting silence, worried suddenly that the plan had failed, but then he heard the sound of footsteps on the metal floor.

Someone at least had bought into the ruse.

He dared a look around the corner and was treated with

the sight of the captain's retreating back. No Khamis. But at least the odds were more evenly spread. Payton would be waiting for Khamis's stooge, so now all Nigel had to do was storm the fortress and rescue the princess.

Easier said than done, but the plan was in motion and there could be no turning back. He made his way around the corner, careful to stay low and close to the wall. The captain never looked back, his attention entirely on the radio room.

In another second, he'd disappeared inside, Payton waiting to surprise him. Nigel pushed all thoughts of his friend from his mind, focusing instead on the open doorway. There was no sound, but he knew they were inside.

Risking a quick look, he pivoted so that he could see through the hinges of the door. Khamis was still holding Melissa. His gun, however, was trained on the door. Not exactly a walk in the park, but at least if Khamis fired instinctively, it would be at Nigel and not Melissa. And if Nigel did his job, Khamis wouldn't be firing at anyone at all.

With a quick inhale of breath, he gathered his strength and, on an internal count of three, launched himself through the doorway, hitting stance and firing as soon as he had Khamis in his sights.

He heard Melissa scream his name, heard the second report of a gun and instinctively dove for her position. His body met nothing but floor, and even before he made full contact, he'd rolled back to his feet, crouching behind the wing chair, his eyes searching for Melissa and Khamis.

They lay together, the big man partially on top of her. Some part of Nigel twisted at the sight, anger and agony combining to fill him with black rage. He crossed the room in seconds, oblivious to any possible danger, his only thought to get the bastard off her.

Grabbing Khamis with his left hand, he pulled the man away, shoving his gun against his temple, his desire to pull the trigger only slightly less than his need to know that she was okay. "Melissa, can you hear me?"

There was a heartrending moment of silence, and then she rolled over and looked up at him. "I'm fine."

"Not shot?"

She closed her eyes for a moment, taking mental inventory, then opened them again and shook her head. "I'm really fine."

Nigel nodded and returned his attention to the man he held, noticing for the first time the blood spreading across the man's shirt.

"Is he dead?" Melissa whispered.

Khamis was slumped against him, but Nigel could feel the faint signs of a pulse beneath his fingertips. "No, he's alive." Nigel looked again at the wound. There was a hell of a lot of blood, but he could see the point of entry in the man's abdomen. "But not for long."

Melissa's gaze followed his to the hole in Khamis's gut, her expression hardening as she assessed the situation. "He's bleeding out."

Nigel nodded.

As if aware of their conversation, Khamis's eyes flickered open, his dark gaze locking on Melissa—his hatred almost a palpable thing.

"Game's over," Nigel hissed in the man's ear.

Khamis shook his head, his eyes seeing only Melissa. "Believe me—it has only just begun." He coughed once, blood trickling down the corner of his mouth, his body sagging against Nigel.

"Where is the nerve gas?" Melissa asked, moving to stand only inches from the dying man. "Tell me where it is." Desperation mixed with anger colored her voice, and Nigel again felt the urge to pull the trigger.

But it would only mean killing a dead man, and Nigel had never been one for overkill. Instead he released Khamis, leaving him lying on the floor.

"He's not going to tell us anything." Nigel moved to Melissa's side, reaching out to caress her bruised cheek, needing to touch her, to know that she was in truth all right.

"But he has to." She shook her head, stepping away from him, her attention still riveted on Khamis. "Tell me where the R-VX is."

"You are too late." Khamis's voice was weak now, as if every word was an effort.

"That's not good enough." Melissa's voice was pleading now.

Khamis ignored the outburst, his gaze shifting upward to stare into empty space. It was almost as if there were someone there, and Nigel watched as the man's lips curved upward into a smile.

"It is as I promised, my love." The words were so soft now that Nigel and Melissa had to move closer, Nigel bending so that he could hear. "The guilty shall suffer," Khamis whispered, "and in so doing, your death shall have been avenged." He sighed once, and then there was nothing more.

Khamis al-Rashid was dead.

THE FREIGHTER WAS AWASH with activity. A rescue helicopter occupied the midship deck area, and two Coast Guard cutters were anchored only a hundred yards or so from the ship. Melissa sat on a folding chair in the bridge area, clutching a cup of hot coffee.

She'd tried pacing, but the motion jarred her aching head, and at least for the moment, it seemed better to stay seated.

Gabe was being prepped for evacuation, St. Vincent's hospital already alerted as to his condition. He'd lost a lot of blood, but Sam assured her that he was going to be fine. The remaining crew members, including the captain, had already been off-loaded onto one of the cutters, their destination Homeland Security.

Nigel and Payton were standing in the corner discussing something, Nigel waving his hands in a very un-English fashion. She watched as they talked for several more minutes, then finally with a nod, Nigel turned to walk in her direction.

There was something in the set of his shoulders that sent alarm bells flashing. She set the coffee on the table, and stood up, already bracing for whatever it was he had to tell her.

"How're you feeling?"

"I'm fine," Melissa insisted, countering her words by lifting her hand to her injured cheek. "It's just a bruise."

Nigel looked for a moment as if he wanted to argue, then seemed to think better of it. "Payton and I have been talking. About Khamis and what he said."

"The bit about the guilty being punished?" Melissa asked. "I know, I haven't been able to get it out of my head, either."

"Payton thinks he meant you."

She nodded, the thought having already occurred to her. "But it wasn't true. I mean, I'm still here. He didn't kill me."

"That's just what's been bothering me. He had every opportunity, Melissa, so why the hell didn't he?"

She frowned for a moment, trying to follow his train of thought, then suddenly everything became clear. The idea sent fresh panic racing along her nerve endings. "To punish me, he has to hurt the people I love."

"I'm afraid that's a distinct possibility."

"Oh, God, there are only two ways for him to do that." She tightened her grip, pulling him closer. "He could hurt you. Or he could hurt Alicia. And Nigel, he didn't know about you."

"Have you tried to reach your sister?"

"Cell phones aren't working and with the storm, the Coast Guard couldn't patch me through." She released his shirt, reaching instead for his hand. "I can't lose her, Nigel. I just can't."

"You won't. I promise. We're not even sure there's a real threat. Payton still believes the bomb is here on the ship. Or if not here, then on another ship somewhere. There simply wasn't time for him to have gotten it into position."

"But we can't know that for sure."

"No. That's why we're redoubling efforts to find it. Payton and Sam here on the freighter, and the Coast Guard coordinating a search of all ships in the area that could conceivably be carrying the warheads. In addition, Homeland Security has issued alerts to up security on all high-profile targets."

"But if he's after Alicia, it won't be a high-profile target. I know you both think it would be overkill to use stolen nerve gas on my sister, but maybe it's meant to kill two birds with one stone." She winced at her words but forced herself to continue. "A strike for the holy war and for Khamis's personal vengeance. I'm betting the R-VX is out there somewhere, primed and ready for Alicia. It's the only way he could be sure I would suffer."

"Look, there's no point in imagining the worst. We won't know anything until we find your sister. Which is why I've arranged to take the speedboat. Payton and Sam can catch a ride with the Coast Guard when they finish here."

"Okay, then let's go." She tossed off the blanket the medic had wrapped around her, her thoughts centered firmly now on Alicia.

"I don't suppose you'd be willing to trust the job of finding Alicia to me while you let a doctor check you out? There's room on Gabe's transport." Nigel nodded his head toward the helicopter.

"No way in hell."

"I figured as much." His smile flickered, then died. "So let's get going. The sooner we find Alicia, the sooner you can put this all to rest. Any idea where she might be?"

"Most likely at home." Melissa quickened her pace. "Their apartment is on East Eighty-ninth, across from Central Park. I'll know more as soon as we're in cell-phone range."

"All right, then, let's go. If Khamis did manage to plant the nerve gas, there won't be much time. I saw his face when he died. Whatever the hell he was looking for, he'd found it. And that doesn't bode well for us."

"Or Alicia."

CHAPTER TWENTY-NINE

"SHE'S STILL NOT ANSWERING." Melissa clicked her cell phone closed with a snap. "And I've called Aaron's numbers, as well." Panic laced through her, but Melissa held on, determined not to let her terror take hold. All it would do was distract from what was important—finding Alicia.

The cabdriver honked as a car pulled out in front of them, the resulting swerve throwing Melissa against Nigel. Automatically his arm came around her, and even though it was merely reaction, she took comfort in his closeness.

"Look," he said, settling back against the seat, not bothering to remove his arm, "this is still all just supposition."

"But you should have heard him," Melissa said. "He blamed me. He said I was responsible for the deaths of his wife and sons. So what better way to punish me than to hurt the people I love?"

"I agree with your logic. It's just that if Khamis's principal goal was to hurt you by killing Alicia, it seems like there are a hell of lot easier ways than stealing old Soviet warheads to do it."

"Like I said, maybe he's piggybacking on someone else's plans. Maybe his affiliation with terrorists is driving the overall agenda, and Khamis saw a chance to get to me at the same time."

"If that's true, then he had to have targeted more than just your sister."

"Aaron's a diplomat, maybe it's about him, too."

Nigel shook his head. “Still not a big enough impact to be worth the effort that had to go into obtaining the R-VX and transporting it here.”

“Well, they live in one of the wealthiest areas of the city. Maybe there’s something in that?” She tried to process the information, to arrange it into a logical whole, but her brain was so flooded with adrenaline she was finding it difficult to think.

“Could be, but again, there are easier ways to take out a block. I just can’t shake the feeling that it’s got to be something higher profile than that.”

“Oh, my God.” Melissa’s heart seemed to stop, her exclamation so tortured even the cabdriver looked back. She reached over for Nigel’s hand, her eyes wide. “Alicia’s at a fund-raiser tonight. To raise money for cancer research. The event is top-shelf. Anyone who is anyone will be there. Plates were something like five thousand a piece. Alicia even wanted me to go, but I told her I couldn’t—not in light of everything that was happening.”

“Where is the event?” Nigel asked, already leaning forward toward the driver.

“The Waldorf. The party is in the main ballroom, the Starlight Roof.”

Nigel reached for the phone, dialing a number. He waited a few minutes then disconnected with a curse. “I can’t reach Payton. Probably something to do with the storm.”

“How about Harrison? He and Cullen are back in the city by now surely.”

Nigel nodded and dialed again, while Melissa leaned forward to tell the cabdriver they’d switched destinations.

Nigel explained their fears, nodded at the phone a couple of times and disconnected again. “He’s going to alert the Waldorf that there may be a problem, as well as the police, and then he’ll try to contact Sam. In the meantime, we’ll need to get there as quickly as possible and assess the situation. This isn't the kind of thing to be handled by rank-and-file security."

Melissa leaned back against the leather seat, her mind racing. Outside, she could see the lights of Grand Central Station as they turned to circumnavigate it, a giant gold eagle seeming to momentarily block their path. Just around the curve they would merge onto Park Avenue. Only a few blocks away. But traffic was backed up to a crawl, commuters trying to get home out of the weather. Melissa knew it could easily take them forty minutes just to get beyond Grand Central.

"Just stop here," Nigel told the driver, flinging a fifty through the sliding window. The man opened his mouth to argue, saw the size of the bill and nodded at the door. They jumped out of the cab, dodging traffic, ignoring shouted curses and honking horns until they'd safely reached Park and Forty-sixth. The rain was falling again, making the sidewalks an obstacle course of bobbing umbrellas.

The traffic light on Forty-seventh cooperated and they ran across it, pushing through the crowds almost as if they weren't there. Nigel reached for her hand, dashing out into oncoming traffic on Forty-eighth, the squeal of brakes echoing in her ears.

Safe on the north side, they headed across Park, dodging between idling cars and taxis in both lanes, oblivious to the light, the traffic jam actually playing to their advantage. Melissa could see the Waldorf ahead, her breathing coming easier when she realized it was unharmed. At least to the naked eye. She could see a couple of taxis out front, and a liveried doorman helping someone out of a car.

She glanced at her watch. It was almost eight. The fundraiser had begun at seven, but would only just now be reaching full swing. It was a dinner affair, which meant people seated at tables, listening to speakers as they talked about the dangers of cancer and the importance of continuing research.

A captive audience if ever there was one.

"Where do we start?" she asked as they slowed to a brisk walk, the doorman giving them a curious look but refraining from comment as they made their way through the revolving door. "The place is huge. If the R-VX is here, it could be anywhere."

"It'll be somewhere high," Nigel said, ushering her through the ornate lobby toward an elevator marked Star Roof. "R-VX is heavier than air, so if you want maximum effect you need it to detonate as far off the ground as possible. That way it has the capability of raining down on the target. Saturating it, so to speak. If the nerve gas is in the hotel, I'm betting it's up there." He shot a look toward the ceiling. "Not only is it on target as far as your sister is concerned, but the room's got a glass ceiling."

"Meaning if it blows, the gas will be disseminated throughout the area."

"Exactly," Nigel said, cupping her elbow to move her forward.

The elevator door dinged open, but before they could move inside, a blue-jacketed security man stepped in front of the elevator, blocking their way.

"I'm sorry. I think maybe you have the wrong elevator." He eyed them dubiously, obviously taking in their bedraggled appearance, and Melissa's now-quite-pronounced bruise.

She swallowed a bubble of hysteria, wondering if after everything they'd been through they were going to fail because some over-testosteroned yahoo in an ill-fitting suit was going to insist they be thrown out of the hotel. Fortunately Nigel had no such reaction.

"I'm with British intelligence." He held out a hand, open-palmed, just in front of his jacket.

The man's eyes narrowed, but he nodded, his hand on the holstered gun at his hip.

Nigel produced his identification, and handed it to the man. "We've reason to believe there may be a problem upstairs. All we need to do is take a look around. Someone should have called to let you know we're coming." He produced a business card and handed it to the man.

The security man read the card and examined the credentials, and then read the card again. Finally he pulled out a two-way and had a whispered conversation with someone at the other end. Melissa could feel the seconds ticking away and had to forcibly keep herself from making a dash for the elevator.

Everything in its time, her granny used to say.

Finally, the man disconnected and handed the credentials back with enough deference to make Melissa feel as if she'd fallen down the rabbit hole. With something akin to awe, he ushered them toward the elevator. "Will you require backup? All I have to do is call it in and my men can converge on the floor in five minutes."

"I'll keep you apprised." Nigel nodded with the formality of a king granting favors, and pulled Melissa onto the elevator.

"What did you give him?" she asked as the doors swooshed shut.

"Cullen's business card." Nigel shrugged. "Apparently it did the trick. He'd obviously had time to talk to someone in power here, or they'd never have let us pass."

"We're not exactly looking our superspy best." She shot him a watery smile, and he reached over to squeeze her hand. "How come you didn't tell him the truth about what we suspect?"

"Cullen and I agreed that it was need-to-know only. And the guard's knowing would only have made things worse. We don't know what we're going to find up there. So there's no sense in causing a panic until we understand what it is we're facing."

"But surely we should evacuate." She was thinking of her sister. Of her unborn baby.

"To where? You heard them talking about the R-VX. It'll kill everything within at least forty miles. And that's best-case. Evacuating isn't going to do a damn bit of good. All it will do is cause panic, and that's the last thing we need right now."

Melissa nodded, swallowing the fear rising inside her. She had so much to lose. More than she'd ever thought possible. Her sister and Aaron. Her unborn nephew or niece—and most importantly, she could lose Nigel. "All right then, so how do we handle this?"

"My guess is that Khamis planted the device somewhere on the periphery of the ballroom. Out of the main flow of party traffic but still close enough to be capable of taking out the entire floor."

"So we start with any outlying rooms."

"Right. But first let me check with Cullen. See where we are as far as reinforcements. If we find anything, we need Sam here ASAP. Or at the very least, someone from the NYPD bomb squad."

"Are they trained to deal with chemical weapons?" she asked.

"Yes. Although at the end of the day, I'd much rather have Sam."

The doors opened, and they stepped into the vestibule. Nigel dialed the phone, and Melissa restrained the urge to go running into the ballroom, screaming for her sister to run. She could see the ballroom from here, but was too far away to make out individuals. Waiters were moving in between tables, trays full of plates balanced carefully in their hands. Dinner was just beginning.

Nigel clicked the phone shut, his expression inscrutable. "Cullen patched me through to Sam. They found nothing on the ship. No sign at all of the R-VX."

"What about the crew? Did anyone say anything?"

"Nothing. Either they don't know or they're willing to die keeping the secret. To hear Sam tell it, I don't think Payton was particularly restrained in trying to obtain the information."

"How soon can she get here?"

"It's not looking good. The storm's gotten worse, so they can't land a helicopter. That means she'll have to come by boat. I'd say it'll be at least an hour."

"And the NYPD?" Melissa stepped back into the shadow of a corner as a guest passed by, her perfectly arched eyebrows rising at the sight of Melissa's shiner.

"Cullen says they've dispatched uniforms, but I'm afraid the bomb squad's hampered by the storm, as well. No one can fly, and traffic's jammed all over the city."

"So for the moment at least, we're on our own."

"Looks that way. But not to worry. We make a pretty good team." His smile was endearing and heartrending all at the same time.

Emotion swamped through her with the force of a riptide, but she didn't allow herself the luxury of defining it. There simply wasn't time. Not now. Maybe later, when they'd safely reached the other side, she'd face it square on, call it for what it was. But not now.

Not here.

"Where first?" she asked, eyeing the room with trepidation. "Obviously we can't just march into the ballroom."

"No. As I said, if it's here, I'm betting it's in an adjoining room. I think we're better off sticking together. Two sets of eyes and all that." He looked over for confirmation, and she nodded. "All right, then, why don't we start here—" he pointed to a room opening off to their left "—and work clockwise back to the elevators. There can't be more than four or five rooms besides the ballroom, I'd think."

"Sounds like a plan. Any idea what we're looking for?" They walked into the first room, and Melissa let her gaze wander around the scattered tables and chairs. Each table was draped in a red cloth, an unlit candle sitting in the center.

"I'm not really sure. Sam said something in plain sight. Something that seems normal but on second consideration is out of place somehow."

"That could be anything." Melissa frowned, trying to reassess the room from Sam's point of view. All the tables looked exactly the same.

Nigel reached over and pinched the wick of a candle. "It's cold. And there are no stains on the cloths. My guess is that they'll be used later, or they're for another function altogether."

"So if the room isn't being used, it seems like the perfect place to slip in something unnoticed."

"Maybe." Nigel bent to lift a cloth and look under the table. "But it's too far from the ballroom to achieve maximum effect. And from the looks of things, I'm betting it was set up recently. Maybe even after the party started. And we know that Khamis couldn't possibly have had access after that. He was on the freighter with us."

"So maybe someone else did his dirty work?"

"No way. Khamis is a hands-on kind of guy. He'd never trust someone else to deliver the package. He'd have done it himself."

"All right, so do we skip this room or check the tables just to be sure?"

Nigel sighed. "We check."

Fifteen minutes later, they'd checked three rooms and found nothing. Melissa could hear the keynote speaker, a prominent senator, making her case for breast cancer research. As always the talk sent shivers of loss racing through Melissa, memories of her mother in her final days still as clear in her mind now as they'd been when she was a kid.

"She didn't leave on purpose." Nigel turned to face her, his tired eyes full of love and comfort.

"I know." Melissa nodded. "It's just that it still hurts so damn bad. I needed her. And even if it wasn't her fault, she's still gone. That's why I never come to these things."

"Sometimes the only way to deal with loss is to face it head-on, Melissa."

There was wisdom in his words, but she wasn't willing to analyze her pain, not even with Nigel. And especially not now. "Shall we tackle the last room?"

Nigel reached over to touch her face, the gentle gesture almost her undoing. Then he moved away, his mind clearly shifting back to the business at hand. "I'm right behind you."

So far the rooms they'd explored had either been set up with candle-topped tables, or completely empty of all extraneous materials. The last room, however, had clearly been used—quite recently.

A bar at the far end was closed now, but there were still a couple of bottles, a stack of ashtrays and a spray can of air freshener gracing the counter. Evidently, if the attendees were rich enough, the mayor's smoking ban was only treated as a suggestion. Behind the bar, Melissa could see a couple of lower tables and a cart that must have held the alcohol.

A scatter of abandoned glasses and plates littered a couple dozen tables, the waist-high kind meant to be used with barstools or standing. Melissa walked over to one, picking up a pink swizzle stick shaped like a ribbon. Similar sticks littered neighboring tables. "This must have been where they had pre-dinner drinks." She held up the stir stick. "Definitely breast cancer awareness."

Nigel nodded, already inspecting the underside of the tables. Chairs were lined up against two walls, and Melissa started to check them, but stopped short as her brain caught up with the images she'd seen. The tables behind the bar were covered with gold-spangled cloths, making the bar itself seem regal, but the cart to the left had been covered with a plain white cloth.

The kind used for room service.

Frowning, she turned from the chairs and crossed over to the bar, her eyes confirming what her mind had brought to her attention. There was nothing intrinsically wrong with the picture. Someone could simply have rolled a cart with ice or additional beverages off the elevator and over to the bar, but somehow it didn't feel right.

The cloth seemed too long, and the cart just felt out of place. She walked behind the bar, trying to figure out what it was that bugged her, and finally she realized the problem. The rest of the room was totally trashed, the remains of the party scattered everywhere.

But the cart wasn't dirty at all. Except for a single wineglass and a napkin, there was nothing on it. And despite the fact that it had initially appeared to be behind the bar, Melissa realized now that it was in actuality about three feet to the left in a corner. As if it had simply been abandoned there.

Something that appeared to fit but didn't. Sam's words echoed through her brain, and she called to Nigel as she knelt to lift the cloth. Her heart pounded against her temples as she bent her head to peer under the cart, instinctively certain of what she would find.

It was surprisingly small. No more than a foot and a half total. A silvery box that at first glance appeared to be made completely of plastic. It was deceptively simple looking, and easy to overlook, the color blending into the muted metal of the cart's underside. Harder to miss were the red numerals of the LED readout.

According to the steadily decreasing numbers, Khamis's device was set to detonate in less then fifteen minutes. Time, it seemed, was about to run out.

CHAPTER THIRTY

"I CAN'T TELL ANYTHING without flipping this thing over." Nigel was lying on his back looking up at the steadily decreasing numbers, but it was impossible to see anything in the half-light. He swallowed a curse and pulled out from under the cart. "What's Sam saying?"

Melissa shook her head, holding up her hand, so that she could hear Sam on the other end of the line. "No way she can make it in time. She's still at least twenty minutes out, and that's not counting the traffic."

"So what the hell are we supposed to do?" He hadn't meant to voice his fear, but now that he'd verbalized it, it lost some of its power, allowing him to focus. "Let me talk to her."

Melissa nodded, handing him the phone, then looked toward the ballroom, the sound of applause filtering into the room.

"I know it's hard, Melissa. But it's better if we don't cause a panic. You know that." He waited for her nod, then concentrated on the phone. "Tell me what to do, Sam." They'd already described the device to her. Wasting precious seconds. They were currently at t-minus ten and counting.

"The device should be stable," Sam said, her voice sounding tinny over the cell phone. "The nerve gas won't be viable until detonation. So if you're careful and don't drop it, you should be able to flip the cart and remove the device."

"There's not enough time to get it the hell out of here." Frustration was building. Nigel wasn't a take-instructions kind of guy. He much preferred action.

"I know that," Sam said, her voice reassuring. "I'm going to walk you through disarming it. It's not the best of situations, but it beats the alternative."

"Right," Nigel said, bending down to look at the bomb again. "So I'll pass you off to Melissa again, and she can relay instructions." He held the phone out for Melissa, and then carefully began to flip the cart onto its back.

Every inch seemed to take a year or more, but in less than thirty seconds, he had the thing upended on a table, the device now clearly visible. Ten seconds after that he'd removed all the duct tape.

"Okay," Melissa said. "First thing to do is remove the casing. Sam says it's probably glued into place, or maybe held together with a latch. First check to be sure there's not a trigger wire attached, then you can break the seals to open it."

Nigel gingerly ran his hands around the edges of the plastic box containing the explosives and nerve gas. Two latches resembling a briefcase were aligned in the center of each end of the box. The only wire protruding from the box was attached to the timer. "I'm going to open it."

Melissa nodded her acceptance and relayed the information to Sam. The box, which was about ten inches deep, opened without incident. The inner workings of the device consisted of a jumble of wire attached in turn to a nine-volt battery and a series of circuit boards, which were welded to what looked like an old motherboard. The board covered the length and width of the box, concealing the nerve agent below.

Melissa moved closer, staring down at the array, using her photographer's eye to paint a verbal picture for Sam. Once she'd described it, seconds ticked away as Sam considered the device. Finally Melissa relayed her thoughts. "She says it's really simple."

"Well, that's a point in our favor at least." Nigel had worked with ordnance before, but he'd never actually been solely responsible for disarming a bomb. Still, he had to agree with Sam, the thing looked pretty straightforward. The LED display signaled seven minutes, and Nigel blew out a slow breath, forcing a calm he didn't feel.

"She says to find the wire connecting to the power source. If you can sever it, then that should kill the timer, and without the timer there'll be no detonation."

Nigel studied the wires, and picked up one, carefully tracing it to its source. Not the battery. It took almost thirty seconds and way too many missteps, but finally he isolated the wire, carefully keeping it between his thumb and forefinger.

With his other hand, he reached into his pocket and retrieved his knife. "Can you open this for me?"

Melissa balanced the phone between her ear and shoulder, and took the knife case, opening it to reveal a tiny pair of scissors. "Should have known you'd be the MacGyver type," she commented, handing him the scissors.

"British Boy Scout," Nigel said. "Always prepared and all that. Tell her I'm about to cut the wire."

Melissa relayed the information, waited a moment as she listened to Sam, then nodded. "Stay close to the battery end. And don't let it touch any of the other wires."

Without giving himself time to think, Nigel slid the scissors into place and squeezed. The wire held for a moment, then severed. The LED went black, and after a heart-stopping three seconds, nothing else happened.

"Did we do it?" Melissa asked, hope blossoming in her voice.

Nigel opened his mouth to respond, but before he could do so, a series of high-pitched beeps sounded, a panel on the floor of the bomb sliding back to reveal another LED counter, its numbers at four minutes and counting.

"Shit," Nigel said. "We've triggered a secondary bomb. Give me the phone."

Mutely Melissa handed it to him, her eyes locked on the flashing green LED. Nigel explained the situation to Sam, trying to speak as quickly as he could.

"I should have guessed," Sam said, her frustration echoing his own. "Looks like the first panel was just a decoy. An inside joke."

"At the moment I'm not finding it all that funny."

"You need to figure out a way to remove the false bottom. The real device is below," Sam said. "Are there screws or latches or anything you can see that might separate the two?"

He leaned over the bomb, his eyes searching for some way to access the area below.

"I see screws," Melissa said, pointing to the corners of the box. Nigel nodded, and after handing the phone back to Melissa, opened the knife again to reveal a screwdriver. Working as quickly as possible without risking motion that would jar the box, he worked the screws free and then carefully removed the false top.

"Sam's right. There's another bomb here." There was nothing homemade about this one. Two titanium cylinders were connected by welded brackets, the space between them housing the actual mechanism for detonation. Two cones faced each other across the open area between the canisters, a metal rod on the left one telescoped down so that there was about an inch of space between the two.

While Melissa described the bomb to Sam, Nigel continued to study it. The mechanism was clearly complex and high-tech, but despite all of that the method of firing was remarkably simple. The metal rod would expand in the breath of a nanosecond, slamming into the metal plate adorning the end of the opposite cone.

Contact would trigger detonation, the force of the blast mixing the contents of the canisters, and propelling the nerve gas out into the skies of New York, an instant death sentence for the world's most populated city—along with the woman he loved. Hell of a price to pay for a life lived on the edge.

"Sam wants to talk to you." She handed him the phone

again, bending so that she too could study the device, the LED readout reminding them they now had under three minutes to find a way out.

"You've got to find a way to block detonation," Sam said. "Something to keep the rod from completing the circuit."

"Sounds easy in theory, but not so much when you're standing in front of the damn thing."

Melissa reached out a hand, finger extended to check out the metal rod.

"Stop," Nigel ordered. "It's probably booby-trapped."

With a sharp intake of breath, Melissa straightened, her hands visibly shaking now.

"I'm betting lasers," Sam said, "or some kind of motion sensors. They won't be activated unless you break the plane. But once you do, there won't be a second chance."

"So we're screwed." Nigel hated to admit defeat, but the bloody LED was determined to remind him in one-second intervals.

"Not necessarily. If you can find something to illuminate the lasers you can see the pathway. And then maybe you can find something to keep the rod from moving upon detonation. All you need to do is keep the—"

Static replaced the sound of her voice, sending alarm coursing through him. "Sam? Can you hear me?" Nigel said, repeating the phrase like the stupid guy on the telephone commercial. The static continued, then abruptly went dead. "I've lost her."

The LED blinked two minutes.

"Then we'll have to handle it on our own." Melissa met his gaze, determination etched clearly on her face. "What did she say?"

He quickly explained about the possibility of lasers, and Sam's suggestion of finding something to reveal the pathway.

"Aerosol," Melissa said, already crossing to the bar. "The tiny drops of liquid will act like prisms, picking up the light and providing us with a picture of what's going on between the two canisters."

"What if it triggers the device?"

"It won't." She shook her head. "There's not enough weight. It's just a mist, essentially. Shouldn't do anything but give us our road map."

"And once we know what we're up against, all we have to do is get something into place to stop the rod from extending to finish the circuit."

Melissa studied the device again, then nodded. "Something plastic or rubber. Anything metal will just act as a conductor."

The LED showed ninety seconds.

Melissa sprayed the air freshener between the cylinders and immediately lines of intersecting green light flashed against the ensuing fog of pine-scented mist.

"How the hell are we supposed to get something in between all that?" The mist cleared, the lines wavering, then disappearing.

"We'll use this." Melissa held up the pink plastic swizzle stick. "Puts a new spin on the idea of nuking cancer, don't you think?"

Again he felt a swell of emotion that had nothing at all to do with the situation at hand, and everything to do with the woman standing in front of him. Their gazes met and held, time standing still for just an instant.

"Nigel, I need to tell you—"

He raised a hand, cutting her off before she could start. "No near-death protestations of love. I'll wait until after this. When we're facing a very long and boring life together."

"Never boring, Nigel." Melissa smiled. "Never boring."

Nigel picked up the aerosol and aimed at the bomb. The clock showed just over forty seconds left. "All right. I'm going to spray this stuff as continuously as possible. Your job is going to be to maneuver the swizzle stick through the spaces between the lasers so that it's in place in front of the pad. Then if we're lucky when the rod fires, the plastic will prevent it from hitting the metal and no circuit. No bomb. We'll do it on my go."

Melissa gripped the pink plastic stick in her hand, moving so that she could see the pathway as soon as he hit the nozzle on the air freshener.

Nigel glanced at the clock—twelve seconds. "All right, this is it." He hit the nozzle, and the mist erupted on a hiss, the protective grid highlighted again in green.

Melissa began to move the swizzle stick between the lines, twisting her wrist now and again to accommodate her line of vision. "Almost there," she whispered. "How much time now?"

"Five seconds."

She moved the stick forward a tiny bit more. It was only millimeters away now. "Nigel, I have to say it. You have to know."

"I do know, Melissa. I've always known, I think. I just didn't know how to combat your fear."

"And you do now?"

Three seconds.

"I'd sure as bloody hell like to find out."

The aerosol hissed and then stopped, the can empty, the green lines already fading from view. Two seconds.

"This is it. Can you see well enough?"

She was chewing the side of her lip, but her hand was steady. "I don't really have a choice."

"One second, Melissa. It's now or never."

She shoved the stick forward into place just as the LED clicked zero. The metal rod shot out of its hole, trapping the plastic permanently in place between the cones.

There was a click as the mechanism finished moving. And then nothing.

Nothing at all.

"Score one for breast cancer awareness," Melissa said as

she dropped to the floor, her breathing coming in gasps. "We did it."

"We sure as hell did," Nigel said, falling down beside her, exhausted beyond caring. "And it sounds to me like we're getting a standing ovation."

Melissa rolled over, lifting her head so that she could listen to the applause coming from the ballroom. "If only they knew."

Nigel watched as the horrors of the past few days played across her face, his heart constricting with her pain. The cost of any war was high, but terrorism in particular threatened so many who were innocent—on both sides of the game. "Khamis may not have his revenge, Melissa. But we can hope that somewhere in eternity he's found peace."

"And maybe his family." The words were soft, almost a whisper.

"It wasn't your fault." Nigel reached up to stroke the soft contour of her cheek. "His choices were what set tragedy in motion, not yours."

"I know that somewhere up here—" she pointed to her head and then her heart "—but in here it's harder to deal with, you know?"

"Yes. I do know. Because if I'd lost you today, I honestly believe I'd have wanted to take out anyone who had even the slightest connection to your death. So in that respect, I understand Khamis. But that doesn't mean either of us would have been right in our actions."

"You're an amazing man," she said, looking down at him, her eyes warm with the hint of promise.

"Then why not tell me what it was you wanted to say earlier?" he asked, working to hold his voice steady.

"You mean now that we've got a lifetime to share?" she answered, her eyes crinkling with laughter. "I seem to have forgotten."

With a loud groan, he flipped her over so that her body was beneath his, his lips finding hers in a kiss filled with passion.

Lifting his head, he reverently traced the edge of her bruised cheek, cherishing all over again the fact that they were together and alive.

Melissa's eyes filled with tears, and she reached up to cup his face in her hands. "I've loved you for fifteen years, Nigel Ferris. And if I have my way I'll love you for a hundred more."

"So," Sam's familiar voice broke into the moment, "I see you managed to disarm the bomb."

"Along with a few other things." Payton's voice was laced with laughter. "What did I tell you, sweetheart? There's just something about Last Chance—it's like *The Love Boat.* Take a case and find your heart's desire. Maybe Cullen is really Mr. Roarke."

"You're mixing up your television shows," Sam said, deftly moving the dead bomb into a lead-lined container. "Mr. Roarke is from *Fantasy Island.*"

Nigel leaned back down to kiss Melissa, shutting out the banter of his friends, the rustle of people as they were evacuated from the ballroom, and the thought that this wasn't the time or the place. All that mattered at the moment was the fact that they were alive, together and in love.

They had been given a second chance—make that a last chance—and he was bound and determined to make the most of every minute.

EPILOGUE

LAVERSHAM HAD NEVER LOOKED so grand. Everyone from the first under butler to the village parson was saying so. Not to mention most of the gossip columnists in England. It was as if the estate had been infused with new life. But then again, Melissa supposed, it had in a way. Somehow, in marrying her, Nigel had finally come to terms with his heritage. Not exactly in a lord-of-the-manor kind of way, but still, he seemed to have found peace.

Or as much peace as anyone could have when surrounded by noisy family and friends. The late-spring grass was just turning green, the roses on the trellis beginning to bloom, white and crimson weaving together in a topiary salute to the Laversham crest.

Considering she'd never had much of a past, Melissa found it a bit overwhelming at times to be known as Lady Laversham with all that entailed. Fortunately, however, it was clear that her husband felt exactly the same, and for the most part they avoided the titles altogether.

"Hey, aren't you going to play?" Madison called from the croquet lawn, little Andrea balanced between her legs, determinedly holding the mallet that was several inches taller than she was.

"Not right now." Melissa smiled. "It's too much fun watching you."

"And it's not fair at all," Payton grumbled. "You can't croquet a toddler. She's got the run of the course."

"About time someone got the better of you on that course. You've already whipped anyone else who dared to give it a go." Sam, pregnant to the bursting point, lifted her lemonade in a toast.

It had been almost a year. A whirlwind of activity. There'd been assignments of course, for the CIA and for Last Chance. But she'd curtailed both because she hadn't wanted to be apart from Nigel. They'd wasted far too much time to let anything stand in their way.

He'd taken to working only the odd case for MI6, preferring instead the idea of making Laversham a home. She had no doubt that eventually he'd tire of playing house husband and head back into the field, but she understood his wanderlust better than most and knew it was part and parcel of the man she'd chosen to spend her life with.

"Penny for your thoughts?" Andrew asked, tipping his head to one side, the gesture almost identical to his brother. Along with inheriting Laversham, she'd also come into Andrew. As brothers went he was a handful, constantly finding trouble and then exacerbating it, but, like Nigel, he was easy to love. And she cherished the fact that her family now included so many wonderful people.

"I was just thinking about how happy I am."

"And that better had be because of me, and not my oh-so-roguish brother," Nigel said with a grin, perching on the arm of her chair.

She reached for his hand, her smile answering him without words.

"Looks like Payton's got more competition," Sam said, pointing to Aaron, holding baby Micah in his arms as he tried to play. "It's all good practice for him, really," she said, patting her belly.

"Somehow, I don't think Payton's going to need any help. He'll make an amazing father." Nigel's voice held a wistful note. Or maybe Melissa was just transferring her feelings. Either way, his hand tightened on hers, and she felt a wash of desire, the heady feeling always surprising her with its power.

"All right, I've made the hamburgers." Gabe strode across the lawn, balancing a giant platter of meat, and sporting an apron emblazoned with Kiss The Cook. A Father's Day present from Andrea, according to Madison. Although exactly why it had made the journey across the Atlantic was still somewhat of a mystery.

"I couldn't find the ketchup, and your cook was a bit disgruntled to be sharing her kitchen, but I've done the best I can." Gabe opened the barbecue grill with a flourish. English to its core, the machine resembled an oversize griddle far more than an American grill, but Nigel had assured him it would suffice.

"There aren't any hot dogs, though." Harrison arrived with a plate of buns and assorted condiments.

"We have hot dogs," Andrew protested.

"Not the American kind," Harrison assured him. "Yours are more like really pregnant sausages."

"Hey, watch it, Harrison," Sam groused with a smile. "I resemble that remark."

"Not even a little," her husband reassured, although the gesture was diluted by the fact that he failed to look up from the wicket.

The burgers sizzled as Gabe placed them on the fire, the smell enticing. All that was missing was the hand-cranked ice cream, but Cook had drawn a line at that, insisting on red, white and blue custard in its stead. Melissa wouldn't put it past her to add little British soldiers for decoration. The woman wasn't exactly thrilled to be celebrating a war they'd lost.

Still, as Fourth of July celebrations went, especially ones in Gloucestershire, it was shaping into everything it should be. Good food, good friends and family. There were even fireworks. Nigel had arranged for them as a surprise, but Melissa and Harrison had stumbled on the men setting them up when she'd showed him the maze.

"Guess what I've found?" Alicia asked, setting a fresh pitcher of lemonade on the table along with a pot of tea.

"I sincerely hope it's something alcoholic," Andrew said, casting a suspicious eye on the new beverages.

"There's beer in the ice chest over by the croquet." Nigel nodded toward a red plastic cooler full of beer. "Payton hates to be in short supply."

"He thinks it helps his game," Sam laughed, "but in truth it's the only thing that gives the rest of us a chance."

"So maybe it's time to show him how it's really done." Andrew stood up with a grin. "I mean, after all, just because you won the blasted war doesn't mean you're better at everything."

Melissa watched Andrew striding toward the croquet lawn, feeling absurdly contented. Everything right with the world. She leaned against Nigel and smiled up at her sister. "You said you'd found something?"

"Actually it's not a *something,* it's a *somebody.*" With a flourish of her hand, she stepped aside to reveal a man striding toward them, his sports shirt a bright shade of turquoise.

"You didn't think you could possibly have a Fourth of July celebration without me, did you?" Cullen smiled at the assembled group, ignoring Harrison's groan. "I flew in especially for the occasion."

Cullen had in large part been responsible for Melissa's being able to fill her sister in about her past, a favor she'd be forever grateful for. He'd even convinced the powers that be that Alicia was not only trustworthy, but an asset in Melissa's cover—since her sister was often traveling about Europe in the company of her husband.

"It's a wonderful surprise," Melissa said, standing up to give Cullen a hug. "Just as long as you haven't got any other news."

"Like what?" he said, his eyes full of mischief.

“Something involving murder and mayhem, if I’m to guess,” Andrew said with a wry grin. “I’ve heard it’s your stock-in-trade.”

“That and matchmaking.” Cullen’s gaze embraced them all. “I do seem to be rather good at that.”

Andrew blanched, taking an involuntary step backward.

“Not your cup of tea, I take it?” Cullen laughed.

“Doesn’t even recognize it as a beverage,” Nigel said, bending to drop a kiss on Melissa’s head. “Poor bloke doesn’t know what he’s missing.”

“So you really flew out here just to be with us?” Harrison was still eyeing Cullen with suspicion, studying the older man for traces of ulterior motive.

“Well,” Cullen said, accepting the beer Gabe offered. “Now that you mention it. The President is having a bit of a problem. You see there are these Colombian warlords…”

* * * * *